WARRIOR WOMEN

Other Anthologies Edited by
Paula Guran

Embraces
Best New Paranormal Romance
Best New Romantic Fantasy
Zombies: The Recent Dead
The Year's Best Dark Fantasy & Horror: 2010
Vampires: The Recent Undead
The Year's Best Dark Fantasy & Horror: 2011
Halloween
New Cthulhu: The Recent Weird
Brave New Love
Witches: Wicked, Wild & Wonderful
Obsession: Tales of Irresistible Desire
The Year's Best Dark Fantasy & Horror: 2012
Extreme Zombies
Ghosts: Recent Hauntings
Rock On: The Greatest Hits of Science Fiction & Fantasy
Season of Wonder
Future Games
Weird Detectives: Recent Investigations
The Mammoth Book of Angels & Demons
The Year's Best Dark Fantasy & Horror: 2013
Halloween: Magic, Mystery, & the Macabre
Once Upon a Time: New Fairy Tales
Magic City: Recent Spells
The Year's Best Dark Fantasy & Horror: 2014
Zombies: More Recent Dead
Time Travel: Recent Trips
New Cthulhu 2: More Recent Weird
Blood Sisters: Vampire Stories by Women
The Year's Best Dark Fantasy & Horror: 2015
The Year's Best Science Fiction & Fantasy Novellas: 2015

WARRIOR WOMEN

EDITED BY PAULA GURAN

PRIME BOOKS

Contents

INTRODUCTION

Paula Guran

WHAT IS NOT WITHIN

IF YOU ARE LOOKING FOR STORIES of warrior women wearing chain-mail bikinis, brass bras, tight leather bodices, "boob-plate" armor, skin-tight spacesuits, or latex bodysuits . . . move along. *Warrior Women* offers no women battling while showing obvious cleavage, toned midriffs, exposed booty, bare or booted thighs, or even tank tops that showcase nipples. Nor will you find long unbound hair that has never known a split end, flapping fringe, or flowing robes to get in the way while fighting. Three prisoners excluded, there's no nudity.

As much as I appreciate the fantasy women portrayed by Frank Frazetta, Boris Vallejo, Julie Bell, and others; glorious old pulp pin-ups; the work of many gaming and comic artists; and the astounding engineering (and challenge of wearing) costumes like Seven of Nine's silver catsuit—the women in these stories have no need of enhanced anatomy or sexy costumes. Like all viable warriors they wear functional clothing and/or protective gear.

The very fact I am addressing *physical appearance* first says something about the history of female fantasy and science fiction characters. They were once seldom found doing much more than being supportive, sexy, in need of rescue, victims, or an occasionally a sidekick who screamed before she remembered to draw her sword or push the right button on the starship console. She could also be inhumanly evil, overwhelmingly immoral, a man-eating maniac, or turned from her wicked ways by the love of a good man.

To be fair: until recently, many male fantasy and science fiction characters have not been overly realistic either. These guys oozed virility, looked like they were pumped up on steroids, had far more testosterone than any human could manage, displayed manly thews in nothing more than a loincloth, or wore spandex as they held off the invaders with a single ray-gun. Despite being prone to risk-taking, more eager to fight than philosophize, allowed to be roguish yet redeemable, and tending to self-serving ambition but turning out to be unselfishly brave after all—they still got to be the heroic protagonist. (If they served the darkside, they also got to be the most dreaded and brilliant of villains.)

Fiction—especially science fiction and fantasy—certainly does not need to adhere to reality. But science fiction does need to be plausible and at least rational enough to be considered possible. As for fantasy, it follows its own rules; to be effective fiction, those rules should be logical and thus internally cohesive. So, the role of women as warriors must also be credible within the context of the world the writer has built.

In every era of human history (and, no doubt, prehistory), women—as with every other task a human can perform—have fought. This is no longer an arguable point. We may have lost a great deal of the evidence of women in history, but examples still abound. Modern historians are expanding our knowledge of the real women warriors of the past.

Despite women performing in an increasingly wide range of military duties, war—particularly combat—is still perceived as being primarily the prerogative of men. Our culture assumes women are physically weaker and psychologically less aggressive—therefore less likely to kill—than men. Beyond that generalization, the specific pros and cons of women serving in combat positions are currently being, maybe for the first time, seriously debated. Slowly but surely, women are proving—again—they are physically, mentally, and morally capable of being warriors.

There is no theoretical consensus on why we wage war. Some see it as a ubiquitous and even genetic facet of human nature. Others feel warfare is the result of specific circumstances: the interaction of the social and the cultural; battles over ideology, resources, or territory; a response to ecological challenges.

Whatever the reasons, humans fight. Although we supposedly yearn for peace rather than war, I doubt humanity will ever completely abandon warfare. But, perhaps, we eventually will at least realize that war—and the role of the warrior—is equally the province of some men and some women, but that it is the preserve of neither.

Science fiction and fantasy's inclusion of women warriors—and women in general, as both characters and writers—has progressed in some ways in the last forty or fifty years. In other ways, it hasn't. I have a lot to say about the subject, but *that* is not a topic that I'm commenting on here

Ursula K. Le Guin wrote: "Science fiction is not prescriptive; it's descriptive." It's a commentary on the present that allows the reader to examine current issues.

Fantasy? Le Guin again: " . . . fantasy is true, of course. It isn't factual, but it is true. Children know that. Adults know it too, and that is precisely why many of them are afraid of fantasy. They know that its truth challenges, even threatens, all that is false, all that is phony, unnecessary, and trivial in the life they have let themselves be forced into living. They are afraid of dragons because they are afraid of freedom . . . "

What (I Hope) Is Within

In gathering stories for this theme, I wanted (of course) top quality and entertainment value, but I also wanted a wide range of styles and subject matter. A "woman warrior" can be many things. As I discovered stories and authors submitted stories or recommended the stories of others, I realized the definition could be even broader than I'd initially envisioned. Not only did I want both science fiction and fantasy, but stories that blurred the lines between (one is neither) . . . stories of adventure as well as deeper contemplation . . . some lightness scattered amongst the inevitable dark . . . new voices and esteemed authors . . . diverse points of view . . . plus, I wanted some surprises.

Although these stories are reprints, the overall tone, if there is just one, was shaped by what the writers had written rather than any editorial agenda. If this anthology had come together when it was first proposed (about ten years ago), I think it would have been a *very* different book. As far as I know, there has not been an original trade anthology with this theme since 2005 (*Women of War*, edited by Tanya Huff and Alexander Potter from DAW Books). One wonders what a volume of original stories on this theme would be like now.

Putting pondering aside and returning to the present pages . . . I wound up sorting the stories into five very loose categories so as not to jar the reader too abruptly (if reading in order) as they journey from one story to another. The titles of each section, I hope, provide guidance to . . . or at least enticement to try . . . the content:

I. Swords (& Spears & Arrows & Axes) and Sorcery
II. Just Yesterday & Perhaps Just Beyond Tomorrow
III. Somewhere Between Myth & Possibility
IV. Space Aria
V. Will No War End All War?

Enough preamble. Onward!

Paula Guran
Women's Equality Day 2015

≫•≪

Tanith Lee wrote "Northern Chess"—featuring Jaisel, a woman warrior—
for Amazons!, *a World Fantasy Award-winning anthology edited by*
Jessica Amanda Salmonson and published in 1979. Another Jaisel story,
"Southern Lights," appeared in Amazons II *in 1982. Published during*
the heyday of feminist Sword and Sorcery, I think this story is one of the
best examples of the sub-genre.

NORTHERN CHESS

Tanith Lee

SKY AND LAND had the same sallow bluish tinge, soaked in cold light from a
vague white sun. It was late summer, but summer might never have come here.
The few trees were bare of leaves and birds. The cindery grass-less hills rolled
up and down monotonously. Their peaks gleamed dully, their dips were full of
mist. It was a land for sad songs and dismal rememberings, and, when the night
came, for nightmares and hallucinations.

Fifteen miles back, Jaisel's horse had died. Not for any apparent cause. It
had been healthy and active when she rode from the south on it, the best the
dealer had offered her, though he had tried to cheat her in the beginning. She
was aiming to reach a city in the far north, on the seacoast there, but not for
any particular reason. She had fallen into the casual habit of the wandering
adventurer. Destination was an excuse, never a goal. And when she saw the
women at their looms or in their greasy kitchens, or tangled with babies, or
broken with field work, or leering out of painted masks from shadowy town
doorways, Jaisel's urge to travel, to ride, to fly, to run away, increased. Generally

she was running from something in fact as well as in the metaphysical. The last city she had vacated abruptly, having killed two footpads who had jumped her in the street. One had turned out to be a lordling, who had taken up robbery and rape as a hobby. In those parts, to kill a lord, with whatever justice, meant hanging and quartering. So Jaisel departed on her new horse, aiming for a city in the north. And in between had come this bleak northern empty land where her mount collapsed slowly under her and died without warning. Where the streams tasted bitter and the weather looked as if it wished to snow in summer.

She had seen only ruins. Only a flock of grayish wild sheep materialized from mist on one hand and plunged away into mist on the other. Once she heard a raven cawing. She was footsore and growing angry—with the country, with herself, and with God. While her saddle and pack gained weight on her shoulders with every mile.

Then she reached the top of one of the endless slopes, looked over and saw something new.

Down in a pool of the yellowish-bluish mist lay a village. Primitive and melancholy it was, but alive, for smokes spiraled from roof-holes, drifting into the cloudless sky. Mournful and faint, too, there came the lowing of cattle. Beyond the warren of cots, a sinister unleafed spider web of trees. Beyond them, barely seen, transparent in mist, something some distance away, a mile perhaps—a tall piled hill, or maybe a stony building of bizarre and crooked shape . . .

Jaisel started and her eyes refocused on the closer vantage of the village and the slope below.

The fresh sound was unmistakable: jingle-jangle of bells on the bridles of war horses. The sight was exotic, also, unexpected here. Two riders on steel-blue mounts, the scarlet caparisons flaming up through the quarter-tone atmosphere like bloody blades. And the shine of mail, the blink of gems.

"Render your name!" one of the two knights shouted, She half smiled, visualizing what they would see, what they would assume, the surprise in store.

"My name is Jaisel," she shouted back.

And heard them curse.

"What sort of a name is that, boy?"

Boy. Yes, and neither the first nor the only time.

She started to walk down the slope toward them.

And what they had supposed to be a boy from the top of the incline, gradually resolved itself into the surprise. Her fine flaxen hair was certainly short as a boy's, somewhat shorter.

A great deal shorter than the curled manes of knights. Slender in her tarnished chain mail, with slender strong hands dripping with frayed frosty lace at the wrists. The white lace collar lying out over the mail with dangling drawstrings each ornamented by a black pearl. The left earlobe pierced and a gold sickle moon flickering sparks from it under the palely electric hair. The sword belt was gray leather, worn and stained. Dagger on right hip with a fancy gilt handle, thin sword on left hip, pommel burnished by much use. A girl knight with intimations of the reaver, the showman, and, (for what it was worth), the prince.

When she was close enough for the surprise to have commenced, she stopped and regarded the two mounted knights.

She appeared gravely amused, but really the joke had palled by now. She had had twelve years to get bored with it. And she was tired, and still angry with God.

"Well," one of the knights said at last, "it takes all kinds to fill the world. But I think you've mistaken your road, lady." He might mean an actual direction. He might mean her mode of living.

Jaisel kept quiet, and waited. Presently the second knight said chillily: "Do you know of this place? Understand where you are?"

"No," she said. "It would be a courteous kindness if you told me."

The first knight frowned. "It would be a courteous kindness to send you home to your father, your husband, and your children."

Jaisel fixed her eyes on him. One eye was a little narrower than the other. This gave her face a mocking, witty slant.

"Then, sir," she said, "send me. Come. I invite you." The first knight gesticulated theatrically.

"I am Renier of Towers," he said. "I don't fight women."

"You do," she said. "You are doing it now. Not successfully."

The second knight grinned; she had not anticipated that.

"She has you, Renier. Let her be. No girl travels alone like this one, and dressed as she is, without skills to back it. Listen, Jaisel. This land is cursed. You've seen, the life's sucked out of it. The village here. Women and beasts birth monsters. The people fall sick without cause. Or with some cause. There was an alchemist who claimed possession of this region. Maudras. A necromancer, a worshipper of old unholy gods. Three castles of his scabbed the countryside between here and Towers in the west. Those three are no more—taken and razed. The final castle is here, a mile off to the northeast. If the mist would lift, you might see it. The Prince of Towers means to expunge all trace of Maudras from the earth. We are the prince's knights, sent here to deal with the fourth castle as with the rest."

"And the castle remains untaken," said Renier. "Months we've sat here in this unwholesome plague-ridden wilderness."

"Who defends the castle?" Jaisel asked. "Maudras himself?"

"Maudras was burned in Towers a year ago," the second knight said. "His familiar, or his curse, holds the castle against God's knights." His face was pale and grim. Both knights indeed were alike in that. But Renier stretched his mouth and said to her sweetly: "Not a spot for a maid. A camp of men. A haunted caste in a blighted country. Better get home."

"I have no horse," said Jaisel levelly. "But coins to buy one."

"We've horses and to spare," said the other knight. "Dead men don't require mounts. I am called Cassant. Vault up behind me and I'll bring you to the camp."

She swung up lightly, despite the saddle and pack on her shoulders.

Renier watched her, sneering, fascinated.

As they turned the horses' heads into the lake of mist, he rode near and murmured: "Beware, lady. The women in the village are sickly and revolting. A knight's honor may be forgotten. But probably you have been raped frequently."

"Once," she said, "ten years back. I was his last pleasure. I dug his grave myself, being respectful of the dead." She met Renier's eyes again and added gently, "and when I am in the district I visit his grave and spit on it."

THE MIST was denser below than Jaisel had judged from the slope. In the village a lot was hidden, which was maybe as well. At a turning among the cots she thought she spied a forlorn hunched-over woman, leading by a tether a shadowy animal, which seemed to be a cow with two heads.

They rode between the trees and out the other side, and piecemeal the war camp of Towers evolved through the mist.

Blood-blotch red banners hung lankly; the ghosts of tents clawed with bright heraldics that penetrated the obscurity. Horses puffed breath like dragon-smoke at their pickets. A couple of Javelot-cannon emplacements, the bronze tubes sweating on their wheels, the javelins stacked by, the powder casks wrapped in sharkskin but probably damp.

At this juncture, suddenly the mist unraveled. A vista opened away from the camp for two hundred yards northeast, revealing the castle of the necromancer-alchemist, Maudras.

It reared up, stark and peculiar against a tin-colored sky.

The lower portion was carved from the native rock-base of a conical hill. This rose into a plethora of walls and craning, squinnying towers, that seemed somehow like the petrification of a thing once unnaturally growing. A causeway flung itself up the hill and under an arched doormouth, barricaded by iron.

No movements were discernible on battlements or roofs. No pennant flew. The castle had an aura of the tomb. Yet not necessarily a tomb of the dead.

It was the camp that had more of the feel of a mortuary about it. From an oblique quarter emanated groanings. Where men were to be found outside the tents, they crouched listlessly over fires. Cook-pots and heaps of accouterments plainly went unattended. By a scarlet pavilion two knights sat at chess. The game was sporadic and violent and seemed likely to end in blows.

Cassant drew rein a space to the side of the scarlet pavilion, whose cloth was blazoned with three gold turrets—the insignia of Towers. A boy ran to take charge of the horse as its two riders dismounted. But Renier remained astride his horse, staring at Jaisel. Soon he announced generally, in a herald's carrying tone: "Come, gentlemen, welcome a new recruit. A peerless knight. A damsel in breeches."

All around, heads lifted. A sullen interest bloomed over the apathy of the camp: the slurred spiteful humor of men who were ill, or else under sentence of execution. They began to get up from the pallid fires and shamble closer. The fierce paused and gazed arrogantly across with extravagant oaths.

"Mistress, you're in for trouble," said Cassant ruefully. "But be fair, he warned you of it."

Jaisel shrugged. She glanced at Renier, nonchalantly posed on the steel-blue horse, right leg loose of the stirrup now and hooked across the saddle-bow. At ease, malevolently, he beamed at her. Jaisel slipped the gaudy dagger from her belt, let him catch the flash of the gilt, then tossed it at him. The little blade, with its wasp-sting point, sang through the air, singeing the hairs on his right cheek. It buried itself, where she had aimed it, in the picket post behind him. But Renier, reacting to the feint as she had intended, lunged desperately aside for the sake of his pretty face, took all his own weight on the yet-stirruped leg and off the free one, unbalanced royally, and plunged crashing to the ground. At the same instant, fully startled, the horse tried to rear. Still left-leggedly trapped in the stirrup, Renier of Towers went slithering through the hot ashes of a fire.

A hubbub resulted—delighted unfriendly mirth. The soldiers were as prepared to make sport of a boastful lord on his ears in the ash as of a helpless girl.

And the helpless girl was not quite finished. Renier was fumbling for his sword. Jaisel leaped over him like a lion, kicking his hands away as she passed. Landing, she wrenched his foot out of the stirrup and, having liberated him, jumped to the picket to retrieve her dagger. As Renier gained his knees, he beheld her waiting for him, quiet as a statue, her pack slung on the ground, the thin sword, slick with light, ready as a sixth long murderous finger to her hand.

A second he faltered, while the camp, ferociously animated, buzzed. Then his ringed hand went to the hilt of his own sword. It was two to three thirds its length from the scabbard when a voice bellowed from the doorway of the scarlet and gold pavilion: "Dare to draw upon a woman, Renier, and I'll flay you myself."

Gasping, Renier let the sword grate home again. Jaisel turned and saw a man incarnadine with anger as the tent he had stepped from. Her own dormant anger woke and filled her, white anger not red, bored anger, cold anger.

"Don't fear him slain, sir," she said. "I will give him only a slight cut, and afterward spare him."

The incarnadine captain of the camp of Towers bent a baleful shaggy lour on her.

"Strumpet, or witch?" he thundered.

"Tell me first," said Jaisel coolly, "your title. Is it coward or imbecile?"

Silence was settling like flies on honey.

The captain shook himself.

"I never yet struck a wench—" he said.

"Nor will you now, by God's wounds."

His mouth dropped ajar. He disciplined it and asked firmly: "Why coward and why imbecile?"

"Humoring me, are you?" she inquired. She strolled toward him and let the sword tip weave a delicate pattern about his nose. To his credit, having calmed himself, he retained the calm. "Coward or imbecile," she said, drawing lines of glinting fire an inch from his nostrils, "because you cannot take a castle that offers no defenders."

A response then. A beefy paw thrust up to flick the sword away from him and out of her hand. But the sword was too quick. Now it rested horizontally on the air, tip twitching a moment at his throat. And now it was gone back into its scabbard, and merely a smiling strange-eyed girl was before him.

"I already know enough of you," the captain said, "that you are a trial to men and an affront to heaven is evident. Despite that, I will answer your abuse. Maudras' last castle is defended by some sorcery he conjured to guard it. Three assaults were attempted. The result you shall witness. Follow, she-wolf."

And he strode off through the thick of the men who parted to let him

by, and to let the she-wolf by in his wake. No one touched her but one fool, who had observed, but learned nothing. The pommel of her dagger in his ribs, bruising through mail and shirt, put pain to his flirtation.

"Here," the captain barked.

He drew aside the flap of a dark tent, and she saw twenty men lying on rusty mattresses and the two surgeons going up and down. The casualties of some savage combat. She beheld things she had beheld often, those things which sickened less but appalled more with repetition. Near to the entrance a boy younger than herself, dreaming horribly in a fever, called out.

Jaisel slipped into the tent. She set her icy palm on the boy's forehead and felt his raging heat burn through it. But her touch seemed to alleviate his dream at least. He grew quieter.

"Again," she said softly, "coward, or imbecile. And these are the sacrificial victims on the altar of cowardice or imbecility."

Probably, the captain had never met such merciless eyes. Or, perhaps not so inexplicably, from between the smooth lids of a young girl.

"Enchantment," he said gruffly. "And sorcery. We were powerless against it. Do you drink wine, you virago? Yes, no doubt. Come and drink it with me then in my pavilion and you shall have the full story. Not that you deserve it. But you are the last thrown stone that kills a man. Injustice atop all the rest, and from a *woman*."

Abruptly she laughed at him, her anger spent.

RED WINE AND RED MEAT were served in the red pavilion. All the seven knights of the Towers camp were present, Cassant and Renier among the rest. Outside, their men went on sitting around the fires. A dreary song had been struck up, and was repeated, over and over, as iron snow-light radiated from the northern summer sky.

The captain of the knights had told again the story Cassant had recounted to Jaisel on the slope: The three castles razed, the final castle which proved unassailable. Gruff and bellicose, the captain found it hard to speak of supernatural items and growled the matter into his wine.

"Three assaults were offered the walls of the castle. Montaube led the first of these. He died, and fifty men with him. Of what? We saw no swordsmen on the battlements, no javelots were fired, no arrows. Yet men sprinkled the ground, bloody and dying, as if an army twice our numbers had come to grips with them unseen. The second assault, I led. I escaped by a miracle. I saw a man, his mail split as if by a bolt shot from a great distance. He dropped with a cry and blood bursting from a terrible wound. Not a soul was near but I, his captain. No weapon or shot was visible. The third assault—was planned, but never carried through. We reached the escarpment, and my soldiers began falling like scythed grain. No shame in our retreat. Another thing. Last month, three brave fools, men of dead Montaube's, decided secretly to effect entry by night over the walls. A sentry perceived them vanish within. They were not attacked. Nor did they return."

There was a long quiet in the pavilion. Jaisel glanced up and encountered the wrathful glare of the captain.

"Ride home to Towers, then," she said. "What else is there to do?"

"And what other council would you predict from a woman?" broke in Renier. "We are *men*, madame. We'll take that rock, or die. Honor, lady. Did you never hear of it in the whorehouse where you were whelped?"

"You have had too much wine, sir," said Jaisel. "But by all means have some more." She poured her cup, measured and deliberate, over his curling hair. Two or three guffawed, enjoying this novelty. Renier leapt up. The captain bellowed familiarly, and Renier again relapsed.

Wine ran in rosy streams across his handsome brow.

"Truly, you do right to reprove me, and the she-wolf is right to anoint me with her scorn. We sit here like cowards, as she mentioned. There's one way to take the castle. A challenge. Single combat between God and Satan. Can the haunting of Maudras refuse that?" Renier got to his feet with precision now.

"You are drunk, Renier," the captain snapped.

"Not too drunk to fight." Renier was at the entrance. The captain roared. Renier only bowed. "I am a knight. Only so far can you command me."

"You fool—" said Cassant.

"I am, however, my own fool," said Renier.

The knights stood, witnesses to his departure. Respect, sorrow, and dread showed in their eyes, their nervous fingers fiddled with jewels, wine cups, chess figures.

Outside, the dreary song had broken off. Renier was shouting for his horse and battle gear.

The knights crowded to the flap to watch him armed. Their captain elect joined them. No further protest was attempted, as if a divine ordinance were being obeyed.

Jaisel walked out of the pavilion. The light was thickening as if to hem them in. Red fires, red banners, no other color able to pierce the gloom. Renier sat his horse like a carved chess figure himself, an immaculate knight moving against a castle on a misty board.

The horse fidgeted, trembled. Jaisel ran her hand peacefully down its nose amid the litter of straps and buckles. She did not look at Renier, swaggering above her. She sensed too well his panic under the pride.

"Don't," she said to him softly, "ride into the arms of death because you think I shamed your manhood. It's too large a purge for so small an ill."

"Go away, girl," he jeered at her. "Go and have babies as God fashioned you to do."

"God did not fashion you to die, Renier of Towers."

"Maybe you're wrong in that," he said wildly, and jerked the horse around and away from her.

He was galloping from the camp across the plain toward the rock. A herald dashed out following, but prudently hung some yards behind. When he sounded the brass, the notes cracked, and his horse shied at the noise. But Renier's horse threw itself on as if in preparation for a massive jump at the end of its running.

"He's mad; will die," Cassant mumbled.

"And my fault," Jaisel answered.

A low horrified moan went through the ranks of the watchers. The iron barricades of the huge castle's mouth were sluggishly folding aside. Nothing rode forth. It was, on the contrary, patently an invitation.

One man yelled to Renier across a hundred yards of gray ground. Several swelled the cry. Suddenly, three quarters of the camp of Towers was howling. To make sport of a noble was one thing. To see him seek annihilation was another. They screamed themselves hoarse, begging him to choose reason above honor.

Jaisel, not uttering a word, turned from the spectacle. When she heard Cassant swearing, she knew Renier had galloped straight in the iron portal. The commotion of shouting crumbled into breathings, oaths. And then came the shock and clangor of two iron leaves meeting together again across the mouth of hell.

Impossible to imagine what he might be confronting now. Perhaps he would triumph, re-emerge in glory. Perhaps the evil in Maudras' castle had faded, or had never existed. Was an illusion. Or a lie.

They waited. The soldiers, the knights. The woman. A cold wind blew up, raking plumes, pennants, the long curled hair, plucking bridle bells, the gold sickle moon in Jaisel's left ear, the fragile lace at her wrists, and the foaming lace at the wrists of others.

The white sun westered, muddied, disappeared. Clouds like curds forming in milk formed in the sky.

Darkness slunk in on all fours. Mist boiled over, hiding the view of the castle. The fires burned, the horses coughed at their pickets.

There was the smell of a wet rottenness, like marshland—the mist—or rotting hope.

A young knight whose name Jaisel had forgotten was at her elbow. He thrust in her face a chess piece of red amber.

"The white queen possessed the red knight," he hissed at her. "Put him in the box then. Slam the lid. Fine chess game here in the north. Castles unbreachable and bitches for queens. Corpses for God's knights."

Jaisel stared him down till he went away. From the corner of her eye, she noticed Cassant was weeping tears, frugally, one at a time.

It was too easy to get by the sentries in the mist and dark.

Of course, they were alert against the outer environs, not the camp itself. But, still too easy. Discipline was lax. Honor had become everything, and honor was not enough.

Yet it was her own honor that drove her, she was not immune. Nor immune to this sad region. She was full of guilt she had no need to feel, and full of regret for a man with whom she had shared only a mutual dislike, distrust, and some quick verbal cuts and quicker deeds of wrath. Renier had given himself to the castle, to show himself valiant, to shame her. She was duly shamed. Accordingly, she was goaded to breach the castle also, to plumb its vile secret. To save his life if she could, avenge him if not. And die if the castle should outwit her? No. Here was the strangest fancy of all. Somewhere in her bones she did not believe Maudras' castle could do that. After all, her entire life had been a succession of persons, things, fate itself, trying to vanquish her and her aims. From the first drop of menstrual blood, the first husband chosen for her at the age of twelve, the first (and last) rape, the first swordmaster who had mocked her demand to learn and ended setting wagers on her—there had been so many lions in her way. And she had systematically overcome each of them. Because she did not, would not, accept that destiny was unchangeable. Or that what was merely named unconquerable could not be conquered.

Maudras' castle then, just another symbol to be thrown down. And the sick-sweet twang of fear in her vitals was no more than before any battle, like an old scar throbbing, simple to ignore.

She padded across the plain noiselessly in the smoky mist.

Sword on left hip, dagger on the right. Saddle and pack had been left behind beneath her blanket. Some would-be goat might suffer astonishment if he ventured to her sleeping place. Otherwise they would not detect her absence till sunrise.

The mist ceased thirty feet from the causeway.

She paused a moment, and considered the eccentric edifice pouring aloft into overcast black sky. Now the castle had a choice. It could gape invitingly as it had before Renier the challenger. Or leave her to climb the wall seventy feet high above the doormouth.

The iron barricades stayed shut.

She went along the causeway.

Gazing up, the cranky towers seemed to reel, sway. Certainly it had an aura of wickedness, of impenetrable lingering hate . . .

White queen against bishop of darkness.

Queen takes castle, a rare twist to an ancient game.

The wall.

Masonry jutted, stonework creviced, protruded. Even weeds had rooted there. It was a gift, this wall, to any who would climb it. Which implied a maleficent joke, similar to the opening doors. *Enter. Come, I welcome you. Enter me and be damned within me.*

She jumped, caught hold, began to ascend. Loose-limbed and agile from a hundred trees, some other less lordly walls, one cliff-face five years ago—Jaisel could skim up vertical buildings like a cat. She did not really require all the solicitous help Maudras' wall pressed on her.

She gained the outer battlements in minutes and was looking in. Beyond this barrier, the curtain, a courtyard with its central guard—but all pitch black, difficult to assess. Only that configuration of turrets and crooked bastions breaking clear against the sky. As before, she thought of a growth, petrified.

The sound was of ripped cloth. But it was actually ripped atmosphere. Jaisel threw her body flat on the broad parapet and something kissed the nape of her neck as it rushed by into the night. Reminiscent of a javelot bolt. Or the thicker swan-righted arrows of the north. Without sentience, yet meant for the heart, and capable of stilling it.

She tilted herself swiftly over the parapet, hung by her fingers, and dropped seven feet to a platform below. As she landed, the tearing sound was reiterated. A violent hand tugged her arm. She glanced and beheld shredded lace barely to be seen in the blackness. The mail above her wrist was heated.

Some power that could make her out when she was nearly blind, but which seemed to attack randomly, inaccurately. She cast herself flat again and crawled on her belly to the head of a stair.

Here, descending, she became the perfect target. No matter. Her second swordmaster had been something of an acrobat—

Jaisel launched herself into air and judging where the rims of the steps should be, executed three bold erratic somersaults, arriving ultimately in a hedgehog-like roll in the court.

As she straightened from this roll, she was aware of a sudden dim glow. She spun to meet it, sword and dagger to hand, then checked, heart and gorge passing each other as they traveled in the wrong directions.

The glow was worse than sorcery. It was caused by a decaying corpse half propped in a ruined niche under the stairs. Putrescent, the remnants gave off a phosphorescent shine, matched by an intolerable stench that seemed to intensify with recognition. And next, something else. Lit by the witch-light of dead flesh, an inscription apparently chiseled in the stone beside it. Against her wits, Jaisel could not resist studying it. In pure clerical calligraphy it read:

MAUDRAS SLEW ME

One of Montaube's men.

Only the fighter's seventh sense warned Jaisel. It sent her ducking, darting, her sword arm sweeping up—and a great blow smashed against the blade, singing through her arm into her breast and shoulder. A great invisible blow.

The thought boiled in her—*How can I fight what I cannot see?* And the second inevitable thought: *I have always fought that way, combat with abstracts.* And in that extraordinary instant, wheeling to avoid the slashing lethal blows of a murderous nonentity, Jaisel realized that though she could not *see*, she could *sense*.

Perhaps twenty further hackings hailed against her sword, chipped the stones around. Her arm was almost numbed, but organized and obedient as a war machine, kept up its parries, feints, deflectings, thrusts. And then, eyes nearly closed, seeing better through instinct with a hair's breadth, dancing-with-death accuracy, she paid out her blade the length of her arm, her body hurtling behind it, and *felt* tissue part on either side of the steel. And immediately there followed a brain-slicing shriek, more like breath forced from a bladder than the protest of a dying throat.

The way was open. She sensed this too, and shot forward, doubled over, blade swirling with precaution. A fresh doorway, the gate into the guard, yawning unbarred, and across this gate, to be leaped, a glow, a reeking skeleton, the elegant chiseling in the stone floor on this occasion:

MAUDRAS SLEW ME

"Maudras!" Jaisel shouted as she leaped.

She was in the wide hollow of the castle guard. In the huge black, which tingled and burned and flashed with colors thrown by her own racing blood against the discs of her eyes.

Then the darkness screamed, an awful shattering of notes, which brought on an avalanche, a cacophony, as if the roof fell. It took her an extra heartbeat to understand, to fling herself from the path of charging destruction no less potent for being natural. As the guard wall met her spine, the screaming nightmare, Renier's horse, exploded by her and out into the court beyond the floor.

She lay quiet, taking air, and something stirred against her arm. She wrenched away and raised her sword, but Montaube's ultimate glowing soldier was there, draped on the base of what looked to be a pillar trunk. A lamp, he shone for her as the circulatory flashes died from the interior of her eyes. So she saw Renier of Towers sprawled not a foot from her.

The corpse (MAUDRAS SLEW ME inscribed on the pillar) appeared to glow brighter to enable her to see the mark on Renier's forehead, like the bruise caused by some glancing bolt. A trickle of blood where formerly wine had trickled. The lids shivering, the chest rising and falling shallowly.

She leaned to him and whispered: "You live then. Your luck's kinder than I reckoned. To be stunned rather than slaughtered. And Maudras' magic waiting for you to get up again. Not liking to kill when you would not know it. Preferring to make a meal of killing you, unfair and unsquare."

Then, without preface, terror swamped the hollow pillared guard of Maudras' castle.

A hundred, ten hundred, whirling slivers of steel carved the nothingness. From the blind vault, blades swooped, seared, wailed. Jaisel was netted in a sea of death. Waves of death broke over her, gushed aside, were negated by vaster waves. She sprang from one edge and reached another. The slashing was like the beaks of birds, scoring hands, cheeks; scratches as yet, but pecking, diligent. While, in its turn, her sword sank miles deep in substances like mud, like powder. Subhuman voices squalled. Unseen shapes tottered. But the rain of bites, of pecks, of scratches, whirled her this way, that way, against pillars, broken stones, downward, upward. And she was in terror. Fought in terror. Terror lent her miraculous skills, feats, a crazy flailing will to survive, and a high wild cry which again and again she smote the darkness with, along with dagger and sword.

Till abruptly she could no longer fight. Her limbs melted and terror melted with them into a worse state of abject exhaustion, acceptance, resignation. Her spirit sank, she sank, the sword sank from one hand, the dagger from the other. Drowning, she thought stubbornly: Die fighting at least. But she did not have the strength left her.

Not until that moment did she grow aware of the cessation of blows, the silence.

She had stumbled against, was partly leaning on, some upright block of stone that had been in her way when she dropped. Dully, her mind struggled with a paradox that would not quite resolve. She had been battling shadows, which had slain others instantly, but had not slain Jaisel. Surely what she supposed was a game had gone on too long for a game. While in earnest, now she was finished, the mechanism for butchery in this castle might slay her, yet did not. And swimming wonder surfaced scornfully: Am I charmed?

There was a light. Not the phosphorus of Montaube's soldiers. It was a light the color the wretched country had been by day, a sallow snow-blue glaze, dirty silver on the columns, coming up like a Sabbat moon from out of nowhere.

Jaisel stared into the light, and perceived a face floating in it. No doubt. It must be the countenance of burned Maudras, the last malicious dregs of his spirit on holiday from hell to effect menace. More skull than man. Eye sockets faintly gleaming, mouth taut as if in agony.

With loathing and aversion, and with horror, the skull regarded her. It seemed, perversely, to instruct her to shift her gaze downward, to the stone block where she leaned powerlessly.

And something in the face ridiculously amused her, made her shake with laughter, shudder with it, so that she knew before she looked.

The light was snuffed a second later.

Then the castle began, in rumbling stages, to collapse on every side. Matter of factly, she went to Renier and lay over his unconscious body to protect him from the cascading granite.

HE WAS NOT GRATEFUL as she bathed his forehead at the chill pool equidistant between the ruin and the camp of Towers.

Nearby, the horse licked the grudging turf. The mist had fled, and a rose-crimson sun was blooming on the horizon. A hundred yards off, the camp gave evidence of enormous turmoil. Renier swore at her.

"Am I to credit that a strumpet nullified the sorcery of Maudras? Don't feed me that stew."

"You suffer it too hardly. As ever," said Jaisel, honed to patience by the events of the night. "Any woman might have achieved this thing. But women warriors are uncommon."

"There is one too many, indeed."

Jaisel stood. She started to walk away. Renier called after her huskily:

"Wait. Say to me again what was written in the stone."

Her back to him, she halted. Concisely, wryly smiling, she said: " 'I, Maudras, to this castle do allot my everlasting bane, that no man shall ever approach its walls without hurt, nor enter it and live long. Nor, to the world's ending, shall it be taken by any man.' "

Renier snarled.

She did not respond to that, but walked on.

Presently he caught up to her, and striding at her side, said: "How many other prophecies could be undone, do you judge, Lady Insolence, that dismiss women in such fashion?"

"As many as there are stars in heaven," she said.

Brooding, but no longer arguing, he escorted her into the camp.

≫•≪

In Ash: A Secret History—*a truly epic and unflinchingly gritty novel—*
Mary Gentle created Ash, a woman warrior with intelligence, strength,
and guts—along with weaknesses and flaws. In this short work, we meet
Rax. Among her people, Rax must fight to be what she is: a warrior. She
finds acceptance, but acceptance does not necessarily bring happiness.

ANUKAZI'S DAUGHTER

Mary Gentle

"OUR INFORMATION was correct," Ukurri said, pointing. The ship was just visible, its prow appearing out of the dawn haze, already in the calm water of the bay. "Let them come ashore. Attack as soon as the light's good."

"Prisoners?" Rax asked.

He grinned at her. "Try to keep one or two alive. They might have things to tell us. These Islanders are weak-willed." Low chuckles came from the mounted company that formed Bazuruk's first Order of the Axe.

"Ready yourselves," he ordered.

Rax knotted the war-horse's reins on the saddle. She breathed deeply, excitement cold in her gut. Her palms were damp. She wiped them on the black surcoat, feeling cold links of mail underneath, and adjusted the buckles on her leg and arm greaves. The shaft of the war-axe was familiar under her hand. The shield hung ready at her side.

The ship nosed close inshore. Sea foam went from gray to white. A cold wind blew. Here great shelves of rock jutted out into the sea, channels worn between them by the waves, so that at low tide a ship could put into what was a natural quay.

There were thirty men—no more—she estimated. Our numbers are equal, then.

"There!" She saw the flash of light from the cliffs at the far end of the bay: a signal-mirror in the hands of the Third Axe, telling them that the other half of the company was in position.

"*Now!*" Ukurri shouted.

Her heels dug into the horse's flanks. For a few strides she was out in the open, ahead of them all. The rocks echoed. Sparks struck from flying hooves.

Rax, cold clear through, hefted the great axe. Ukurri and Azu-anuk and Lilazu rode with her, and the rest of the Order behind, but she spurred forward and outdistanced them all.

The war-mount cleared a channel where crimson weed hung delicate and fragile in clear water. She heard cries, shouts; she saw the men half ashore from the ship and heard the thunder of the riders from the far end of the bay. She rose up in the saddle sweating, cold as death under her mail, excitement drying her lips—and caught a spear-thrust on her shield. She struck. The great blade sheared up under the man's helmet. The jaw, ear, half the skull ripping away.

Another struck at her, jabbing with a barbed spear. Her blow, which seemed only to brush him, spilled a crimson trail.

On the backstroke she put the axe's spike through another man's eye socket and left him screaming. The horse reared, came down, crushing with iron hooves. Smooth rock became treacherous, slick with blood. The sun hit her eyes. Her face was wet, and her black surcoat had turned rust-colored with blood—not hers. An Islander fled. She leaned dangerously far out of the saddle to slice through his leather jerkin and left him face down on the rock. She smelled burning and heard flames crackle. A dozen of the Order were at the ship. The pitch that caulked its seams burned fiercely. A man screamed. She saw Ukurri strike, hurling the man back into the blaze. Flames were invisible in the sunlight; only the shimmering air betrayed them.

"Bazuruk!" She heard the war call behind her.

She wheeled, lifted the axe—it was heavy, and her arm was stiff—and saw Lilazu fighting on one of the narrow rock spurs. His horse shifted uneasily. It was no help now to be mounted. Two Islanders had him pinned against the water's edge.

Her thrown hand-axe took one in the back. Rax struck with the flat of the axe, sending the other man full-length into the shallow pool. Lilazu acknowledged Rax's aid with a raised hand, guiding his horse delicately onto solid rock, then galloping off toward the last knot of fighting.

Rax leaned down from the saddle, using the spike of the axe to hook the stunned man ashore.

The crackling of the flames was loud. Surf beat on the rocks. Gulls cried. The air smelled of dank weed, of burning, of blood. Rax's hands were red, her arms streaked with blood that dried and cracked. She hauled the Islander over her saddle, clicking to the weary horse, and rode over to where Ukurri watched the burning ship. The early sun was already hot. A warming relaxation spread through her. If she had not been exhausted, she would have sung.

"Rax Keshanu!" Ukurri slapped her leg and pulled the Islander down from her saddle. "A live one . . . and not half-killed. Good! That's four."

She was grinning amiably at nothing in particular: she recognized the after-battle euphoria. "Shall I bring him with me?" she asked.

Ukurri hesitated. Rax's light mood faded.

"Do you think I'm stupid enough to let him escape?"

"Women have soft hearts," Ukurri said and then laughed as Rax held up her bloody hands. "But not in the Order of the Axe, no—though we've only you to judge by. Bring him with us to the Tower, then."

The others were rifling the dead, leaving the bodies unburied on the rocks. If the stink offended any of the nearby settlements, they'd send a burial party. If not, enemy bones would bleach in the cove, and the storm tides would carry them home to Shabelit and the Hundred Isles.

AT THEIR FIRST CAMP, she tended the unconscious Islander's head wound. He was young, no more than twenty, she judged: Ukurri's age, ten summers younger than Rax. He had pale skin, red-brown hair, and green eyes in a face marred by plague-scars.

She felt an indefinable pang: not of desire or pity, but somehow familiar. If I'd seen him, I couldn't have killed him, she realized. Anukazi! What's the matter with me?

She had fought before, taken prisoners for ransom; none had ever disturbed her the way this Islander boy did.

The Order headed north, resting in the heat of noon, crossing the humid, insect-ridden flats of the Shantar marshes. Rax guarded the Islander closely. After the first day his rage and grief—displayed beyond what a Bazuruki considered proper subsided into quiet. She thought that meant loss of spirit until she caught him cutting himself and the other survivors free with a stolen knife. After that she watched him constantly.

"I didn't think he had the wits to try it," she admitted to Ukurri, as they rode on north.

"You served on the barbarian frontier, the Crystal Mountains. They're cunning in the cold south," he said. "The Islanders are the worst of all. That one's a Vanathri—you can tell by the cropped hair. The others are mercenaries, from the Cold Lands, I'd guess."

Rax shrugged. "It's not our concern. They'll discover the truth in the Tower."

That night she took a water flask for the Islander. He regarded her with disgust.

"Bazuruki killer," he said.

She pulled off her helmet, letting the coarse black hair fall free. She grinned, feral, content.

"Yes," she said, "I am a woman and a warrior."

She realized that he wasn't shocked or even surprised. That sent her back to Ukurri with oblique questions, and he told her that in the Hundred Isles a woman was barred from no profession, not even that of warrior.

ON THE THIRD DAY they rode through rice fields to the river estuary and came to the city.

"That's Anukazi?" The Islander rode beside her on a remount, bound securely. "A great city, Rax . . . "

"Wherever you heard my name, keep it out of your mouth." She almost regretted her harshness. Her curiosity was stirred. "Why did you come here—one ship's company against all Bazuruk?"

"You have my freemate there." His voice was rough. "I would have fought my way to the city—but I used mercenaries. It is no surprise that I was betrayed."

The Order rode down the brick-paved way that led to the South Gate. Ox-carts drew aside. Insects whirred in the dustclouds. The heat made Rax thirsty. As the shadow of Anukazi's squat square buildings fell across her, she became aware that her joy at returning was less than usual.

"You have women-warriors in your islands, then, Vanathri?"

"If you can recognize a Vanathri, you know we don't bind ourselves with useless laws." His body tensed as they rode down the wide streets. "Though it seems your laws aren't as strict as I'd heard."

"You don't think so?" Her bitterness was never far below the surface. Her long fight to be accepted in an Order had been successful, but the struggle robbed her of half her satisfaction. At last she said, "I've spent most of my life in the northern mountains. All I know of the Archipelago is rumors."

"That can be remedied."

He was talking to keep his fears at bay, she guessed. He didn't look at her. She studied his familiar features. What does he see when he looks at me? Rax wondered.

She listened while he spoke of the Shabelit Archipelago, which began in the sandbars off Bazuruk's coast and ended as far south as the Cold Lands. He talked about the Hundred Isles, where life was trade and where half a hundred petty lordlings engaged their private quarrels, with no Tower to bind them into one nation . . .

"Rax," Ukurri called, as they entered the Tower walls, "take that one down to the cells with the mercenaries before you go off duty."

She acknowledged his order curtly. While the rest of the Order dismounted at the stables, she made her way with the prisoners to the dungeons. The underground shadow was cool.

"You've got another Islander in here," she told the jailer, keeping charge of the Vanathri man. "Put them in together. They might talk."

Brick walls were scarred with nitre. Pitch-torches flared, blackening the ceiling. The jailer searched down the entry scroll.

"Three-five-six," he announced. "Let him sweat. They won't get to him for a while."

"Why not?"

"A conspiracy was discovered against the Firsts of the Orders." He glanced fearfully at her. "The guards are interrogating everyone in the Tower and executing traitors."

"Anukazi save the Tower from harm," Rax said, and the man echoed her fervently. "Give me the keys, I'll take this one down for you."

Shadows leapt as they descended the long stairways. Rax held the torch high, searching for the right cell.

"I'll send a physician to look at you."

"No." He was hostile.

"You're young," she said, "but you're not stupid. If you've no friends, you won't live long here, Vanathri. These cells are plague-pits."

"I'll do without Bazuruk's help."

She fitted the key in the lock, thrust the torch in a wall-socket, and pulled the heavy door open. There was only one other Islander listed—a Shabelitan—so this must be his freemate. It would be interesting to see a warrior-woman, Rax thought.

The Islander came into the torchlight, dragging his chain.

Rax was disappointed. It was a man: stocky, in his forties, with a lined face and mocking smile. This is the wrong cell, she thought, or the Islander woman's already dead—

"Devenil," Vanathri said, holding out his bound hands. The other man stepped forward and kissed him on the mouth with a lover's kiss.

"So here you are to rescue me. Again." The older man smiled tightly. Behind his mockery there was pain. "Vanathri are impetuous, I know, Kel. But this is stupidity."

"Did you think I wouldn't come?" Kel Vanathri asked, looking younger than ever.

"Did you come for me or for Shabelit's heir? Vanathri's not a rich island, and if ever I inherit Shabelit—though lord knows my mother may outlive us all—then I can see why you'd want to be Shabelit's freemate."

"I'd stay with you even if I thought you'd never inherit—or if you weren't heir at all. You should know that by now."

Cynicism marked Devenil's face, but his voice was tired and uncertain. "Would you? Yes, I think you would."

"I should have managed this better." Anger darkened Kel's eyes. "I'm a fool, and I've paid for it. I've lost a mercenary company and my freedom. But a chance will come. We're not dead yet."

Rax crept away from the spy-hole, leaving the torch to burn itself out.

I SHOULD REPORT IT.

Lost in thought, Rax made her way to the Axe Order's building in the Tower complex. Devenil, that was the name: heir of Shabelit of the Hundred Isles. They can't know, or they'd be asking a ransom for him. But they'll know as soon as they start interrogating him, as soon as this purge is over.

Anukazi keep them from me!

She reached her own chambers, a bare brick-walled room divided by rice-paper screens. Through the window she could see across the flat roofs and ziggurats of the city. She pulled the thin linen shutters closed in order to keep flies and a degree of heat out. Then she shed her mail, bathed, and donned a silk robe.

She sat on the pallet. A brush and paper lay on the low table, unfinished calligraphy spidering across the page. She wasn't yet calm enough to write. She called the house slave and ordered rice and herb tea.

The Islanders had reeked of dead meat. So they eat animal flesh, Rax thought with revulsion. The men couple with one another, and the women too, I suppose; and women are warriors, and men—but he's a fighter, that Kel Vanathri.

Seated cross-legged before the carved Keshanu mask that hung on the wall, she gazed at the abstract face and tried to achieve harmony. Patterns of light and shade entered her eyes. Her breathing slowed.

She was free, then, of Rax. She could stand outside herself and see the tall strong-limbed woman whose skin was lined with exposure to wind and sun. With black hair, green eyes, red-brown skin, she was born of hot Keshanu in the Crystal Mountains . . .

But then she thought of Kel Vanathri and Devenil, Shabelit's heir.

She tried to consider them dispassionately. The image that came to her was not Vanathri's but Ukurri's. Of an age with the young Islander, Ukurri was already First Axe of this Order, her commander, and sometime bedfriend. And she, a decade older, with experience gained on the barbarian frontier . . .

You'll never be First Axe, a voice said in her mind. No matter how good you are, how many successes you have, they won't give you an Order because the men wouldn't accept you as commander. You're good, better than Ukurri, but you're a woman.

In Vanathri, Kel said, there are women-warriors; and in Zu and Orindol and Shamur, and all the Hundred Isles . . .

She cursed Kel for disturbing her peace of mind.

He's young to end in the Tower. He, she thought, has courage, too; he crossed the sea, which is more than I'd do.

Outside, the gongs sounded for evening prayer. She belted her hand-axe over her robe and put on her sandals, preparing to go down to the main hall.

Keep low, Rax thought. There have been conspiracies and interrogations before. I'm loyal to the Tower. They'll take Anukazi's sons but I don't think they'll take Anukazi's only daughter.

SHE FOLLOWED the disciplines of the Tower, attended weapons practice and theory classes and services for the preservation of Anukazi's priests. She knew better than to ask about missing faces or empty places. Finally the atmosphere of tension eased: the purge was—for this time at least—finished.

THE DICE were kind. Rax found herself on a winning streak for the first time in a long while. She was able to bribe extra rations for the Islanders without touching her own pay. When she heard that the Guard had begun interrogating the mercenaries, she went back to the Tower and paid for an undisturbed time in the cells.

The torch burned bright. Kel had fallen against Devenil while he slept, and the older man sat with his back to the wall, supporting Kel. All the mockery was gone from his worn face.

Rax was noisy with the lock, and when she had the door open, hostile stares greeted her.

"What do you want?" Kel Vanathri demanded.

Rax shook her head. The calmness that was a discipline of the Order deserted her. She couldn't name the influence the Islanders had over her.

"They're starting the questioning soon," she said.

"Bring me a knife," Kel said, "I won't ask more, Bazuruki." It was pointless to tell them that one day their rations would be drugged, that they would wake in the upper chambers—in the hands of the Anukazi Guard.

"Say you're only mercenaries, pirates, whatever," she pleaded. "As for freemates, for the love of Anukazi himself, keep that quiet!"

"There's no love in your Orders?" Devenil asked skeptically.

"I—" The Order denied love fanatically and practiced it covertly. Every Order had its pretty boys, vying for favor and carrying rumors. Looking now at Kel and Devenil, she thought no, it's not the same thing at all.

"What they forgive themselves, they hate in others."

"Take advice," Kel Vanathri said, "stay out of here." She knew they had plans to escape, or to invite a quick death.

The thought bothered her more than it should. She slammed the door and walked away. In a little while they'd be dead.

They'd be good companions in an Order, she thought. It's a senseless waste . . .

To kill Bazuruk's enemies?

No!

What am I thinking? We're caught between the northern barbarians and these damned islands, which, if they could ever unite, could crush Bazuruk. We can't afford mercy, not even for those two. Ah, Anukazi! Why should I care?

Rax couldn't sleep that night. She rose and dressed—in mail, with her war-axe—and went down to the main hall. But even dice-games couldn't ease her spirit.

All the city slept. There were no lights in the squat buildings, no noise from the beast markets, no carts in the street. She went by way of the river wall and entered the Tower as the guards changed shift.

Torches burned low in the guardroom.

"Jailer—" Some instinct held her hand, when she reached to shake him awake. A thin thread of blood ran out from under his head, bowed on the table.

Movement caught her eye, where the torch guttered. The axe slid into her hands. A scuffed noise came from down the passage. She tensed. The jailer had no knife or sword. They would be armed, then.

Softly she said "Vanathri?"

"Be silent."

"Devenil." The strength of her relief was alarming. "Where's Kel?"

"Put down your axe!"

She rested the spike on the floor, hands clasping the shaft. "Now I'll tell you something. You're not the first to kill a jailer and come this far. But can you fight your way out past every guard in Anukazi's Tower?"

"If we have to." It was Kel Vanathri's voice.

"Wait." She sensed movement. "Suppose you were taken out of here by a guard? There are riverboats. You might cross the sea to the Hundred Isles."

"And let you sound the alarm?" Kel said. "Put down the axe. I can throw a knife as well as any Bazuruki."

"You're not listening to me, Islander. Take the jailer's uniform."

They stepped forward into the light. Devenil nodded, watching her with a curious expression. "We'll lock you in one of the cells, unless you prefer a glorious death—as Bazuruki do, I've heard."

"And how will you get past the gates? I'll have to speak for you. Trust me," Rax said. "Only be quick!"

It was only then that she knew her long career with the Order of the Axe had ended in betrayal.

A FISHING BOAT was moored with sails still raised. The man aboard answered Rax's hail from the dock.

"Stay back," she said to the Islanders. The man's head came above the rail, and she drove her knife up under the soft part of his jaw. Blood spilled over her hands. She wrenched the blade loose, feeling it grate against bone, and shoved the body off the side. It sank quickly. She led the Islanders down the stone steps.

"Now, Devenil, Shabelit's heir," she said, "take this young fool with you and get out of Bazuruk. The alarm's out, I expect, but the tide's in your favor. Go!"

"They know who brought us out," Kel Vanathri said. "You can't stay."

"But my Order—"

"You should have thought of that." Devenil gave a sardonic grin. The early sun showed dirt, blood, the traces of long confinement; he looked a good ten years older than his age. His mocking face disturbed and attracted her. She felt he understood motives she herself didn't recognize.

"We owe a debt we'll never pay you," said Vanathri. His young face looked vulnerable. "But if you come with us to the Hundred Isles, we'll try."

From the first moment I saw you, she thought. That lover's kiss between you and Devenil . . . how could I leave you two innocents in the Tower? You remind me of—

Yes. Is it that simple? He'd have been very like you, if he'd lived: my son Tarik.

"I'll come," Rax said.

THE SUN BURNED, and the sea shimmered. The stars hung like a mist of diamonds, and the night wind cut to the bone.

Cotton-wool fog hugged the coast. The deep swells rolled like hills. They headed south, into ever-colder seas.

Rax lay moaning in the coffin-sized cabin, sweating, heaving with every lurch and dip of the sea. Days passed. Kel and Devenil sailed, fished, fed her fresh water. Once she woke to see them lying together, Kel's pale arm across Devenil's scarred body.

Solitude and loss and sickness frightened her. She slept with the war-axe tight in her grip. No Tower discipline, no skill learned in battle helped her now.

On the tenth day, when they sighted the coast of Dhared, she barely stirred, and at noon, when they passed it and came to Vanathri itself, she was too weak to do more than stare. She saw a green land, chill under a gray sky and lashing rain, where slant-roofed buildings hugged a narrow harbor. They sailed into it and were recognized.

Rax stood on the quay, swaying, seeing Kel and Devenil in each other's arms—in broad daylight, she thought dizzily. Then they pulled her into their embrace. The gathering crowd of Vanathri Islanders cheered, and every bell in the town rang out.

WHEN SHE WAS WELL, they crossed the straits to Shabelit, and there Devenil took her before the Island lords and the head of the Council.

"Lady Sephir," he said to her, "here is our rescuer, Rax Keshanu of Bazuruk, axe-warrior of Anukazi's Tower." The chamber was full of brightly dressed men and women and children, she saw, appalled. The air stank of old cooking, new perfumes, and the sea. Rax pulled her stained surcoat over her mail and kept the axe close to her hand. Shabelitans jabbered and pointed while Kel Vanathri told what had happened in Bazuruk.

"We do not welcome Bazuruki," Sephir said, when she had heard his story, "but you have brought my son back to me and restored Kel to Vanathri. You are welcome, Rax Keshanu, in all the Hundred Isles!"

The woman, white-haired, had Devenil's face with more delicate lines. She stood as Rax bowed—the formal acknowledgment of a Bazuruki warrior—and embraced and kissed her.

Rax froze, smelling the scent of a meat-eater.

Amid the general applause, the Lady Sephir pronounced her an honorary captain of Shabelit. It was then, identifying the white scars on the old woman's arms as ancient sword-cuts, that Rax realized she had met her first Shabelit woman-warrior.

COLD SPRING turned to cool summer. Rax moved into rooms in Shabelit, a city founded on trade and almost as big as Anukazi.

She lived with Islander customs as much as was possible for her but followed her version of Bazuruk's discipline. One midsummer day Devenil found her in the practice courts using the war-axe.

"Come up and talk," he said, and she joined him on the seafort's wall.

"I see too little of you both lately," Rax said as she pulled on a tunic against the Archipelago's cold wind. "I suppose Kel's back on Vanathri or another of your damned rocks."

"Kel offered you a place on his ship," Devenil said. "Why don't you take it?"

"The sea, with that sickness?" she scowled.

A brisk wind blew across the sea-fort, spattering her face with dampness. She watched the light on the straits.

"If you wanted to come, sickness wouldn't stop you."

"I'm a soldier," she said at last. "You people . . . I didn't expect anything like the Orders, but you've no standing army at all. You don't understand. I'm a warrior. It's what I do, and I do it better than most. You're asking me to drop it and ship out as some kind of deck hand—"

"A guard. You'd work on the ship, but so do Kel and I. Even Bazuruki aren't killed by honest work."

"Damned Islanders," she said.

Devenil smiled. "You're not the first person to perform a generous act and regret the consequences."

"I don't regret what I did!"

In her mind's eye, Rax saw her chambers in the Tower of Anukazi. The cool light, the shade, the fine carving of the Keshanu mask. Ever since I came to the islands, she thought, my mind's been in a fog.

"Let us pay our debt to you," Devenil said. "Come with us on the *Luck of Vanathri*, if not for our sake, then for your own."

"You love him, don't you?" The thought still amazed her.

"I'll do anything I can for him, including ordering you aboard the *Luck* if it eases his mind. I'm still Shabelit's heir. I can do that."

I got you out of the Tower, she thought. How much more must I give?

"You don't order me. I'm Bazuruki."

"Not any more! You have to see that."

She sighed. Eventually she asked, "When do you sail? I'll come if I can, Devenil, but don't wait for me."

They waited anyway, but she never came.

"You've got company," Garad said. "At least I'd swear it's you he's looking at."

Rax glanced up from the dice. Sun and windburned from his months at sea, brown hair grown untidy, wrapped against the cold of a Shabelit winter night—Kel Vanathri.

"Stay here," she said, "we'll continue our discussion later." Garad smiled, shuttling the dice from hand to hand. "Don't leave. I have your debt-slips—"

She gave him a look that stopped his voice in his throat, then crossed to the doorway.

"Rax!" Kel gripped her hands, then let them fall, puzzled by her lack of response. "The time it's taken me to find you—"

"Did I ask you to come looking?"

"I came anyway. It's a strange place to find a Bazuruk warrior. With mercenaries."

"Mercenaries and gamblers are no worse company than traders' sons and lords' heirs with nothing better on their minds than piracy."

Her message hit home. She sensed that he was on the edge of violence, and she grinned. He studied her closely.

"You're drunk," he said, amazed.

"Am I? It's a custom we could do with in Bazuruk."

He frowned. "Devenil said you'd end in a place like this. I'm sorry he was right."

"Listen." Rax laid one long finger on the center of his chest, leaning closer. The spirit-fumes blocked his meat-eater scent.

"I'm a soldier by profession and choice. I had no quarrel with Bazuruk, except they wouldn't make me First Axe, which I earned. I'll practice my skills where I please. You were glad enough of them in Anukazi."

"You can't live on old debts." His anger was under tight control. "I see you have new ones. I'll leave you to settle them, if you can."

She waited until he'd left the smoke-filled inn before she went back to the table.

"That's a rich trading house," Garad said. "The Vanathri."

"Shut your lying mouth." She fell into the seat, draining the mug of spirits. "Gratitude doesn't last."

I'm trapped, Rax thought foggily. Money doesn't last, honorary captaincy carries no pay—and I won't beg from Kel or Devenil! How else, in Anukazi's name, can I live? And to sneer at me for being with mercenaries . . .

She missed the act of violence, the revulsion that, in the cold moment before battle, transmuted to recklessness; the empathy that made her imagine each blow, each wound. It was not skill nor craft, but art—an ache and an addiction.

"I can find the people you need." Garad interrupted her thoughts. "There are lords in the Cold Lands who'll pay well for a mercenary company, but first you need money to equip them."

"And pay off my debts," Rax said, grinning. "We'll talk. Call to mind three or four men you can trust, and a good lockpick. I've a plan to pay off my debts and get all the gold I need to go to war."

The house was dark. Rax led them cautiously. Her hand clamped over the mouth of a guard, and her long knife cut his throat. She wiped her hands. Garad came forward with the lockpick. Their breath was white in the icy air. Rax took another drink from the flask to warm herself.

"It's open." The lockpick stood back.

Her heel skidded in blood. She cursed and regained her balance. Darkness cloaked them. She led the way to the cellars.

Above, the house slept. Rax hummed under her breath.

"It's a fine revenge on Vanathri," Garad said as his men searched the stacked chests. Silver glinted in the lantern's light.

"It's only a joke," Rax corrected him. "Try that one there—yes, and there. Good."

After a few skirmishes in the Cold Lands, I'll come and pay back what I've taken. I wonder if he'll see the joke? she thought.

The flare of the lanterns took her totally by surprise.

The war-axe slid into her right hand, the throwing-axe into her left. One man yelled. Dazzled, she struck by instinct. Garad heaved up a chest and threw it at the advancing men. She let fly with the throwing-axe, heard a scream as it found a target.

Garad screeched—

New lights from five or six bright lanterns blinded her. Something struck a paralyzing blow to her arm. The men, out of her striking reach, held crossbows.

Fear sobered her. Even mail could not stop the crossbow bolts pointing at her breast.

A familiar voice shouted, and no one fired.

Garad bubbled out his life at her feet. The lockpick breathed harshly in the sudden silence. Her other men, and several guards, lay dead. Kel Vanathri stood at the head of the steps, in night robes, carrying an unsheathed sword.

He cried out.

Devenil slumped against the wall. Blood matted his hair and soaked his shirt; his flesh was laid open, and white bone showed in the redness. The throwing axe's blade was buried under his ribs. He was dead.

"HE WAS ALWAYS a light sleeper." Kel sounded stunned. "He said he'd see what the disturbance was. By the time I could follow—"

"I'm sorry," Rax said. "I liked Devenil."

"I loved him!" Kel's agony flared. "He was the best. The Island will never see another like him. That you could kill him . . . "

"His rescuer in Bazuruk is his killer in Shabelit," Rax said, rubbing her face wearily. Chains clinked. "He'd appreciate the irony."

It was less complex in Bazuruk, she thought. That is what comes of charity. I'd never have hurt him if I'd seen it was Devenil.

"You're nothing more than a butcher. I thought you were different because of what you did in Anukazi, but you're just another Bazuruki killer."

"Of course I'm Bazuruki." She was bewildered. "I was born in Keshanu. I spent ten years defending the borders of the Crystal Mountains. What else would I be?"

It took time for the anger to leave him. Almost to himself, he said, "That's the tragedy. I know you have compassion, but it doesn't matter, does it? The Bazuruki training is what matters."

"I am what I am," Rax said, "and so are you. And so was he. We can't change."

"I can't believe that." He stood, pacing the cell. The guard looked in and went away again. They wouldn't stop him from visiting his own justice on her, she guessed. Not on Shabelit, Sephir's island. She knew how a mother felt for a dead son.

"What will you do?"

"Nothing. You will answer to the law for theft, murder, Devenil."

"Not a cell. Not caged. You owe me that."

"I owe you nothing!" Leaving, he stopped. "He—loved you, Devenil did, for fighting to be what you were. He would have given you a lord's inheritance if you'd asked. You were his friend."

She watched him with Bazuruki eyes, Rax Keshanu, Anukazi's daughter.

"Tarik—Kel, I mean—"

"Better we'd died in Bazuruk."

"I'm a long way from home," Rax said. "I'm tired, Kel."

"I won't cage you," he said from the doorway. "But I won't let them free you, not after what you've done. If you leave, there's only one other way from here."

"Yes," she agreed.

After a time, she knew he had left.

She stood looking down through fine rain into the prison courtyard, where soon they would raise a block, and Rax Keshanu would for the last time behold the clean stroke of an axe.

≫•≪

Revenge is a literary theme that often proves, in lesser hands, trite. Jane Yolen's story, however, provides insight into the power of vengeance to shape a girl's psyche and map a pathway she follows resolutely.

BECOME A WARRIOR

Jane Yolen

Both the hunted and the hunter pray to God.

THE MOON HUNG like a bloody red ball over the silent battlefield. Only the shadows seemed to move. The men on the ground would never move again. And their women, sick with weeping, did not dare the field in the dark. It would be morning before they would come like crows to count their losses.

But on the edge of the field there was a sudden tiny movement, and it was no shadow. Something small was creeping to the muddy hem of the battleground.

Something knelt there, face shining with grief. A child, a girl, the youngest daughter of the king who had died that evening surrounded by all his sons.

The girl looked across the dark field and, like her mother, like her sisters, like her aunts, did not dare put foot on to the bloody ground. But then she looked up at the moon and thought she saw her father's face there. Not the father who lay with his innards spilled out into contorted hands. Not the one who had braided firesticks in his beard and charged into battle screaming. She thought she saw the father who had always sung her to sleep against the night terrors. The one who sat up with her when Great Graxyx haunted her dreams.

"I will do for you, Father, as you did for me," she whispered to the moon. She prayed to the goddess for the strength to accomplish what she had just promised.

Then foot by slow foot, she crept onto the field, searching in the red moon's light for the father who had fallen. She made slits of her eyes so she would not see the full horror around her. She breathed through her mouth so that she would not smell all the deaths. She never once thought of the Great Graxyx who lived—so she truly believed—in the black cave of her dressing room. Or any of the hundred and six gibbering children Graxyx had sired. She crept across the landscape made into a horror by the enemy hordes. All the dead men looked alike. She found her father by his boots.

She made her way up from the boots, past the gaping wound that had taken him from her, to his face which looked peaceful and familiar enough, except for the staring eyes. He had never stared like that. Rather his eyes had always been slitted, against the hot sun of the gods, against the lies of men. She closed his lids with trembling fingers and put her head down on his chest, where the stillness of the heart told her what she already knew.

And then she began to sing to him.

She sang of life, not death, and the small gods of new things. Of bees in the hive and birds on the summer wind. She sang of foxes denning and bears shrugging off winter. She sang of fish in the sparkling rivers and the first green uncurlings of fern in spring. She did not mention dying, blood, or wounds, or the awful stench of death. Her father already knew this well and did not need to be recalled to it.

And when she was done with her song, it was as if his corpse gave a great sigh, one last breath, though of course he was dead already half the night and made no sound at all. But she heard what she needed to hear.

By then it was morning and the crows came. The human crows as well as the black birds, poking and prying and feeding on the dead.

So she turned and went home and everyone wondered why she did not weep. But she had left her tears out on the battlefield.

She was seven years old.

Dogs bark, but the caravan goes on.

BEFORE THE MEN who had killed her father and who had killed her brothers could come to take all the women away to serve them, she had her maid cut her black hair as short as a boy's. The maid was a trembling sort, and the haircut was ragged. But it would do.

She waited until the maid had turned around and leaned down to put away the shears. Then she put her arm around the woman and, with a quick knife's cut across her throat, killed her, before the woman could tell on her. It was a mercy, really, for she was old and ugly and would be used brutally by the soldiers before being slaughtered, probably in a slow and terrible manner. So her father had warned before he left for battle.

Then she went into the room of her youngest brother, dead in the field and lying by her father's right hand. In his great wooden chest she found a pair of trews that had probably been too small for him, but were nonetheless too long for her. With the still-bloody knife she sheared the legs of the trews a hand's width, rolled and sewed them with a quick seam. All the women of her house could sew well, even when it had to be done quickly. Even when it had to be done through half-closed eyes. Even when the hem was wet with blood. Even then.

When she put on the trews, they fit, though she had to pull the drawstring around the waist quite tight and tie the ribbands twice around her. She shrugged into one of her brother's shirts as well, tucking it down into the waistband. Then she slipped her bloody knife into the shirtsleeve. She wore her own riding boots, which could not be told from a boy's, for her brother's boots were many times too big for her.

Then she went out through the window her brother always used when he set out to court one of the young and pretty maids. She had watched him often enough through he had never known she was there, hiding beside the bed, a dark little figure as still as the night.

Climbing down the vine, hand over hand, was no great trouble either. She had done it before, following after him. Really, what a man and a maid did together was most interesting, if a bit odd. And certainly noisier than it needed to be.

She reached the ground in moments, crossed the garden, climbed over the outside wall by using a twisted tree as her ladder. When she dropped to the ground, she twisted her ankle a bit, but she made not the slightest whimper. She was a boy now. And she knew they did not cry.

In the west a cone of dark dust was rising up and advancing on the fortress, blotting out the sky. She knew it for the storm that many hooves make as horses race across the plains. The earth trembled beneath her feet. Behind her, in their rooms, the women had begun to wail. The sound was thin, like a gold filament thrust into her breast. She plugged her ears that their cries could not recall her to her old life, for such was not her plan.

Circling around the stone skirting of the fortress, in the shadow so no one could see her, she started around toward the east. It was not a direction she knew. All she knew was that it was away from the horses of the enemy.

Once she glanced back at the fortress that had been the only home she had ever known. Her mother, her sisters, the other women stood on the battlements looking toward the west and the storm of riders. She could hear their wailing, could see the movement of their arms as they beat upon their breasts. She did not know if that were a plea or an invitation.

She did not turn to look again.

To become a warrior, forget the past.

THREE YEARS SHE WORKED as a serving lad in a fortress not unlike her own but many days' travel away. She learned to clean and to carry, she learned to work after a night of little sleep. Her arms and legs grew strong. Three years she worked as the cook's boy. She learned to prepare geese and rabbit and bear for the pot, and learned which parts were salty, which sweet. She could tell good mushrooms from bad and which greens might make the toughest meat palatable.

And then she knew she could no longer disguise the fact that she was a girl for her body had begun to change in ways that would give her away. So she left the fortress, starting east once more, taking only her knife and a long loop of rope which she wound around her waist seven times.

She was many days hungry, many days cold, but she did not turn back. Fear is a great incentive.

She taught herself to throw the knife and hit what she aimed at. Hunger is a great teacher.

She climbed trees when she found them in order to sleep safe at night. The rope made such passages easier.

She was so long by herself, she almost forgot how to speak. But she never forgot how to sing. In her dreams she sang to her father on the battlefield. Her songs made him live again. Awake she knew the truth was otherwise. He was dead. The worms had taken him. His spirit was with the goddess, drinking milk from her great pap, milk that tasted like honey wine.

She did not dream of her mother or of her sisters or of any of the women in her father's fortress. If they died, it had been with little honor. If they still lived, it was with less.

So she came at last to a huge forest with oaks thick as a goddess' waist. Over all was a green canopy of leaves that scarcely let in the sun. Here were many streams, rivulets that ran cold and clear, torrents that crashed against rocks, and pools that were full of silver trout whose meat was sweet. She taught herself to fish and to swim, and it would be hard to say which gave her the greater pleasure. Here, too, were nests of birds, and that meant eggs. Ferns curled and then opened, and she knew how to steam them, using a basket made of willow strips and a fire from rubbing sticks against one another. She followed bees to their hives, squirrels to their hidden nuts, ducks to their watered beds.

She grew strong, and brown, and—though she did not know it—very beautiful.

Beauty is a danger, to women as well as to men. To warriors most of all. It steers them away from the path of killing. It softens the soul.

When you are in a tree, be a tree.

SHE WAS THREE YEARS ALONE in the forest and grew to trust the sky, the earth, the river, the trees, the way she trusted her knife. They did not lie to her. They did not kill wantonly. They gave her shelter, food, courage. She did not remember her father except as some sort of warrior god, with staring eyes, looking as she had seen him last. She did not remember her mother or sisters or aunts at all.

It had been so long since she had spoken to anyone, it was as if she could not speak at all. She knew words, they were in her head, but not in her mouth, on her tongue, in her throat. Instead she made the sounds she heard every day— the grunt of boar, the whistle of duck, the trilling of thrush, the settled cooing of the wood pigeon on its nest.

If anyone had asked her if she was content, she would have nodded.

Content.

Not happy. Not satisfied. Not done with her life's work.

Content.

And then one early evening a new sound entered her domain. A drumming on the ground, from many miles away. A strange halloing, thin, insistent, whining.

The voices of some new animal, packed like wolves, singing out together.

She trembled. She did not know why. She did not remember why. But to be safe from the thing that made her tremble, she climbed a tree, the great oak that was in the very center of her world.

She used the rope ladder she had made, and pulled the ladder up after. Then she shrank back against the trunk of the tree to wait. She tried to be the brown of the bark, the green of the leaves, and in this she almost succeeded.

It was in the first soft moments of dark, with the woods outlined in muzzy black, that the pack ran yapping, howling, belling into the clearing around the oak.

In that instant she remembered dogs.

There were twenty of them, some large, lanky grays; some stumpy browns with long muzzles; some stiff-legged spotted with pushed-in noses; some thick-coated; some smooth. Her father, the god of war, had had such a motley pack. He had hunted boar and stag and hare with such. They had found him bear and fox and wolf with ease.

Still, she did not know why the dog pack was here, circling her tree. Their jaws were raised so that she could see their iron teeth, could hear the tolling of her death with their long tongues.

She used the single word she could remember. She said it with great authority, with trembling.

"Avaunt!"

At the sound of her voice, the animals all sat down on their haunches to stare up at her, their own tongues silenced. Except for one, a rat terrier, small and springy and unable to be still. He raced back up the path toward the west like some small spy going to report to his master.

Love comes like a thief, stealing the heart's gold away.

IT WAS in the deeper dark that the dogs' master came, with his men behind him, their horses' hooves thrumming the forest paths. They trampled the grass, the foxglove's pink bells and the purple florets of selfheal, the wine-colored burdock flowers and the sprays of yellow goldenrod equally under the horses' heavy feet. The woods were wounded by their passage. The grass did not spring back nor the flowers rise up again.

She heard them and began trembling anew as they thrashed their way across her green haven and into the very heart of the wood.

Ahead of them raced the little terrier, his tail flagging them on, till he led them right to the circle of dogs waiting patiently beneath her tree.

"Look, my lord, they have found something," said one man.

"Odd they should be so quiet," said another.

But the one they called *lord* dismounted, waded through the sea of dogs, and stood at the very foot of the oak, his feet crunching on the fallen acorns. He stared up, and up, and up through the green leaves and at first saw nothing but brown and green.

One of the large gray dogs stood, walked over to his side, raised its great muzzle to the tree, and howled.

The sound made her shiver anew.

"See, my lord, see—high up. There is a trembling in the foliage," one of the men cried.

"You fool," the lord cried, "that is no trembling of leaves. It is a girl. She is dressed all in brown and green. See how she makes the very tree shimmer." Though how he could see her so well in the dark, she was never to understand. "Come down, child, we will not harm you."

She did not come down. Not then. Not until the morning fully revealed her. And then, if she was to eat, if she was to relieve herself, she had to come down. So she did, dropping the rope ladder, and skinning down it quickly. She kept her knife tucked in her waist, out where they could see it and be afraid.

They did not touch her but watched her every movement, like a pack of dogs. When she went to the river to drink, they watched. When she ate the bit of journeycake the lord offered her, they watched. And even when she relieved herself, the lord watched. He would let no one else look then, which she knew honored her, though she did not care.

And when after several days he thought he had tamed her, the lord took her on his horse before him and rode with her back to the far west where he lived. By then he loved her, and knew that she loved him in return, though she had yet to speak a word to him.

"But then, what have words to do with love," he whispered to her as they rode.

He guessed by her carriage, by the way her eyes met his, that she was a princess of some sort, only badly used. He loved her for the past which she could not speak of, for her courage which showed in her face, and for her beauty. He would have loved her for much less, having found her in the tree, for she was something out of a story, out of a prophecy, out of a dream.

"I loved you at once," he whispered. "When I knew you from the tree."

She did not answer. Love was not yet in her vocabulary. But she did not say the one word she could speak: *avaunt.* She did not want him to go.

When the cat wants to eat her kittens, she says they look like mice.

His father was not so quick to love her.

His mother, thankfully, was long dead.

She knew his father at once, by the way his eyes were slitted against the hot sun of the gods, against the lies of men. She knew him to be a king if only by that.

And when she recognized her mother and her sisters in his retinue, she knew who it was she faced.

They did not know her, of course. She was no longer seven but nearly seventeen. Her life had browned her, bronzed her, made her into such steel as they had never known. She could have told them but she had only contempt for their lives. As they had contempt now for her, thinking her some drudge run off to the forest, some sinister trowling from a forgotten clan.

When the king gave his grudging permission for their marriage, when the prince's advisors set down in long scrolls what she should and should not have, she only smiled at them. It was a tree's smile, giving away not a bit of the bark.

She waited until the night of her wedding to the prince, when they were couched together, the servants a-giggle outside their door. She waited until he had covered her face with kisses, when he had touched her in secret places that made her tremble, when he had brought blood between her legs. She waited until he had done all the things she had once watched her brother do to the maids, and she cried out with pleasure as she had heard them do. She waited until he was asleep, smiling happily in his dreams, because she did love him in her warrior way.

Then she took her knife and slit his throat, efficiently and without cruelty, as she would a deer for her dinner.

"Your father killed my father," she whispered, soft as a love token in his ear as the knife carved a smile on his neck.

She stripped the bed of its bloody offering and handed it to the servants who thought it the effusions of the night. Then she walked down the hall to her father-in-law's room.

He was bedded with her mother, riding her like one old wave atop another.

"Here!" he cried as he realized someone was in the room. "You!" he said when he realized who it was.

Her mother looked at her with half-opened eyes and, for the first time, saw who she really was, for she had her father's face, fierce and determined.

"No!" her mother cried. "Avaunt!" But it was a cry that was ten years late.

She killed the king with as much ease as she had killed his son, but she let the knife linger longer to give him a great deal of pain. Then she sliced off one of his ears and put it gently in her mother's hand.

In all this she had said not one word. But wearing the blood of the king on her gown, she walked out of the palace and back to the woods, though she was many days getting there.

No one tried to stop her, for no one saw her. She was a flower in the meadow, a rock by the roadside, a reed by the river, a tree in the forest.

And a warrior's mother by the spring of the year.

>⦁≪

In medieval romances (and, to some extent, history) a knight-errant wandered (errant means "traveling, roving") about searching for evil to defeat, dragons and other monsters to slay, and fair maidens to rescue. Such adventures are all well and good, but honor only goes so far: a knight needs reward as well. The main character of Caitlín Kiernan's tale is not a knight because she is a woman; otherwise she fills the role of knight errant quite well.

THE SEA TROLL'S DAUGHTER

Caitlín R. Kiernan

1.

IT HAD BEEN THREE DAYS since the stranger returned to Invergó, there on the muddy shores of the milky blue-green bay where the glacier met the sea. Bruised and bleeding, she'd walked out of the freezing water. Much of her armor and clothing were torn or altogether missing, but she still had her spear and her dagger, and claimed to have slain the demon troll that had for so long plagued the people of the tiny village.

Yet, she returned to them with no *proof* of this mighty deed, except her word and her wounds. Many were quick to point out that the former could be lies, and that she could have come by the latter in any number of ways that did not actually involve killing the troll, or anything else, for that matter. She might have been foolhardy and wandered up onto the wide splay of the glacier, then taken a bad tumble on the ice. It might have happened just that way. Or she might have only slain a bear, or a wild boar or auroch, or a walrus, having mistook one of these beasts for the demon. Some even suggested it may have been an honest mistake, for bears and walrus, and even boars and aurochs, can be quite fearsome when angered, and if encountered unexpectedly in the night, may have easily been confused with the troll.

Others among the villagers were much less gracious, such as the blacksmith and his one-eyed wife, who went so far as to suggest the stranger's injuries may have been self-inflicted. She had bludgeoned and battered herself, they argued, so that she might claim the reward, then flee the village before the creature showed itself again, exposing her deceit. This stranger from the south, they argued, thought them all feeble-minded. She intended to take their gold and leave them that much poorer and still troubled by the troll.

The elders of Invergó spoke with the stranger, and they relayed these concerns, even as her wounds were being cleaned and dressed. They'd arrived at a solution by which the matter might be settled. And it seemed fair enough, at least to them.

"Merely deliver unto us the body," they told the stranger. "Show us this irrefutable testament to your handiwork, and we will happily see that you are compensated with all that has been promised to whomsoever slays the troll. All the monies and horses and mammoth hides, for ours was not an idle offer. We would not have the world thinking we are liars, but neither would we have it thinking we can be beguiled by make-believe heroics."

But, she replied, the corpse had been snatched away from her by a treacherous current. She'd searched the murky depths, all to no avail, and had been forced to return to the village empty-handed, with nothing but the scars of a lengthy and terrible battle to attest to her victory over the monster.

The elders remained unconvinced, repeated their demand, and left the stranger to puzzle over her dilemma.

So, penniless and deemed either a fool or a charlatan, she sat in the moldering, broken-down hovel that passed for Invergó's one tavern, bandaged and staring forlornly into a smoky sod fire. She stayed drunk on whatever mead or barley wine the curious villagers might offer to loosen her tongue, so that she'd repeat the tale of how she'd purportedly bested the demon. They came and listened and bought her drinks, almost as though they believed her story, though it was plain none among them did.

"The fiend wasn't hard to find," the stranger muttered, thoroughly dispirited, looking from the fire to her half-empty cup to the doubtful faces of her audience. "There's a sort of reef, far down at the very bottom of the bay. The troll made his home there, in a hall fashioned from the bones of great whales and other such leviathans. How did I learn this?" she asked, and when no one ventured a guess, she continued, more dispirited than before.

"Well, after dark, I lay in wait along the shore, and there I spied your monster making off with a ewe and a lamb, one tucked under each arm, and so I trailed him into the water. He was bold, and took no notice of me, and so I swam down, down, down through the tangling blades of kelp and the ruins of sunken trees and the masts of ships that have foundered—"

"Now, exactly how did you hold your breath so long?" one of the men asked, raising a skeptical eyebrow.

"Also, how did you not succumb to the chill?" asked a woman with a fat goose in her lap. "The water is so dreadfully cold, and especially—"

"*Might* it be that someone here knows this tale *better* than I?" the stranger growled, and when no one admitted they did, she continued. "Now, as *I* was saying, the troll kept close to the bottom of the bay, in a hall made all of bones, and it was there that he retired with the ewe and the lamb he'd slaughtered and dragged into the water. I drew my weapon," and here she quickly slipped her dagger from its sheath for effect. The iron blade glinted dully in the firelight. Startled, the goose began honking and flapping her wings.

"I *still* don't see how you possibly held your breath so long as that," the man said, raising his voice to be heard above the noise of the frightened goose. "Not to mention the darkness. How did you see anything at all down there, it being night and the bay being so silty?"

The stranger shook her head and sighed in disgust, her face half hidden by the tangled black tresses that covered her head and hung down almost to the tavern's dirt floor. She returned the dagger to its sheath and informed the lot of them they'd hear not another word from her if they persisted with all these questions and interruptions. She also raised up her cup, and the woman with the goose nodded to the barmaid, indicating a refill was in order.

"I *found* the troll there inside its lair," the stranger continued, "feasting on the entrails and viscera of the slaughtered sheep. Inside, the walls of its lair glowed, and they glowed rather *brightly*, I might add, casting a ghostly phantom light all across the bottom of the bay."

"Awfully bloody convenient, that," the woman with the goose frowned, as the barmaid refilled the stranger's cup.

"*Sometimes,* the Fates, they do us a favorable turn," the stranger said and took an especially long swallow of barley wine. She belched, then went on. "I watched the troll, I did, for a moment or two, hoping to discern any weak spots it might have in its scaly, knobby hide. That's when it espied me, and straightaway the fiend released its dinner and rushed towards me, baring a mouth filled with fangs longer even than the tusks of a bull walrus."

"Long as that?" asked the woman with the goose, stroking the bird's head.

"Or longer," the stranger told her. "Of a sudden, it was upon me, all fins and claws, and there was hardly time to fix every detail in my memory. As I said, it *rushed* me, and bore me down upon the muddy belly of that accursed hall with all its weight. I thought it might crush me, stave in my skull and chest, and soon mine would count among the jumble of bleached skeletons littering that floor. There were plenty enough human bones, I *do* recall that much. Its talons sundered my armor, and sliced my flesh, and soon my blood was mingling with that of the stolen ewe and lamb. I almost despaired, then and there, and I'll admit that much freely and suffer no shame in the admission."

"Still," the woman with the goose persisted, "awfully damned convenient, all that light."

The stranger sighed and stared sullenly into the fire.

And for the people of Invergó, and also for the stranger who claimed to have done them such a service, this was the way those three days and those three nights passed. The curious came to the tavern to hear the tale, and most of them went away just as skeptical as they'd arrived. The stranger only slept when the drink overcame her, and then she sprawled on a filthy mat at one side of the hearth; at least no one saw fit to begrudge her that small luxury.

But then, late on the morning of the fourth day, the troll's mangled corpse fetched up on the tide, not far distant from the village. A clam-digger and his three sons had been working the mudflats where the narrow aquamarine bay meets the open sea, and they were the ones who discovered the creature's remains. Before midday, a group had been dispatched by the village constabulary to retrieve the body and haul it across the marshes, delivering it to Invergó, where all could see and judge for themselves. Seven strong men were required to hoist the carcass onto a litter (usually reserved for transporting strips of blubber and the like), which was drawn across the mire and through the rushes by a team of six oxen. Most of the afternoon was required to cross hardly a single league. The mud was deep and the going slow, and the animals strained in their harnesses, foam flecking their lips and nostrils. One of the cattle perished from exhaustion not long after the putrefying load was finally dragged through the village gates and dumped unceremoniously upon the flagstones in the common square.

Before this day, none among them had been afforded more than the briefest, fleeting glimpse of the sea devil. And now, every man, woman, and child who'd heard the news of the recovered corpse crowded about, able to peer and gawk and prod the dead thing to their hearts' content. The mob seethed with awe and morbid curiosity, apprehension and disbelief. For their pleasure, the enormous head was raised up and an anvil slid underneath its broken jaw, and, also, a fishing gaff was inserted into the dripping mouth, that all could look upon those protruding fangs, which did, indeed, put to shame the tusks of many a bull walrus.

However, it was almost twilight before anyone thought to rouse the stranger, who was still lying unconscious on her mat in the tavern, sleeping off the proceeds of the previous evening's storytelling. She'd been dreaming of her home, which was very far to the south, beyond the raw black mountains and the glaciers, the fjords and the snow. In the dream, she'd been sitting at the edge of a wide green pool, shaded by willow boughs from the heat of the noonday sun, watching the pretty women who came to bathe there. Half a bucket of soapy, lukewarm seawater was required to wake her from this reverie, and the stranger spat and sputtered and cursed the man who'd doused her (he'd drawn the short straw). She was ready to reach for her spear when someone hastily explained that a clam-digger had come across the troll's body on the mudflats, and so the people of Invergó were now quite a bit more inclined than before to accept her tale.

"That means I'll get the reward and can be shed of this sorry one-whore piss-hole of a town?" she asked. The barmaid explained how the decision was still up to the elders, but that the scales *did* seem to have tipped somewhat in her favor.

And so, with help from the barmaid and the cook, the still half-drunken stranger was led from the shadows and into what passed for bright daylight, there on the gloomy streets of Invergó. Soon, she was pushing her way roughly through the mumbling throng of bodies that had gathered about the slain sea troll, and when she saw the fruits of her battle—when she saw that everyone *else* had seen them—she smiled broadly and spat directly in the monster's face.

"Do you doubt me *still?*" she called out and managed to climb onto the creature's back, slipping off only once before she gained secure footing on its shoulders. "Will you continue to ridicule me as a liar, when the evidence is right here before your own eyes?"

"Well, it *might* conceivably have died some other way," a peat-cutter said without looking at the stranger.

"Perhaps," suggested a cooper, "it swam too near the glacier, and was struck by a chunk of calving ice."

The stranger glared furiously and whirled about to face the elders, who were gathered together near the troll's webbed feet. "Do you truly mean to *cheat* me of the bounty?" she demanded. "Why, you ungrateful, two-faced gaggle of sheep-fuckers," she began, then almost slipped off the cadaver again.

"Now, now," one of the elders said, holding up a hand in a gesture meant to calm the stranger. "There will, of course, be an inquest. Certainly. But, be assured, my fine woman, it is only a matter of formality, you understand. I'm sure not one here among us doubts, even for a moment, it was *your* blade returned this vile, contemptible spirit to the nether pits that spawned it."

For a few tense seconds, the stranger stared warily back at the elder, for she'd never liked men, and especially not men who used many words when only a few would suffice. She then looked out over the restless crowd, silently daring anyone present to contradict him. And, when no one did, she once again turned her gaze down to the corpse, laid out below her feet.

"I cut its throat, from ear to ear," the stranger said, though she was not entirely sure the troll *had* ears. "I gouged out the left eye, and I expect you'll come across the tip end of my blade lodged somewhere in the gore. I am Malmury, daughter of my Lord Gwrtheyrn the Undefeated, and before the eyes of the gods do I so claim this as *my* kill, and I know that even *they* would not gainsay this rightful averment."

And with that, the stranger, whom they at last knew was named Malmury, slid clumsily off the monster's back, her boots and breeches now stained with blood and the various excrescences leaking from the troll. She returned immediately to the tavern, as the salty evening air had made her quite thirsty. When she'd gone, the men and women and children of Invergó went back to examining the corpse, though a disquiet and guilty sort of solemnity had settled over them, and what was said was generally spoken in whispers. Overhead, a chorus of hungry gulls and ravens cawed and greedily surveyed the troll's shattered body.

"Malmury," the cooper murmured to the clam digger who'd found the corpse (and so was, himself, enjoying some small degree of celebrity). "A *fine* name, that. And the daughter of a lord, even. Never questioned her story in the least. No, not me."

"Nor I," whispered the peat-cutter, leaning in a little closer for a better look at the creature's warty hide. "Can't imagine where she'd have gotten the notion any of us distrusted her."

Torches were lit and set up round about the troll, and much of the crowd lingered far into the night, though a few found their way back to the tavern to listen to Malmury's tale a third or fourth time, for it had grown considerably more interesting, now that it seemed to be true. A local alchemist and astrologer, rarely seen by the other inhabitants of Invergó, arrived and was permitted to take samples of the monster's flesh and saliva. It was he who located the point of the stranger's broken dagger, embedded firmly in the troll's sternum, and the artifact was duly handed over to the constabulary. A young boy in the alchemist's service made highly detailed sketches from numerous angles, and labeled anatomical features as the old man had taught him. By midnight, it became necessary to post a sentry to prevent fisherman and urchins slicing off souvenirs. But only half an hour later, a fishwife was found with a horn cut from the sea troll's cheek hidden in her bustle, and a second sentry was posted.

In the tavern, Malmury, daughter of Lord Gwrtheyrn, managed to regale her audience with increasingly fabulous variations of her battle with the demon. But no one much seemed to mind the embellishments, or that, partway through the tenth retelling of the night, it was revealed that the troll had summoned a gigantic, fire-breathing worm from the ooze that carpeted the floor of the bay, which Malmury also claimed to have dispatched in short order.

"Sure," she said, wiping at her lips with the hem of the barmaid's skirt. "And now, there's something *else* for your muckrakers to turn up, sooner or later."

By dawn, the stench wafting from the common was becoming unbearable, and a daunting array of dogs and cats had begun to gather round about the edges of the square, attracted by the odor, which promised a fine carrion feast. The cries of the gulls and the ravens had become a cacophony, as though all the heavens had sprouted feathers and sharp, pecking beaks and were descending upon the village. The harbormaster, two physicians, and a cadre of minor civil servants were becoming concerned about the assorted noxious fluids seeping from the rapidly decomposing carcass. This poisonous concoction spilled between the cobbles and had begun to fill gutters and strangle drains as it flowed downhill, towards both the waterfront and the village well. Though there was some talk of removing the source of the taint from the village, it was decided, rather, that a low bulwark or levee of dried peat would be stacked around the corpse.

And, true, this appeared to solve the problem of seepage, for the time being, the peat acting both as a dam and serving to absorb much of the rot. But it did nothing whatsoever to deter the cats and dogs milling about the square, or the raucous cloud of birds that had begun to swoop in, snatching mouthfuls of flesh before they could be chased away by the two sentries, who shouted at them and brandished brooms and long wooden poles.

Inside the smoky warmth of the tavern—which, by the way, was known as the Cod's Demise, though no sign had ever borne that title—Malmury knew nothing of the trouble and worry her trophy was causing in the square or the talk of having the troll hauled back into the marshes. But neither was she any longer precisely carefree, despite her drunkenness. Even as the sun was rising over the village and peat was being stacked about the corpse, a stooped and toothless old crone of a woman had entered the Cod's Demise. All those who'd been enjoying the tale's new wrinkle of a fire-breathing worm turned towards her. Not a few of them uttered prayers and clutched tightly to the fetishes they carried against the evil eye and all manner of sorcery and malevolent spirits. The crone stood near the doorway, and she leveled a long, crooked finger at Malmury.

"*Her,*" she said ominously, in a voice that was not unlike low tide swishing about rocks and rubbery heaps of bladder wrack. "She is the stranger? The one who has murdered the troll who for so long called the bay his home?"

There was a brief silence as eyes drifted from the crone to Malmury, who was blinking and peering through a haze of alcohol and smoke, trying to get a better view of the frail, hunched woman.

"That I am," Malmury said at last, confused by this latest arrival and the way the people of Invergó appeared to fear her. Malmury tried to stand, then thought better of it and stayed in her seat by the hearth, where there was less chance of tipping over.

"Then she's the one I've come to see," said the crone, who seemed less like a living, breathing woman and more like something assembled from bundles of twigs and scraps of leather, sloppily held together with twine, rope, and sinew. She leaned on a gnarled cane, though it was difficult to be sure if the cane were wood or bone or some skillful amalgam of the two. "She's the interloper who has doomed this village and all those who dwell here."

Malmury, confused and growing angry, rubbed at her eyes, starting to think this was surely nothing more than an unpleasant dream, born of too much drink and the boiled mutton and cabbage she'd eaten for dinner.

"How *dare* you stand there and speak to me this way?" she barked back at the crone, trying hard not to slur as she spoke. "Aren't I the one who, only five days ago, *delivered* this place from the depredations of that demon? Am I not the one who risked her *life* in the icy brine of the bay to keep these people safe?"

"*Oh,* she thinks much of herself," the crone cackled, slowly bobbing her head, as though in time to some music nobody else could hear. "Yes, she thinks herself gallant and brave and favored by the gods of her land. And who can say? Maybe she is. But she should know, this is not *her* land, and we have our *own* gods. And it is one of *their* children she has slain."

Malmury sat up as straight as she could manage, which wasn't very straight at all, and, with her sloshing cup, jabbed fiercely at the old woman. Barley wine spilled out and spattered across the toes of Malmury's boots and the hard-packed dirt floor.

"Hag," she snarled, "how dare you address me as though I'm not even present. If you have some quarrel with me, then let's hear it spoken. Else, crab, scuttle away and bother this good house no more."

"This good *house?*" the crone asked, feigning dismay as she peered into the gloom, her stooped countenance framed by the morning light coming in through the opened door. "Beg pardon. I thought possibly I'd wandered into a rather ambitious privy hole, but that the swine had found it first."

Malmury dropped her cup and drew her chipped dagger, which she brandished menacingly at the crone. "You *will* leave now, and without another insult passing across those withered lips, or we shall be presenting you to the swine for their breakfast."

At this, the barmaid, a fair woman with blondish hair, bent close to Malmury and whispered in her ear, "Worse yet than the blasted troll, this one. Be cautious, my lady."

Malmury looked away from the crone, and, for a long moment, stared, instead, at the barmaid. Malmury had the distinct sensation that she was missing some crucial bit of wisdom or history that would serve to make sense of the foul old woman's intrusion and the villagers' reactions to her. Without turning from the barmaid, she furrowed her brow and again pointed at the crone with her dagger.

"This slattern?" she asked, almost laughing. "This shriveled harridan not even the most miserable of harpies would claim? I'm to *fear* her?"

"No," the crone said, coming nearer now. The crowd parted to grant her passage, one or two among them stumbling in their haste to avoid the witch. "*You* need not fear *me*, Malmury Trollbane. Not this day. But, you *would* do well to find some ounce of sobriety and fear the consequences of your actions."

"She's insane," Malmury sneered, than spat at the floor between herself and the crone. "Someone show her a mercy, and find the hag a root cellar to haunt."

The old woman stopped and stared down at the glob of spittle, then raised her head, flared her nostrils, and fixed Malmury in her gaze.

"There was a balance here, Trollbane, an equity, decreed when my great-grandmothers were still infants swaddled in their cribs. The debt paid for a grave injustice born of the arrogance of men. A tithe, if you will, and if it cost these people a few souls now and again, or thinned their bleating flocks, it also kept them safe from that greater wrath, which watches us always from the Sea at the Top of the World. But this selfsame balance have you undone, and, foolishly, they name you a hero for that deed. For their damnation and their doom."

Malmury cursed, spat again, and tried then to rise from her chair, but was held back by her own inebriation and by the barmaid's firm hand upon her shoulder.

The crone coughed and added a portion of her own jaundiced spittle to the floor of the tavern. "They will *tell* you, Trollbane, though the tales be less than half remembered among this misbegotten legion of cowards and imbeciles. You *ask* them, they will tell you what has not yet been spoken, what was never freely uttered for fear no hero would have accepted their blood-gold. Do not think *me* the villain in this ballad they are spinning around you."

"You would do well to *leave,* witch," answered Malmury, her voice grown low and throaty, as threatful as breakers before a storm tide or the grumble of a chained hound. "They might fear you, but I do not, and I'm in an ill temper to suffer your threats and intimations."

"Very well," the old woman replied, and she bowed her head to Malmury, though it was clear to all that the crone's gesture carried not one whit of respect. "So be it. But you *ask* them, Trollbane. You ask after the *cause* of the troll's coming, and you ask after his daughter, too."

And with that, she raised her cane, and the fumy air about her appeared to shimmer and fold back upon itself. There was a strong smell, like the scent of brimstone and of smoldering sage, and a sound, as well. Later, Malmury would not be able to decide if it was more akin to a distant thunderclap or the crackle of burning logs. And, with that, the old woman vanished, and her spit sizzled loudly upon the floor.

"Then she *is* a sorceress," Malmury said, sliding the dagger back into its sheath.

"After a fashion," the barmaid told her and slowly removed her grip upon Malmury's shoulder. "She's the last priestess of the Old Ways and still pays tribute to those beings who came before the gods. I've heard her called Grímhildr, and also Gunna, though none among us recall her right name. She is powerful and treacherous, but know that she has also done great *good* for Invergó and all the people along the coast. When there was plague, she dispelled the sickness—"

"What did she *mean,* to ask after the coming of the troll and its daughter?"

"These are not questions I would answer," the barmaid replied and turned suddenly away. "You must take them to the elders. They can tell you these things."

Malmury nodded and sipped from her cup, her eyes wandering about the tavern, which she saw was now emptying out into the morning-drenched street. The crone's warnings had left them in no mood for tales of monsters and had ruined their appetite for the stranger's endless boasting and bluster. No matter, Malmury thought. They'd be back come nightfall, and she was weary, besides, and needed sleep. There was now a cot waiting for her upstairs, in the loft above the kitchen, a proper bed complete with mattress and pillows stuffed with the down of geese, even a white bearskin blanket to guard against the frigid air that blew in through the cracks in the walls. She considered going before the council of elders, after she was rested and merely hungover, and pressing them for answers to the crone's questions. But Malmury's head was beginning to ache, and she entertained the proposition only in passing. Already, the appearance of the old woman and what she'd said was beginning to seem less like something that had actually happened, and Malmury wondered, dimly, if she were having trouble discerning where the truth ended and her own generous embroidery of the truth began. Perhaps she'd invented the hag, feeling the tale needed an appropriate epilogue, and then, in her drunkenness, forgotten that she'd invented her.

Soon, the barmaid—whose name was Dóta—returned to lead Malmury up the narrow, creaking stairs to her small room and the cot, and Malmury forgot about sea trolls and witches and even the gold she had coming. For Dóta was a comely girl, and free with her favors, and the stranger's sex mattered little to her.

2.

THE DAUGHTER OF THE SEA TROLL lived among the jagged, windswept highlands that loomed above the milky blue-green bay and the village of Invergó. Here had she dwelt for almost three generations, as men reckoned the passing of time, and here did she imagine she would live until the long span of her days was at last exhausted.

Her cave lay deep within the earth, where once had been only solid basalt. But over incalculable eons, the glacier that swept down from the mountains, inching between high volcanic cliffs as it carved a wide path to the sea, had worked its way beneath the bare and stony flesh of the land. A ceaseless trickle of meltwater had carried the bedrock away, grain by grain, down to the bay, as the perpetual cycle of freeze and thaw had split and shattered the stone. In time (and then, as now, the world had nothing but time), the smallest of breaches had become cracks, cracks became fissures, and intersecting labyrinths of fissures collapsed to form a cavern. And so, in this way, had the struggle between mountain and ice prepared for her a home, and she dwelt there, alone, almost beyond the memory of the village and its inhabitants, which she despised and feared and avoided when at all possible.

However, she had not always lived in the cave, nor unattended. Her mother, a child of man, had died while birthing the sea troll's daughter, and, afterwards, she'd been taken in by the widowed conjurer who would, so many years later, seek out and confront a stranger named Malmury who'd come up from the southern kingdoms. When the people of Invergó had looked upon the infant, what they'd seen was enough to guess at its parentage. And they would have put the mother to death, then and there, for her congress with the fiend, had she not been dead already. And surely, likewise, would they have murdered the baby, had the old woman not seen fit to intervene. The villagers had always feared the crone, but also they'd had cause to seek her out in times of hardship and calamity. So it gave them pause, once she'd made it known that the infant was in her care, and this knowledge stayed their hand, for a while.

In the tumbledown remains of a stone cottage at the edge of the mudflats, the crone had raised the infant until the child was old enough to care for herself. And until even the old woman's infamy, and the prospect of losing her favors, was no longer enough to protect the sea troll's daughter from the villagers. Though more human than not, she had the creature's blood in her veins. In the eyes of some, this made her a greater abomination than her father.

Finally, rumors had spread that the girl was a danger to them all, and, after an especially harsh winter, many become convinced that she could make herself into an ocean mist and pass easily through windowpanes. In this way, it was claimed, had she begun feeding on the blood of men and women while they slept. Soon, a much-prized milking cow had been found with her udder mutilated, and the farmer had been forced to put the beast out of her misery. The very next day, the elders of Invergó had sent a warning to the crone, that their tolerance of the half-breed was at an end, and she was to be remanded to the constable forthwith.

But the old woman had planned against this day. She'd discovered the cave high above the bay, and she'd taught the sea troll's daughter to find auk eggs and mushrooms and to hunt the goats and such other wild things as lived among the peaks and ravines bordering the glacier. The girl was bright and had learned to make clothing and boots from the hides of her kills, and also she had been taught herb lore, and much else that would be needed to survive on her own in that forbidding, barren place.

Late one night in the summer of her fourteenth year, she'd fled Invergó, and made her way to the cave. Only one man had ever been foolish enough to go looking for her, and his body was found pinned to an iceberg floating in the bay, his own sword driven through his chest to the hilt. After that, they left her alone, and soon the daughter of the sea troll was little more than legend and a tale to frighten children. She began to believe, and to hope, that she would never again have cause to journey down the slopes to the village.

But then, as the stranger Malmury, senseless with drink, slept in the arms of a barmaid, the crone came to the sea troll's daughter in her dreams, as the old woman had done many times before.

"Your father has been slain," she said, not bothering to temper the words.

"His corpse lies desecrated and rotting in the village square, where all can come and gloat and admire the mischief of the one who killed him."

The sea troll's daughter, whom the crone had named Sæhildr, for the ocean, had been dreaming of stalking elk and a shaggy herd of mammoth across a meadow. But the crone's voice had startled her prey, and the dream animals had all fled across the tundra.

The sea troll's daughter rolled over onto her back, stared up at the grizzled face of the old woman, and asked, "Should this bring me sorrow? Should I have tears, to receive such tidings? If so, I must admit it doesn't, and I don't. Never have I seen the face of my father, not with my waking eyes, and never has he spoken unto me, nor sought me out. I was nothing more to him than a curious consequence of his indiscretions."

"You and he lived always in different worlds," the old woman replied, but the one she called Sæhildr had turned back over onto her belly and was staring forlornly at the place where the elk and mammoth had been grazing, only a few moments before.

"It is none of my concern," the sea troll's daughter sighed, thinking she should wake soon, that then the old woman could no longer plague her thoughts. Besides, she was hungry, and there was fresh meat from a bear she'd killed only the day before.

"Sæhildr," the crone said, "I've not come expecting you to grieve, for too well do I know your mettle. I've come with a warning, as the one who slew your father may yet come seeking you."

The sea troll's daughter smiled, baring teeth that effortlessly cracked bone to reach the rich marrow inside. With the hooked claws of a thumb and forefinger, she plucked the yellow blossom from an arctic poppy, and held it to her wide nostrils.

"Old mother, knowing my mettle, you should know that I am not afraid of men," she whispered, then she let the flower fall back to the ground.

"The one who slew your father was not a man, but a woman, the likes of which I've never seen," the crone replied. "She is a warrior, of noble birth, from the lands south of the mountains. She came to collect the bounty placed upon the troll's head. Sæhildr, this one is strong, and I fear for you."

In the dream, low clouds the color of steel raced by overhead, fat with snow, and the sea troll's daughter lay among the flowers of the meadow and thought about the father she'd never met. Her short tail twitched from side to side, like the tail of a lazy, contented cat, and she decapitated another poppy.

"You believe this warrior will hunt *me* now?" she asked the crone.

"What I think, Sæhildr, is that the men of Invergó have no intention of honoring their agreement to pay this woman her reward. Rather, I believe they will entice her with even greater riches, if only she will stalk and destroy the bastard daughter of their dispatched foe. The woman is greedy, and prideful, and I hold that she will hunt you, yes."

"Then let her come to me, Old Mother," the sea troll's daughter said. "There is little enough sport to be had in these hills. Let her come into the mountains and face me."

The old woman sighed and began to break apart on the wind, like sea foam before a wave. "She's not a fool," the crone said. "A braggart, yes, and a liar, and also a drunk. But by her own strength and wits did she undo your father. I'd not see the same fate befall you, Sæhildr. She will lay a trap."

"Oh, I know something of traps," the troll's daughter replied, and then the dream ended. She opened her black eyes and lay awake in her freezing den, deep within the mountains. Not far from the nest of pelts that was her bed, a lantern she'd fashioned from walrus bone and blubber burned unsteadily, casting tall, writhing shadows across the basalt walls. The sea troll's daughter lay very still, watching the flame, and praying to all the beings who'd come before the gods of men that the battle with her father's killer would not be over too quickly.

3.

As it happened, however, the elders of Invergó were far too preoccupied with other matters to busy themselves trying to conceive of schemes by which they might cheat Malmury of her bounty. With each passing hour, the clam-digger's grisly trophy became increasingly putrid, and the decision not to remove it from the village's common square had set in motion a chain of events that would prove far more disastrous to the village than the *living* troll ever could have been. Moreover, Malmury was entirely too distracted by her own intoxication and with the pleasures visited upon her by the barmaid, Dóta, to even recollect she had the reward coming. So, while there can be hardly any doubt that the old crone who lived at the edge of the mudflats was, in fact, both wise and clever, she had little cause to fear for Sæhildr's immediate well-being.

The troll's corpse, hauled so triumphantly from the marsh, had begun to swell in the mid-day sun, distending magnificently as the gases of decomposition built up inside its innards. Meanwhile, the flock of gulls and ravens had been joined by countless numbers of fish crows and kittiwakes, a constantly shifting, swooping, shrieking cloud that, at last, succeeded in chasing off the two sentries who'd been charged with the task of protecting the carcass from scavengers and souvenir hunters. And, no longer dissuaded by the men and their jabbing sticks, the cats and dogs that had skulked all night about the edges of the common grew bold and joined in the banquet (though the cats proved more interested in seizing unwary birds than in the sour flesh of the troll). A terrific swarm of biting flies arrived only a short time later, and there were ants, as well, and voracious beetles the size of a grown man's thumb. Crabs and less savory things made their way up from the beach. An order was posted that the citizens of Invergó should retreat to their homes and bolt all doors and windows until such time as the pandemonium could be resolved.

There was, briefly, talk of towing the body back to the salt marshes from whence it had come. But this proposal was soon dismissed as impractical and hazardous. Even if a determined crew of men dragging a litter or wagon and armed with the requisite hooks and cables, the block and tackle, could fight their way through the seething, foraging mass of birds, cats, dogs, insects, and crustaceans, it seemed very unlikely that the corpse retained enough integrity that it could now be moved in a single piece. And just the thought of intentionally breaking it apart, tearing it open and thereby releasing whatever foul brew festered within, was enough to inspire the elders to seek some alternate route of ridding the village of the corruption and all its attendant chaos. To make matters worse, the peat levee that had been hastily stacked around the carcass suddenly failed partway through the day, disgorging all the oily fluid that had built up behind it. There was now talk of pestilence, and a second order was posted, advising the villagers that all water from the pumps was no longer potable, and that the bay, too, appeared to have been contaminated. The fish market was closed, and incoming boats forbidden to offload any of the day's catch.

And then, when the elders thought matters were surely at their worst, the alchemist's young apprentice arrived bearing a sheaf of equations and ascertainments based upon the samples taken from the carcass. In their chambers, the old men flipped through these pages for some considerable time, no one wanting to be the first to admit he didn't actually understand what he was reading. Finally, the apprentice cleared his throat, which caused them to look up at him.

"It's simple, really," the boy said. "You see, the various humors of the troll's peculiar composition have been demonstrated to undergo a predictable variance during the process of putrefaction."

The elders stared back at him, seeming no less confused by his words than by the spidery handwriting on the pages spread out before them.

"To put it more plainly," the boy said, "the creature's blood is becoming volatile. Flammable. Given significant enough concentrations, which must certainly exist by now, even explosive."

Almost in unison, the faces of the elders of Invergó went pale. One of them immediately stood and ordered the boy to fetch his master forthwith, but was duly informed that the alchemist had already fled the village. He'd packed a mule and left by the winding, narrow path that led west into the wilderness. He hoped, the apprentice told them, to observe for posterity the grandeur of the inevitable conflagration, but from a safe distance.

At once, a proclamation went out that all flames were to be extinguished, all hearths and forges and ovens, every candle and lantern, in Invergó. Not so much as a tinderbox or pipe must be left smoldering anywhere, so dire was the threat to life and property. However, most of the men dispatched to see that this proclamation was enforced, instead fled into the marshes, or towards the foothills, or across the milky blue-green bay to the far shore, which was reckoned to be sufficiently remote that sanctuary could be found there. The calls that rang through the streets of the village were not so much "Douse the fires," or "Mind your stray embers," as "Flee for your lives, the troll's going to explode."

In their cot, in the small but cozy space above the Cod's Demise, Malmury and Dóta had been dozing. But the commotion from outside, both the wild ruckus from the feeding scavengers and the panic that was now sweeping through the village, woke them. Malmury cursed and groped about for the jug of fine apple brandy on the floor, which Dóta had pilfered from the larder. Dóta lay listening to the uproar, and, being for the most part sober, began to sense that something, somewhere, somehow had gone terribly wrong, and that they might now be in very grave danger.

Dóta handed the brandy to Malmury, who took a long pull from the jug and squinted at the barmaid.

"They have no intention of paying you," Dóta said flatly, buttoning her blouse. "We've known it all along. All of us. Everyone who lives in Invergó."

Malmury blinked and rubbed at her eyes, not quite able to make sense of what she was hearing. She had another swallow from the jug, hoping the strong liquor might clear her ears.

"It was a dreadful thing we did," Dóta admitted. "I know that now. You're brave, and risked much, and—"

"I'll *beat* it out of them," Malmury muttered.

"That might have worked," Dóta said softly, nodding her head. "Only, they don't have it. The elders, I mean. In all Invergó's coffers, there's not even a quarter what they offered."

Beyond the walls of the tavern, there was a terrific crash, then, and, soon thereafter, the sound of women screaming.

"Malmury, listen to me. You stay here and have the last of the brandy. I'll be back very soon."

"I'll beat it out of them," Malmury declared again, though this time with slightly less conviction.

"Yes," Dóta told her. "I'm sure you will do just that. Only now, wait here. I'll return as quickly as I can."

"Bastards," Malmury sneered. "Bastards and ingrates."

"You finish the brandy," Dóta said, pointing at the jug clutched in Malmury's hands. "It's excellent brandy, and very expensive. Maybe not the same as gold, but . . . " and then the barmaid trailed off, seeing that Malmury had passed out again. Dóta dressed and hurried downstairs, leaving the stranger, who no longer seemed quite so strange, alone and naked, sprawled and snoring loudly on the cot.

In the street outside the Cod's Demise, the barmaid was greeted by a scene of utter chaos. The reek from the rotting troll, only palpable in the tavern, was now overwhelming, and she covered her mouth and tried not to gag. Men, women, and children rushed to and fro, many burdened with bundles of valuables or food, some on horseback, others trying to drive herds of pigs or sheep through the crowd. And, yet, rising above it all, was the deafening clamor of that horde of sea birds and dogs and cats squabbling amongst themselves for a share of the troll. Off towards the docks, someone was clanging the huge bronze bell reserved for naught but the direst of catastrophes. Dóta shrank back against the tavern wall, recalling the crone's warnings and admonitions, expecting to see, any moment now, the titanic form of one of those beings who came before the gods, towering over the rooftops, striding towards her through the village.

Just then, a tinker, who frequently spent his evenings and his earnings in the tavern, stopped and seized the barmaid by both shoulders, gazing directly into her eyes.

"You must *run!*" he implored. "Now, this very minute, you must get away from this place!"

"But why?" Dóta responded, trying to show as little of her terror as possible, trying to behave the way she imagined a woman like Malmury might behave. "What has happened?"

"It *burns*," the tinker said, and before she could ask him *what* burned, he released her and vanished into the mob. But, as if in answer to that unasked question, there came a muffled crack and then a boom that shook the very street beneath her boots. A roiling mass of charcoal-colored smoke shot through with glowing red-orange cinders billowed up from the direction of the livery, and Dóta turned and dashed back into the Cod's Demise.

Another explosion followed, and another, and by the time she reached the cot upstairs, dust was sifting down from the rafters of the tavern, and the roofing timbers had begun to creak alarmingly. Malmury was still asleep, oblivious to whatever cataclysm was befalling Invergó. The barmaid grabbed the bearskin blanket and wrapped it about Malmury's shoulders, then slapped her several times, hard, until the woman's eyelids fluttered partway open.

"*Stop that*," Malmury glowered, seeming now more like an indignant girl child than the warrior who'd swum to the bottom of the bay and slain their sea troll.

"We have to *go*," Dóta said, almost shouting to be understood above the racket. "It's not safe here anymore, Malmury. We have to get out of Invergó."

"But I've done *killed* the poor, sorry wretch," Malmury mumbled, shivering and pulling the bearskin tighter about her. "Have you lot gone and found another?"

"Truthfully," Dóta replied, "I do not *know* what fresh devilry this is, only that we can't stay here. There is fire, and a roar like naval cannonade."

"I was sleeping," Malmury said petulantly. I was dreaming of—"

The barmaid slapped her again, harder, and this time Malmury seized her wrist and glared blearily back at Dóta. "I *told* you not to do that."

"Aye, and I told *you* to get up off your fat ass and get moving." There was another explosion then, nearer than any of the others, and both women felt the floorboards shift and tilt below them. Malmury nodded, some dim comprehension wriggling its way through the brandy and wine.

"My horse is in the stable," she said. "I cannot leave without my horse. She was given me by my father."

Dóta shook her head, straining to help Malmury to her feet. "I'm sorry," she said. "It's too late. The stables are all ablaze." Then neither of them said anything more, and the barmaid led the stranger down the swaying stairs and through the tavern and out into the burning village.

4.

FROM A ROCKY CRAG HIGH ABOVE INVERGÓ, the sea troll's daughter watched as the town burned. Even at this distance and altitude, the earth shuddered with the force of each successive detonation. Loose stones were shaken free of the talus and rolled away down the steep slope. The sky was sooty with smoke, and beneath the pall, everything glowed from the hellish light of the flames.

And, too, she watched the progress of those who'd managed to escape the fire. Most fled westward, across the mudflats, but some had filled the hulls of doggers and dories and ventured out into the bay. She'd seen one of the little boats lurch to starboard and capsize, and was surprised at how many of those it spilled into the icy cove reached the other shore. But of all these refugees, only two had headed south, into the hills, choosing the treacherous pass that led up towards the glacier and the basalt mountains that flanked it. The daughter of the sea troll watched their progress with an especial fascination. One of them appeared to be unconscious and was slung across the back of a mule, and the other, a woman with hair the color of the sun, held tight to the mule's reins and urged it forward. With every new explosion the animal bucked and brayed and struggled against her; once or twice, they almost went over the edge, all three of them. By the time they gained the wider ledge where Sæhildr crouched, the sun was setting and nothing much remained intact of Invergó, nothing that hadn't been touched by the devouring fire.

The sun-haired woman lashed the reigns securely to a boulder, then sat down in the rubble. She was trembling, and it was clear she'd not had time to dress with an eye towards the cold breath of the mountains. There was a heavy belt cinched about her waist and from it hung a sheathed dagger. The sea troll's daughter noted the blade, then turned her attention to the mule and its burden. She could see now that the person slung over the animal's back was also a woman, unconscious and partially covered with a moth-eaten bearskin. Her long black hair hung down almost to the muddy ground.

Invisible from her hiding place in the scree, Sæhildr asked, "Is the bitch dead, your companion?"

Without raising her head, the sun-haired woman replied. "Now, why would I have bothered to drag a dead woman all the way up here?"

"Perhaps she is dear to you," the daughter of the sea troll replied. "It may be you did not wish to see her corpse go to ash with the others."

"She's *not* a corpse," the woman said. "Not yet, anyway." And as if to corroborate the claim, the body draped across the mule farted loudly and then muttered a few unintelligible words.

"Your sister?" the daughter of the sea troll asked, and when the sun-haired woman told her no, Sæhildr said, "She seems far too young to be your mother."

"She's not my mother. She's . . . a friend. More than that, she's a hero."

The sea troll's daughter licked at her lips, then glanced back to the inferno by the bay. "A hero," she said, almost too softly to be heard.

"Well, that's the way it started," the sun-haired woman said, her teeth chattering so badly she was having trouble speaking. "She came here from a kingdom beyond the mountains, and, single-handedly, she slew the fiend that haunted the bay. But—"

"—then the fire came," Sæhildr said, and, with that, she stood, revealing herself to the woman. "My *father's* fire, the wrath of the Old Ones, unleashed by the blade there on your hip."

The woman stared at the sea troll's daughter, her eyes filling with wonder and fear and confusion, with panic and awe. Her mouth opened, as though she meant to say something or to scream, but she uttered not a sound. Her hand drifted towards the dagger's hilt.

"*That,* my lady, would be a very poor idea," Sæhildr said calmly. Taller by a head than even the tallest of tall men, she stood looking down at the shivering woman, and her skin glinted oddly in the half light. "Why do you think I mean you harm?"

"You," the woman stammered. "You're the troll's whelp. I have heard the tales. The old witch is your mother."

Sæhildr made an ugly, derisive noise that was partly a laugh. "Is that how they tell it these days, that Gunna is my mother?"

The sun-haired woman only nodded once and stared at the rocks.

"*My* mother is dead," the troll's daughter said, moving nearer, causing the mule to bray and tug at its reigns. "And now, it seems, my father has joined her."

"I cannot let you harm her," the woman said, risking a quick sidewise glance at Sæhildr. The daughter of the sea troll laughed again and dipped her head, almost seeming to bow. The distant firelight reflected off the small curved horns on either side of her head, hardly more than nubs and mostly hidden by her thick hair, and it shone off the scales dappling her cheekbones and brow, as well.

"What you *mean* to say is that you would have to *try* to prevent me from harming her."

"Yes," the sun-haired woman replied, and now she glanced nervously towards the mule and her unconscious companion.

"If, of course, I *intended* her harm."

"Are you saying that you don't?" the woman asked. "That you do not desire vengeance for your father's death?"

Sæhildr licked her lips again, then stepped past the seated woman to stand above the mule. The animal rolled its eyes, neighed horribly, and kicked at the air, almost dislodging its load. But then the sea troll's daughter gently laid a hand on its rump, and immediately the beast grew calm and silent once more. Sæhildr leaned forward and grasped the unconscious woman's chin, lifting it, wishing to know the face of the one who'd defeated the brute who'd raped her mother and made of his daughter so shunned and misshapen a thing.

"This one is drunk," Sæhildr said, sniffing the air.

"Very much so," the sun-haired woman replied.

"A *drunkard* slew the troll?"

"She was sober that day," said Dóta. "I think."

Sæhildr snorted and said, "Know that there was no bond but blood between my father and I. Hence, what need have I to seek vengeance upon his executioner? Though, I will confess, I'd hoped she might bring me some measure of sport. But even that seems unlikely in her current state." The troll's daughter released the sleeping woman's jaw, letting it bump roughly against the mule's ribs, and stood upright again. "No, I think you need not fear for your lover's life. Not this day. Besides, hasn't the utter destruction of your village counted as a more appropriate reprisal?"

The sun-haired woman blinked and said, "Why do you say that, that she's my lover?"

"Liquor is not the only stink on her," answered the sea troll's daughter. "Now, *deny* the truth of this, my lady, and I may yet grow angry."

The woman from doomed Invergó didn't reply, but only sighed and continued staring into the gravel at her feet.

"This one is practically naked," Sæhildr said. "And you're not much better. You'll freeze, the both of you, before morning."

"There was no time to find proper clothes," the woman protested, and the wind shifted then, bringing with it the cloying reek of the burning village.

"Not very much farther along this path, you'll come to a small cave," the sea troll's daughter said. "I will find you there, tonight, and bring what furs and provisions I can spare. Enough, perhaps, that you may yet have some slim chance of making your way through the mountains."

"I don't understand," Dóta said, exhausted and near to tears, and when the troll's daughter made no response, the barmaid discovered that she and the mule and Malmury were alone on the mountain ledge. She'd not heard the demon take its leave, so maybe the stories were true, and it could become a fog and float away whenever it so pleased. Dóta sat a moment longer, watching the raging fire spread out far below them. And then she got to her feet, took up the mule's reins, and began searching for the shelter that the troll's daughter had promised her she would discover. She did not spare a thought for the people of Invergó, not for her lost family, and not even for the kindly old man who'd owned the Cod's Demise and had taken her in off the streets when she was hardly more than a babe. They were the past, and the past would keep neither her nor Malmury alive.

Twice, she lost her way among the boulders, and by the time Dóta stumbled upon the cave, a heavy snow had begun to fall, large wet flakes spiraling down from the darkness. But it was warm inside, out of the howling wind. And, what's more, she found bundles of wolf and bear pelts, sealskins and mammoth hide, some sewn together into sturdy garments. And there was salted meat, a few potatoes, and a freshly killed rabbit spitted and roasting above a small fire. She would never again set eyes on the sea troll's daughter, but in the long days ahead, as Dóta and the stranger named Malmury made their way through blizzards and across fields of ice, she would often sense someone nearby, watching over them. Or only watching.

>>•<<

Elaine Isaak's Joenna, like Yolen's anonymous princess, is driven by vengeance. Unlike the princess, though, her entire life has not been shaped by it. She becomes a warrior to find revenge for the loss of a beloved son. Her perspicacity and loyalty are weapons even sharper than her axe.

JOENNA'S AXE

Elaine Isaak

KILLING A DEMON was almost as difficult as being a man, Joenna reflected as she jerked free her axe from the corpse. Crouching in its vast shadow, she scanned the battlefield, hoping to spot her captain or the banner of their company. The darting figures of men could be seen between the hulking figures of the demons. There! She saw the crimson banner held aloft, its bearer defended by three soldiers. A demon towered over them, smacking the feeble standard down before it sliced the bearer in two.

Joenna cried out, then cursed herself as a group of demons broke off from the mass and sprang to the attack, their tattered leather wings darkening her view.

Gritting her teeth against the throb of muscles too long abused, she fended off the first sword. With the backswing, she hacked the leg off the next demon, the huge creatures blocking each other in their eagerness for blood.

Momentum swung her around to face a third, the reek of its breath staggering her as she ducked the poisoned blade. With a sweep of its ragged wings, the demon sprang into the sky. It howled and a chorus of replies answered.

Joenna stumbled back from the waves of sound, both hands flying to cover her ears. The axe-haft she still gripped gave her a nasty knock. "Blue Lady smother me for a fool!"

Across the ruined field, warriors dropped to their knees, hands pressed to their ears. Like her captain, Joenna had stuffed hers with wads of wool, but the sound came on, rattling her teeth and aching her bones.

"Shut up, shut up," she chanted through clenched teeth. As she swung wildly, she scanned the corpses and stones, searching for her company and hoping they fared better than the poor sots tossed on the points of demons swords. She had been doing this too long now to feel sick any more, or even to feel much sympathy.

Distantly a horn-blast called her back. The demon's weak wings gave out and it dropped heavily, slamming to the earth in her path. The others shifted away, leaving her to face the shrieker. Its knobbed face split into the parody of a grin, the blood-spattered skin more red than brown.

Snarling, Joenna raised her axe and roared. She roared as if she were giving birth and this monster was the bastard who'd got her there.

For a moment, the beast hesitated, its dripping jaws gaping, and Joenna charged, swinging the axe for all she was worth and more. Short and quick, she ducked the demon blade and carved into its belly.

The creature gave a horrid scream, and Joenna said a prayer of thanksgiving for the wool that cut the sound. Dark viscera spilled out as the demon struggled backward and fell.

"Come on! Joseph, come!" shouted a hurrying figure.

Thank the Lady, it was the captain! Propping the axe on her shoulder, Joenna leapt the thrashing of the demon's tail to join the retreat. Grabbing wounded comrades and stumbling over the dead, the scattered army fled. They flung themselves over the ridge of stone, a barrage of flaming arrows fending off the demons in pursuit, letting the soldiers burrow into tunnels too small for demons to follow.

Into the cavern where they had their camp, men straggled by twos and threes. Joenna bent over, hands on knees, catching her breath.

Beside her, the captain stopped to clap her on the shoulder. "Good work, Joseph—if we'd a few more like you, we'd rout those bastards, eh?"

Despite her exhaustion, Joenna snorted her laughter. "There aren't any more like me, Gavin. You've got the original." She plucked the wool from her ears and wiggled her jaw to clear out the stuffed-up feeling.

He laughed in reply, pushing a sandy shag of hair from his face, leaving it red with blood. "Aye, well, if more men were inspired . . . " he trailed off, his excitement fading. "Gods, I'm sorry, Joseph. I don't mean . . . "

She straightened and nodded once. "Aye, Gavin, I know. If every man who lost a son joined battle with us today, we'd be a mighty force indeed."

He lowered his gaze. In a softer voice, he asked, "Have you made your mark yet?"

Grunting, Joenna lifted the axe once more and stroked the smooth wood of its handle. A dozen years ago, she taught her boy to hew logs with this very axe, the weapon she now used to avenge him. The head had none of the fancy work some smiths were prone to, but it kept a good edge and was not so large that a boy—or a woman—would have trouble wielding it. Just below the head, twelve notches chinked the wood. She wiped away the new sheen of blood already turning the notches to the dark, aged brown of the rest of the wood. Slipping a knife from her belt, Joenna hesitated. "Two for sure . . . and a leg wound." Raising an eyebrow at Gavin she offered a smile. "To be honest, the morning's a bit of a blur, isn't it?"

"I saw you take one by the river, early on, then we were hard-pressed for a while. I lost track of you." He sighed. "We're down four men today, that's only six of us from our troop remaining." Again, he scrubbed a hand over his face. More red streaked his ruddy cheeks and trailed down into his beard.

Joenna frowned, then turned back to her axe. "Makes three, then." Carefully, she cut three new notches. Fifteen. Seven more to go to make the total of his years, her son's life cut short in this damnable war. "That your own blood, Cap'n?" The urge to care for his wound prodded at her conscience but four months of playing her role kept her still.

Gavin stared into his hand. "Aye, it may be. I keep wiping it off, but I feel only the dirtier for it." He stiffened, his glance sharpening. "Oh, Gods." He turned abruptly, striding away.

Tracking his gaze, Joenna found a small party approaching. Dressed in the dull camouflage of scouts, they walked stooped over, black hair sticking out in tufts from misshapen heads. Heavy swords that would have reached her breast were strapped across their backs. Her stomach knotted when she saw them, but she merely nodded acknowledgment, seeing the slant of exhaustion in their long limbs.

The leader stopped and blinked at her, then gave a queer grin, wide open to show his snagged teeth. "Don't you run with your captain when the orcs come calling?" His guttural voice grated on her ears, but she stood her ground.

When the orcs come calling. Joenna shuddered and swallowed hard, her eyes dropping for a moment, then she shook her head. "Your mother was no orc, was she?"

"Doesn't matter to your kind, does it?"

Growling, his two companions trotted off, their long arms dangling dangerous fists.

Joenna gave them a sidelong glance, then faced the half-orc before her. "What's your name, then?"

"Are we playing at questions?" He shook back his hair—longer than her own, and more comely since she had hacked hers off without a thought to appearance. The face revealed, once he closed his mouth, looked nearly human. To be sure, his nose was over-large and flat, and his eyes a curious dull black, like two cauldrons freshly scrubbed.

Now that she stood still, the aches returned with full ferocity and Joenna groaned, dropping the axe to put her hands at her back. She was too old for this. "Get on with you—if you can't have a civil conversation, I've done with it."

The half-orc's fingers twitched and his big nostrils flared as if he smelled magic. His eyes narrowed, then widened over another grin. "Valanor, like the hero of old. My mother read the classics." He hissed the last word, drawing it out. His mother was a lady, then, and if he had been another son, he would have been a knight riding with the king's men rather than a scout derided by the very men he served.

Joenna nodded her understanding. "Mine's Joseph. You know a lad named Loref?"

Pulling himself up almost straight and a good deal taller than she, Valanor replied, "Aye. He rode with the ones who went after the dragon, and died there, I'm told."

"He was a friend of mine."

Valanor regarded her, his black eyes unblinking, then he tossed back his head and laughed, the sound raucous and brutal in its bitterness. "Cor—I didn't think you full-bloods could turn your spite so subtle. A friend of yours? What's that make me, your brother?" His cackling broke off and he spat on the ground at her feet. With a snarl low in his throat, he spun away and caught up with his kin in long, loping strides.

"What'd they have to say to you, eh? Nothing good, I'll warrant," Gavin rumbled, returning with a fresh bandage wrapped around his forehead.

Joenna opened her mouth to answer from her anger and exhaustion, then clamped it shut again when the general stomped up. She dropped a short bow, gasping against the confines of the breastplate, which held her too tightly. Breastplate—now there was an irony!

"Captain, Joseph." The general nodded to each in turn. "Good work out there."

"Thank you, sir," Gavin replied, then hesitated until the general prompted, "What is it?"

"Had a thought just now, sir." He looked off where the half-orcs had gone, a little enclave surrounding a grubby pond where they set about their compulsive bathing. "Demons don't care for that sort any more than we do, do they?"

The general gave a noncommittal *whuff* through his graying mustache.

"Well, what if we put them in a vanguard attack, get the demons so bent on ripping them up that we might get an edge on them?"

"You can't do that," Joenna blurted, drawing the officers' keen eyes to her. She floundered, then finally said, "They're our scouts, sir. Without their noses, we'd not know where the demons are."

The general snapped, "But we know where the damn things are—" he thrust his arm toward the roof—"they're at our very doorstep!"

"Just so!" Gavin matched the general's fervor.

"And we need a change of tactics. This may be the very thing. Good thinking, Gavin." He gave the captain an approving smile, tight-lipped and regal, then ruffled his mustache, staring toward the scouts and nodding to himself.

Across the cave, Valanor hitched a thumb in their direction, gesturing to his comrades as he told his tale, the new joke some full-blood had tried on him. Joenna, despite her age and uniform, felt her cheeks flush. She gritted her teeth, then said, "Sir?"

"Mmm?" A gray eyebrow arched at her.

She took a deep breath. "These half-breeds—they'll need a leader, someone brighter than they are to bring this thing off."

"Mmm." The general frowned, flicking his glance to Gavin, then around the cavern to the other commanders minding the battered remnants of the army.

Joenna, too, looked to Gavin, noting the sudden pallor of his wounded face. "I was thinking, sir, that you'll not like to waste a good officer on this, and I know I'm no officer at all—and not like to be—" she chuckled, hoping to strike a note of humor, and failing, she plunged ahead "—but I'll do it, sir, if that's your will." For her son's sake she stood firm.

"Joseph," Gavin muttered, "it's suicide," but the general focused down his long nose at her, mustaches bristling.

"You raise a point, though," the general mused. "You do raise a point."

"Please, sir," she glanced toward the scouts. "What better way to avenge my son?"

"Yes, yes." He looked her up and down, frowning at the top of her head, but nodding at the heft of her axe. "Good lad, your boy. Keep the rabble together, eh, Joseph, and if you win through, there might be a commission in it for you." He slapped her shoulder and she hid her wince. "Meantime," he drawled, "Get some rest, we'll work out the details. Come, Captain."

She bowed again as they drew away, Gavin looking back at her for a moment. The general leaned over to him and whispered, "What's the name of Joseph's son?" as they left earshot.

At last, Joenna flopped on her aching buttocks and loosened the breastplate. Her breasts underneath seemed to protest their freedom almost as much as they had protested the close-quarters. She drew a long, shaky breath and lay back, pillowing her head on her sack of worthless belongings. They'd tell her the plan some time, and probably tell her troops when they kicked them out of bed for the assault—why bother to warn the rabble? Her mouth tasted sour, and the backs of her eyes throbbed to the pulse of her heart. Tomorrow, she would lead the half-orcs in a feint against the demons, hoping to kill her seven, even if she never again notched her axe. Tomorrow, she would die.

The thought was still in her mind as Gavin introduced her to the company she would lead, with the general looking down his nose at the lot of them. The half-orcs, awakened early to this news, glared at her from their kettle-black eyes. They squatted on their haunches, long arms dangling, long fingers working into fists and back again as if they sought a throat to close over.

"And if we don't?" said Valanor. "If we refuse to follow that—" a sharp gesture at Joenna "—to this slaughter?"

"You shall be ignoring a direct order and I shall have you slaughtered by your own army. They may be only too happy to comply. Have I made myself clear?" the general said, the three feathers of his golden helmet bobbing over his shoulders. "I am giving you the unprecedented opportunity to die with an honor you do not deserve, and to see that our forces win out." He pivoted on his heel to give Joenna the benefit of his regard. "This charge shall be known as Joseph's Charge. Best of luck. We'll be an hour behind you." He gave a stiff nod and left them.

"You're a brave man, and a good soldier," Gavin murmured close to her ear. "Lady be with you."

Straightening, Joenna found thirty glaring half-orcs shifting before her. A few glanced toward the archers whose job it was to be sure they followed orders, then back to her, baring their sharp teeth.

"What's it to be, frontal assault? Shall we bother with swords, or will that only make it harder for the demons to rip us to shreds?" Valanor loomed over her.

Joenna hefted her axe and propped it on her shoulder. "Blue Lady, there's got to be a way through this," she muttered.

"Yeah," cried a harsh voice, "kill the general!"

The half-breeds stilled as nearby archers drew their bows, searching for the joker. "Who said it?" called a sergeant. "Point him out, or we'll open on the lot of you."

"Not if we get you first," snarled one of the half-orcs. They crowded together as the archers advanced. Beyond the bowmen, the mass of the army—sharpening swords and checking the buckles on their armor—paused to watch.

More arrows were nocked and bowstrings tightened; the soldiers behind stood at the ready as the half-orcs fingered their swords, weighing the odds. The half-orcs, with their agility and strength, could wreak considerable damage if they tore into the soldiers, but sorely outnumbered, all thirty would soon be slain.

Valanor kept himself still, addressing his comrades. "Think, would you! Better to die on the field than in this cave."

The dark group swayed as if they weren't so sure.

A crew pushed through the army, carrying the barrel of rotten meat they used to keep the scouts in line. Its stink preceded them, and the half-orcs recoiled, giving ground before the archers.

"Enough!" Joenna shouted. "Enough, we've got a job to do." She glanced sharply toward the archer-sergeant, who offered a curt nod and swung his men away, providing an opening for the company to move out of the cavern. They gulped in the breeze across the caves, the fetid barrel brought behind as an encouragement, then they scrambled up the steep slope toward their death.

Above, the air reeked of fire and blood, and the unmistakable sickly stench of demons not far off. At her back, the half-orcs retched and gasped for breath. Thirty young men, the age of her own boy, marred by the hideous orc features. Their knuckles whitened on their sword-hilts just like any other men. "There's got to be a way."

Close by, Valanor snorted. "Don't fool yourself, full-blood. We face one army or the other and you get the glory when we're dead—twice as much for volunteering to serve with us. As appealing as it sounds, killing the general would only confuse the issue."

"Aye, killing the general. Pity we can't kill theirs."

"You know how they fight, better than we do, I'll warrant. They're like insects, one leader dies and another takes its place with a damnable shriek. They don't wear feathered hats to tell us who's in charge." He tossed his shaggy head, growling low in his throat.

As they started the long trudge up the slope, Joenna turned over in her mind the events of the previous day. She had cut down one demon, and another came, leaping up with that shriek. "But they can't all fly," she mumbled to herself.

"They've all got bloody wings, but can't none of them fly more than a few feet straight up."

"Those're the ones that shriek, though," she said, hesitating, looking to the field. Dawn's light began to creep over the shapes of the dead. Somewhere across the field, the enemy hunched down, waiting. "The shriekers are the leaders, I think, not just one of them, but any one of them. We kill one, another takes his place and they fight on like nothing's happened."

"You're talking nonsense," Valanor snapped. "And it doesn't matter anyhow to a company of the dead."

But the idea took form, and Joenna waved away his despair. "Do they smell different?"

"What?"

"The ones that can fly, do they smell different?"

"They all stink like a week-old murder."

"Come on," she tipped her head toward the battlefield, then faced her surly crew. "You lot stay a minute, and keep low. Come on," she urged Valanor again.

With a shrug that rolled from one shoulder to the other, he followed, crouching among the rubble as they shifted their way through the corpses and scorched trees. In moments, they came to the site of yesterday's stand, where Joenna slew the shrieking demon. "This one," she pointed. "Does it smell different than the others?"

Losing his grin, Valanor glanced at the wreck of the demon, and his face in the vague light looked pale. She, too, looked down where the flood of fluids and intestines clogged the path. To her, the thing smelled much the same as a live one, it hadn't had enough time to rot in the short hours they had been sleeping. Catching Valanor's eye, she grimaced. "Sorry. Hard to imagine what it's like for you, with that sensitive nose and all."

His eyes narrowed and he bent over the demon's head, then over that of her first victim. Immediately, he rose again, his throat working as if he fought down bile.

She set a hand on his arm. "Gods, I am sorry, mate."

Snarling, he shook her away, then leaned in close, taking a sniff of her and baring his teeth. "You're a lying, stinking bastard like the rest of them—woman."

Joenna jerked back from him, catching her breath.

Valanor advanced and she dare not move again, dare not reveal them before they were ready. "Aye, this sack of stink smells different. Rotten, with a hint of evil a little sharper than the rest. He does, but so do you." He shot out a long finger, the claw scratching her breastplate. "You smell like baby-making and kitchen-cooking and stitching on a pillow. Paugh! I thought yesterday there was something odd about you." He tapped his blunt nose with a hooked nail. "Now I sense it, you bloody liar. What if I go back in and tell your captain? Or is he the reason you're here? No, I'll take it to the general—if he'd hear me—" a cackle passed his smirking lips. "Maybe that'd give us time to get out of here without all of us losing our necks." He rose away from her, still hunched, and started to turn.

Lunging forward, Joenna caught his arm and yanked him down. Both landed hard on the slimy stones. Valanor knocked her away, sweeping the sword from his back, his teeth bared as he stooped over her. Joenna flipped up her axe, catching his blade and turning it, a new and unintended chink appearing through the stain of the haft.

Hooking her feet on a stone she yanked herself downward and out from under, ramming aside his sword with the flat of her axe. Despite his strength, the half-orc was a scout, not a soldier, and Joenna smiled.

With a heave, he flung her off again, propelling himself back toward the line.

Joenna dove, the axe ahead of her, catching his ankle and toppling him even as their archers took aim.

She pushed herself up beside him, proving her conquest to the rearguard as she faced him. "Watch yourself, you bloody bastard!"

His cauldron eyes glinted fire as his lips twisted. "Will I be the next notch on your axe, oh mighty woman? You do your captain proud."

She lowered her weapon, arms shaking with the rush of fighting. Mastering herself, she whispered, "It's not Gavin I'm fighting for, it's my son. Don't you see?" She wiped back her hair, matching his fierce expression with her own.

His face, inches from hers, looked more awry than ever, the heavy single brow furrowing in his disgust. "Oh, aye, nobility, honor, sacrifice. I know all about that from those accursed stories my mammy tossed aside. I think she died from the shame of it, or maybe from the sight of me, as if it were my fault the orcs took her, my fault what they did to her." His fist rapped against his narrow chest as his voice moved into a hushed wail of unanswered pain.

Joenna snatched his fist, the hairy strength of it captured by her two small hands. "What they did to me," she said. "To me."

After a moment, Valanor let out a breath through flaring nostrils. He swallowed, his shaking fist twisting in her grasp, but not yet applying his strength to freedom.

"The orcs came to my house, too. I never saw a brute so awful, not until this war. That raiding party, they broke and beat and took what they would." She gave a short, nasty laugh. "Look at me, Valanor. I make a better man than a woman—I'm so ugly, no man would take me to wife. But I was good enough for orc-bedding, wasn't I? My parents cast me out. And there I was with child—this gangly, screaming little baby." Dropping his hand, she scrubbed tears from her face. "And I thought two things as ugly as us, we might as well love each other." Her chin rapped against her breastplate as she wept, her ragged hair flopping around her face. Cursing herself, she fought the tears, drawing long breaths, snorting like an ass.

Nearby, Valanor remained silent except the quick rhythm of his breathing. After a long time, he said, "Loref. He was your son."

"Aye."

"He's the reason you fight, the reason you've got those notches in your axe."

More calmly, the tears trickling away at last. "Aye."

"He was like me." His voice became a hot breath across her damp face.

Joenna faced him fully. "Aye," she said. "Like you."

They sat in the growing light, surrounded by demon filth and Valanor stared at her from his dull-black eyes, so like her son's. "You've got a plan, haven't you? You've thought of something."

"I don't think it'll save us, but it may cause confusion enough that the others can win. Valanor—" she took a deep breath and expelled it, along with the grief she could not afford "—it may be enough to show those bastards you're not to be spat on."

A grin started at the corners of his thin lips. "I doubt it."

She sighed. "Me, too, but at least we'll know we did our best. We'll have to convince the company."

"That we will." He cocked his head at her. "What's your name, Loref's mother?"

"Joenna."

"So, Joenna's Charge."

"Naw." She touched the head of her axe. "Better to call it, Half-orc's Revenge."

The troop had few complaints—any plan was better than their orders—and they fanned out around Joenna and Valanor. Quickly, closely, they began their advance. They rippled over the stones and bodies like a shadow not yet dispelled by the feeble light of day. It felt like miles, jogging over the rough ground when the demons rose up, shrieking before them.

The vile wind of their voices slapped back the attackers, but the troop shifted and swirled around her. Instead of attacking, Valanor and Joenna threw themselves under the first swords. They dodged and sprinted and Valanor sniffed. Wherever he pointed, there they struck.

The company plunged in with them, knocking aside the demons as best they could, crying out to block the sound of demon shrieking. One demon leapt up, flapping, over and over, its voice howling out commands. Three of her orcs went down in the first strike and Joenna set her jaw against the dread.

Rather than driving straight on, Joenna's force moved as if at random, following the whims of Valanor's nose. The shrieking filled her ears and echoed inside her aching skull. Grimly she followed where the half-orc led.

Joenna's axe defended him—cleaving the arm from one demon, slicing the leg of another—until he spotted a shrieker and they set-to and brought it down.

The half-orcs swirled around them, slaying the marked demons, themselves falling beneath the poison blades—hacked in two or crushed by taloned arms. The gray garb of the scouts vanished beneath a wash of red. The distant sound of horns announced the army's advance; Joenna doubted if any of hers would be alive to see.

A great demon sprang up before them, outspread wings heaving to lift off as it shrieked. Its lashing tail caught Joenna broadside and she tumbled over the ground, sprawling with her axe underneath. "Blue Lady!" she cried, as the demon thudded down again.

The demon leapt away, a wail of pain escaping it. Demon blood spattered Joenna's face as she rolled and snatched up her axe.

Bellowing, it snatched at Valanor, slapping aside his sword at the cost of its own claws. It lunged again at the half-orc scrambling across the ground.

Matching its bellow, Joenna buried her axe in the demon's side. She slammed to earth as it spun around, and its sword bit into her shoulder.

The demon's head filled her vision, its fangs dripping as it gaped over its prize. The head reared back for another shriek and dove toward her.

With her left hand, Joenna whipped free her knife and rammed it home into a smoldering eye.

Blood spurted, obscuring her own vision; the breath whoofed from her lungs as the demon collapsed on top of her.

For a long time, the world went silent. Joenna thanked the Lady for this reprieve, promising to visit Her temples the first chance she got. She struggled to drag air into her lungs past the steaming corpse that covered her.

Thunk! Thunk! The sound penetrated her fog, and Joenna cracked open her eyes. *Thunk!* The steady sound of an axe into wood. "Loref?" she croaked.

The weight bearing down on her fell aside and Valanor stood over her, axe in hand, shoving the severed demon from her chest.

Letting the axe-head rest beside hers, Valanor bent down. Agile, hairy fingers stroked the blood from her eyes. "Praise the Gods, you're alive!"

"You, too," she managed, sucking in great breaths. "Like to smothered me, that beast." She moved as if she could rise, but Valanor plucked the wool from her ears.

"Listen!" He shouted.

"Can't hear a damn thing." Joenna slapped her ear with her right hand. The left hand only twitched numbly.

"No shrieking! They're retreating from us, a bunch of half-breeds, before the damned army even got here!" His laughter sparkled with hope, echoing the horns drawing the army past. Valanor leaned in closer. "You're wounded, Joenna. I'll get you to the surgeons." He bent to gather her up.

Slapping his hand she rattled, "Don't. They'll know."

"Aye. They'll send you home to get over all this, you fool woman."

She shook her head. "How many?" she asked.

"How many what?"

"Demons I killed."

Tilting back his head, Valanor considered. "Five."

"Then I'm not through yet." She shoved herself into a sitting position, his arm hovering near her. "Don't haul me from here like a fragile woman. If you want to be useful, raise me up like a man."

"But you're wounded! Surely this battle is honor enough."

Joenna shook her head again. "I've two more notches yet to carve, my friend." Then she grinned up at him. "Valanor, hand me my axe."

>•≪

By the end of Elizabeth Bear's story, I hope you will agree that it is not always the number of battles fought or the frequency of fighting that makes a warrior. To quote Sun Tzu: "The wise warrior avoids the battle."

LOVE AMONG THE TALUS

Elizabeth Bear

YOU CANNOT REALLY KEEP a princess in a tower. Not if she has no brothers and must learn statecraft and dancing and riding and poisons and potions and the passage of arms, so that she may eventually rule.

But you can do the next best thing.

In the land of the shining empire, in a small province north of the city of Messaline and beyond the great salt desert, a princess with a tip-tilted nose lived with her mother, Hoelun Khatun, the Dowager Queen. The princess—whose name, it happens, was Nilufer—stood tall and straight as an ivory pole, and if her shoulders were broad and out of fashion from the pull of her long oak-white bow, her dowry would no doubt compensate for any perceived lack of beauty. Her hair was straight and black, as smooth and cool as water, and even when she did not ride with her men-at-arms, she wore split, padded skirts and quilted, paneled robes of silk satin, all emerald and jade and black and crimson embroidered with gold and white chrysanthemums.

She needed no tower, for she was like unto a tower in her person, a fastness as sure as the mountains she bloomed beside, her cool reserve and mocking half-lidded glances the battlements of a glacial virginity.

Her province compassed foothills, and also those mountains (which were called the Steles of the Sky). And while its farmlands were not naturally verdant, its mineral wealth was abundant. At the moderate elevations, ancient terraced slopes had been engineered into low-walled, boggy paddies dotted with unhappy oxen. Women toiled there, bent under straw hats, the fermenting vegetation and glossy leeches which adhered to their sinewy calves unheeded. Farther up, the fields gave way to slopes of scree. And at the bottoms of the sheer, rising faces of the mountains, opened the nurturing mouths of the mines.

The mines were not worked by men; the miners were talus, living boulders with great stone-wearing mouths. The talus consumed ore and plutonic and metamorphic rocks alike (the sandstones, slates, schists, and shales, they found to be generally bereft of flavor and nutrition, but they would gnaw through them to obtain better) and excreted sand and irregular ingots of refined metal. The living rocks were gentle, stolid, unconcerned with human life, although casualties occurred sometimes among the human talus-herders when their vast insensate charges wholly or partially scoured over them. They were peaceful, though, as they grazed through stone, and their wardens would often lean against their rough sides, enjoying the soothing vibrations caused by the grinding of their gizzards, which were packed with the hardest of stones. Which is to say carborundum—rubies and sapphires—and sometimes diamonds, polished by ceaseless wear until they attained the sheen of tumbled jewels or river rock.

Of course, the talus had to be sacrificed to retrieve those, so it was done only in husbandry. Or times of economic hardship or unforeseen expense. Or to pay the tithe to the Khagan, the Khan of Khans might-he-live-forever, who had conquered Nilufer's province and slain her father and brother when Nilufer was but a child in the womb.

There had been no peace before the Khagan. Now the warring provinces could war no longer, and the bandits were not free to root among the spoils like battle ravens. Under the peace of the Khanate and protection of the Khagan's armies, the bandit lords were often almost controlled.

So they were desperate, and they had never been fastidious. When *they* caught one of the talus, they slaughtered it and butchered the remains for jewels, and gold, and steel.

As has been mentioned, the princess of the land had no brothers, and the Khatun, finding it inexpedient to confine her only daughter until marriage (as is the custom of overzealous guardians in any age), preferred to train her to a terrifying certainty of purpose and to surround her with the finest men-at-arms in the land. To the princess and to her troop of archers and swordsmen, not incidentally, fell the task of containing the bandit hordes.

Now, the bandits, as you may imagine, had not been historically well-organized. But in recent years they had fallen under the sway of a new leader, a handsome strong-limbed man who some said had been a simple talus-herder in his youth, and others said was a Khanzadeh, a son of the Khagan, or the son in hiding of one of the Khagan's vanquished enemies, who were many. Over the course of time, he brought the many disparate tribes of bandits together under one black banner, and taught them to fletch their arrows with black feathers.

Whether it was the name he had been given at the cradleboard, none knew, but what he called himself was Temel.

To say that Nilufer could not be *kept* in a tower implies unfairly that she did not *dwell* in one, and that, of course, would be untrue. Her mother's palace had many towers, and one of those—the tallest and whitest of the lot—was entirely Nilufer's own. As has been noted, the Khatun's province was small—really no more than a few broad plateaus and narrow valleys—and so she had no need of more than one palace. But as has also been described, the Khatun's province was wealthy, and so that palace was lavish, and the court that dwelled within it thrived.

Nilufer, as befitted a princess who would someday rule, maintained her own court within and adjacent her mother's. This retinue was made up in part of attendants appointed by the Khatun—a tutor of letters, a tutor of sciences, a tutor of statecraft and numbers; a dancing-master; a master of hawk and horse and hound; a pair of chaperones (one old and smelling of sour mare's milk, the other middle-aged and stern); three monkish warrior women who had survived the burning of their convent by the Khagan some seventeen years before, and so come into the Khatun's service—and in part of Nilufer's own few retainers and gentlewomen, none of whom would Nilufer call friend.

And then of course there was the Witch, who came and went and prophesied and slept and ate as she pleased, like any cat.

On summer evenings, seeking mates, the talus crept from the mines to sing great eerie harmonies like the wails of wetted crystal. Nilufer, if she was not otherwise engaged, could hear them from her tower window. Sometimes, she would reply, coaxing shrill satiny falls of music from the straight white bone of her reed flute. Sometimes, she would even play for them on the one that was made of silver.

Late one particular morning in spring, Nilufer turned from her window six towering stories above the rocky valley. The sun was only now stretching around the white peaks of the mountains, though gray twilight had given a respectable light for hours. Nilufer had already ridden out that morning, with the men-at-arms and the three monkish women, and had practiced her archery at the practice stumps and at a group of black-clad bandits, slaying four of seven.

Now, dressed for ease in loose garments protected by a roll-sleeved smock, she stood before an easel, a long, pale bamboo brush dipped in rich black ink disregarded in her right hand as she examined her medium. The paper was absorbent, thick. Soft, and not glossy. It would draw the ink well, but might feather.

All right for art, for a watercolor wash or a mountainscape where a certain vagueness and misty indirection might avail. But to scribe a spell, or a letter of diplomacy, she would have chosen paper glazed lightly with clay, to hold a line crisply.

Nilufer turned to the Witch, darting her right hand unconsciously at the paper. "Are you certain, old mother?"

The Witch, curled on a low stool beside the fire although the day was warm, lifted her head so her wiry gray braids slid over the motley fur and feathers of her epaulets. The cloak she huddled under might be said to be gray, but that was at best an approximation. Rather it was a patchwork thing, taupes and tans and grays and pewters, bits of homespun wool and rabbit fur and fox fur all sewed together until the Witch resembled nothing so much as a lichen-crusted granite boulder.

The Witch showed tea-stained pegs of teeth when she smiled. She was never certain. "Write me a love spell," she said.

"The ink is too thin," Nilufer answered. "The ink is too thin for the paper. It will feather."

"The quality of the paper is irrelevant to your purpose," the Witch said. "You must use the tools at hand as best you can, for this is how you will make your life, your highness."

Nilufer did not turn back to her window and her easel, though the sun had finally surmounted the peaks behind her, and slanted light suffused the valley. "I do not care to scribe a love spell. There is no man I would have love me, old mother."

The Witch made a rude noise and turned back to the fire, her lids drawing low over eyes that had showed cloudy when the dusty light crossed them. "You will need to know the how of it when you are Khatun, and you are married. It will be convenient to command love then, your highness."

"I will not marry for love," said the princess, cold and serene as the mountains beyond her.

"Your husband's love is not the only love it may be convenient to command, when you are Khatun. Scribe the spell."

The Witch did not glance up from the grate. The princess did not say *but I do not care to be Khatun.*

It would have been a wasted expenditure of words.

Nilufer turned back to her easel. The ink had spattered the page when she jerked her brush. The scattered droplets, like soot on a quartz rock, feathered there.

THE PRINCESS did not sleep alone; royalty has not the privilege of privacy. But she had her broad white bed to herself, the sheets and featherbed tucked neatly over the planks, her dark hair and ivory face stark against the snowy coverlet. She lay on her back, her arms folded, as composed for slumber as for death. The older chaperone slept in a cot along the east side of the bed, and the youngest and most adamant of the monkish warrior women along the west side. A maid in waiting slept by the foot.

The head of the bed stood against the wall, several strides separating it from the window by which stood Nilufer's easel.

It was through this window—not on the night of the day wherein the princess remonstrated with the Witch, but on another night, when the nights had grown warmer—that the bandit Temel came. He scaled the tower as princes have always come to ladies, walking up a white silken rope that was knotted every arm's-length to afford a place to rest his feet and hands. He slipped over the windowsill and crouched beside the wall, his gloved hands splayed wide as spiders.

He had had the foresight to wear white, with a hood and mask covering his hair and all his face but for his eyes. And so he almost vanished against the marble wall.

The guardians did not stir. But Nilufer sat up, dark in her snowy bed, her hair a cold river over her shoulder and her breasts like full moons beneath the silk of her nightgown, and drew a breath to scream. And then she stopped, the breath indrawn, and turned first to the east and then to the west, where her attendants slumbered.

She let the breath out.

"You are a sorcerer," she told him, sliding her feet from beneath the coverlet. The arches flexed when she touched the cold stone floor: of a morning, her ladies would have knelt by the bed to shoe her. Scorning her slippers, she stood.

"I am but a bandit, princess," he answered, and stood to sweep a mocking courtesy. When he lifted his head, he looked past a crescent-shaped arrowhead, down the shaft into her black, unblinking eye, downcast properly on his throat rather than his face. She would never see him flinch, certainly not in moonlight, but *he* felt his eyelids flicker, his cheeks sting, a sharp contraction between his shoulder blades.

"But you've bewitched my women."

"Anyone can scribe a spell," he answered modestly, and then continued: "And I've come to bring you a gift."

"I do not care for your gifts." She was strong. Her arms, as straight and oak-white as her bow where they emerged from the armscyes of her nightgown, did not tremble, though the bow was a killing weapon and no mere toy for a girl.

His smile was visible even through the white silk of his mask. "This one, you will like."

No answer. Her head was straight upon the pillar of her neck. Even in the moonlight, he could see the whitening of her unprotected fingertips where they hooked the serving. A quarter-inch of steady flesh, that was all that stayed his death.

He licked his lips, wetting silk. "Perhaps I just came to see the woman who would one day be Nilufer Khatun."

"I do not care to be Khatun," Nilufer said.

The bandit scoffed. "What else are you good for?"

Nilufer raised her eyes to his. It was not what women did to men, but she was a princess, and he was only a bandit. She pointed with her gaze past his shoulder, to the easel by the window, on which a sheet of paper lay spread to dry overnight. Today's effort—the ideogram for *foundation*—was far more confident than that for *love* had been. "I want to be a Witch," she said. "A Witch and not a Queen. I wish to be not loved, but wise. Tell your bandit lord, if he can give me that, I might accept his gift."

"Only you can give yourself that, your highness," he said. "But I can give you escape."

He opened his hand, and a scrap of paper folded as a bird slipped from his glove. The serving, perhaps, eased a fraction along the ridges of her fingerprints, but the arrow did not fly.

The bandit waited until the bird had settled to the stones before he concluded, "And the bandit lord, as you call him, has heard your words tonight."

Then the arrow did waver, though she steadied it and trained it on his throat again. "Temel."

"At her highness' service."

Her breath stirred the fletchings. He stepped back, and she stepped forward. The grapnel grated softly on the stone, and before she knew it, he was over the sill and descending, almost silently but for the flutter of slick white silk.

Nilufer came to her window and stood there with the string of her long oak-white bow drawn to her nose and her rosebud lips, her left arm untrembling, the flexed muscles in her right arm raising her stark sinews beneath the skin.

The moonlight gilded every pricked hair on her ivory flesh like frost on the hairy stem of a plant. Until the bandit prince disappeared into the shadow of the mountains, the point of her arrow tracked him. Only then did she unbend her bow and set the arrow in the quiver—her women slept on—and crouch to lift the paper bird into her hand.

Red paper, red as blood, and slick and hard so that it cracked along the creases. On its wings, in black ink, was written the spell-word for *flight*.

Blowing on fingers that stung from holding the arrow drawn so steady, she climbed back into her bed.

In the morning, the Khagan's caravan arrived to collect his tithe. The Khagan's emissary was an ascetic, mustached man, graying at the temples. The Witch said that he and the Khagan had been boys together, racing ponies on the steppes.

Hoelun Khatun arranged for him to watch the butchering of the talus from whose guts the tribute would be harvested, as a treat. There was no question but that Nilufer would also attend them.

They rode out on the Khatun's elderly elephant. An extravagance, on the dry side of the mountains. But one that a wealthy province could support, for the status it conferred.

A silk and ivory palanquin provided shade, and Nilufer thought sourly that the emissary was blind to any irony, but her face remained expressionless under its coating of powder as her feathered fan flicked in her hand. The elephant's tusks were capped with rubies and with platinum, a rare metal so impervious to fire that even a smelting furnace would not melt the ore. Only the talus could refine it, though once they excreted it, it was malleable and could be easily worked.

As the elephant traveled, Nilufer became acquainted with the emissary. She knew he watched her with measuring eyes, but she did not think he was covetous. Rather she thought more tribute might be demanded than mere stones and gold this time, and her heart beat faster under the cold green silk of her robes. Though her blood rushed in her ears, she felt no warmer than the silk, or than the talus' tumbled jewels.

The elephant covered the distance swiftly. Soon enough, they came to the slaughtering ground, and servants who had followed on asses lifted cakes and ices up onto the carpet that covered the elephant's back.

Despite its size and power, the slaughter of the talus was easily done. They could be lured from place to place by laying trails of powdered anthracite mixed with mineral oil; the talus-herders used the same slurry to direct their charges at the rock faces they wished mined. And so the beast selected for sacrifice would be led to the surface and away from others. A master stonemason, with a journeyman and two apprentices, would approach the grazing talus and divine the location of certain vulnerable anatomic points. With the journeyman's assistance, the mason would position a pointed wrecking bar of about six feet in length, which the brawny apprentices, with rapid blows of their sledges, would drive into the heart—if such a word is ever appropriate for a construct made of stone—of the talus, such that the beast would then and there almost instantly die.

This was a hazardous proceeding, more so for the journeyman—rather trapped between the rock and the hammers, as it were—than the master or the apprentices. Masons generally endeavored to produce a clean, rapid kill, for their own safety, as well as for mercy upon the beast. (The bandits were less humane in their methods, Nilufer knew, but they too got the job done.) She licked crystals of ice and beet sugar from her reed straw, and watched the talus die.

On the ride back, the emissary made his offer.

NILUFER SOUGHT HOELUN KHATUN in her hall, after the emissary had been feted through dinner, after the sun had gone down. "Mother," she said, spreading her arms so the pocketed sleeves of her over-robe could sweep like pale gold wings about her, "will you send me to Khara-Khorin?"

The possibility beat in her breast; it would mean dangerous travel, overland with a caravan. It would mean a wedding to Toghrul Khanzadeh, the sixth son of the Khagan, whom Nilufer had never met. He was said to be an inferior horseman, a merely adequate general, far from the favorite son of the Khagan and unlikely, after him, to be elected Khan of Khans.

But the offer had been for a consort marriage, not a morganatic concubinage. And if Toghrul Khanzadeh was unlikely to become Khagan, it was doubly unlikely that when his father died, his brothers would blot out his family stem and branch to preclude the possibility.

Hoelun Khatun rose from her cushions, a gold-rimmed china cup of fragrant tea in her right hand. She moved from among her attendants, dismissing them with trailing gestures until only the Witch remained, slumped like a shaggy, softly snoring boulder before the brazier.

The hall echoed when it was empty. The Khatun paced the length of it, her back straight as the many pillars supporting the arched roof above them. Nilufer fell in beside her, so their steps clicked and their trains shushed over the flagstones.

"Toghrul Khanzadeh would come here, if you were to marry him," said Nilufer's mother. "He would come here, and rule as your husband. It is what the Khagan wants for him—a safe place for a weak son."

Nilufer would have wet her lips with her tongue, but the paint would smear her teeth if she did so. She tried to think on what it would be like, to be married to a weak man. She could not imagine.

She did not, she realized, have much experience of men.

But Hoelun Khatun was speaking again, as they reached the far end of the hall and turned. "You will not marry Toghrul Khanzadeh. It is not possible."

The spaces between the columns were white spaces. Nilufer's footsteps closed them before and opened them behind as she walked beside her mother and waited for her to find her words.

Hoelun Khatun stepped more slowly. "Seventeen years ago, I made a bargain with the Khagan. Seventeen years, before you were born. It has kept our province free, Nilufer. I did what he asked, and in repayment I had his pledge that only you shall rule when I am gone. You must marry, but it is not possible for you to marry his son. Any of his sons."

Nilufer wore her face like a mask. Her mother's training made it possible; another irony no one but she would ever notice "He does not mean to stand by it."

"He means to protect a weak son." Hoelun Khatun glanced at her daughter through lowered lashes. "Parents will go to great lengths to protect their children."

Nilufer made a noncommittal noise. Hoelun Khatun caught Nilufer's sleeve, heedless of the paper that crinkled in the sleeve-pocket. She said, too quickly: "Temel could rise to be Khagan."

Nilufer cast a glance over her shoulder at the Witch, but the Witch was sleeping. They were alone, the princess and her mother. "Khan of Khans?" she said, too mannered to show incredulity. "Temel is a bandit."

"Nonetheless," Hoelun Khatun said, letting the silk of Nilufer's raiment slip between her fingers. "They say the Khagan was a prince of bandits when he was young."

She turned away, and Nilufer watched the recessional of her straight back beneath the lacquered black tower of her hair. The princess folded her arms inside the sleeves of her robes, as if serene.

Inside the left one, the crumpled wings of the red bird pricked her right palm.

THAT NIGHT, in the tower, Nilufer unfolded the spell-bird in the darkness, while her attendants slept. For a rushed breathless moment her nightrobes fell about her and she thought that she might suffocate under their quilted weight, but then she lifted her wings and won free, sailing out of the pile of laundry and into the frost-cold night. Her pinions were a blur in the dark as a dancing glimmer drew her; she chased it, and followed it down, over the rice-paddies where sleepless children watched over the tender seedlings, armed with sticks and rocks so wild deer would not graze them; over the village where oxen slept on their feet and men slept with their heads pillowed in the laps of spinning women; over the mines where the talus-herders mostly slumbered and the talus toiled through the night, grinding out their eerie songs.

It was to the mountains that it led her, and when she followed it down, she found she had lost her wings. If she had been expecting it, she could have landed lightly, for the drop was no more than a few feet. Instead she stumbled, and bruised the soles of her feet on the stones.

She stood naked in the moonlight, cold, toes bleeding, in the midst of a rocky slope. A soft crunching vibration revealed that the mossy thing looming in the darkness beside her was a talus. She set out a hand, both to steady herself on its hide and so it would not roll over her in the dark, and so felt the great sweet chime roll through it when it begin to sing. It was early for the mating season, but perhaps a cold spring made the talus fear a cold and early winter, and the ground frozen too hard for babies to gnaw.

And over the sound of its song, she heard a familiar voice, as the bandit prince spoke behind her.

"And where is your bow now, Nilufer?"

She thought he might expect her to gasp and cover her nakedness, so when she turned, she did it slowly, brushing her fingers down the hide of the hulk that broke the icy wind. Temel had slipped up on her, and stood only a few arm-lengths distant, one hand extended, offering a fur-lined cloak. She could see the way the fur caught amber and silver gleams in the moonlight. It was the fur of wolves.

"Take it," he said.

"I am not cold," she answered, while the blood froze on the sides of her feet. Eventually, he let his elbow flex, and swung the cloak over his shoulder.

When he spoke, his breath poised on the air. Even without the cloak she felt warmer; something had paused the wind, so there was only the chill in the air to consider. "Why did you come, Nilufer?"

"My mother wants me to marry you," she answered. "For your armies."

His teeth flashed. He wore no mask now, and in the moonlight she could see that he was comely and well-made. His eyes stayed on her face. She would not cross her arms for warmth, lest he think she was ashamed, and covering herself. "We are married now," he said. "We were married when you unfolded that paper. For who is there to stop me?"

There was no paint on her mouth now. She bit her lip freely. "I could gouge your eyes out with my thumbs," she said. "You'd make a fine bandit prince with no eyes." He stepped closer. He had boots, and the rocks shifted under them. She put her back to the cold side of the talus. It hummed against her shoulders, warbling. "You would," he said. "If you wanted to. But wouldn't you rather live free, Khatun to a Khagan, and collect the tithes rather than going in payment of them?"

"And what of the peace of the Khanate? It has been a long time, Temel, since there was war. The only discord is your discord."

"What of your freedom from an overlord's rule?"

"My freedom to become an overlord?" she countered.

He smiled. He was a handsome man.

"How vast are your armies?" she asked. He was close enough now that she almost felt his warmth. She clenched her teeth, not with fear, but because she did not choose to allow them to chatter. In the dark, she heard more singing, more rumbling, Another talus answered the first.

"Vast enough." He reached past her and patted the rough hide of the beast she leaned upon. "There is much of value in a talus." And then he touched her shoulder, with much the same affection. "Come, princess," he said. "You have a tiger's heart, it is so. But I would make this easy."

She accepted the cloak when he draped it over her shoulders and then she climbed up onto the talus beside him, onto the great wide back of the ancient animal. There were smoother places there, soft with moss and lichen, and it was lovely to lie back and look at the stars, to watch the moon slide down the sky.

This was a feral beast, she was sure. Not one of the miners. Just a wild thing living its wild slow existence, singing its wild slow songs. Alone, and not unhappy, in the way such creatures were. And now it would mate (she felt the second talus come alongside, though there was no danger; the talus docked side by side like ships, rather than one mounting the other like an overwrought stallion) and it might have borne young, or fathered them, or however talus worked these things.

But Temel warmed her with his body, and the talus would never have the chance. In the morning, he would lead his men upon it, and its lichen and moss and bouldery aspect would mean nothing. Its slow meandering songs and the fire that lay at its heart would be as nothing. It was armies. It was revolution. It was freedom from the Khan.

He would butcher it for the jewels that lay at its heart, and feel nothing.

Nilufer lay back on the cold stone, pressed herself to the resonant bulk and let her fingers curl how they would. Her nails picked and shredded the lichen that grew in its crevices like nervous birds picking their plumage until they bled.

Temel slid a gentle hand under the wolf-fur cloak, across her belly, over the mound of her breast. Nilufer opened her thighs.

She flew home alone, wings in her window, and dressed in haste. Her attendants slept on, under the same small spell which she had left them, and she went to find the Witch.

The Witch crouched beside the brazier, as before, in the empty hall. But now, her eyes were open, wide, and bright.

The Witch did not speak. That fell to Nilufer.

"She killed my father," Nilufer said. "She betrayed my father and my brother, and she slept with the Khagan, and I am the Khagan's daughter, and she did it all so she could be Khatun."

"So you will not marry the Khanzadeh, your brother?"

Nilufer felt a muscle twitch along her jaw. "That does not seem to trouble the Khagan."

The Witch settled her shoulders under the scrofular mass of her cloak. "Before I was the Witch," she said, in a voice that creaked only a little, "I was your father's mother."

Nilufer straightened her already-straight back. She drew her neck up like a pillar. "And when did you become a Witch and stop being a mother?"

The Witch's teeth showed black moons at the root where her gums had receded. "No matter how long you're a Witch, you never stop being a mother."

Nilufer licked her lips, tasting stone grit and blood. Her feet left red prints on white stone. "I need a spell, grandmother. A spell to make a man love a woman, in spite of whatever flaw may be in her." *Even the chance of another man's child?*

The Witch stood up straighter. "Are you certain?"

Nilufer turned on her cut foot, leaving behind a smear. "I am going to talk to the emissary," she said. "You will have, I think, at least a month to make ready."

Hoelun Khatun came herself, to dress the princess in her wedding robes. They should have been red for life, but the princess had chosen white, for death of the old life, and the Khatun would permit her daughter the conceit. Mourning upon a marriage, after all, was flattering to the mother.

Upon the day appointed, Nilufer sat in her tower, all her maids and warriors dismissed. Her chaperones had been sent away. Other service had been found for her tutors. The princess waited alone, while her mother and the men-at-arms rode out in the valley before the palace to receive the bandit prince Temel, who some said would be the next Khan of Khans.

Nilufer watched them from her tower window. No more than a bowshot distant, they made a brave sight with banners snapping.

But the bandit prince Temel never made it to his wedding. He was found upon that day by the entourage and garrison of Toghrul Khanzadeh, sixth son of the Khagan, who was riding to woo the same woman, upon her express invitation. Temel was taken in surprise, in light armor, his armies arrayed to show peace rather than ready for war.

There might have been more of a battle, perhaps even the beginnings of a successful rebellion, if Hoelun Khatun had not fallen in the first moments of the battle, struck down by a bandit's black arrow. This evidence of treachery from their supposed allies swayed the old queen's men to obey the orders of the three monkish warrior women who had been allies of the Khatun's husband before he died. They entered the fray at the Khanzadeh's flank.

Of the bandit army, there were said to be no survivors.

No one mentioned to the princess that the black fletchings were still damp with the ink in which they had been dipped. No one told her that Hoelun Khatun had fallen facing the enemy, with a crescent-headed arrow in her back.

And when the three monkish warrior women came to inform Nilufer in her tower of her mother's death and found her scrubbing with blackened fingertips at the dark drops spotting her wedding dress, they also did not tell her that the outline of a bowstring still lay livid across her rosebud mouth and the tip of her tilted nose.

If she wept, her tears were dried before she descended the stair.

Of the Dowager Queen Nilufer Khatun—she who was wife and then widow of Toghrul Khanzadeh, called the Barricade of Heaven for his defense of his father's empire from the bandit hordes at the foothills of the Steles of the Sky—history tells us little.

But, that she died old.

>⟫•⟪

In this brief but vivid historical fantasy from Nalo Hopkinson, almost everyone in a Caribbean village—one of the free communities formed by escaped slaves—is ready to battle the colonial brigade sent against them with whatever weapons they have. One of those is powerful, but costly: magic.

SOUL CASE

Nalo Hopkinson

MOMENTS AFTER the sun's bottom lip cleared the horizon, the brigade charged down the hill. Kima stood with the rest of the Garfun, ready to give back blow for blow.

The pistoleers descended towards the waiting village compong. Their silence unnerved. Only the paddy thump of the camels' wide feet made any sound. Compong people murmured, stepped back. But Mother Letty gestured to the Garfuns defending them to stand still. So they did. Kima felt her palm slippery on her sharpened hoe.

The pistoleers advanced upon them in five rows; some tens of impeccably uniformed men and women posting up and down in unison on their camels. Each row but the last comprised seven gangly camels, each camel ridden by a soldier, each soldier kitted out à la zouave, in identical and pristine red-and-navy with clean white shirts. Near on four muskets for each of them, and powder, carried by a small boy running beside each camel. There were only twelve muskets in the compong.

Now the first rows of camels stepped onto the pitch road that led into the village. The road was easily wide enough for seven camels across. The cool morning sun had not yet made the surface of the pitch sticky. The camels didn't even break stride. Kima made a noise of dismay. Where was the strong science that the three witches had promised them? Weeks and weeks they'd had them carting reeking black pitch from the deep sink of it that lay in the gully, re-warming it on fires, mixing it with stones and spreading it into this road that led from nowhere to the entrance of the compong, and stopped abruptly there. Had they done nothing but create a smooth paved surface by which the army could enter and destroy them?

From her position at the head of the Garfuns, the black witch, the Obe Acotiren, showed no doubt. She only pursed her lips and grunted, once. Standing beside her, white Mother Letty and the Taino witch Maridowa did not even that. The three should have been behind the Garfuns, where they could be protected. If the villagers lost their Knowledgeables, they would be at the mercy of the whites' fish magic. Yet there the three stood and watched. Acotiren even had her baby grandson cotched on her hip. So the Garfuns took their cue from the three women. Like them, they kept their ground, ready but still.

"Twice five," whispered Mother Letty. "Twice six." She was counting the soldiers as they stepped onto the black road. Kima thought it little comfort to know exactly how many soldiers had come to kill them, but she found herself counting silently along with Mother Letty.

The leading edge of the army was almost upon them, scant yards from the entrance to the compong. Camels covered almost the full length of the road. A few of the Garfuns made ready to charge. "Hold," said Mother Letty. Her voice cut through the pounding of the camels. They held.

Maridowa turned her wide, brown face to the Garfuns and grinned. "Just a little more," she said. She was merry at strange times, the young Taino witch was.

The soldiers had their muskets at the ready. The barrels gleamed in the sun. The Garfuns' muskets were dull and scorched. "So many of them," whispered Kima. She raised her hoe, cocked it ready to strike. Beside her, the white boy Carter whimpered, but clutched his cutlass at the ready, a grim look on his face. He'd said he would rather die than be press-ganged onto the ships once more as a sailor. He had fourteen years. If he survived this, the village would let him join the boys to be circumcised; let him become a man.

Thrice six . . .

The thrice seventh haughty camel stepped smartly onto the battlefield, a little ahead of its fellows. "That will do it," pronounced the Obe Acotiren. It wasn't quite a question.

The pitch went liquid. It was that quick. Camels began to flounder, then to sink. The villagers gasped, talked excitedly to each other. They had laid the pitch only four fingers deep! How then was it swallowing entire camels and riders?

The pitch swamp had not a care for what was possible and what not. It sucked the brigade into its greedy gullet like a pig gobbling slops. Camels mawed in dismay, the pitch snapping their narrow ankles as they tried to clamber out. They sank more quickly than their lighter riders. Soldier men and women clawed at each other, stepped on each others' heads and shoulders to fight free of the melted pitch. To no avail. The last hoarse scream was swallowed by the pitch in scarce the time it took the Obe Acotiren's fifth grandchild—the fat brown boy just past his toddling age, his older sisters and brothers having long since joined the Garfun fighters—to slip from her arms and go running for his favorite mango tree.

The black face of the road of tar was smooth and flat again, as though the army had never been.

One meager row of uniformed soldiers stared back at the Garfuns from the other side of the pitch. Their weapons hung unused from their hands. Then, together, they slapped their camels into a turn, and galloped hard for the foot of the hill.

All but one, who remained a-camelback at the bank of the river of pitch.

The pistoleer slid off her beast. She stood on the edge of where her fellows, suffocated, were slowly hardening. She bent her knees slightly, curling her upper body around her belly. Fists held out in front of her, she screamed full throat at the villagers; a raw howl of grief that used all the air in her lungs, and that went on long after she should have had none remaining. She seemed like to spit those very lungs up. Her camel watched her disinterestedly for a while, then began to wander up the hill. It stopped to crop yellow hog plums from a scraggly tree.

On the hill above, the general sounded the retreat. In vain; most of his army had already dispersed. (Over the next few weeks, many of them would straggle into Garfun compongs—some with their camels—begging asylum. This they would be granted. It was a good land, but mostly harsh scrub. It needed many to tend it.)

Some few of the Garfuns probed the pitch with their weapons. They did not penetrate. Cautiously, the Garfuns stepped onto the pitch. It was hard once more, and held them easily. They began to dance and laugh, to call for their children and their families to join them. Soon there was a celebration on the flat pitch road. An old matron tried to show Carter the steps of her dance. He did his best to follow her, laughing at his own clumsiness.

THE OBE ACOTIREN watched the soldier woman, who had collapsed onto her knees now, her scream hiccuping into sobs. While the army was becoming tar beneath the feet of the villagers, Acotiren had pushed through the crowd and fetched her fearless grandchild from the first branch of the mango tree. He'd fallen out of it thrice before, but every day returned to try again. She hitched him up onto her hip. He clamped his legs at her waist and fisted up a handful of her garment at the shoulder. He brought the fist happily to his mouth.

Acotiren's face bore a calm, stern sadness. "Never you mind," Kima heard her mutter in the direction of the grieving woman. "What we do today going to come back on us, and more besides." Maridowa glanced at the Obe, but said nothing.

Then Acotiren produced her obi bag from wherever she had had it hidden on her person, and tossed it onto the pitch. Mother Letty started forward. "Tiren, no!" cried Mother Letty, her face anguished.

She was too late to intercept the obi bag. It landed on the road. It was a small thing, no bigger than a guinea fowl's egg. It should have simply bounced and rolled. Instead, it sank instantly, as though it weighed as much in itself as the whole tarred army together.

Maridowa was dancing on the road, and hadn't noticed what was happening. It was Kima who saw it all. Acotiren pressed her lips together, then smiled a bright smile at her grandchild. "Come," she said. "Make I show you how to climb a mango tree."

Tranquil, as though she hadn't just tossed her soulcase away to be embalmed forever in tar, she turned her back to go and play with the boy, leaving Mother Letty kneeling there, tears coursing through the lines on her ancient face as she watched her friend go.

In less than a year, Acotiren was frail and bent. There was no more climbing trees for her. Her eyes had grown crystalline with cataracts, her hands tremulous, her body sere and unmuscled. One morning she walked into the bush to die, and never came out again. But by then her daughter's child, Acotiren's fifth grandchild, was so sure-footed from skinning up gru-gru bef palms and mamapom trees with his nana, that he never, ever fell. Wherever he could plant his feet, he could go. His friends called him Goat.

≫•≪

Carrie Vaughn reminds us of some true heroes in this non-genre—well, it is a mystery—story. During World War II, 1,100 women pilots served in the Women Airforce Service Pilots, WASP—the first women to fly American military aircraft. Thirty-eight died while in the program. In 2010, the WASP were awarded the Congressional Gold Medal by the United States Congress. Over 250 surviving WASP were present to receive the honor.

THE GIRLS FROM AVENGER

Carrie Vaughn

JUNE 1943

THE SUN WAS SETTING over Avenger Field when Em and a dozen others threw Mary into the so-called Wishing Well, the wide round fountain in front of the trainee barracks. A couple of the girls grabbed her arms; a couple more grabbed her feet and hauled her off the ground. Mary screamed in surprise, and Em laughed—she should have known this was coming, it happened to everyone after they soloed. But she remembered from her own dunking the week before, it was hard not to scream out of sheer high spirits.

Em halted the mob of cheering women just long enough to pull off Mary's leather flight jacket—then she was right there at Mary's shoulders, lifting her over the stone lip of the pool of water. Mary screamed again—half screamed, half laughed, rather—and splashed in, sending a wave over the edge. On her knees now, her sodden jumpsuit hanging off her like a sack, she splashed them all back. Em scrambled out of the way.

Applause and laughter died down, and Mary started climbing over the edge. "Don't forget to grab your coins," Em told her.

"Oh!" She dived back under the water, reached around for a moment, then showed Em her prize—a couple of pennies in her open palm. Mary was young, twenty-two, and her wide, clear eyes showed it. Her brown hair was dripping over her face and she looked bedraggled, grinning. "I'm the luckiest girl in the world!"

Whenever one of the trainees at the Women's Flight Training Detachment at Avenger Field had a test or a check-out flight, she tossed a coin into the fountain for good luck. When she soloed for the first time, she could take two out, for luck. Em's coins were still in her pocket.

Em reached out, and Mary grabbed her hand. "Come on, get out of there. I think Suze has a fifth of whiskey with your name on it hidden under her mattress."

Mary whooped and scrambled out. She shook out her jumpsuit; sheets of water came off it, and she laughed all over again.

Arm in arm, they trooped to the barracks, where someone had a radio playing and a party had already started.

DECEMBER 1943

IN AN OUTFIT like the WASP, everyone knew everyone and news traveled fast.

Em heard about it as soon as she walked into the barracks at New Castle.

Didn't have time to even put her bag down or slide her jacket off before three of the others ran in from the hall, surrounded her, and started talking. Janey gripped her arm tight like she was drowning, and Em let her bag drop to the floor.

"Did you hear?" Janey said. Her eyes were red from crying, Tess looked like she was about to start, and Patty's face was white. Em's stomach turned, because she already knew what they were going to say.

"Hear what?" she asked. Delaying the inevitable, like if she could draw this moment out long enough, the news wouldn't be true.

"A crash, out at Romulus," Patty said.

Em asked what was always the first question: "Who?"

"Mary Keene."

The world flipped, her heart jumped, and all the blood left her head.

No, there was a mistake, not Mary. Rumors flew faster than anything. She realized Patty didn't look so worried because of the crash; she was worried about Em.

"What happened?" Always the second question.

"I don't know, just that there was a crash."

"Mary, is she—?"

Janey's tears fell and her voice was tight. She squeezed Em harder. "Oh, Em! I'm so sorry. I know you were friends—I'm so sorry."

If Em didn't get out of here now, she'd have to hug them all and start crying with them. She'd have to think about how to act and what to say and what to do next. She'd have to listen to the rumors and try to sort out what had really happened.

She pushed by them, got past their circle, ignored it when Patty touched her arm, trying to hold her back. Left her bag behind, thought that she ought to drag it with her because it had dirty clothing in it. Maybe somebody called to her, but she just wanted to be alone.

She found her room, sat on her cot, and stared at the empty cot against the other wall. She bunked with Mary, right here in this room, just as they had at Avenger. Doubled over, face to her lap, she hugged herself and wondered what to do next.

THIS DIDN'T HAPPEN often enough to think it could happen to you, or even someone you knew. A year of women flying Army planes, and it had happened less than a dozen times. There were few enough of them all together that Em had known some of them, even if they hadn't been friends. Seen them at training or waved on the way to one job or another.

It had happened often enough that they had a system.

Em knocked on the last door of the barracks and collected money from Ruth and Liz. She didn't have to explain what it was for when she held the cup out. It had been like that with everyone, the whole dozen of them on base at the moment. Em would take this hundred and twenty dollars, combine it with the hundred or so sent in from the women at Sweetwater and Houston, and she'd use it to take Mary back to Dayton. None of them were officially Army, so Uncle Sam didn't pay for funerals. It seemed like a little thing to complain about, especially when so many of the boys overseas were dying. But Mary had done her part, too. Didn't that count for something?

"Have you found out what happened yet?" Liz asked. Everyone had asked that, too.

Em shook her head. "Not a thing. I called Nancy, but they're not telling her anything either."

"You think it was bad?" Liz said. "You think that's why they're hushing it up?"

"They're hushing it up because they don't like to think about women dying in airplanes," she said. Earlier in the year, she'd been told point blank by a couple of male pilots that the only women who belonged on planes were the ones painted on the noses. That was supposed to be clever.

She was supposed to laugh and flirt. She'd just walked away.

Running footsteps sounded on the wood floor and they looked up to see Janey racing in. The panic in her eyes made Em think that maybe it had happened again, that someone else had gone and crashed and that they'd have to pass the cup around again, so soon.

Janey stopped herself by grabbing Em's arm and said, "There's a bird in from Romulus, a couple of guys in a B-26. You think maybe they know what happened?"

They'd have a better idea than anyone. They might even have seen something. "Anyone talk to them yet?" Em said. Janey shook her head.

A line on the rumor mill. Em gave her colleagues a grim smile and headed out.

SHE COULDN'T WALK by the flight line without stopping and looking, seeing what was parked and what was roaring overhead. The place was swarming, and it always made her heart race. It was ripe with potential—something big was happening here. *We're fighting a war here, we really are.* She took a deep breath of air thick with the smell of fuel and tarmac. Dozens of planes lined up, all shapes and sizes, a dozen more were taking off and landing.

Hangar doors stood open revealing even more, and a hundred people moved between them all, working to keep the sound of engines loud and sweet.

This time, she wasn't the only one stopping to look, because a new sound was rocketing overhead, a subtly different rumble than the ones she normally heard out here. Sure enough, she heard the engine, followed the sound, and looked up to see a bulldog of a fighter buzz the field, faster than sin. She shaded her eyes against a bright winter sun and saw the P-51 Mustang—so much more graceful and agile than anything else in the sky.

The nose tapered to a sleek point, streamlined and fast, like a rocket. Not like the clunky, snub-nosed trainers. Granted, clunky trainers served a purpose—it was easier for a pilot in training to correct a mistake at a hundred miles an hour than it was at three hundred. But Em had to wonder what it felt like to really *fly*. Some way, somehow, she was going to get up in one of those birds someday. She was going to find out what it was like to have 1,500 horsepower at her command.

If she were male, her training wouldn't stop with the little single-engine trainers the WASP ferried back and forth from training base to training base, where they were flown by the men who would move on to pursuits and bombers, and from there to combat. If she were male, she'd be flying bigger, faster, meaner planes already. Then she'd go overseas to fly them for real.

As Janey had said, a B-26 Marauder—a fast, compact two-engine bomber—crouched out on the tarmac, a couple of mechanics putting fuel into her. She was probably stopped for a refuel on her way to somewhere else. That meant Em probably had only one chance to talk to the pilots.

She continued on to the ops center. The door to the briefing room was closed, but she heard voices inside, muffled. Against her better judgment, she put her ear to the door and listened, but the talk was all routine. The bomber was on its way to Newark for transport overseas, and the pilot was a combat instructor, just off the front.

Em sat in a chair across the hall and waited. Half an hour later, the door opened. The two guys who emerged were typical flyboys, leather jackets, sunglasses tucked in the pockets, khaki uniforms, short cropped hair, and Hollywood faces. Lieutenant bars on the shoulders.

When Em stood at attention, smoothing her trousers and trying not to worry if her collar was straight, the men looked startled. She didn't give them time to try to figure out what to do with her. "I'm sorry to bother you. My name's Emily Anderson, and I'm with the WASP squadron here. I got word that you just flew in from Romulus this morning. I was wondering if I could ask you something."

The taller of the two edged toward the door. "I have to go check on . . . on something. Sorry." His apology was quick and not very sincere.

The remaining pilot looked even more stricken and seemed ready to follow his buddy.

"Please, just a quick question," she said, hating to sound like she was begging. She ought to be charming him.

His wary look deepened, a defensive, thin-lipped frown that made her despair of his taking her seriously. He hesitated, seeming to debate with himself before relenting. "What can I help you with, Miss Anderson?"

She took a deep breath. "I'm trying to find out about a crash that happened near Romulus Field three days ago. A WASP was the pilot. Mary Keene. Sir, she was a friend of mine, and we—the other WASP and I—we just want to know what happened. No one will tell us anything."

He could have denied knowing anything, shaken his head, and walked out, and she wouldn't have been able to do anything, and she wouldn't have been more worried than she already was. But he hesitated. His hands fidgeted with the edge of his jacket, and he glanced at the door, nervous.

He knew. Not just that, it was something he didn't want to talk about, something awful.

She pressed. "You know what it's like when something like this happens and they won't tell you anything."

He shook his head and wouldn't meet her gaze. "I shouldn't tell you this."

"Why not? Because it's classified? Or because I'm female and you think I can't handle it?"

The lieutenant pursed his lips. He'd been in combat, might even have faced down enemy fighters, but he didn't seem to want to stand up to her.

"It was a collision," he said finally.

Em had worked out a dozen scenarios, everything from weather to mechanical failure. She was even braced to hear that Mary had made a mistake. A million things could go wrong in the air. But a collision?

"That doesn't make sense, Mary had almost seven hundred hours in the air, she was too experienced for that."

He got that patronizing look a lot of male pilots had when dealing with WASP, like she couldn't possibly know what she was talking about. "I told you I shouldn't have said anything."

"A collision with whom? Did the other pilot make it? What were they doing that they ran into each other? Did you see it?"

"I don't know the details, I'm sorry."

"The Army won't even tell me what she was flying when she went down," she said.

He stepped closer, conspiratorially, as if afraid that someone was listening in. Like this really was classified.

"Look, Miss Anderson, you seem like a nice girl. Why are you doing this? Why are any of you risking your lives like this? Why not stay home, stay safe—?"

"And plant a Victory Garden like a good girl? Sit by the radio and wait for someone to tell me it's going to be all right, and that my husband'll come home safe? I couldn't do that, Lieutenant. I had to do something."

The arguments against women flyers tended to stall out at this point, into vague statements about what was ladylike, what well-bred girls ought to be doing, how women weren't strong enough to handle the big planes even though they'd proved themselves over and over again. A year of women flying should have shut the naysayers up by now. It hadn't.

The lieutenant didn't say anything.

She said, "Is there someone else I can talk to?"

"Look, I don't know, I'm working off rumors like everyone else. I can't help you. I'm sorry." He fled, backing to the door and abandoning Em to the empty corridor.

THE WASP ALL LIKED COLONEL ROPER, who commanded the Second Ferry Group at New Castle. At some of the other bases, commanders had given

WASP the cold shoulder, but here, he'd treated them with respect and made it policy that the rest of the group do likewise. He didn't constantly ask them if they could do the job—he just gave them the job.

She went to him with the lieutenant's story.

His office door was open and he saw her coming. As he was glancing up, a frown drew lines around his mouth. He was young for a colonel, maybe a little rounder than most guys in the Army, but high-spirited. His uniform jacket was slung over the back of his chair.

"I'm sorry, Anderson, I don't have any news for you," he told her before she'd said a word.

She ducked her gaze and blushed. She'd been in here every day looking for news about Mary's death.

"Sorry, sir," she said, standing at the best attention she knew, back straight and hands at her sides. "But I just talked to the pilots of that B-26 that came in from Romulus. Sir, they told me Mary crashed in a collision. They wouldn't tell me anything else."

Roper's lips thinned, his brow creased. "A collision—Mary wouldn't get herself in that kind of mess."

"I know. Sir, something's not right. If there's anything you can do, anything you can find out—"

He scratched out a note on a pad of paper. "The crash report ought to be filed by now. I'll get a copy sent over."

That meant a few more days of waiting, but it was progress. They'd get the report, and that would be that. But she still wanted to *talk* to someone. Someone who'd seen it, someone who knew her. If there was a collision, another pilot was involved. If she could just find out who.

"Thank you, sir," she said.

"You're welcome. Anderson—try to get some sleep. You look beat." She hadn't even been thinking about being tired. She'd been running on fumes. "Yes, sir."

MARY KEENE came from the kind of family that did everything just so, with all the right etiquette. A car from the funeral home was waiting at the train station, along with Mary's father. Em recognized him from the family picture Mary kept in their room.

Em, dressed in her blue uniform—skirt straight, collar pressed, lapels smooth, insignia pins and wings polished—jumped to the platform before the train slowed to a complete stop and made her way to the luggage car.

She waited again. It should have been raining; instead, a crisp winter sun shone in a blue sky. Perfect flying weather. She was thankful for the wool uniform, because a cold wind blew in over a flat countryside.

Men from the funeral home retrieved the casket while Mr. Keene thanked her for coming, shaking her hand with both of his and frowning hard so he wouldn't cry.

"I thought I'd be meeting one of my boys here like this. Not Mary."

Em bowed her head. No one ever knew quite what to say about a woman coming home from war in a casket. If one of Mr. Keene's sons had been killed, the family would put a gold star in the window to replace the blue one showing loved ones serving in combat. They'd be able to celebrate their war hero. Mary wouldn't get any of that, not even a flag on her casket.

Mr. Keene left in his own car. Em would go with Mary to the funeral home, then call a cab and find a hotel to stay at until the funeral tomorrow.

One of the men from the mortuary took Em aside before they left.

"I'm given to understand Miss Keene passed on in an airplane crash."

"That's right."

He was nervous, not looking at her, clasping his hands. Em thought these guys knew how to deal with anything.

"I'm afraid I have to ask—I wasn't given any information," he said. "The family has traditionally held open-casket services—will this be possible?"

Or had she burned, had she been smashed beyond recognition, was there anything left? . . . Em's lips tightened. Stay numb, stay focused, just like navigating a fogbank.

"No, I don't think it will," she said.

The man lowered his gaze, bowing a little, and returned to his car.

Em logged thirty hours the next week in trainers, two AT-6s and a BT-13, flying from one end of the country to the other. One morning, she'd woken up in the barracks and had to look outside the window to remember where she was. She kept an eye on other logs and flight plans coming in and out of each base, and kept looking for people who'd been at Romulus last week. Everyone knew about the crash, but other than the fact that a WASP had been killed, nobody treated it like anything unusual. This was wartime, after all.

Arriving back at New Castle on the train after ferrying another round of BT-13s to Houston, she dropped her bag off at the barracks and went to see Colonel Roper. She still had her jumpsuit and flight jacket on, and she really needed a shower. And a meal. And sleep. But maybe this time he had news.

"Sir?" she said at his doorway.

He looked hard at her, didn't say a word. Self-consciously, she pushed her hair back behind her ears. Maybe she should have washed up first. She tried again. "Sir?"

"You're right, Anderson," he said finally. "Something's not right. The crash report's been classified."

She stared. "But that doesn't make any sense."

"I have something for you."

He handed her a folded paper that looked suspiciously like orders.

She'd been in the air for three days. She hadn't been back in her own room for a week. She didn't want another mission; she didn't want orders. But you never said no; you never complained.

Her despair must have shown, because Roper gave a thin smile. "I saved this one just for you. I have an AT-11 needs to go to Romulus and I thought you're just the pilot to do it."

Exhaustion vanished. She could fly a month straight if she had to.

He continued, "In fact, you look a little tired. Why don't you spend a few days out there while you're at it? Take a break, meet the locals."

Do some digging, in other words.

"Thank you, sir," she said, a little breathlessly.

"Bring me back some facts, Anderson."

LAST JUNE, right after graduation and before transferring to New Castle, Em and Mary flew together on a cross-country training hop from Sweetwater to Dallas. It was the kind of easy trip where Em could sit back and actually enjoy flying. The kind of trip that reminded her why she was even doing this. She could lean back against the narrow seat, look up and all around through the narrow, boxy canopy at nothing but blue sky. Free as air.

"Hey Em, take the stick for a minute," Mary said, shouting over the rumble of the engine, when they'd almost reached Love Field at Dallas.

From the back seat of their BT-13 Valiant, craning her neck to peer over Mary's shoulder, Em saw her drop the stick and start digging in one of the pockets of her jacket. Em hadn't yet taken over on the dual controls.

The Valiant was a trainer and could be flown from either the front or back seat, and every trainee sitting in front had had the controls yanked away from them by the instructor in back at least once. The plane was flying trim so Em didn't panic too much; she had a little time to put a steadying hand on the stick.

"What are you doing up there?" Em asked. Mary turned just enough so Em could see her putting on lipstick, studying her work in a compact mirror.

She'd had enough practice putting on lipstick in airplanes that the teeth-rattling vibrations of the engine didn't affect her at all. Em laughed. "No one up here cares about your lipstick."

Mary looked a little ridiculous, leather cap mashing down her hair, goggles up on her forehead, painting her lips. So this was why she wanted to fly with the canopy closed on such a warm, beautiful day, making the cockpit hot and stuffy. She didn't want to be all ruffled when they landed.

"I have to be ready. There might be some handsome young officer just waiting for me to catch his eye. Oh, I hope we get there in time for dinner. This bucket's so slow. You think they'll ever give us anything faster to fly?"

"A real plane, you mean?" Em said. It was an old joke.

"I wouldn't say *that*. This bird's real enough. If you don't mind going *slow*."

Em looked out the canopy stuck up top in the middle of the fuselage. "We have to get there and land before you can catch your handsome young officer's eye. Do you know where we are?" They were flying low-level and cross-country; Em searched for landmarks, which was quite a trick in the middle of Texas.

"Don't fret, we're right on course. Bank left—there's the main road, see?" Em nudged the stick and the plane tipped, giving her a wide view past the wing and its Army star to the earth below, and the long straight line of paved road leading to Dallas. Mary seemed to have an instinct for these sorts of things.

"You really do have this all planned out," Em said. "You'll be heading straight from the flight line to the Officer's Club, won't you?"

Mary had a pout in her voice. "I might stop to brush my hair first." Em laughed, and Mary looked over her shoulder. "Don't give me a hard time just because I'm not already married off to a wonderful man like you are."

Em sighed. She hadn't seen her husband in almost a year. The last letter she'd had from him was postmarked Honolulu, three weeks ago. He hadn't said where he was sailing to—couldn't, really. All she knew was that he was somewhere in the middle of a big wide ocean, flying Navy dive-bombers off a carrier. Sometimes she wished she weren't a pilot, because she knew exactly what could go wrong for Michael. Then again, maybe he was flying right now—it was mid-morning in the Pacific—cruising along for practice on a beautiful day and thinking of her, the way she was thinking of him.

"Em?" Mary said, still craned over to took at Em the best she could over the back of her seat.

"Sorry. You just got me thinking about Michael."

Em could just see Mary's wide red smile, her excitable eyes. "You really miss him, don't you?"

"Of course I do."

Mary sighed. "That's so romantic."

Em almost laughed again. "Would you listen to you? There's nothing romantic about waking up every day wondering if he's alive or dead." She was only twenty-four, too young to be a widow, surely. She had to stop this or she'd start crying and have to let Mary land the plane. Shaking her head, she looked away, back to the blue sky outside the canopy, scattered clouds passing by.

"It's just that being in love like that? I've never been in love like that. Except maybe with Clark Gable." She grinned.

Em gratefully kept the joke going. "Don't think for a minute Clark Gable's going to be on the ground when we get there."

"You never know. These are strange times. He enlisted, did you know that? I read about it. Him and Jimmy Stewart both—and Jimmy Stewart's a pilot!"

"And maybe they'll both be at Dallas, just for you."

"Hope springs eternal," Mary said smugly. "I've got my lucky pennies, you know."

"All right, but if they're there, you have to ask them to dance."

"It's a deal," Mary said brightly, knowing she'd never have to make good on it. Because Clark Gable and Jimmy Stewart were not at Dallas. But if something like that was going to happen to anyone, it would happen to Mary.

A few minutes later, Em leaned forward to listen. Sure enough, Mary was singing. "Don't sit under the apple tree, with anyone else but me, anyone else but me . . ."

Em joined in, and they sang until they were circling over the field to land.

AFTER SHUTTING DOWN THE ENGINE, she sat in her cockpit and took a look down the flight line at Romulus, in freezing Michigan. The sight never failed to amaze her—a hundred silver birds perched on the tarmac, all that power, ready and waiting. The buzzing of engines was constant; she could feel the noise in her bones.

This was the last runway Mary took off from.

Sighing, she filled out the plane's 1-A, collected her bag and her logbook, and hoisted herself out of the cockpit and onto the tarmac. Asked the first guy she saw, a mechanic, where the WASP barracks were. The wary look on his face told her all she needed to know about what the men on this base thought of WASP. She'd heard the rumors—they traded stories about which bases welcomed them and which wanted nothing to do with women pilots. She wasn't sure she believed the stories about someone putting sugar in the fuel tank of a WASP's plane at Camp Davis, causing it to crash—mostly because she didn't think anyone would do that to a plane. But those were the sorts of stories people told.

She made her way to the barracks. After a shower, she'd be able to face the day a little easier.

After the shower, Em, dressed in shirt and trousers, was still drying her hair when a group of women came into the barracks—three of them, laughing and windblown, peeling off flight jackets and scrubbing fingers through mussed hair. They quieted when they saw her, and she set her towel aside.

"Hi."

One of them, a slim blonde with mischief in her eyes, the kind of woman the brass liked to use in press photos, stepped forward, hand outstretched.

"Hi. You must be the new kid they were talking about back in ops. I'm Lillian Greshing."

"Em Anderson," she said, shaking her hand. "I'm just passing through. I hope you don't mind, I used one of the towels on the shelf. There weren't any names or labels—"

"Of course not, that's what they're there for. Hey—we were going to grab supper in town after we get cleaned up. Want to come along? You can catch us up on all the gossip."

Em's smile went from polite to warm, as she felt herself among friends again. "That sounds perfect."

THE FOUR WOMEN found a table in the corner of a little bar just off base. The Runway wasn't fancy; it had a Christmas tree decorated with spots of tinsel and glass bulbs in a corner, a pretty good bar, and a jukebox playing swing.

The dinner special was roast chicken, mashed potatoes, and a bottle of beer to wash it down.

"What're they transferring WASP to Camp Davis for?" Betsy, a tall woman with a narrow face and a nervous smile, asked when Em passed on the rumor.

"Don't know," Em said. "Nobody'll say. But Davis is a gunnery school." More speculative murmurs ran around the table.

"Target towing. Wanna bet?" Lillian said.

"I'll stick to the job I have, thank you very much," Betsy said, shivering.

Em felt her smile grow thin and sly. "Not me. Nursing along slowpoke trainers? We can do better than that."

"You *want* to fly planes while some cross-eyed greenhorn shoots at you?"

"Nope," Em said. "I want to transition to pursuits."

"It'll never happen," Lillian said, shaking her head, like she needed the emphasis. "The old cronies like Burnett will never let it happen."

"Burnett?"

"Colonel. Runs this lovely little operation." She gestured in the direction of the airfield. Smoke trailed behind her hand to join the rest of the haze in the air.

"What's he like?" Em asked.

That no one answered with anything more than sidelong glances and rolled eyes told her enough. Romulus was a cold-shoulder base.

Em pressed on. "We'll get there. Nancy Love has five girls in transition out at Palm Springs already. The factories are all working overtime building bombers and fighters, and ATC doesn't have enough pilots to ferry them to port. They're going to have to let us fly 'em, whether they like it or not."

Betsy was still shaking her head. "Those birds are too dangerous."

Mary got killed in a trainer, Em wanted to say. "We can do it. We're capable of it."

Lillian said with a sarcastic lilt, "Burnett would say we're not strong enough. That we wouldn't be able to even get something like a Mustang off the ground."

"He's full of it," Em said. "I can't *wait* to get my hands on one of those."

Betsy, smiling vaguely, looked into her beer. "I don't know how I'd explain flying fighters to my husband. He's barely all right with my flying at all."

"So don't tell him," Lillian said. Shocked giggles met the proclamation.

Round-eyed Molly, blond hair in a ponytail, leaned in. "Don't listen to her, she's got three boyfriends at three different fields. She doesn't understand about husbands." More giggling.

Em smiled. "Betsy, is he overseas?"

"England," she said. "He's a doctor." Her pride was plain.

"You've got a ring there, Em," Molly said to the band on Em's finger. "You married or is that to keep the flyboys off you?"

"He's Navy," Em said. "He's on a carrier in the Pacific."

After a sympathetic hesitation, Lillian continued. "What does he think about you flying?"

Em donned a grin. "I met him when we were both taking flying lessons before the war. He can't argue about me flying. Besides, I have to do something to keep my mind off things."

Lillian raised her bottle. "Here's to the end of the war."

They raised their glasses and the toasts were heartfelt.

The quiet moment gave Em her opening—time to start in on the difficult gossip, what she'd come here to learn. "What do you all know about Mary Keene's crash last week?"

No one would look at her. Betsy bit a trembling lip and teared up, and Molly fidgeted with her glass. Lillian's jaw went taut with a scowl. She ground her cigarette into the ashtray with enough force to destroy what was left of it.

"It happened fifty miles out," Lillian said, her voice quiet. "Nobody saw anything, we just heard it when the fire truck left. All we know is a group of seven planes went out—BT-13s, all of 'em—and an hour later six came back and nobody would tell us a thing. Just that Mary'd been killed. You knew her, I take it?"

"We were in the same class at Avenger," Em said. "We were friends."

"I'm sorry," Lillian said. "She was only here a couple of days but we all liked her a lot."

Molly handed Betsy a handkerchief; she dabbed her eyes with it.

"I was told the accident report was classified, and that doesn't make any sense. Some guys who were here last week told me there was a collision."

Lillian leaned close and spoke softly; like this was some kind of conspiracy. "That's what we heard, and one of the planes came back with a wheel all busted up, but Burnett clamped down on talk so fast, our heads spun. Filed away all the paperwork and wouldn't answer any questions. We don't even know who else was flying that day."

"He can't do that," Em said. "Couldn't you go after him? Just keep pushing—"

"It's Burnett," Lillian said. "Guy's a brick wall."

"Then go over his head."

"And get grounded? Get kicked out? That's what he's threatened us with, for going over his head," Lillian said, and Em couldn't argue. But technically, she wasn't part of his squadron, and he couldn't do anything to her. She could ask her questions.

Another group from the field came in then, flyboys by their leather jackets with silver wings pinned to the chest. Ferry Division, by the insignia. Not so different from the girls, who were wearing trousers and blouses, their jackets hanging off their chairs—a group gathered around a table, calling for beers and talking about the gossip, flying, and the war.

Pretty soon after their arrival, a couple of them went over to the jukebox and put in a few coins. A dance tune came up, something just fast enough to make you want to get out of your seat—Glenn Miller, "Little Brown Jug." Lillian rolled her eyes and Molly hid a smile with her hand; they all knew what was coming next.

Sure enough, the guys sauntered over to their table. Em made sure the hand with her wedding band was out and visible. Not that that stopped some men.

Just a dance, they'd say. But she didn't want to, because it would make her think about Michael.

Lillian leaned back in her chair, chin up and shoulders squared, and met their gazes straight on. The others looked on like they were watching a show.

They weren't bad looking, early thirties maybe. Slightly rumpled uniforms and nice smiles. "Would any of you ladies like a dance?"

The women glanced at each other—would any of them say yes?

Lillian, brow raised, blond curls falling over her ears so artfully she might have pinned them there, said, "What makes you boys think you could keep up with any of us?"

The guys glanced at each other, then smiled back at Lillian. Gauntlet accepted. "We'd sure like to give it a try."

Nobody was making a move to stand, and Lillian again took the lead—breaking the boys' hearts for fun. "Sorry to disappoint you, but the girls and I spent all day putting repaired AT-6s through their paces and we're beat. We were looking forward to a nice, quiet evening."

The guy standing at the first one's shoulder huffed a little. "Lady pilots," he might have muttered.

The first guy seemed a little daunted. "Well, maybe you'll let us pull over a couple of chairs and buy you a round?"

Magic words, right there. Lillian sat up and made a space at the table. "That'll be all right."

Another round of beers arrived a moment later.

The men were nice enough, Ferry Division boys flying pursuits and bombers from the factories. Em asked questions—how many, what kind, where were they going, what was it like?—and ate up the answers. They seemed happy enough to humor her, even if they did come off on the condescending side—isn't that cute, a girl who wants to fly fast planes.

The attitude was easy enough to ignore. Every WASP had a story about being chatted up by some flyboy at a bar, him bragging about piloting hotshot planes and ending with the "I ship out to Europe tomorrow, honey," line; then seeing the look of shock on the guy's face the next day when he spotted her on the flight line climbing into her own cockpit. That was funny every damn time.

Lillian leaned over to Jim, the guy who'd talked to them first, and said, "Do your friends want to come on over and join us? We could make a real party of it."

A couple of the guys already had, but a few remained at the other table, talking quietly and nursing beers. They didn't pay much attention to the other group, except for one guy, with a round face and slicked-back hair, who kept his jacket on even though the room had grown warm.

Grinning, Jim leaned forward and lowered his voice. "I think you all make some of the boys nervous."

Em smiled and ducked her gaze while the other women giggled.

Lillian almost purred. "We're not flying now, I don't see why they should be nervous. We're not going to crash into them." Em looked away at that. It was just a joke, she told herself.

Jim tilted his head to the sullen-looking pilot. "Frank there almost walked back out again when he saw you girls sitting here."

"What, afraid of little old us?" Lillian said, and the others laughed. The sullen-looking pilot at the other table, Frank, seemed to sink into his jacket a little further.

Jim shrugged. "His loss, right?"

Em agreed. Anyone had an issue with women pilots, it was their problem, not hers.

EM HAD TO GO at the mystery backwards. The accident report wasn't available, so she dug through the flight logs to see who else was flying that day. Who else was in the air with Mary.

She made her way to ops, a big square prefab office building off the airstrip, around lunchtime the next day, when she was less likely to run into people. The move paid off—only a secretary, a woman in civilian clothes, was on duty. Em carried her logbook in hand, making her look more official than not, and made up some excuse about being new to the base and needing to log her next flight and where should she go? The secretary directed her to an adjoining room. There, Em found the setup familiar: maps pinned to the wall, chalkboards with instructions written on them, charts showing planes and schedules, and a wall of filing cabinets.

Every pilot taking off from the field was supposed to file a flight plan, which were kept in ops. Mary's plan—and the plans of anyone else who was flying that day and might have collided with her—should be here. She rubbed her lucky pennies together and got to work.

The luck held: the files were marked by day and in order. Flipping through, Em found the pressboard folder containing the forms from that day. Taking the folder to an empty desk by the wall, she began studying, reconstructing in her mind what the flight line had looked like that day.

Mary had been part of a group ferrying seven BT-13 Valiants from Romulus to Dallas. She wasn't originally part of the group; she'd been at Romulus overnight after ferrying a different BT-13. But they had an extra plane, and like just about any WASP, she would fly anything she was checked out on, anything a commander asked her to fly. Those were the bare facts. That was the starting point. Less than an hour after takeoff, Mary had crashed. A collision—which meant it must have been one of the other planes in the group.

WASP weren't authorized for close-formation flying. When they did fly in groups, they flew loose, with enough distance between to prevent accidents—at least five hundred feet. Mary was the only WASP in the group, but the men should have followed the same procedure and maintained a safe distance. Just saying "collision" didn't tell the story, because only one plane hit the ground, and only one pilot died.

The accident had eyewitnesses: the other six pilots in the group, who were flying with Mary when she crashed. She started jotting down names and the ID numbers of the planes they'd been flying.

"What do you think you're doing?"

Startled, Em flinched and looked up to find a lanky man just past forty or so, his uniform starched and perfect, standing in the doorway, hands clenched, glaring. Silver eagles on his shoulders—this must be Colonel Burnett. Reflexively, she crumpled her page of notes and stuffed it in her pocket. The move was too obvious to hide. Gathering her thoughts, she stood with as much attention as she could muster—part of her mind was still on those six pilots.

She'd spent enough time in the Army Air Force to know how men like Burnett operated: they intimidated, they browbeat. They had their opinions and didn't want to hear arguments. She just had to keep from letting herself get cowed.

"Filing a flight plan, sir." She kept the lie short and simple, so he wouldn't have anything to hold against her.

"I don't think so," he said, looking at the pages spread out on the desk.

They were in a standoff. She hadn't finished, and wanted to get those last couple of names. Burnett didn't look like he was going to leave.

"It's true," she bluffed. "BT-13 to Dallas." Mary's last flight plan; that might have been pushing it.

"You going to show me what's in your pocket there?"

"Grocery list," she said, deadpan.

He stepped closer, and Em had to work not to flinch away from the man.

"Those are papers from last week," he said, pointing at the plans she'd been looking at.

"Yes, sir."

His face reddened, and she thought he might start screaming at her, drill-sergeant style. "Who authorized you to look at these?"

Somebody had to speak up. Somebody had to find the truth. That allowed her to face him, chin up. "Sir, I believe the investigation into that crash ended prematurely, that all the information hasn't been brought to light."

"That report was filed. There's nothing left to say. You need to get out of here, missy."

Now he was just making her angry, he probably expected her to wilt—he probably yelled at all the women because he expected them to wilt. She stepped forward, feeling her own flush starting, her own temper rising.

"Why was the report buried? I just want to know what really happened."

"I don't have to explain anything to you. You're a civilian. You're just a civilian."

"What is there to explain, sir?"

"Unless you march out of here right now, I'll have you arrested for spying. Don't think the Army won't shoot a woman for treason!"

Em expected a lot of threats—being grounded, getting kicked out of the WASP, just like Lillian said. But being shot for treason? What the hell was Burnett trying to hide?

Em was speechless, and didn't have any fight left in her after that. She marched out with her logbook, just as Burnett told her to, head bowed, unable to look at him. Even though she really wanted to spit at him. In the corner of her gaze, she thought she saw him smile, like he thought he'd won some kind of victory over her. Bullying a woman, and he thought that made him tough. By the time she left the building, her eyes were watering. Angrily, she wiped the tears away.

Well away from the building, she stopped to catch her breath. Crossed her arms, waited for her blood to cool. Looked up into the sky, turning her face to the clouds. The day was overcast, the ceiling low, a biting wind smelling of snow. Terrible weather for flying. But she'd go up in a heartbeat, in whatever piece-of-junk trainer was available, just to get away from here.

ONE OF THE LESSONS you learned early on: Make friends with the ground crew. When some of the trainers they flew had seen better days and took a lot of attention to keep running, sweet-talking a mechanic about what was wrong went further than complaining. Even if the wreckage from Mary's plane was still around—it would have already been picked over for aluminum and parts—Em wouldn't have been able to tell what had happened without seeing the crash site. She needed to talk to the recovery team.

Lillian told her that a Sergeant Bill Jacobs' crew had been the one to recover Mary's Valiant. He'd know a lot that hadn't made it into the records, maybe even be able to tell her what happened. If she could sweet-talk him. She touched up her lipstick, repinned her hair, and tapped her lucky pennies.

On the walk to the hangar, she tried to pound out her bad mood, to work out her anger and put herself in a sweet-talking frame of mind. *Hey there, mind telling me about a little ol' plane crash that happened last week?* She wasn't so good at sweet-talking, not like Lillian was. Not like Mary had been.

The main door of the hangar was wide open to let in the afternoon light. In the doorway, she waited a moment to let her eyes adjust to the shadows. A B-24 was parked inside, two of its four engines open and half-dismantled. The couple of guys working on each one called a word to the other now and then, asking for a part or advice. A radio played Duke Ellington.

The hangar had a strangely homey feel to it, with its atmosphere of grease and hard work, the cheerful music playing and the friendly banter between the mechanics. This might have been any airport repair shop, if it weren't for the fact they were working on a military bomber.

Em looked around for someone who might be in charge, someone who might be Jacobs. In the back corner, she saw the door to an office and headed there. Inside, she found what she was probably looking for: a wide desk stacked with papers and clipboards. Requisitions, repair records, inventories, and the like, she'd bet. Maybe a repair order for a BT13 wounded in a collision last week?

She was about to start hunting when a man said, "Can I help you, miss?"

A man in Army coveralls and a cap stood at the doorway. Scraping together all the charm she could manage, she straightened and smiled. She must have made quite a silhouette in her trousers and jacket because he looked a bit stricken. He glanced at the insignia on her collar, the patches on her jacket, and knew what, if not who, she was.

"Sergeant Jacobs?" she said, smiling.

"Yes, ma'am."

Her smile widened. "Hi, I'm Emily Anderson, in from New Castle." She gestured vaguely over her shoulder. "They told me you might be able to help me out."

He relaxed, maybe thinking she was only going to ask for a little grease on a squeaky canopy.

She said, "The crash last week. The one the WASP died in. Can you tell me what happened?" Her smile had stiffened; her politeness was a mask.

Jacobs sidled past her in an effort to put himself between her and the desk—the vital paperwork. He began sorting through the mess on the desk, but his movements were random. "I don't know anything about that."

"You recovered the plane. You saw the crash site."

"It was a mess. I can't tell you what happened."

"What about the other plane? How badly was it damaged?"

He looked at her. "How do you know there was another plane?"

"I heard there was a collision. Who was flying that other plane? Can you at least tell me that much?"

"I can't help you, I'm sorry." He shook his head, like he was shaking off an annoying fly.

"Sergeant Jacobs, Mary Keene was my friend."

When he looked at her, his gaze was tired, pitying. "Ma'am, please. Let it go. Digging this up isn't going to fix anything."

"I need to know what really happened."

"The plane crashed, okay? It just crashed. Happens all the time, I hate to say it, but it's so."

Em shook her head. "Mary was a good pilot. *Something* had to have happened."

Jacobs looked away. "She switched off the engine."

"What?"

"She'd lost part of a wing—there was no way she could pull out of it. But before she hit the ground, she had time to turn off the engine so it wouldn't catch fire. So the plane wouldn't burn. She knew what was going to happen and she switched it off."

Mary, sitting in her cockpit, out of control after whatever had hit her, calmly reaching over to turn off the ignition, knowing the whole time she maybe wasn't going to make it—

"Is that supposed to make me feel better?" Em said.

"No. I'm sorry, ma'am. It's just you're right. She was a good pilot."

"Then why won't you—?"

A panicked shouting from the hangar caught their attention—"Whoa whoa, hold that thing, it's gonna drop"—followed by the ominous sound of metal crashing to concrete. Jacobs dashed out of the office to check on his crew.

Em wasn't proud; she went through the stack of papers while he was occupied.

The fact that Mary had crashed and died was becoming less significant to Em than the way everyone was acting about it. Twitchy. Defensive. Like a pilot towing targets for gunnery training, wondering if the wet-behind-the-ears gunners were going to hit you instead. These guys, everyone who knew what had happened, didn't want to talk about it, didn't want her to ask about it, and were doing their damnedest to cover this up. What were all these people hiding? Or, what were they protecting?

It wasn't a hard answer, when she put it like that: the other pilot. They were protecting the pilot who survived the collision.

She dug through repair orders. Mary's plane had crashed—but the other plane hadn't. It still would have been damaged, and there'd be paperwork for that. She looked at the dates, searching for *that* date. Found it, found the work order for a damaged BT-13. Quickly, she retrieved the list of names she'd taken from the flight plans. She'd copied only half of them before Burnett interrupted her. She had a fifty-fifty chance of matching the name on the work order. Heads or tails?

And there it was. When she compared ID numbers with the ones on the work order, she found the match she was looking for: Frank Milliken. The other pilot's name was Frank Milliken.

She marched out of the office and into the hangar. Jacobs was near the B-24 wing, yelling at the guys who had apparently unbolted and dropped a propeller. He might have followed her with a suspicious gaze as she left, but he couldn't do anything about it now, could he?

She kept her eyes straight ahead and didn't give him a chance to stop her.

"You know Frank Milliken?" she asked Lillian when she got back to the barracks.

"By name. He's one of the Third Ferry Group guys—he was part of Jim's bunch of clowns last night," she said.

Em tried to remember the names she'd heard, to match them up with the faces, the guys who talked to them. "I don't remember a Frank," she said.

"He's the sulky guy who stayed at the table."

Ah . . . "You know anything about him?"

"Not really. They kind of run together when they're all flirting with you at once." She grinned. "What about him?"

"I think he was in the plane that collided with Mary's last week."

"What?" she said with a wince and tilted head, like she hadn't heard right.

"I've got a flight plan and a plane ID number on a repair order that says it was him."

Clench-jawed anger and an anxious gaze vied with each other and ended up making Lillian look young and confused. "What do we do?"

"I just want to find out what happened," Em said. She just wanted to sit down with the guy, make him walk her through it, explain who had flown too close to whom, whether it was accident, weather, a gust of wind, pilot error—anything. She just wanted to know.

"You sure?" Lillian said. "This is being hushed up for a reason. It can't be anything good. Not that *anything* is going to make this better, but—well, you know what I mean. Em, what if—what if it was Mary's fault? Are you ready to hear that? Are you ready to hear that this was a stupid accident and Burnett's covering it up to make his own record a little less dusty?" Em understood what Lillian was saying—it didn't matter how many stories you made up for yourself; the truth could always be worse. If something—God forbid—ever happened to Michael, would she really want to know what killed him? Did she really want to picture that? Shouldn't she just let Mary go?

Em's smile felt thin and pained. "We have to look out for each other, Lillian. No one else is doing it for us, and no one else is going to tell our stories for us. I have to know."

Lillian straightened, and the woman's attitude won out over her confusion. "Right, then. Let's go find ourselves a party."

Em and Lillian parked at the same table at the Runway, but didn't order dinner tonight. Em's stomach was churning; she couldn't think of eating.

She and Lillian drank sodas and waited.

"What if they don't come?" Em said.

"They'll be here," Lillian said. "They're here every night they're on base. Don't worry."

As they waited, a few of the other girls came in and joined them, and they all had a somber look, frowning, quiet. Em didn't know how, but the rumor must have traveled.

"Is it true?" Betsy asked, sliding in across from Em. "You found out what happened to Mary?"

"That's what we need to see," she said, watching the front door, waiting.

The men knew something was up as soon as they came in and found the women watching them. The mood was tense, uncomfortable. None of them were smiling. And there he was, with his slicked-back hair, hunched up in his jacket like he was trying to hide. He hesitated inside the doorway along with the rest of the guys—if he turned around to leave this time, Em didn't think Jim or the others would try to stop him.

Em stood and approached them. "Frank Milliken?"

He glanced up, startled, though he had to have seen her coming. The other guys stepped away and left him alone in a space.

"Yeah?" he said warily.

Taking a breath, she closed her eyes a moment to steel herself. Didn't matter how much she'd practiced this speech in her mind, it wasn't going to come out right. She didn't know what to say.

"Last week, you were flying with a group of BT-13s. There was a collision. A WASP named Mary Keene crashed. I'm trying to find out what happened. Can you tell me?"

He was looking around, glancing side to side as if searching for an escape route. He wasn't saying anything, so Em kept on. "Your plane was damaged—I saw the work order. So I'm thinking your plane was involved and you know exactly what happened. Please, I just want to know how a good pilot like Mary crashed."

He was shaking his head. "No. I don't have to talk to you. I don't have to tell you anything."

"What's wrong?" Em pleaded. "What's everyone trying to hide?"

"Let it go. Why can't you just let it go?" he said, refusing to look at her, shaking his head like he could ward her away. Lillian was at Em's shoulder now, and a couple of the other WASP had joined them, standing in a group, staring down Milliken.

If Em had been male, she could have gotten away with grabbing his collar and shoving him to the wall, roughing him up a little to get him to talk.

She was on the verge of doing it anyway; then wouldn't he be surprised? "It was your fault, wasn't it?" She had the sudden epiphany. It was why he couldn't look at her, why he didn't even want to be here with WASP sitting at the next table. "What happened? Did you just lose control? Was something wrong with your plane?"

"It was an accident," he said softly.

"But what happened?" Em said, getting tired of asking, not knowing what else to do. He had six women staring him down now, and a handful of men looking back and forth between them and him. Probably wondering who was going to start crying first.

"Why don't you just tell her, Milliken," Jim said, frowning.

"Please, no one will tell me—"

"It was an accident!" His face was flushed; he ran a shaking hand over his hair. "It was just a game, you know? I only buzzed her a couple of times. I thought it'd be funny—it was supposed to be funny. You know, get close, scare her a little. But—it was an accident."

He probably had repeated it to himself so often, he believed it. But when he spoke it out loud, he couldn't gloss the crime of it: he'd broken regs, buzzed Mary in the air, got closer than the regulation five hundred feet, thought he could handle the stunt—and he couldn't. He'd hit her instead, crunched her wing. She'd lost control, plowed into the earth. Em could suddenly picture it so clearly. The lurch as the other plane hit Mary, the dive as she went out of control. She'd have looked out the canopy to see the gash in her wing, looked the other way to see the ground coming up fast. She'd have hauled on the stick, trying to land nose up, knowing it wasn't going to work because she was going too fast, so she turned off the engine, just in case, and hadn't she always wanted to go faster—

You tried to be respectful, to be a good girl. You bought war bonds and listened to the latest news on the radio. You prayed for the boys overseas, and most of all you didn't rock the boat, because there were so many other things to worry about, from getting a gallon of rationed gas for your car to whether your husband was going to come home in one piece.

They were a bunch of Americans doing their part. She tried to let it go. Let the anger drain away. Didn't work. The war had receded in Em's mind to a small noise in the background. She had this one battle to face.

With Burnett in charge, nothing would happen to Milliken. The colonel had hushed it up good and tight because he didn't want a more involved investigation, he didn't want the lack of discipline among his male flyers to come out. Milliken wouldn't be court-martialed and grounded, because trained pilots were too valuable. Em couldn't do anything more than stand here and stare him down. How could she make that be enough?

"Mary Keene was my friend," she said softly.

Milliken said, his voice a breath, "It was an accident. I didn't mean to hit her. I'm sorry. I'm sorry, all right?"

Silence cut like a blade. None of the guys would look at her.

Em turned and walked out, flanked by the other WASP.

Outside, the sun had set, but she could still hear airplane engines soaring over the airfield, taking off and landing, changing pitch as they roared overhead. The air smelled of fuel, and the field was lit up like stars fallen to earth. The sun would shine again tomorrow no matter what happened, and nothing had changed. She couldn't tell if she'd won. She slumped against the wall, slid to the ground, put her face to her knees and her arms over her head, and cried. The others gathered around her, rested hands on her shoulders, her arms. Didn't say a word, didn't make a big production.

Just waited until she'd cried herself out. Then Lillian and Betsy hooked their arms in hers and pulled her back to the barracks, where one of the girls had stashed a bottle of whiskey.

THE LAST TIME Em saw Mary was four days before she died.

Em reached the barracks after coming off the flight line to see Mary sitting on the front steps with her legs stretched out in front of her, smoking a cigarette and staring into space. Em approached slowly and sat beside her. "What's gotten into you?"

Mary donned a slow, sly smile. "It didn't happen the way I thought it would, the way I planned it."

"What didn't?"

She tipped her head back so her honey brown curls fell behind her and her tanned face looked into the sky. "I was supposed to step out of my airplane, chin up and beautiful, shaking my hair out after I took off my cap, and my handsome young officer would be standing there, stunned out of his wits. That didn't happen."

Em was grinning. This ought to be good. "So what did happen?"

"I'd just climbed out of my Valiant and I wanted to check the landing gear because it was feeling kind of wobbly when I landed. So there I was, bent over when I heard some guy say, 'Hey, buddy, can you tell me where to find ops?' I just about shot out of my boots. I stood up and look at him, and his eyes popped. And I swear to you he looked like Clark Gable. Not *just* like, but close. And I blushed red because the first thing he saw of me was my . . . my fanny stuck up in the air! We must have stood there staring at each other in shock for five minutes. Then we laughed."

Now Em was laughing, and Mary joined in, until they were leaning together, shoulder to shoulder.

"So, what," Em said. "It's true love?"

"I don't know. He's nice. He's a captain in from Long Beach. He's taking me out for drinks later."

"You are going to have the best stories when this is all over," Em said.

Mary turned quiet, thoughtful. "Can I tell you a secret? Part of me doesn't want the war to end. I don't want *this* to end. I just want to keep flying and carrying on like this forever. They won't let us keep flying when the boys come home. Then I'll have to go back home, put on white gloves and a string of pearls and start acting respectable." She shook her head. "I don't really mean that, about the war. It's got to end sometime, right?"

"I hope so," Em said softly. Pearl Harbor had been almost exactly two years ago, and it was hard to see an end to it all.

"Sometimes I wish my crazy barnstormer uncle hadn't ever taken me flying, then I wouldn't feel like this. Oh, my dad was so mad, you should have seen it. But once I'd flown I wasn't ever going to go back. I'm not ever going to quit, Em."

"I know." They sat on the stoop, watching and listening to planes come in over the field, until Mary went to get cleaned up for her date.

EM SAT ACROSS from Colonel Roper's desk and waited while he read her carefully typed report. He read it twice, straightened the pages, and set it aside. He folded his hands together and studied her.

"How are you doing?"

She paused a moment, thinking about it rather than giving the pat "just fine" response. Because it wasn't true, and he wouldn't believe her.

"Is it worth it, sir?" He tilted his head, questioning, and she tried to explain. "Are we really doing anything for the war? Are we going to look back and think she died for nothing?"

His gaze dropped to the desk while he gathered words. She waited for the expected platitudes, the gushing reassurances. They didn't come.

"You want me to tell you Mary's death meant something, that what she was doing was essential for the war, that her dying is going to help us win. I can't do that." He shook his head. Em almost wished he would sugarcoat it. She didn't want to hear this. But she was also relieved that he was telling the truth. Maybe the bad-attitude flyboys were right, and the WASP were just a gimmick.

He continued. "You don't build a war machine so that taking out one cog makes the whole thing fall apart. Maybe we'll look back on this and decide we could have done it all without you. But, Emily—it would be a hell of a lot harder. We wouldn't have the pilots we need, and we wouldn't have the planes where we need them. And there's a hell of a lot of war left to fight."

She didn't want to think about it. You could take all the numbers, all the people who'd died over the last few years and everything they'd died for, and the numbers on paper might add up, but you start putting names and stories to the list and it would never add up, never be worth it. She just wanted it to be over; she wanted Michael home.

Roper sorted through a stack of papers on the corner of his desk and found a page he was looking for. He made a show of studying it for a long moment, giving her time to draw her attention from the wall where she'd been staring blankly. Finally, she met his gaze across the desk.

"I have transfer orders here for you. If you want them."

She shook her head, confused, wondering what she'd done wrong. Wondering if Burnett was having his revenge on her anyway, after all that had happened.

"Sir," she said, confused. "But . . . where? Why?"

"Palm Springs," he said, and her eyes grew wide, a spark in her heart lit, knowing what was at Palm Springs. "Pursuit School. If you're interested."

MARCH 1944

EM SETTLED IN HER SEAT and reached up to close the canopy overhead. This was a one-seater, compact, nestled into a narrow, streamlined fuselage. The old trainers were roomy by comparison. She felt cocooned in the seat, all her controls and instruments at hand.

She started the engine; it roared. She could barely hear herself call the tower. "This is P-51 21054 requesting clearance for takeoff."

Her hands on the stick could feel this thing's power running into her bones. She wasn't going to have to push this plane off the ground. All she'd have to do was give it its head and let it go.

A voice buzzed in her ear. "P-51 21054, this is Tower, you are cleared for takeoff."

This was a crouched tiger preparing to leap. A rocket ready to explode. The nose was higher than the tail; she couldn't even see straight ahead—just straight up, past sleek silver into blue sky.

She eased the throttle forward, and the plane started moving. Then it *really* started moving. The tail lifted—she could see ahead of her now, to the end of the runaway. Her speed increased, and she watched the dials in front of her. At a hundred miles per hour, she pulled back on the stick, *lifted*, and left earth behind. Climbed *fast*, into clear blue sky, like a bullet, like a hawk. She glanced over her shoulder; the airstrip was already tiny.

Nothing but open sky ahead, and all the speed she could push out of this thing.

This was heaven.

"Luckiest girl in the world," she murmured, thinking that Mary would have loved this.

≫•≪

The military definition of collateral damage—as it relates to target selection and prosecution—rests on intent; it is damage apart from that which is intended. There are many ways of inflicting collateral damage during war, and not all of the harm can be immediately determined. In Ken Liu's story, Kyra is motivated to become a warrior in hopes of mitigating such damage; her weapons are algorithms.

IN THE LOOP

Ken Liu

WHEN KYRA WAS NINE, her father turned into a monster.

It didn't happen overnight. He went to work every morning, like always, and when he came in the door in the evening, Kyra would ask him to play catch with her. That used to be her favorite time of the day. But the yesses came less frequently, and then not at all.

He'd sit at the table and stare. She'd ask him questions and he wouldn't answer. He used to always have a funny answer for everything, and she'd repeat his jokes to her friends and think he was the cleverest dad in the whole world.

She had loved those moments when he'd teach her how to swing a hammer properly, how to measure and saw and chisel. She would tell him that she wanted to be a builder when she grew up, and he'd nod and say that was a good idea. But he stopped taking her to his workshop in the shed to make things together, and there was no explanation.

Then he started going out in the evenings. At first, Mom would ask him when he'd be back. He'd look at her like she was a stranger before closing the door behind him. By the time he came home, Kyra and her brothers were already in bed, but she would hear shouts and sometimes things breaking.

Mom began to look at Dad like she was afraid of him, and Kyra tried to help with getting the boys to bed, to make her bed without being asked, to finish her dinner without complaint, to do everything perfectly, hoping that would make things better, back to the way they used to be. But Dad didn't seem to pay any attention to her or her brothers.

Then, one day, he slammed Mom into the wall. Kyra stood there in the kitchen and felt the whole house shake. She didn't know what to do. He turned around and saw Kyra, and his face scrunched up like he hated her, hated her mother, hated himself most of all. And he fled the house without saying another thing.

Mom packed a suitcase and took Kyra and her brothers to Grandma's place that evening, and they stayed there for a month. Kyra thought about calling her father but she didn't know what she would say. She tried to imagine herself asking the man on the other end of the line *what have you done with Daddy?*

A policeman came, looking for her mother. Kyra hid in the hall so she could hear what he was telling her. *We don't think it was a homicide.* That was how she found out that her father had died. They moved back to the house, where there was a lot to do: folding up Dad's uniforms for storage, packing up his regular clothes to give away, cleaning the house so it could be sold, getting ready to move away permanently. She caressed Dad's medals and badges, shiny and neatly laid out in a box, and that was when she finally cried.

They found a piece of paper at the bottom of Dad's dresser drawer.

"What is it?" she asked Mom.

Mom read it over. "It's from your Dad's commander, at the Army." Her hands shook. "It shows how many people he had killed."

She showed Kyra the number: one thousand two-hundred and fifty-one.

The number lingered in Kyra's mind. As if that gave his life meaning. As if that defined him—and them.

KYRA WALKED QUICKLY, pulling her coat tight against the late fall chill. It was her senior year in college, and on-campus recruiting was in full swing. Because Kyra's school was old and full of red brick buildings named after families that had been wealthy and important even before the founding of this republic, its students were desirable to employers.

She was on her way back to her apartment from a party hosted by a small quantitative trading company in New York that was generating good buzz on campus. Companies in management consulting, financial services, and Silicon Valley had booked hotel rooms around the school and were hosting parties for prospective interviewees every night, and Kyra, as a comp sci major, found herself in high demand. This was the night when she would need to finalize her list of ranked preferences, and she had to strategize carefully to have a shot at getting one of the interview slots for the most coveted companies in the lottery.

"Excuse me," a young man stepped in her way. "Would you sign this petition?"

She looked at the clipboard held in front of her. *Stop the War.*

Technically, America wasn't at war. There had been no declaration of war by Congress, just the president exercising his office's inherent authority. But maybe the war had never stopped. America left; America went back; America promised to leave again some time. A decade had passed; people kept on dying far away.

"I'm sorry," Kyra said, not looking the boy in the eyes. "I can't."

"Are you *for* the war?" The boy's voice was tired, the incredulity almost an act. He was there canvassing for signatures alone in the evening because no one cared. When so few Americans died, the "conflict" didn't seem real.

How could she explain to him that she did not believe in the war, did not want to have anything to do with it, and yet, signing the petition the boy held would seem to her tantamount to a betrayal of the memory of her father, would seem a declaration that what he had done was wrong? She did not want him to be defined by the number on that piece of paper her mother kept hidden at the bottom of the box in the attic.

So all she said was, "I'm not into politics."

Back in her apartment, Kyra took off her coat and flipped on the TV.

. . . the largest protest so far in front of the American Embassy. Protesters are demanding that the U.S. cease the drone strikes, which so far have caused more than three hundred deaths in the country this year, many of whom the protesters claim were innocent civilians. The U.S. Ambassador . . .

Kyra turned off the TV. Her mood had been ruined, and she could not focus on the task of ranking her interview preferences. Agitated, she tried to clean the apartment, scrubbing the sink vigorously to drive the images in her mind away.

As she had grown older, Kyra had read and seen every interview with other drone operators who suffered from PTSD. In the faces of those men, she had searched for traces of her father.

I sat in an air-conditioned office and controlled the drone with a joystick while watching on a monitor what the drone camera saw. If a man was suspected of being the enemy, I had to make a decision and pull the trigger and then zoom in and watch as the man's body parts flew around the screen as the rest of him bled out, until his body cooled down and disappeared from the infrared camera.

Kyra turned on the faucet and held her hands under the hot water, as if she could wash off the memory of her father coming home every evening: silent, sullen, gradually turning into a stranger.

Every time, you wonder: Did I kill the right person? Was the sack on that man's back filled with bombs or just some hunks of meat? Were those three men trying to set up an ambush or were they just tired and taking a break behind those rocks by the road? You kill a hundred people, a thousand people, and sometimes you find out afterwards that you were wrong, but not always.

"You were a hero," Kyra said. She wiped her face with her wet hands. The water was hot against her face and she could pretend it was all just water.

No. You don't understand. It's different from shooting at someone when they're also shooting at you, trying to kill you. You don't feel brave pushing a button to kill people who are not in uniform, who look like they're going for a visit with a friend, when you're sitting thousands of miles away, watching them through a camera. It's not like a video game. And yet it also is. You don't feel like a hero.

"I miss you. I wish I could have understood."

Every day, after you're done with killing, you get up from your chair and walk out of the office building and go home. Along the way you hear the birds chittering overhead and see teenagers walking by, giggling or moping, self-absorbed in their safe cocoons, and then you open the door to your home. Your spouse wants to tell you about her annoying boss and your children are waiting for you to help them with their homework, and you can't tell them a thing you've done.

I think either you become crazy or you already were.

She did not want him to be defined by the number on that piece of paper her mother kept hidden at the bottom of the box in the attic.

"They counted wrong, Dad," Kyra said. "They missed one death."

KYRA WALKED DOWN THE HALL dejectedly. She was done with her last interview of the day—a hot Silicon Valley startup. She had been nervous and distracted and had flubbed the brainteaser. It had been a long day and she didn't get much sleep the night before.

She was almost at the elevator when she noticed an interview schedule posted on the door of the suite next to the elevator for a company named AWS Systems. It hadn't been completely filled. A few of the slots on the bottom were blank; that generally meant an undesirable company.

She took a closer look at the recruiting poster. They did something related to robotics. There were some shots of office buildings on a landscaped, modern campus. Bullet points listed competitive salary and benefits. Not flashy, but it seemed attractive enough. Why weren't people interested?

Then she saw it: "Candidates need to pass screening for security clearance." That would knock out many of her classmates who weren't U.S. citizens. And it likely meant government contracts. Defense, probably. She shuddered. Her family had had enough of war.

She was about to walk away when her eyes fell on the last bullet point on the poster: "Relieve the effects of PTSD on our heroes."

She wrote her name on one of the blank lines and sat down on the bench outside the door to wait.

"You have impressive credentials," the man said, "the best I've seen all day, actually. I already know we'll want to talk to you some more. Do you have any questions?"

This was what Kyra had been waiting for all along. "You're building robotic systems to replace human-controlled drones, aren't you? For the war."

The recruiter smiled. "You think we're Cyberdyne Systems?"

Kyra didn't laugh. "My father was a drone operator."

The man became serious. "I can't reveal any classified information. So we have to speak only in hypotheticals. Hypothetically, there may be advantages to using autonomous robotic systems over human-operated machines. Robots."

"Like what? It can't be about safety. The drone operators are perfectly safe back here. You think machines will fight better?"

"No, we're not interested in making ruthless killer robots. But we shouldn't make people do the jobs that should be done by machines."

Kyra's heart beat faster. "Tell me more."

"There are many reasons why a machine makes a better soldier than a human. A human operator has to make decisions based very limited information: just what he can see from a video feed, sometimes alongside intelligence reports. Deciding whether to shoot when all you have to go on is the view from a shaking camera and confusing, contradictory intel is not the kind of thinking humans excel at. There's too much room for error. An operator might hesitate too long and endanger an innocent, or he might be too quick on the trigger and violate the rules of engagement. Decisions by different operators would be based on hunches and emotions and at odds with each other. It's inconsistent and inefficient. Machines can do better."

Worst of all, Kyra thought, *a human can be broken by the experience of having to decide.*

"If we take these decisions away from people, make it so that individuals are out of the decision-making loop, the result should be less collateral damage and a more humane, more civilized form of warfare."

But all Kyra could think was: *No one would have to do what my father did.*

The process of getting security clearance took a while. Kyra's mother was surprised when Kyra called to tell her that government investigators might come to talk to her, and Kyra wasn't sure how to explain why she had taken this job when there were much better offers from other places. So she just said, "This company helps veterans and soldiers."

Her mother said, carefully, "Your father would be proud of you."

Meanwhile, they assigned her to the civilian applications division, which made robots for factories and hospitals. Kyra worked hard and followed all the rules. She didn't want to mess up before she got to do what she really wanted. She was good at her job, and she hoped they noticed.

Then one morning Dr. Stober, the head roboticist, called her to join him in a conference room.

Kyra's heart was in her throat as she walked over. Was she going to be let go? Had they decided that she couldn't be trusted because of what had happened to her father? That she might be emotionally unstable? She had always liked Dr. Stober, who seemed like a good mentor, but she had never worked with him closely.

"Welcome to the team," said a smiling Dr. Stober. Besides Kyra, there were five other programmers in the room. "Your security clearance arrived this morning, and I knew I wanted you on this team right away. This is probably the most interesting project at the company right now."

The other programmers smiled and clapped. Kyra grinned at each of them in turn as she shook their outstretched hands. They all had reputations as the stars in the company.

"You're going to be working on the AW-1 Guardians, one of our classified projects."

One of the other programmers, a young man named Alex, cut in: "These aren't like the field transport mules and remote surveillance crafts we already make. The Guardians are unmanned, autonomous flying vehicles about the size of a small truck armed with machine guns and missiles."

Kyra noticed that Alex was really excited by the weapons systems.

"I thought we make those kinds already," Kyra said.

"Not exactly," Dr. Stober said. "Our other combat systems are meant for surgical strikes in remote places or are prototypes for frontline combat, where basically anything that moves can be shot. But these are designed for peacekeeping in densely populated urban areas, especially places where there are lots of Westerners or friendly locals to protect. Right now we still have to rely on human operators."

Alex said in a deadpan voice, "It would be a lot easier if we didn't have to worry about collateral damage."

Dr. Stober noticed that Kyra didn't laugh and gestured for Alex to stop. "Sarcasm aside, as long as we're occupying their country, there will be locals who think they can get some advantage from working with us and locals who wish we'd go away. I doubt that dynamic has changed in five thousand years. We have to protect those who want to work with us from those who don't, or else the whole thing falls apart. And we can't expect the Westerners doing reconstruction over there to stay holed up in walled compounds all the time. They have to mingle."

"It's not always easy to tell who's a hostile," Kyra said.

"That's the heart of the issue. Most of the time, the population is ambivalent. They'll help us if they think it's safe to do so, and they'll help the militants if they think that's the more convenient choice."

"I've always said that if they choose to help the militants blend in, I don't see why we need to be that careful. They made a decision," Alex said.

"I suppose some interpretations of the rules of engagement would agree with you. But we're telling the world that we're fighting a new kind of war, a clean war, one where we hold ourselves to a higher standard. How people see the way we conduct ourselves is just as important nowadays."

"How do we do that?" Kyra asked, before Alex could further derail the conversation.

"The key piece of software we have to produce needs to replicate what the remote operators do now, only better. The government has supplied us with thousands of hours of footage from the drone operations during the last decade or so. Some of them got the bad guys, and some of them got the wrong people. We'll need to watch the videos and distill the decision-making process of the operators into a formal procedure for identifying and targeting militants embedded in urban conditions, eliminate the errors, and make the procedure repeatable and applicable to new situations. Then we'll improve it by tapping into the kind of big data that individual operators can't integrate and make use of."

The code will embody the minds of my father and others like him so that no one would have to do what they did, endure what they endured.

"Piece of cake," said Alex. And the room laughed, except for Kyra and Dr. Stober.

KYRA THREW HERSELF into her work, a module they called the ethical governor, which was responsible for minimizing collateral damage when the robots fired upon suspects. She was working on a conscience for killing machines.

She came in on the weekends and stayed late, sometimes sleeping in the office. She didn't view it as a difficult sacrifice to make. She couldn't talk about what she was working on with the few friends she had, and she didn't really want to spend more time outside the office with people like Alex.

She watched videos of drone strikes over and over. She wondered if any were missions her father had flown. She understood the confusion, the odd combination of power and powerlessness experienced when watching a man one is about to kill through a camera, the pressure to decide.

The hardest part was translating this understanding into code. Computers require precision, and the need to articulate vague hunches had a way of forcing one to confront the ugliness that could remain hidden in the ambiguity of the human mind.

To enable the robots to minimize collateral damage, Kyra had to assign a value to each life that might be endangered in a crowded urban area. One of the most effective ways for doing this—at least in simulations—also turned out to be the most obvious: profiling. The algorithm needed to translate racial characteristics and hints about language and dress into a number that held the power of life and death. She felt paralyzed by the weight of her task.

"Everything all right?" Dr. Stober asked.

Kyra looked up from her keyboard. The office lights were off; it was dark outside. She was practically the last person left in the building.

"You've been working a lot."

"There's a lot to do."

"I've reviewed your check-in history. You seem to be stuck on the part where you need the facial recognition software to give you a probability on ethnic identity."

Kyra gazed at Dr. Stober's silhouette in the door to her office, back-lit by the hall lights. "There's no API for that."

"I know, but you're resisting the need to roll your own."

"It seems . . . wrong."

Dr. Stober came in and sat down in the chair on the other side of her desk. "I learned something interesting recently. During World War II, the U.S. Army trained dogs for warfare. They would act as sentries, guards, or maybe even as shock troops in an island invasion."

Kyra looked at him, waiting.

"The dogs had to be trained to tell allies apart from enemies. So they used Japanese-American volunteers to teach the dogs to profile, to attack those with certain kinds of faces. I've always wondered how those volunteers felt. It was repugnant, and yet it was also necessary."

"They didn't use German-American or Italian-American volunteers, did they?"

"No, not that I'm aware of. I'm telling you this not to dismiss the problematic nature of your work, but to show you that the problem you're trying to solve isn't entirely new. The point of war is to prefer the lives of one group over the lives of another group. And short of being able to read everyone's minds, you must go with shortcuts and snap heuristics to tell apart those who must die from those who must be saved."

Kyra thought about this. She could not exempt herself from Dr. Stober's logic. After all, she had lamented her father's death for years, but she had never shed a tear for the thousands he had killed, no matter how many might have been innocent. His life was more valuable to her than all of them added together. His suffering meant more. It was why she was here.

"Our machines *can* do a better job than people. Attributes like appearance and language and facial expressions are but one aspect of the input. Your algorithm can integrate the footage from citywide surveillance by thousands of other cameras, the metadata of phone calls and social visits, individualized suspicions built upon data too massive for any one person to handle. Once the programming is done, the robots will make their decisions consistently, without bias, always supported by the evidence."

Kyra nodded. Fighting with robots meant that no one had to feel responsible for killing.

KYRA'S ALGORITHM had to be specified exactly and submitted to the government for approval. Sometimes the proposals came back marked with questions and changes.

She imagined some general (advised, perhaps, by a few military lawyers) looking through her pseudocode line by line.

A target's attributes would be evaluated and assigned numbers. Is the target a man? Increase his suspect score by thirty points. Is the target a child? Decrease his suspect score by twenty-five points. Does the target's face match any of the suspected insurgents with at least a fifty-percent probability? Increase his suspect score by five hundred points.

And then there was the value to be assigned to the possible collateral damage around the target. Those who could be identified as Americans or had a reasonable probability of being Americans had the highest value. Then came native militia forces and groups who were allied with U.S. forces and the local elites. Those who looked poor and desperate were given the lowest values. The algorithm had to formalize anticipated fallout from media coverage and politics.

Kyra was getting used to the process. After the specifications had gone back and forth a few times, her task didn't seem so difficult.

KYRA LOOKED at the number on the check. It was large.

"It's a small token of the company's appreciation for your efforts," said Dr. Stober. "I know how hard you've been working. We got the official word on the trial period from the government today. They're very pleased. Collateral damage has been reduced by more than eighty percent since they started using the Guardians, with zero erroneous targets identified." Kyra nodded. She didn't know if the eighty percent was based on the number of lives lost or the total amount of points assigned to the lives. She wasn't sure she wanted to think too hard about it. The decisions had already been made.

"We should have a team celebration after work."

And so, for the first time in months, Kyra went out with the rest of the team. They had a nice meal, some good drinks, sang karaoke. And Kyra laughed and enjoyed hearing Alex's stories about his exploits in war games.

"AM I BEING PUNISHED?" Kyra asked. "No, no, of course not," Dr. Stober said, avoiding her gaze. "It's just administrative leave until . . . the investigation completes. Payroll will still make bi-weekly deposits and your health insurance will continue, of course. I don't want you to think you're being scapegoated. It's just that you did most of the work on the ethical governor. The Senate Armed Forces Committee is really pushing for our methodology, and I've been told that the first round of subpoenas is coming down next week. You won't be called up, but we'll likely have to name you."

Kyra had seen the video only once, and once was enough. Someone in the market had taken it with a cellphone, so it was shaky and blurry. No doubt the actual footage from the Guardians would be much clearer, but she wasn't going to get to see that. It would be classified at a level beyond her clearance.

The market was busy, the bustling crowd trying to take advantage of the cool air in the morning. It looked, if you squinted a bit, like the farmer's market that Kyra sometimes went to, to get her groceries. A young American man, dressed in the distinctive protective vest that expat reconstruction advisors and technicians wore over there, was arguing with a merchant about something, maybe the price of the fruits he wanted to buy.

Reporters had interviewed him afterwards, and his words echoed in Kyra's mind: *"All of a sudden, I heard the sound made by the Guardians patrolling the market change. They stopped to hover over me, and I knew something was wrong."*

In the video, the crowd was dispersing around him, pushing, jostling with each other to get out of the way. The person who took the video ran, too, and the screen was a chaotic blur.

When the video stabilized, the vantage point was much further. Two black robots about the size of small trucks hovered in the air above the kiosk. They looked like predatory raptors. Metal monsters.

Even in the cellphone video, it was possible to make out the recorded warning in the local language the robots projected via loudspeakers. Kyra didn't know what the warnings said.

A young boy, seemingly oblivious to the hovering machines above him, was running at the American man, laughing and screaming, his arms opened wide as if he wanted to embrace the man.

"I just froze. I thought, oh God, I'm going to die. I'm going to die because this kid has a bomb on him."

The militants had tried to adapt to the algorithms governing the robots by exploiting certain weaknesses. Because they realized that children were assigned a relatively high value for collateral damage purposes and a relatively low value for targeting purposes, they began to use more children for their missions. Kyra had had to tweak the algorithm and the table of values to account for these new tactics.

"All of your changes were done at the request of the Army and approved by them," said Dr. Stober. "Your programming followed the updated rules of engagement and field practices governing actual soldiers. Nothing you've done was wrong. The Senate investigation will be just be a formality."

In the video, the boy kept on running towards the American. The warnings from the hovering Guardians changed, got louder. The boy did not stop.

A few more boys and girls, some younger, some older, came into the area cleared by the crowd. They ran after the first boy, shouting.

The militants had developed an anti-drone tactic that was sometimes effective. They'd send the first bomber out, alone, to draw the fire of the drones. And while the drone operators were focused on him and distracted, a swarm of backup bombers would rush out to get to the target while the drones shot up the first man.

Robots could not be distracted. And Kyra had programmed them to react correctly to such tactics.

The boy was now only a few steps away from the lone American. The Guardian hovering on the right took a single shot. Kyra flinched at the sound from the screen.

"It was so loud," said the young man in his interview. "I had heard the Guardians shoot before, but only from far away. Up close was a completely different experience. I heard the shot with my bones, not my ears."

The child collapsed to the ground immediately. Where his head had been, there was now only empty space. The Guardians had to be efficient when working in a crowd. Clean.

A few more loud shots came from the video, making Kyra jump involuntarily. The cellphone owner panned his camera over, and there were a few more bundles of rags and blood on the ground. The other children.

The crowd stayed away, but a few of the men were coming back into the clearing, moving closer, raising their voices. But they didn't dare to move too close to the stunned young American, because the two Guardians were still hovering overhead. It took a few minutes before actual American soldiers and the local police showed up at the scene and made everyone go home. The video ended there.

"When I saw that dead child lying in the dust, all I could feel was relief, an overwhelming joy. He had tried to kill me, and I had been saved. Saved by our robots."

Later, when the bodies were searched by the bomb-removal robots, no explosives were found.

The child's parents came forward. They explained that their son wasn't right in the head. They usually locked him in the house, but that day, somehow he had gotten out. No one knew why he ran at that American. Maybe he thought the man looked different and he was curious.

All the neighbors insisted to the authorities that the boy wasn't dangerous. Never hurt anyone. His siblings and friends had been chasing after him, trying to stop him before he got into any trouble.

His parents never stopped crying during the interview. Some of the commenters below the interview video said that they were probably sobbing for the camera, hoping to get more compensation out of the American government. Other commenters were outraged. They constructed elaborate arguments and fought each other in a war of words in the comment threads, trying to score points.

Kyra thought about the day she'd made the changes in the programming. She had been sipping a frappé because the day was hot. She remembered deleting the old value of a child's life and putting in a new one. It had seemed routine, just another change like hundreds of other tweaks she had already made. She remembered deleting one IF and adding another, changing the control flow to defeat the enemy. She remembered feeling thrilled at coming up with a neat solution to the nested logic. It was what the Army had requested, and she had decided to do her best to give it to them faithfully.

"Mistakes happen," said Dr. Stober. "The media circus will eventually end, and all the hand-wringing will stop. News cycles are finite, and something new will replace all this. We just have to wait it out. We'll figure out a way to make the system work better next time. This *is* better. This is the future of warfare."

Kyra thought about the sobbing parents, about the dead child, about the dead children. She thought about the eighty-percent figure Dr. Stober had quoted. She thought about the number on her father's scorecard, and the parents and children and siblings behind those numbers. She thought about her father coming home.

She got up to leave.

"You must remember," said Dr. Stober from behind her, "You're not responsible."

She said nothing.

It was rush hour when Kyra got off the bus to walk home. The streets were filled with cars and the sidewalks with people. Restaurants were filling up quickly; waitresses flirted with customers; men and women stood in front of display windows to gawk at the wares.

She was certain that most of them were bored with coverage of the war. No one was coming home in body bags any more. The war was clean. This was the point of living in a civilized country, wasn't it? So that one did not have to think about wars. So that somebody else, something else, would.

She strode past the waitress who smiled at her, past the diners who did not know her name, into the throng of pedestrians on the sidewalk, laughing, listening to music, arguing and shouting, oblivious to the monster who was walking in their midst, ignorant of the machines thousands of miles away deciding who to kill next.

>•≪

The aliens are destroying Earth and its inhabitants with ease. Doom is inevitable . . . unless Seanan McGuire's heroic band of plucky young warriors can use the powers of spell-chants and captromancy to summon supernatural aid. Fighting Pumpkins forever! Go, team, go!

DYING WITH HER CHEER PANTS ON

Seanan McGuire

BRIDGET DUCKED behind the remains of a burned-out Impala, crouching low as the *zap-zap-zap* of blaster fire split the October night. The sound was already familiar enough to turn her stomach. Not just because it meant another survivor had been spotted—because there was nothing she could do to help whoever it was. She huddled against the wheel, making herself as small as possible. She didn't think she'd been seen. She'd know for sure in a few minutes, when the patrol reached her position. There was nothing to do but wait.

It was still hard to believe that aliens were real, not just science-fiction bullshit for the geeks in the computer club to obsess over. Maybe they'd been science-fiction bullshit once, but not anymore. This was real. Some guy on CNN had called them *blasters* when the aliens first landed, before anybody had a clue how destructive their quaint-looking little ray guns really were. He'd laughed when he said it.

That was sixteen hours ago, nine hours before the start of the homecoming game and eleven hours before the game's untimely end. Nobody was laughing now, least of all Bridget, who'd been chosen for the unenviable duty of leaving the safety of the gym and crossing the ruins of town to get what Amy was saying the squad would need.

(They'd all put their names into the sacred gym bag, and when Maddy— who was Squad Leader, even though there was barely any squad left—pulled out Bridget's name, she couldn't argue. The gym bag's word was law.)

She wished she'd been allowed to stay in uniform. She would have felt safer that way, more confident, more in-control . . . more like herself. A Fighting Pumpkin was always a cheerleader on the inside, but there was still an undeniable security in being a cheerleader on the *outside*, a safety of sorts in their matching orange and green uniforms. Present a united front. Look your best, and you'll be the best. But she would have been too visible if she'd worn the school colors outside; they would have stood out like a floodlight against the scorch marks and gummy ash covering everything in town. Better to blend in. Better to make it back to the gym alive.

The blaster fire tapered off. Bridget managed to huddle down even further as she waited to hear the slithering sound the aliens made when they moved. She didn't want to see them almost as badly as she wanted them not to see *her*. She'd seen the aliens on the morning news, before the shooting had started, but it hadn't prepared her for the reality of them. The TV couldn't show the way they smelled, or the way their sticky-looking skins seemed to bend the light, as if even it didn't want to touch them.

(Amy had described them best. She'd looked at the pictures being flashed across the emergency broadcasts, sniffed, and said they looked like what you'd get if you let Dr. Frankenstein play with a giant squid, a spider, and a Pomeranian. She then went on to explain that Frankenstein was the doctor, not the monster. As if anybody cared. She would never have made the squad if she weren't the only one who could do a perfect back-handspring every single time. Plus, it was good to have a brain around, if only because the principal kept refusing to cancel finals.)

Finals were canceled now, along with Homecoming, cheerleading, and everything else about the world that mattered. The only question left was whether the human race was getting canceled. Things didn't look good for the home team.

The sound of tentacles slapping against broken pavement drew closer to Bridget's hiding place. She clapped a hand over her mouth to block the sound of her breathing, squeezing her eyes shut. They'd pass or they wouldn't. If they passed, she'd start running. If they didn't . . .

If they didn't, the sacred gym bag had been wrong. She wasn't the one.

The slapping sounds passed the car, getting softer as the alien patrol moved on to search for more survivors. *You missed one,* thought Bridget. She still stayed where she was, counting slowly to a hundred. The sounds didn't resume. Uncurling herself, she rose, her precious burden clutched against her chest.

Bridget ran.

THE INVASION STARTED at 5:30 a.m. Central Time on the third Saturday in October—Homecoming Weekend for high schools across America. The aliens came in enormous saucer-shaped ships before scattering out in smaller vessels that looked sort of like flying Winnebagos. Those outer space motor homes touched down wherever there were people, opening their doors and spilling dozens of squid-spider *things* into the streets. Some people panicked. Some people fired guns at them, but the bullets just bounced off their invisible shields. The aliens kept moving, seeming to ignore the people of Earth, no matter what those people did.

The adults promptly went out of their minds, which is basically what adults are for. At least half the squad was under house arrest, but of the fifteen girls on the Fighting Pumpkins Varsity Cheerleading Squad, fourteen were at the locker room on time. Jeanne was fifteen minutes late; her father actually locked her in her bedroom when she said she was going to the game with or without his permission.

("I waited until he went back to the living room and snuck out my bedroom window," bragged Jeanne, after she'd finally shown up. Her pride turned into hysteria when halftime turned into a bloodbath and she realized she'd never see her family again. It was almost a mercy when one of the blasters caught her in the back, reducing her to ash and blackened bones. Almost. Annoying or not, she'd been a Fighting Pumpkin, and Fighting Pumpkins were supposed to take care of their own.)

The entire football team showed up for the game—naturally—and so did enough of the opposing team for the coaches to decide they should go ahead and play. "We'll show those aliens what it means to be American!" said Coach Ackley, and everyone applauded.

It was a good game. It would have been a better one if the aliens hadn't shown up at halftime and opened fire on the crowd. It took them less than five minutes to kill almost a hundred people and send the survivors scattering like quail.

(According to the videos Amy had downloaded to her phone, the aliens actually attacked at the same time all over the world. Bridget really didn't care. She didn't have to smell the entire world getting fried, just the people on the field. So much for the home-team advantage.)

They never even got to finish the game. Funny, the things that stop seeming like the end of the world when the world is really ending.

BRIDGET PRESSED HERSELF against the gym wall outside the locker room door, praying she'd managed to get the secret knock right. One missed beat and they might leave her outside, alone, in the dark, with the aliens.

She'd been waiting just long enough to be on the verge of total panic when the door creaked open and Amy whispered, urgently, "Get in here before you're spotted."

Bridget was only too happy to oblige.

Maddy, Betsy, and Kathryn were waiting in the shower room. The power was out all over town, but they had flashlights, and the screensaver on Amy's laptop gave off a soothing glow. The girls were sitting on a pile of gymnastic mats they'd dragged over from the equipment cage. Bridget blinked back sudden tears as she realized, again, that this was it; this was the squad. This might even be the entire high school. She hadn't seen any survivors in her trek across the town.

Maddy rose as Bridget and Amy approached. Her eyes were only for the bag Bridget clutched against her chest. "Is that it?" she demanded. "Did you get it?"

"Right where Amy said it would be." Bridget held out the bag, opening it to display the contents: a box of dinner candles and a shabby old book in a plastic library dust jacket. The word WITHDRAWN was stamped across the width of the pages in gory red. "I got matches, too."

"Good," said Amy, taking the bag from Bridget's unresisting hands. "We'll need them."

Maddy looked Bridget up and down. "Go get your uniform on. You're going to want to be in your colors for this."

Maddy was the Squad Leader, and she was a senior. Questioning her went against every bone in Bridget's body. She still found the strength, somehow, to ask timidly, "Is this really going to work?"

"It has to." Maddy shrugged. "There's nothing else left to try."

Bridget nodded, accepting Maddy's words as truth. According to what Amy was able to find before the school wireless cut out, the aliens had taken out everything that was thrown at them, including most of the United States Armed Forces and a Chinese nuclear bomb. They'd been most of the way to conquering the planet when the connection died. Everything had been tried, and everything had failed.

Everything except the impossible. Bridget glanced at the three girls now sitting cross-legged on the shower floor, all of them focused on the book in Amy's hands. It would work. It had to. If it didn't . . .

Well, if it didn't, it wouldn't be their problem anymore. With that reassuring thought at the front of her mind, Bridget turned to creep back to her locker. If she was going to die, she was going to do it with her cheer pants on.

FIVE GIRLS in orange and green uniforms stood in a circle in the center of the shower room, their eyes fixed on the gym bag on the floor in front of them. Inside the bag were five slips of Betsy's rose-scented pink notebook paper, each with a girl's name written on it. No one moved. Bridget was barely breathing.

For the second time in a single night, and the second time in her entire life, she was afraid of what the sacred bag might ask of her.

"Everybody understands what they need to do?" asked Amy, eyes still fixed on the bag. She'd taken out her contacts, replacing them with the glasses she was only allowed to wear when nobody outside the squad would see her. Aliens didn't count.

Nods from the other girls. Bridget forced herself to nod with them. The bag was going to pick her. She knew the bag was going to pick her. Why were they even bothering?

Because it was tradition, and tradition must be observed, even at the end of the world—maybe especially at the end of the world. "Then it's time," said Maddy. She picked up the bag, giving it a shake. "Who wants to pull the name?" No hands were raised. This wasn't like deciding who was going to go pick up the pizzas, or who had to go tell Coach Ackley the freshmen had been peeping in the girls' locker room again. This was too big.

"You do it, Maddy," said Kathryn. A murmur of agreement ran through the other girls. Maddy was Captain. She'd pick the one the gym bag wanted. That was how the power worked.

"All right." Expression grave, Maddy plunged her hand into the gym bag, rummaged around, and came up with a single slip of paper and the strong smell of roses.

Please, thought Bridget.

"Bridget," read Maddy. As one, the five sighed. "I'm sorry."

"Don't be." Bridget wiped the back of her hand across her eyes, smearing tears and mascara. No one was going to say anything. Not now. "I came to tryouts on my own, remember? I cheered my heart out. That's why I'm here."

"Fighting Pumpkins forever," said Betsy.

It was a good thing to say. "Fighting Pumpkins forever," said Maddy. One by one, they took up the cheer, chanting it in a whisper barely louder than a sigh. Amy passed out the candles and the books of matches, while the other girls dug out their compacts, with their tiny, perfect mirrors. Only Bridget didn't bother. Her mirror was going to be bigger than that.

"It will work," Amy said, folding Bridget's fingers around the matchbook. "Believe it's going to work like you always believed the home team was going to win. Home team advantage."

"Home team advantage," Bridget echoed, and stayed where she was as the others stepped forward, one by one, to hug her and head for the exits. Maddy was the last to go.

"She'll make them pay for this," she said, squeezing Bridget's shoulder, and then was gone.

Not allowing herself to look at the candle in her hand, Bridget turned and walked after the others. She wasn't heading for the exit. She was heading for the bathroom, and the full-length mirror on the bathroom wall.

EVERYTHING WAS SILENT. Bridget looked at her reflection, wishing she looked braver, or at least less afraid. Portrait of a cheerleader about to die. Maddy was right; she felt better knowing she was going to do it in the school colors. Other schools could laugh about their stupid mascot and garish uniforms, but real school spirit wasn't being badass with a mascot like a Tiger or a Wolf. It was being proud to be a Pumpkin.

Her hands were shaking hard enough that it took three tries to light the candle. The match flared orange, even brighter than her uniform, before dimming into candlelight that bleached her reflection phantom-pale. She mustered a wavering smile, and waited, still watching her reflection.

The bathroom window was open, just a crack. Enough for her to hear the first handclaps, like gunshots breaking the night, followed by Maddy's well-conditioned voice bellowing, "Ready? *Okay!*"

That was the signal. Doing her best to tune out the rest of the squad cheering outside the gym, Bridget fixed her eyes on her reflection. *Don't look away; Amy's book says you can't look away.* If you looked away, it wouldn't work.

("We've all played that stupid game," Kathryn had said before they voted, before the squad agreed to try Amy's crazy suggestion. "It never works. She never comes."

"That was before we knew what the rules were," said Amy.

"What are they?" asked Betsy.

But it was Maddy who answered. Maddy, who'd seen her boyfriend die on the football field; the only Squad Leader in Fighting Pumpkins history to lose a homecoming game and the majority of her squad in a single night. "There aren't any," she said, and that was when Bridget had known they were going to go through with Amy's plan, desperate and strange as it was.)

"Bloody Mary," whispered Bridget. "Bloody Mary, Bloody Mary—" The sound of blaster fire was starting up outside; the aliens were taking the bait, drawn by the irresistible lure of four teenage girls in skimpy pleated skirts cheering their hearts out. It didn't matter what part of the galaxy you were from. No one could resist a cheerleader.

"BLOODY MARY, SHE'S THE ONE!" screamed the Pumpkins outside the

gym. *"BLOODY MARY, I KILLED YOUR SON!"* Each of them would have a compact on the ground in front of her, but they couldn't be sure they'd be able to maintain eye contact long enough to call her name the required thirteen times. That was why one of them had to stay behind, and miss the final cheer. Dying sucked. Dying without your squad around you was worse.

"—Bloody Mary, Bloody Mary, Bloody Mary—" That was six. The blasters were still firing. Betsy wasn't cheering anymore, and neither was Kathryn. It was just Amy and Maddy outside, cheering their hearts out for the last, and least appreciative, audience they would ever have. Was the mirror getting blurry, or was she just crying again?

("See, if you hold a candle and look in the mirror while you say her name thirteen times, she'll come." Amy had been talking nonsense, but they were taking her seriously because after you'd seen your teammates fried by giant alien squid with ray guns, *ray guns*, for God's sake, nonsense didn't sound so bad. "She'll scratch your eyes out. That's the bad part."

"So what's the good part?" demanded Maddy.

"If you tell her you're the one who killed her son, she'll kill everybody she can get her hands on."

They'd gotten very quiet after that.)

"Bloody Mary." Amy wasn't cheering anymore. It was just Maddy, and the sound of blasters. "Bloody Mary, Bloody Mary, Bloody Mary." That was ten, and Maddy screamed, just once, before the cheering from outside stopped completely. That horrible slithering sound was everywhere, coming from every direction. They were inside the gym. *They were inside the gym.*

(She was really going to die. No last minute reprieve. No third-act hero. She was going to die with her Fighting Pumpkins cheer pants on, and she wouldn't even get one of those stupid yearbook memorials, because there was no one left to write it.)

"Bloody Mary." Eleven. The mirror was definitely getting blurry, and it definitely wasn't tears. "Bloody Mary." She could almost see the face behind her own, and oh, God, if she was going to stop, it had to be now, but how could she stop, when she'd heard the squad gunned down, and the slithering just kept getting closer? Alien or evil ghost-witch-woman from inside the mirror?

Bloody Mary might be evil. But this was homecoming weekend, and on the Planet Earth, she by-God had the home team advantage.

"BLOODY MARY!" Bridget shouted, abandoning all pretense of quiet. *"BLOODY MARY, I KILLED YOUR SON!"*

She only saw Mary for an instant as she lunged out of the mirror, hands hooked into claws and descending toward Bridget's eyes. Then came the searing pain, and she was falling, candle wax covering her hand in a spray of burning droplets. Her head slammed against the tile floor hard enough that she heard bone cracking.

"Go Pumpkins," Bridget whispered, as the sound of the blasters started up again. A new sound came with it, dentist's-drill sharp and inhuman. She smiled despite the pain as she realized what it was. The sound of aliens, screaming. "Gimme a 'B' . . . "

Bridget kept cheering in a whisper as she bled to death on the bathroom floor, not caring that there was no one left to hear her. The sound of Bloody Mary laughing and the screams of the aliens stood in well for the roar of the crowd. She died with her cheer pants on, knowing to the last that she'd done what every cheerleader dreams of.

She'd cheered the home team to victory.

>•≪

Robert Reed writes of a young insurgent in Occupied Toronto who lucks upon a cognitive railgun developed by the enemy Americans. The fourteen-year-old warrior believes she has shaped this astonishing instrument of mayhem into a loyal agent of the insurgency. But the weapon is even more remarkable than she knows, and—like war—it is far more complex than she can imagine.

PRAYER

Robert Reed

FASHION MATTERS. In my soul of souls, I know that the dead things you carry on your body are real, real important. Grandma likes to call me a clotheshorse, which sounds like a good thing. For example, I've always known that a quality sweater means the world. I prefer soft organic wools woven around Class-C nanofibers—a nice high collar with sleeves riding a little big but with enough stopping power to absorb back-to-back kinetic charges. I want pants that won't slice when the shrapnel is thick, and since I won't live past nineteen, probably, I let the world see that this body's young and fit. (Morbid maybe, but that's why I think about death only in little doses.) I adore elegant black boots that ignore rain and wandering electrical currents, and everything under my boots and sweater and pants has to feel silky-good against the most important skin in my world. But essential beyond all else is what I wear on my face, which is more makeup than Grandma likes, and tattooed scripture on the forehead, and sparkle-eyes that look nothing but ordinary. In other words, I want people to see an average Christian girl instead of what I am, which is part of the insurgency's heart inside Occupied Toronto.

To me, guns are just another layer of clothes, and the best day ever lived was the day I got my hands on a barely-used, cognitively damaged Mormon railgun. They don't make that model anymore, what with its willingness to change sides. And I doubt that there's ever been a more dangerous gun made by the human species. Shit, the boy grows his own ammo, and he can kill anything for hundreds of miles, and left alone he will invent ways to hide and charge himself on the sly, and all that time he waits waits waits for his master to come back around and hold him again.

I am his master now.

I am Ophelia Hanna Hanks, except within my local cell, where I wear the randomly generated, perfectly suitable name:

Ridiculous.

The gun's name is Prophet, and until ten seconds ago, he looked like scrap conduit and junk wiring. And while he might be cognitively impaired, Prophet is wickedly loyal to me. Ten days might pass without the two of us being in each other's reach, but that's the beauty of our dynamic: I can live normal and look normal, and while the enemy is busy watching everything else, a solitary fourteen-year-old girl slips into an alleyway that's already been swept fifty times today.

"Good day, Ridiculous."

"Good day to you, Prophet."

"And who are we going to drop into Hell today?"

"All of America," I say, which is what I always say.

Reliable as can be, he warns me, "That's a rather substantial target, my dear. Perhaps we should reduce our parameters."

"Okay. New Fucking York."

Our attack has a timetable, and I have eleven minutes to get into position.

"And the specific target?" he asks.

I have coordinates that are updated every half-second. I could feed one or two important faces into his menu, but I never kill faces. These are the enemy, but if I don't define things too closely, then I won't miss any sleep tonight.

Prophet eats the numbers, saying, "As you wish, my dear."

I'm carrying him, walking fast towards a fire door that will stay unlocked for the next ten seconds. Alarmed by my presence, a skinny rat jumps out of one dumpster, little legs running before it hits the oily bricks.

"Do you know it?" I ask.

The enemy likes to use rats as spies.

Prophet says, "I recognize her, yes. She has a nest and pups inside the wall."

"Okay," I say, feeling nervous and good.

The fire door opens when I tug and locks forever once I step into the darkness.

"You made it," says my gun.

"I was praying," I report.

He laughs, and I laugh too. But I keep my voice down, stairs needing to be climbed and only one of us doing the work.

SHE FOUND ME after a battle. She believes that I am a little bit stupid. I was damaged in the fight and she imprinted my devotions to her, and then using proxy tools and stolen wetware, she gave me the cognitive functions to be a loyal agent to the insurgency.

I am an astonishing instrument of mayhem, and naturally her superiors thought about claiming me for themselves.

But they didn't.

If I had the freedom to speak, I would mention this oddity to my Ridiculous. "Why would they leave such a prize with little you?"

"Because I found you first," she would say.

"War isn't a schoolyard game," I'd remind her.

"But I made you mine," she might reply. "And my bosses know that I'm a good soldier, and you like me, and stop being a turd."

No, we have one another because her bosses are adults. They are grown souls who have survived seven years of occupation, and that kind of achievement doesn't bless the dumb or the lucky. Looking at me, they see too much of a blessing, and nobody else dares to trust me well enough to hold me.

I know all of this, which seems curious.

I might say all of this, except I never do.

And even though my mind was supposedly mangled, I still remember being crafted and calibrated in Utah, hence my surname. But I am no Mormon. Indeed, I'm a rather agnostic soul when it comes to my interpretations of Jesus and His influence in the New World. And while there are all-Mormon units in the U.S. military, I began my service with Protestants—Baptists and Missouri Synods mostly. They were bright clean happy believers who had recently arrived at Fort Joshua out on Lake Ontario. Half of that unit had already served a tour in Alberta, guarding the tar pits from little acts of sabotage. Keeping the Keystones safe is a critical but relatively simple duty. There aren't many people to watch, just robots and one another. The prairie was depopulated ten years ago, which wasn't an easy or cheap process; American farmers still haven't brought the ground back to full production, and that's one reason why the Toronto rations are staying small.

But patrolling the corn was easy work compared to sitting inside Fort Joshua, millions of displaced and hungry people staring at your walls.

Americans call this Missionary Work.

Inside their own quarters, alone except for their weapons and the Almighty, soldiers try to convince one another that the natives are beginning to love them. Despite a thousand lessons to the contrary, Canada is still that baby brother to the north, big and foolish but congenial in his heart, or at least capable of learning manners after the loving sibling delivers enough beat-downs.

What I know today—what every one of my memories tells me—is that the American soldiers were grossly unprepared. Compared to other units and other duties, I would even go so far as to propose that the distant generals were aware of their limitations yet sent the troops across the lake regardless, full of religion and love for each other and the fervent conviction that the United States was the empire that the world had always deserved.

Canada is luckier than most. That can't be debated without being deeply, madly stupid. Heat waves are killing the tropics. Acid has tortured the seas. The wealth of the previous centuries has been erased by disasters of weather and war and other inevitable surprises. But the worst of these sorrows haven't occurred in the Greater United States, and if they had half a mind, Canadians would be thrilled with the mild winters and long brilliant summers and the supportive grip of their big wise master.

My soldiers' first recon duty was simple: Walk past the shops along Queen.

Like scared warriors everywhere, they put on every piece of armor and every sensor and wired back-ups that would pierce the insurgent's jamming. And that should have been good enough. But by plan or by accident, some native let loose a few molecules of VX gas—just enough to trigger one of the biohazard alarms. Then one of my brother-guns was leveled at a crowd of innocents, two dozen dead before the bloody rain stopped flying.

That's when the firefight really began.

Kinetic guns and homemade bombs struck the missionaries from every side. I was held tight by my owner—a sergeant with commendations for his successful defense of a leaky pipeline—but he didn't fire me once. His time was spent yelling for an orderly retreat, pleading with his youngsters to find sure targets before they hit the buildings with hypersonic rounds. But despite those good smart words, the patrol got itself trapped. There was a genuine chance that one of them might die, and that's what those devout men encased in body armor and faith decided to pray: Clasping hands, they opened channels to the Almighty, begging for thunder to be sent down on the infidels.

The Almighty is what used to be called the Internet—an American child reclaimed totally back in 2027.

A long stretch of shops and old buildings was struck from the sky.

That's what American soldiers do when the situation gets dicey. They pray, and the locals die by the hundreds, and the biggest oddity of that peculiar day was how the usual precise orbital weaponry lost its way, and half of my young men were wounded or killed in the onslaught while a tiny shaped charge tossed me a hundred meters down the road.

There, I was discovered in the rubble by a young girl.

As deeply unlikely as that seems.

I DON'T WANT THE ROOF. I don't need my eyes to shoot. An abandoned apartment on the top floor is waiting for me, and in particular, its dirty old bathroom. As a rule, I like bathrooms. They're the strongest part of any building, what with pipes running through the walls and floor. Two weeks ago, somebody I'll never know sealed the tube's drain and cracked the faucet just enough for a slow drip, and now the water sits near the brim. Water is essential for long shots. With four minutes to spare, I deploy Prophet's long legs, tipping him just enough toward the southeast, and then I sink him halfway into the bath, asking, "How's that feel?"

"Cold," he jokes.

We have three and a half minutes to talk.

I tell him, "Thank you."

His barrel stretches to full length, its tip just short of the moldy plaster ceiling. "Thank you for what?" he says.

"I don't know," I say.

Then I laugh, and he sort of laughs.

I say, "I'm not religious. At least, I don't want to be."

"What are you telling me, Ridiculous?"

"I guess . . . I don't know. Forget it."

And he says, "I will do my very best."

Under the water, down where the breech sits, ammunition is moving. Scrap metal and scrap nanofibers have been woven into four bullets. Street fights require hundreds and thousands of tiny bullets, but each of these rounds is bigger than most carrots and shaped the same general way. Each one carries a brain and microrockets and eyes. Prophet is programming them with the latest coordinates while running every last-second test. Any little problem with a bullet can mean an ugly shot, or even worse, an explosion that rips away the top couple floors of this building.

At two minutes, I ask, "Are we set?"

"You're standing too close," he says.

"If I don't move, will you fire anyway?"

"Of course."

"Good," I say.

At ninety-five seconds, ten assaults are launched across southern Ontario. The biggest and nearest is fixated on Fort Joshua—homemade cruise missiles and lesser railguns aimed at that artificial island squatting in our beautiful lake. The assaults are meant to be loud and unexpected, and because every soldier thinks his story is important, plenty of voices suddenly beg with the Almighty, wanting His godly hand.

The nearby battle sounds like a sudden spring wind.

"I'm backing out of here," I say.

"Please do," he says.

At sixty-one seconds, most of the available American resources are glancing at each of these distractions, and a brigade of AIs is studying past tendencies and elaborate models of insurgency capabilities, coming to the conclusion that these events have no credible value toward the war's successful execution.

Something else is looming, plainly.

"God's will," says the nonbeliever.

"What isn't?" says the Mormon gun.

At seventeen seconds, two kilometers of the Keystone John pipeline erupt in a line of smoky flame, microbombs inside the heated tar doing their best to stop the flow of poisons to the south.

The Almighty doesn't need prayer to guide His mighty hand. This must be the main attack, and every resource is pulled to the west, making ready to deal with even greater hazards.

I shut the bathroom door and run for the hallway.

Prophet empties his breech, the first carrot already moving many times faster than the speed of sound as it blasts through the roof. Its three buddies are directly behind it, and the enormous release of stored energy turns the bathwater to steam, and with the first shot the iron tub is yanked free of the floor while the second and third shots kick the tub and the last of its water down into the bathroom directly downstairs. The final shot is going into the wrong part of the sky, but that's also part of the plan. I'm not supposed to be amazed by how many factors can be juggled at once, but they are juggled and I am amazed, running down the stairs to recover my good friend.

THE SCHEDULE *is meant to be secret and followed precisely. The Secretary of Carbon rides her private subway car to the UN, but instead of remaining indoors and safe, she has to come into the sunshine, standing with ministers and potentates who have gathered for this very important conference. Reporters are sitting in rows and cameras will be watching from every vantage point, and both groups are full of those who don't particularly like the Secretary. Part of her job is being despised, and fuck them. That's what she thinks whenever she attends these big public dances.*

Journalists are livestock, and this is a show put on for the meat. Yet even as the scorn builds, she shows a smile that looks warm and caring, and she carries a strong speech that will last for three minutes, provided she gives it. Her words are meant to reassure the world that full recovery is at hand. She will tell everyone that the hands of her government are wise and what the United States wants is happiness for every living breathing wonderful life on this great world—a world that with God's help will live for another five billion years.

For the camera, for the world, the Secretary of Carbon and her various associates invest a few moments in handshakes and important nods of the head.

Watching from a distance, without knowing anything, it would be easy to recognize that the smiling woman in brown was the one in charge.

The UN president shakes her hand last and then steps up to the podium. He was installed last year after an exhaustive search. Handsome and personable, and half as bright as he is ambitious, the President greets the press and then breaks from the script, shouting a bland "Hello" to the protesters standing outside the blast screens.

Five thousand people are standing in the public plaza, holding up signs and generated holos that have one clear message:

"END THE WARS NOW."

The Secretary knows the time and the schedule, and she feels a rare ache of nervousness, of doubt.

When they hear themselves mentioned, the self-absorbed protesters join together in one rehearsed shout that carries across the screens. A few reporters look at the throng behind them. The cameras and the real professionals focus on the human subjects. This is routine work. Reflexes are numb, minds lethargic. The Secretary picks out a few familiar faces, and then her assistant pipes a warning into her sparkle-eyes. One of the Keystones has been set on fire.

In reflex, the woman takes one step backward, her hands starting to lift to cover her head.

A mistake.

But she recovers soon enough, turning to her counterpart from Russia, telling him, "And congratulations on that new daughter of yours."

He is flustered and flattered. With a giddy nod, he says, "Girls are so much better than boys these days. Don't you think?"

The Secretary has no chance to respond.

A hypersonic round slams through the atmosphere, heated to a point where any impact will make it explode. Then it drops into an environment full of clutter and one valid target that must be acquired and reached before the fabulous energies shake loose from their bridle.

There is no warning sound.

The explosion lifts bodies and pieces of bodies, and while the debris rises, three more rounds plunge into the panicked crowd.

Every person in the area drops flat, hands over their heads.

Cameras turn, recording the violence and loss—more than three hundred dead and maimed in a horrific attack.

The Secretary and new father lie together on the temporary stage.

Is it her imagination, or is the man trying to cop a feel?

She rolls away from him, but she doesn't stand yet. The attack is finished, but she shouldn't know that. It's best to remain down and act scared, looking at the plaza, the air filled with smoke and pulverized concrete while the stubborn holos continue to beg for some impossible gift called Peace.

MY GRANDMOTHER IS SHARP. She is. Look at her once in the wrong way, and she knows something is wrong. Do it twice and she'll probably piece together what makes a girl turn quiet and strange.

But not today, she doesn't.

"What happened at school?" she asks.

I don't answer.

"What are you watching, Ophelia?"

Nothing. My eyes have been blank for half a minute now.

"Something went wrong at school, didn't it?"

Nothing is ever a hundred percent right at school, which is why it's easy to harvest a story that might be believed. Most people would believe it, at least. But after listening to my noise about snippy friends and broken trusts, she says, "I don't know what's wrong with you, honey. But that isn't it."

I nod, letting my voice die away.

She leaves my little room without closing the door. I sit and do nothing for about three seconds, and then the sparkle eyes take me back to the mess outside the UN. I can't count the times I've watched the impacts, the carnage. Hundreds of cameras were working, government cameras and media cameras and those carried by the protesters. Following at the digitals' heels are people talking about the tragedy and death tolls and who is responsible and how the war has moved to a new awful level.

"Where did the insurgents get a top-drawer railgun?" faces ask.

But I've carried Prophet for a couple years and fired him plenty of times. Just not into a public target like this, and with so many casualties, and all of the dead on my side of the fight.

That's the difference here: The world suddenly knows about me.

In the middle of the slaughter, one robot camera stays focused on my real targets, including the Secretary of Fuel and Bullshit. It's halfway nice, watching her hunker down in terror. Except she should have been in pieces, and there shouldn't be a face staring in my direction, and how Prophet missed our target by more than fifty meters is one big awful mystery that needs solving.

I assume a malfunction.

I'm wondering where I can take him to get his guidance systems recalibrated and ready for retribution.

Unless of course the enemy has figured out how to make railgun rounds fall just a little wide of their goals, maybe even killing some troublemakers in the process.

Whatever is wrong here, at least I know that it isn't my fault.

Then some little thing taps at my window.

From the next room, my grandmother asks, "What are you doing, Ophelia?"

I'm looking at the bird on my windowsill. The enemy uses rats, and we use robins and house sparrows. But this is a red-headed woodpecker, which implies rank and special circumstances.

The bird gives a squawk, which is a coded message that my eyes have to play with for a little while. Then the messenger flies away.

"Ophelia?"

"I'm just thinking about a friend," I shout.

She comes back into my room, watching my expression all over again.

"A friend, you say?"

"He's in trouble," I say.

"Is that what's wrong?" she asks.

"Isn't that enough?"

Two rats in this alley don't convince me. I'm watching them from my new haven, measuring the dangers and possible responses. Then someone approaches the three of us, and in the best tradition of ratdom, my companions scurry into the darkness under a pile of rotting boards.

I am a plastic sack filled with broken machine parts.

I am motionless and harmless, but in my secret reaches, inside my very busy mind, I'm astonished to see my Ridiculous back again so soon, walking toward the rat-rich woodpile.

Five meters behind her walks an unfamiliar man.

To him, I take an immediate dislike.

He looks prosperous, and he looks exceptionally angry, wearing a fine suit made stiff with nano-armor and good leather shoes and a platoon of jamming equipment as well as two guns riding in his pockets, one that shoots poisoned ice as well as the gun that he trusts—a kinetic beast riding close to his dominant hand.

Ridiculous stops at the rot pile.

The man asks, "Is it there?"

"I don't know," she says, eyes down.

My girl has blue sparkle eyes, much like her original eyes—the ones left behind in the doctor's garbage bin.

"It looks like boards now?" he asks.

"He did," she lies.

"Not he," the man says, sounding like a google-head. "The machine is an It."

"Right," she says, kicking at the planks, pretending to look hard. "It's just a big gun. I keep forgetting."

The man is good at being angry. He has a tall frightful face and neck muscles that can't stop being busy. His right hand thinks about the gun in his pocket. The fingers keep flexing, wanting to grab it.

His gun is an It.

I am not.

"I put it here," she says.

She put me where I am now, which tells me even more.

"Something scared it," she says. "And now it's moved to another hiding place."

The man says, "Shit."

Slowly, carefully, he turns in a circle, looking at the rubble and the trash and the occasional normal object that might still work or might be me. Then with a tight slow voice, he says, "Call for it."

"Prophet," she says.

I say nothing.

"How far could it move?" he asks.

"Not very," she says. "The firing drained it down to nothing, nearly. And it hasn't had time to feed itself, even if it's found food."

"Bullshit," he says, coming my way.

Ridiculous watches me and him, the tattooed Scripture above her blue eyes dripping with sweat. Then the man kneels beside me, and she says, "I put the right guidance codes into him."

"You said that already." Then he looks back at her, saying, "You're not in trouble here. I told you that already."

His voice says a lot.

I have no power. But when his hands reach into my sack, what resembles an old capacitor cuts two of his fingers, which is worth some cursing and some secret celebration.

Ridiculous' face is twisted with worry, up until he looks back at her again. Then her expression turns innocent, pure and pretty and easy to believe.

Good girl, I think.

The man rises and pulls out the kinetic gun and shoots Ridiculous in the chest. If not for the wood piled up behind her, she would fly for a long distance. But instead of flying, she crashes and pulls down the wood around her, and one of those very untrustworthy rats comes out running, squeaking as it flees.

Ridiculous sobs and rolls and tries saying something.

He shoots her in the back, twice, and then says, "We never should have left it with you. All that luck dropping into our hands, which was crazy. Why should we have trusted the gun for a minute?"

She isn't dead, but her ribs are broken. And by the sound of it, the girl is fighting to get one good breath.

"Sure, it killed some bad guys," he says. "That's what a good spy does. He sacrifices a few on his side to make him look golden in the enemy's eyes."

I have no strength.

"You can't have gone far," he tells the alley. "We'll drop ordinance in here, take you out with the rats."

I cannot fight.

"Or you can show yourself to me," he says, the angry face smiling now. "Reveal yourself and we can talk."

Ridiculous sobs.

What is very easy is remembering the moment when she picked up me out of the bricks and dust and bloodied bits of human meat.

He gives my sack another good kick, seeing something.

And for the first time in my life, I pray. Just like that, as easy as anything, the right words come out of me, and the man bending over me hears nothing coming and senses nothing, his hands playing with my pieces when a fleck of laser light falls out of the sky and turns the angriest parts of his brain into vapor, into a sharp little pop.

I'm still not breathing normally. I'm still a long way from being able to think straight about anything. Gasping and stupid, I'm kneeling in a basement fifty meters from where I nearly died, and Prophet is suckling on an unsecured outlet, endangering both of us. But he needs power and ammunition, and I like the damp dark in here, waiting for my body to come back to me.

"You are blameless," he says.

I don't know what that means.

He says, "You fed the proper codes into me. But there were other factors, other hands, and that's where the blame lies."

"So you are a trap," I say.

"Somebody's trap," he says.

"The enemy wanted those civilians killed," I say, and then I break into the worst-hurting set of coughs that I have ever known.

He waits.

"I trusted you," I say.

"But Ridiculous," he says.

"Shut up," I say.

"Ophelia," he says.

I hold my sides, sipping my breaths.

"You assume that this war has two sides," he says. "But there could be a third player at large, don't you see?"

"What should I see?"

"Giving a gun to their enemies is a huge risk. If the Americans wanted to kill their political enemies, it would be ten times easier to pull something out of their armory and set it up in the insurgency's heart."

"Somebody else planned all of this, you're saying."

"I seem to be proposing that, yes."

"But that man who came with me today, the one you killed . . . he said the Secretary showed us a lot with her body language. She knew the attack was coming. She knew when it would happen. Which meant that she was part of the planning, which was a hundred percent American."

"Except whom does the enemy rely on to make their plans?"

"Tell me," I say.

Talking quietly, making the words even more important, he says, "The Almighty."

"What are we talking about?" I ask.

He says nothing, starting to change his shape again.

"The Internet?" I ask. "What, you mean it's conscious now? And it's working its own side in this war?"

"The possibility is there for the taking," he says.

But all I can think about are the dead people and those that are hurt and those that right now are sitting at their dinner table, thinking that some fucking Canadian bitch has made their lives miserable for no goddamn reason.

"You want honesty," Prophet says.

"When don't I?"

He says, "This story about a third side . . . it could be a contingency buried inside my tainted software. Or it is the absolute truth, and the Almighty is working with both of us, aiming toward some grand, glorious plan."

I am sort of listening, and sort of not.

Prophet is turning shiny, which happens when his body is in the middle of changing shapes. I can see little bits of myself reflected in the liquid metals and the diamonds floating on top. I see a thousand little-girl faces staring at me, and what occurs to me now—what matters more than anything else today—is the idea that there can be more than two sides in any war.

I don't know why, but that's the biggest revelation of all.

When there are more than two sides, that means that there can be too many sides to count, and one of those sides, standing alone, just happens to be a girl named Ophelia Hanna Hanks.

>•≪

*Theodora Goss' narrator-warrior was only a child when the Empress came.
Like many women, her mother enlists in the northern queen's army and
soon the Empress rules England by might and magic, eternal winter and
fearsome wolves. Her promises of security, equality, and peace are fulfilled
and her frigid empire spreads . . . but at what cost?*

ENGLAND UNDER THE WHITE WITCH

Theodora Goss

IT IS ALWAYS WINTER NOW.

WHEN SHE CAME, I was only a child—in ankle socks, my hair tied back with a
silk ribbon. My mother was a seamstress working for the House of Alexandre.
She spent the days on her knees, saying Yes, madame has lost weight, what has
madame been doing? When madame had been doing nothing of the sort. My
father was a photograph of a man I had never seen in a naval uniform. A medal
was pinned to the velvet frame.

My mother used to take me to Kensington Gardens, where I looked for
fairies under the lilac bushes or in the tulip cups.

In school, we studied the kings and queens of England, its principal imports
and exports, and home economics. Even so young, we knew that we were living
in the waning days of our empire. That after the war, which had taken my
father and toppled parts of London, the sun was finally setting. We were a
diminished version of ourselves.

At home, my mother told me fairy tales about Red Riding Hood (never
talk to wolves), Sleeping Beauty (your prince will come), Cinderella (choose

the right shoes). We had tea with bread and potted meat, and on my birthday there was cake made with butter and sugar that our landlady, Mrs. Stokes, had bought as a present with her ration card.

Harold doesn't hold with this new Empress, as she calls herself, Mrs. Stokes would tell my mother. Coming out of the north, saying she will restore us to greatness. She's established herself in Edinburgh, and they do say she will march on London. He says the King got us through the war, and that's good enough for us. And who believes a woman's promises anyway?

But what I say is, England has always done best under a queen. Remember Elizabeth and Victoria. Here we are, half the young men dead in the war, no one for the young women to marry so they work as typists instead of having homes of their own. And trouble every day in India, it seems. Why not give an Empress a try?

One day Monsieur Alexandre told my mother that Lady Whortlesham had called her impertinent and therefore she had to go. That night, she sat for a long time at the kitchen table in our bedsit, with her face in her hands. When I asked her the date of the signing of the Magna Carta, she hastily wiped her eyes with a handkerchief and said, As though I could remember such a thing! Then she said, Can you take care of yourself for a moment, Ann of my heart? I need to go talk to Mrs. Stokes.

The next day, when I ran home from school for dinner, she was there, talking to Mrs. Stokes and wearing a new dress, white tricotine with silver braid trim. She looked like a princess from a fairy tale.

It's easy as pie, she was saying. I found the office just where you said it was, and they signed me right up. At first I'm going to help with recruitment, but the girl I talked to said she thought I should be in the rifle corps. They have women doing all sorts of things, there. I start training in two days.

You're braver than I am, said Mrs. Stokes. Aren't you afraid of being arrested?

If they do arrest me, will you take care of Ann? she asked. I know it's dangerous, but they're paying twice what I was making at the shop, and I have to do something. This world we're living in is no good, you and I both know that. Nothing's been right since the war. Just read this pamphlet they gave me. It makes sense, it does. I'm doing important work, now. Not stitching some Lady Whortlesham into her dress. I'm with the Empress.

In the end, the Empress took London more easily than anyone could have imagined. She had already taken Manchester, Birmingham, Oxford. We had heard how effective her magic could be against the remnants of our Home

Forces. First, she sent clouds that covered the sky, from horizon to horizon. It snowed for days, until the city was shrouded in white. And then the sun came out just long enough to melt the top layer of snow, which froze during the night. The trees were encased in ice. They sparkled as though made of glass, and when they moved I heard a tinkling sound.

Then, she sent wolves. Out of the mist they came, white and gray, with teeth as sharp as knives. They spoke in low, guttural voices, telling the Royal Guards to surrender or have their throats ripped out. Most of the guards stayed loyal. In the end, there was blood on the snow in front of Buckingham Palace. Wolves gnawed the partly frozen bodies.

Third and finally came her personal army, the shop girls and nursemaids and typists who had been recruited, my mother among them. They looked magnificent in their white and silver, which made them difficult to see against the snow. They had endured toast and tea for supper, daily indignity, the unwanted attention of employers. Their faces were implacable. They shot with deadly accuracy and watched men die with the same polite attention as they had shown demonstrating a new shade of lipstick.

Buckingham Palace fell within a day. On the wireless, we heard that the King and his family had fled to France, all but one of his sisters, who it turned out was a sympathizer. By the time the professional military could mobilize its troops, scattered throughout our empire, England was already hers to command.

I stood by Mrs. Stokes, watching the barge of the Empress as it was rowed down the Thames. She stood on the barge, surrounded by wolves, with her white arms bare, black hair down to her feet, waving at her subjects.

No good will come of this, you mark my words, said Mr. Stokes.

Hush! Isn't she lovely? said Mrs. Stokes.

You have seen her face in every schoolroom, every shop. Perhaps in your dreams. It is as familiar to you as your own. But I will never forget that first glimpse of her loveliness. She looked toward us, and I believed that she had seen me, had waved particularly to me.

The next day, our home economics teacher said, From now on, we are not going to learn about cooking and sewing. Instead, we are going to learn magic. There was already a picture of our beloved Empress over her desk, where the picture of the King used to be.

At first, there were resistance movements. There were some who fought for warmth, for light. Who said that as long as she reigned, spring would never come again. We would never see violets scattered among the grass, never hear a river run. Never watch young lovers hold each other on the embankment, kiss each other not caring who was watching. There was the Wordsworth Society, which tried to effect change politically. And there were more radical groups: the Children of Albion, the Primrose Brigade.

But we soon learned that our Empress was as ruthless as she was beautiful. Those who opposed her were torn apart by wolves, or by her girl soldiers, who could tear men apart with their bare hands and were more frightening than any wolves. Sympathizers were rounded up and imprisoned, encased in ice. Or worse, they were left free but all the joy was taken from them, so that they remained in a prison of their own perpetual despair.

Her spies were everywhere. Even the trees could not be trusted. The hollies were the most dangerous, the most liable to inform. But resistance groups would not meet under pines, firs, or hemlocks. In many households, the cats were on her side. Whispers of disloyalty would bring swift retribution.

And many said, such traitors deserved punishment. That winter was good for England, that we needed cold, needed toughening. We had grown soft after the war, allowed our dominions to rebel against us, allowed the world to change. But she would set things right. And so the resistance movements were put down, and our soldiers marched into countries under a white flag that did not mean surrender. Those who had tried to be free of us were confronted with winter, and sorceresses, and wolves. Their chiefs and rajahs and presidents came to London, bringing jewels and costly fabrics to lay before her feet, and pledged their loyalty.

Our empire spread, as indeed it must. A winter country must import its food, and as winter spreads, the empire must expand to supply the lands under snow, their waters locked in ice. That is the terrible, inescapable logic of empire.

I was a Snowflake, in a white kerchief with silver stars. Then, I was an Ice Maiden. The other girls in school nodded to me as I walked by. If they did not wear the white uniform, I asked them why they had not joined up yet, and if they said their parents would not let them, I told them it was their responsibility to be persuasive. I won a scholarship to university, where I was inducted into the Sisterhood of the Wolf.

My den mother encouraged me to go into the sciences. Scientists will be useful to the Empress in the coming war, she said. Science and magic together are more powerful, are greater weapons, than they are apart. And there is a war coming, Ann. We hear more and more from our spies in Germany. A power is rising in that part of the world, a power that seeks to oppose the reign of the Empress. Surely not, I said. Who would oppose her? A power that believes in fire, she said. A fire that will burn away the snow, that will scorch the earth. That does not care about what we have already achieved—the security, the equality, the peace we will achieve when her empire spreads over the earth.

When I graduated, the Empress herself handed me a diploma and the badge of our order. My mother, who had been promoted to major-general, was so proud! All of us in the Sisterhood had been brought to Buckingham Palace, in sleighs drawn by reindeer with silver bells on their antlers. We waited in a long room whose walls were painted to look like a winter forest, nibbling on almond biscuits and eating blancmange from silver cups with small bone spoons. At last, we were summoned into her presence.

You have seen our beloved Empress from far away, from below while she stands on a balcony, or from a sidewalk as she is drawn through the city streets in her sleigh. But I have met her, I have kissed her hand. It was white and cold, with the blue veins visible. Her grip was strong—stronger than any man's, as she was taller than any man. Her face was so pale that I could only look at it for a moment without pain. Her black hair trailed on the floor.

You have done well, she said to me, and I could hear her voice in my head as well as with my ears. To hear that voice again, I would consent to being torn apart by wolves.

You have never seen, you will never see, anything as magnificent as our Empress.

WHERE DID SHE COME FROM? Some say she came from the stars, that she is an alien lifeform. Some say that she is an ancient goddess reborn. Some say she is an ordinary woman, and that such women have always lived in the north: witches who command the snows.

The question is whispered, in secret places where there are no hemlocks, no cats: does human blood flow in her veins? Can our Empress die?

I MET JACK in the basic physical training program required for all recruits to the war effort. My mother had used her influence to have me chosen for the Imperial Guard, the Empress' personal girl army, which could be deployed throughout the empire. After basic training, I was going to advanced training in the north, and then wherever the war effort needed me. He was a poet, assigned to the Ministry of Morale. He had been conscripted after university—this was in the early days of general conscription. He was expected to write poetry in praise of the Empress, and England, and those who served the empire. But first, we all had to pass basic training.

We stayed in unheated cabins, bathed in cold water, all to make us stronger, to bring the cold inside us. Each morning, we marched through the woods. The long marches, hauling weapons and equipment through the snow, were not difficult for me. I had been training since my university days, waking at dawn to run through the snow or swim in the icy rivers with the Sisterhood. But he was not as strong as I was. He would stumble over roots or boulders beneath the snow, and try to catch himself with chilled, chapped hands—the woolen gloves we had been issued were inadequate protection against the cold. I would help him up, holding him by the elbow, and sometimes I would carry part of his equipment, transferring it into my pack surreptitiously so the Sergeant did not see me.

Why are you so kind to me, Ann? he asked me once. Someone has to be, I said, smiling.

The other girls laughed at him, but I thought his large, dark eyes were beautiful. When he looked at me, I did not feel the cold. One day, I sat next to him at dinner. He told me about Yorkshire, where he was born—about the high hills, the sheep huddled together, their breaths hanging on the air.

Perhaps I should have been more like my father, he said. It was my headmaster at school who first read my poems and told me to apply for a scholarship. There I was, a farmer's son, studying with the children of ministers and generals, who talked about going to the palace the way I talked about going to the store. I kept to myself, too proud or ashamed to approach them, to presume they might be my friends. But my tutor sent my poems to the university literary magazine, and they were published. Then, I was invited to join the literary society. I thought it was an honor—until we all received letters from the war office. So here I am, losing my toes to frostbite so I can write odes for the dead in Africa—or for the war they say is coming.

We all believed that war was coming. The newspapers were already talking about a fire rising in the east, burning all before it.

It's a great honor to write for the Empress, I said.

Yes, of course it is, he said after a moment. He looked at me intently with those dark eyes. Of course, he said again, before finishing the thin broth with dumplings that we were told was Irish stew.

WE SPENT more and more time together, huddled in the communal showers when we could, telling each other about our childhoods, the foods we liked, the books we had read. We wondered about the future. He hoped that after his compulsory service, he could work as a schoolteacher, publish his poems. I did not know where I would be assigned—Australia? South America? There was always unrest in some part of the empire.

One day, the sergeant said to me, Ann, I'm not going to tell you what to do. I'm just going to warn you—there's something not right about Jack Kirby. I don't know what it is, but Thule—who was her wolf—can't stand him. I don't think a general's daughter should show too much interest in that boy. You don't want anyone questioning your loyalty, do you?

Her words made me angry. He was going into the Ministry—wasn't that good enough? That night, we met in the showers. I don't want to talk, I said. I kissed him—slid my hands under his jacket, sweater, undershirt. His body was bony, but I thought it had its own particular grace. He told me that I was beautiful, breathing it into my neck as we made love, awkwardly, removing as few layers of clothing as possible. You're beautiful, Ann—I hear it in my mind and remember the warmth of his breath in that cold place. There had been others, not many, but he may as well have been my first. He is the one I remember.

During our week of leave, he asked me to come home with him, to Yorkshire. His father met us at the train station. He was a large, quiet man who talked mostly of sheep. Look at these pelts, he told me. Feel the weight of them. Didn't use to get wool like this, in Yorkshire. It's the perpetual winter as does it. Grows twice as thick and twice as long. But he grumbled about the feed from the communal granaries—not as nourishing as the grass that used to grow on the hillsides, never seen such sickly lambs. And the wolves—not allowed to shoot them anymore. Those who complained were brought before a committee.

We had suppers of Yorkshire pudding and gravy, and walked out over the fields holding hands. I asked Jack about his mother. She had died in the influenza epidemic, which he had barely survived. That was before the coming of the Empress. I could see, from the photograph of her on the bureau, that he had inherited her delicacy, her dark eyes and thick, dark hair. Late at night, when his father was asleep, he would sneak into the guest room and we would make love under the covers, as quietly as possible, muffling our laughter, whispering to one another.

The day before we were to return from leave, his father told him that a ewe was giving birth in the snow. She had become trapped in a gully, and could not be lifted out in her condition. There was no chance of bringing her into the barn, so he and his father, one of the two farm hands, and the veterinarian went out, grumbling about the cold.

I wandered through the house, then sat in his room for a while, looking through the books he had read as a child. Books from before the Empress came, and from after—*Prince Frost and the Giants*, the Wolf Scout series, the *Treasury of English Poems* we had all studied in school. I can't tell you why I chose to look though the battered old desk he had used as a schoolboy. It was wrong, a base impulse. But I loved him, and on this last day before we went back to the camp, I wanted to feel close to him. I wanted to know his secrets, whatever they were—even if they included love letters from another girl. I tortured myself for a moment with that thought, knowing how unlikely it was that I would find anything but old school books and pens. And then I pulled open the drawer.

In the desk was a notebook, and in the notebook were his poems—in his handwriting, with dates at the tops of the pages indicating when they had been written. The latest of them was dated just before camp. They spoke of sunlight and warmth and green fields. Next to the notebook was a worn copy of one of the forbidden books: *The Complete Poetical Works of Wordsworth*. I opened to the page marked with a ribbon and read,

> *I wandered lonely as a cloud*
> *That floats on high o'er vales and hills,*
> *When all at once I saw a crowd,*
> *A host, of golden daffodils . . .*

I slammed the book shut. My hands were shaking. I remembered what the sergeant had said: You don't want anyone questioning your loyalty, do you?

By the time Jack, his father, and the other men had returned, I was composed enough to seem almost normal. That night, he came to my room. We made love as though nothing had happened, but all the time I could hear it in my head: *I wandered lonely as a cloud—a host of golden daffodils.* I remembered daffodils. I could almost see them, bright yellow against the blue sky.

The next morning, as Jack and his father were loading our bags into the sleigh that would take us to the train station, I told them I had forgotten something. I ran back into the house, up the stairs and into Jack's room, then quickly slid the notebook and book into my backpack.

When we arrived back at camp, I went to the sergeant and denounced Jack Kirby as a traitor.

I told myself that I was doing the right thing. He would be sent for reeducation. He would become a productive citizen, not a malcontent longing for what could never be. Perhaps some day he would even thank me.

He was sent to a reeducation camp in the north of Scotland. I graduated from basic training, went on to advanced training for the Imperial Guard, and was eventually given my wolf companion, Ulla. Together, we were sent to France, where the war had already started. We were among the first to enter Poland. We were in the squadron that summoned ice to cover the Black Sea so our soldiers could march into Turkey. My den mother had been right: science and magic together created powerful weapons. It took five years, but the fire in the east was defeated, and our empire stretched into the Russian plains, into the deserts of Arabia.

When I returned to England, I asked for Jack's file. It told me that he had died in the camp, shortly after arriving. The causes of death were listed as cold and heartbreak.

DURING THE EMPRESS' REIGN, England has changed for the better, some say. There is always food in the shops, although it has lost its flavor. Once, carrots were not pale, like potatoes. Cabbages were green. They were not grown in great glass houses. The eggs had bright yellow centers, and all meat did not taste like mutton. Once, there were apple trees in England, and apples, peaches, plums were not imported from the distant reaches of our empire, where winter has not yet permanently settled. There was a sweetness in the world that you have never tasted. There was love and joy, and pain sharp as knives, rather than this blankness.

Our art, our stories, our poems have changed, become ghosts of their former selves. Mothers tell their daughters about Little White Hood and her wolf companion. About Corporal Cinder, who joined the liberation army and informed on her wicked sisters.

Our soldiers move on from conquest to conquest, riding white bears, white camels. Parts of the world that had never seen snow have seen it now. I myself have sent snowdrifts to cover the sands of the Sahara, so we could deploy our sleighs. I have seen the Great Pyramid covered in ice, and crocodiles lying lethargic on ice-floes in the Nile.

Our empire stretches from sea to sea to sea. Eventually, even the republics that now fight against us will come under our dominion. And then perhaps the only part of the world that has not bowed down to our Empress, the wild seas themselves, will be covered in ice. What will happen to us then, when there are no more lands to send provisions to the empire? I do not know. Our Empress has promised us a perfect world, but the only perfection is death.

You have heard stories of primroses and daffodils, and you do not believe them. You have heard that there were once green fields, and rivers that ran between their banks, and a warm sun overhead. You have never seen them, and you believe they are merely tales. I am here to tell you that they are true, that in my childhood these existed. And cups of tea that were truly hot, and Christmas trees with candles on their branches, and church bells. Girls wore ribbons in their hair rather than badges on their lapels. Boys played King Arthur or Robin Hood rather than Wolf Scout.

I'm here to tell you that the fairy tales are true.

And that, sitting in this secret place, looking at each other in fear, wondering who among you is an informant, you must decide whether to believe in the fairy tales, whether to fight for an idea. Ideas are the most powerful things—beauty, freedom, love. But they are harder to fight for than things like food, or safety, or power. You can't eat freedom, you can't wield love over another.

You are so young, with your solemn faces, your thin bodies, nourished on pale cabbage and soggy beef and slabs of flavorless pudding! I do not know if you have the strength. But that, my children, you will have to find out for yourselves.

Your leaders, who have asked me here tonight, believe that winter can end, if you have the courage to end it. They are naive, as revolutionaries always are. Looking at your faces, I wonder. You have listened so intently to an old soldier, a woman who has seen much, felt much, endured. I have no strength left to fight, either for or against the Empress. Everyone I have ever loved—my mother, Mrs. Stokes, Jack Kirby, Ulla—is dead. I have just enough strength to tell you what the world was once, and could be again: imperfect, unequal, and in many ways unjust. But there was warmth and light to counteract the cold, the darkness.

What do I believe? Entropy is the law of the universe. All things run down, all things eventually end. Perhaps, after all, she is not an alien, not a witch, but a universal principal. Perhaps all you can do is hold back the cold, the darkness, for a while. Is a temporary summer worth your lives? But if you do not fight, you will never feel the warmth of the sun on your cheeks, or smell lilacs, or bite into a peach picked directly from the tree. You will never hold each other on the embankment, watching the waters of the Thames run below. The old stories will be forgotten. Our empire will spread over the world, and it will be winter, everywhere, forever.

>>•<<

"'Laren Dorr,'" according to George R. R. Martin, "probably counts as my first foray into high fantasy . . ." The tale is profoundly romantic, but Sharra is very powerful: she does, after all, travel between worlds. Except for one, her battles are "offstage" in the story, but that she is a warrior is evident.

THE LONELY SONGS OF LAREN DORR

George R. R. Martin

THERE IS A GIRL who goes between the worlds.

She is gray-eyed and pale of skin, or so the story goes, and her hair is a coal-black waterfall with half-seen hints of red. She wears about her brow a circlet of burnished metal, a dark crown that holds her hair in place and sometimes puts shadows in her eyes. Her name is Sharra; she knows the gates.

The beginning of her story is lost to us, with the memory of the world from which she sprang. The end? The end is not yet, and when it comes we shall not know it.

We have only the middle, or rather a piece of that middle, the smallest part of the legend, a mere fragment of the quest. A small tale within the greater, of one world where Sharra paused, and of the lonely singer Laren Dorr and how they briefly touched.

ONE MOMENT there was only the valley, caught in twilight. The setting sun hung fat and violet on the ridge above, and its rays slanted down silently into a dense forest whose trees had shiny black trunks and colorless ghostly leaves. The only sounds were the cries of the mourning-birds coming out for the night, and the swift rush of water in the rocky stream that cut the woods.

Then, through a gate unseen, Sharra came tired and bloodied to the world of Laren Dorr. She wore a plain white dress, now stained and sweaty, and a heavy fur cloak that had been half-ripped from her back. And her left arm, bare and slender, still bled from three long wounds. She appeared by the side of the stream, shaking, and she threw a quick, wary glance about her before she knelt to dress her wounds. The water, for all its swiftness, was a dark and murky green. No way to tell if it was safe, but Sharra was weak and thirsty. She drank, washed her arm as best she could in the strange and doubtful water, and bound her injuries with bandages ripped from her clothes. Then, as the purple sun dipped lower behind the ridge, she crawled away from the water to a sheltered spot among the trees and fell into exhausted sleep.

She woke to arms around her, strong arms that lifted her easily to carry her somewhere, and she woke struggling. But the arms just tightened and held her still. "Easy," a mellow voice said, and she saw a face dimly through gathering mist, a man's face, long and somehow gentle.

"You are weak," he said, "and night is coming. We must be inside before darkness."

Sharra did not struggle, not then, though she knew she should. She had been struggling a long time, and she was tired. But she looked at him, confused. "Why?" she asked. Then, not waiting for an answer, "Who are you? Where are we going?"

"To safety," he said.

"Your home?" she asked, drowsy.

"No," he said, so soft she could scarcely hear his voice. "No, not home, not ever home. But it will do." She heard splashing then, as if he were carrying her across the stream, and ahead of them on the ridge she glimpsed a gaunt, twisted silhouette, a triple-towered castle etched black against the sun. Odd, she thought, that wasn't there before.

She slept.

WHEN SHE WOKE, he was there, watching her. She lay under a pile of soft, warm blankets in a curtained, canopied bed. But the curtains had been drawn back, and her host sat across the room in a great chair draped by shadows. Candlelight flickered in his eyes, and his hands locked together neatly beneath his chin. "Are you feeling better?" he asked, without moving.

She sat up and noticed she was nude. Swift as suspicion, quicker than thought, her hand went to her head. But the dark crown was still there, in place, untouched, its metal cool against her brow. Relaxing, she leaned back against the pillows and pulled the blankets up to cover herself. "Much better," she said, and as she said it she realized for the first time that her wounds were gone.

The man smiled at her, a sad, wistful sort of smile. He had a strong face, with charcoal-colored hair that curled in lazy ringlets and fell down into dark eyes somehow wider than they should be. Even seated, he was tall. And slender. He wore a suit and cape of some soft gray leather, and over that he wore melancholy like a cloak. "Claw marks," he said speculatively, while he smiled.

"Claw marks down your arm, and your clothes almost ripped from your back. Someone doesn't like you."

"Something," Sharra said. "A guardian, a guardian at the gate." She sighed. "There is always a guardian at the gate. The Seven don't like us to move from world to world. Me they like least of all."

His hands unfolded from beneath his chin and rested on the carved wooden arms of his chair. He nodded, but the wistful smile stayed. "So, then," he said. "You know the Seven, and you know the gates." His eyes strayed to her forehead. "The crown, of course. I should have guessed."

Sharra grinned at him. "You did guess. More than that, you knew. Who are you? What world is this?"

"My world," he said evenly. "I've named it a thousand times, but none of the names ever seem quite right. There was one once, a name I liked, a name that fit. But I've forgotten it. It was a long time ago. My name is Laren Dorr, or that was my name, once, when I had use for such a thing. Here and now it seems somewhat silly. But at least I haven't forgotten it."

"Your world," Sharra said. "Are you a king, then? A god?"

"Yes," Laren Dorr replied, with an easy laugh. "And more. I'm whatever I choose to be. There is no one around to dispute me."

"What did you do to my wounds?" she asked.

"I healed them." He gave an apologetic shrug. "It's my world. I have certain powers. Not the powers I'd like to have, perhaps, but powers nonetheless."

"Oh." She did not look convinced.

Laren waved an impatient hand. "You think it's impossible. Your crown, of course. Well, that's only half right. I could not harm you with my, ah, powers, not while you wear that. But I can help you." He smiled again, and his eyes grew soft and dreamy. "But it doesn't matter. Even if I could I would never harm you, Sharra. Believe that. It has been a long time."

Sharra looked startled. "You know my name. How?"

He stood up, smiling, and came across the room to sit beside her on the bed. And he took her hand before replying, wrapping it softly in his and stroking her with his thumb. "Yes, I know your name. You are Sharra, who moves between the worlds. Centuries ago, when the hills had a different shape and the violet sun burned scarlet at the very beginning of its cycle, they came to me and told me you would come. I hate them, all Seven, and I will always hate them, but that night I welcomed the vision they gave me. They told me only your name, and that you would come here, to my world. And one thing more, but that was enough. It was a promise. A promise of an ending or a start, of a change. And any change is welcome on this world. I've been alone here through a thousand sun-cycles, Sharra, and each cycle lasts for centuries. There are few events to mark the death of time."

Sharra was frowning. She shook her long, black hair, and in the dim light of the candles the soft red highlights glowed. "Are they that far ahead of me, then?" she said. "Do they know what will happen?" Her voice was troubled. She looked up at him. "This other thing they told you?"

He squeezed her hand, very gently. "They told me I would love you," Laren said. His voice still sounded sad. "But that was no great prophecy. I could have told them as much. There was a time long ago—I think the sun was yellow then—when I realized that I would love any voice that was not an echo of my own."

SHARRA WOKE AT DAWN, when shafts of bright purple light spilled into her room through a high arched window that had not been there the night before. Clothing had been laid out for her: a loose yellow robe, a jeweled dress of bright crimson, a suit of forest green. She chose the suit, dressed quickly. As she left, she paused to look out the window.

She was in a tower, looking out over crumbling stone battlements and a dusty triangular courtyard. Two other towers, twisted matchstick things with pointed conical spires, rose from the other corners of the triangle. There was a strong wind that whipped the rows of gray pennants set along the walls, but no other motion to be seen.

And, beyond the castle walls, no sign of the valley, none at all. The castle with its courtyard and its crooked towers was set atop a mountain, and far and away in all directions taller mountains loomed, presenting a panorama of black stone cliffs and jagged rocky walls and shining clean ice steeples that gleamed with a violet sheen. The window was sealed and closed, but the wind *looked* cold.

Her door was open. Sharra moved quickly down a twisting stone staircase, out across the courtyard into the main building, a low wooden structure built against the wall. She passed through countless rooms, some cold and empty save for dust, others richly furnished, before she found Laren Dorr eating breakfast.

There was an empty seat at his side; the table was heavily laden with food and drink. Sharra sat down and took a hot biscuit, smiling despite herself. Laren smiled back.

"I'm leaving today," she said, in between bites. "I'm sorry, Laren. I must find the gate."

The air of hopeless melancholy had not left him. It never did. "So you said last night," he replied, sighing. "It seems I have waited a long time for nothing."

There was meat, several types of biscuits, fruit, cheese, milk. Sharra filled a plate, face a little downcast, avoiding Laren's eyes. "I'm sorry," she repeated.

"Stay awhile," he said. "Only a short time. You can afford it, I would think. Let me show you what I can of my world. Let me sing to you." His eyes, wide and dark and very tired, asked the question.

She hesitated. "Well . . . it takes time to find the gate."

"Stay with me for a while, then."

"But Laren, eventually I must go. I have made promises. You understand?"

He smiled, gave a helpless shrug. "Yes. But look. I know where the gate is. I can show you, save you a search. Stay with me, oh, a month. A month as you measure time. Then I'll take you to the gate." He studied her. "You've been hunting a long, long time, Sharra. Perhaps you need a rest."

Slowly, thoughtfully, she ate a piece of fruit, watching him all the time. "Perhaps I do," she said at last, weighing things. "And there will be a guardian, of course. You could help me, then. A month . . . that's not so long. I've been on other worlds far longer than a month." She nodded, and a smile spread slowly across her face. "Yes," she said, still nodding. "That would be all right."

He touched her hand lightly. After breakfast he showed her the world they had given him.

They stood side by side on a small balcony atop the highest of the three towers, Sharra in dark green and Laren tall and soft in gray. They stood without moving, and Laren moved the world around them. He set the castle flying over restless, churning seas, where long, black serpent-heads peered up out of the water to watch them pass. He moved them to a vast, echoing cavern under the earth, all aglow with a soft green light, where dripping stalactites brushed down against the towers and herds of blind white goats moaned outside the battlements. He clapped his hands and smiled, and steam-thick jungle rose around them; trees that climbed each other in rubber ladders to the sky, giant flowers of a dozen different colors, fanged monkeys that chittered from the walls. He clapped again, and the walls were swept clean, and suddenly the courtyard dirt was sand and they were on an endless beach by the shore of a bleak gray ocean, and above the slow wheeling of a great blue bird with tissue-paper wings was the only movement to be seen. He showed her this, and more, and more, and in the end as dusk seemed to threaten in one place after another, he took the castle back to the ridge above the valley. And Sharra looked down on the forest of black-barked trees where he had found her and heard the mourning-birds whimper and weep among transparent leaves.

"It is not a bad world," she said, turning to him on the balcony.

"No," Laren replied. His hands rested on the cold stone railing, his eyes on the valley below "Not entirely. I explored it once, on foot, with a sword and a walking stick. There was a joy there, a real excitement. A new mystery behind every hill." He chuckled. "But that, too, was long ago. Now I know what lies behind every hill. Another empty horizon."

He looked at her and gave his characteristic shrug. "There are worse hells, I suppose. But this is mine."

"Come with me, then," she said. "Find the gate with me, and leave. There are other worlds. Maybe they are less strange and less beautiful, but you will not be alone."

He shrugged again. "You make it sound so easy," he said in a careless voice. "I have found the gate, Sharra. I have tried it a thousand times. The guardian does not stop me. I step through, briefly glimpse some other world, and suddenly I'm back in the courtyard. No. I cannot leave."

She took his hand in hers. "How sad. To be alone so long. I think you must be very strong, Laren. I would go mad in only a handful of years."

He laughed, and there was a bitterness in the way he did it. "Oh, Sharra. I have gone mad a thousand times, also. They cure me, love. They always cure me." Another shrug, and he put his arm around her. The wind was cold and rising. "Come," he said. "We must be inside before full dark."

They went up in the tower to her bedroom, and they sat together on her bed and Laren brought them food; meat burned black on the outside and red within, hot bread, wine. They ate, and they talked.

"Why are you here?" she asked him, in between mouthfuls, washing her words down with wine. "How did you offend them? Who were you, before?"

"I hardly remember, except in dreams," he told her. "And the dreams—it has been so long, I can't even recall which ones are truth and which are visions born of my madness." He sighed. "Sometimes I dream I was a king, a great king in a world other than this, and my crime was that I made my people happy. In happiness they turned against the Seven, and the temples fell idle. And I woke one day, within my room, within my castle, and found my servants gone. And when I went outside, my people and my world were also gone, and even the woman who slept beside me.

"But there are other dreams. Often I remember vaguely that I was a god. Well, an almost-god. I had powers, and teachings, and they were not the teachings of the Seven. They were afraid of me, each of them, for I was a match for any of them. But I could not meet all Seven together, and that was what they forced me to do. And then they left me only a small bit of my power, and set me here. It was cruel irony. As a god, I'd taught that people should turn to each other, that they could keep away the darkness by love and laughter and talk. So all these things the Seven took from me.

"And even that is not the worst. For there are other times when I think that I have always been here, that I was born here some endless age ago. And the memories are all false ones, sent to make me hurt the more."

Sharra watched him as he spoke. His eyes were not on her, but far away, full of fog and dreams and half-dead rememberings. And he spoke very slowly, in a voice that was also like fog, that drifted and curled and hid things, and you knew that there were mysteries there and things brooding just out of sight and far-off lights that you would never reach.

Laren stopped, and his eyes woke up again. "Ah, Sharra," he said. "Be careful how you go. Even your crown will not help you should they move on you directly. And the pale child Bakkalon will tear at you, and Naa-Slas feed upon your pain, and Saagael on your soul."

She shivered and cut another piece of meat. But it was cold and tough when she bit into it, and suddenly she noticed that the candles had burned very low. How long had she listened to him speak?

"Wait," he said then, and he rose and went outside, out the door near where the window had been. There was nothing there now but rough, gray stone; the windows all changed to solid rock with the last fading of the sun. Laren returned in a few moments, with a softly shining instrument of dark black wood slung around his neck on a leather cord. Sharra had never quite seen its like. It had sixteen strings, each a different color, and all up and down its length brightly glowing bars of light were inlaid amid the polished wood. When Laren sat, the bottom of the device rested on the floor and the top came to just above his shoulder. He stroked it lightly, speculatively; the lights glowed, and suddenly the room was full of swift-fading music.

"My companion," he said, smiling. He touched it again, and the music rose and died, lost notes without a tune. And he brushed the light-bars and the very air shimmered and changed color. He began to sing.

> I am the lord of loneliness,
> Empty my domain . . .

. . . the first words ran, sung low and sweet in Laren's mellow far-off fog voice. The rest of the song—Sharra clutched at it, heard each word and tried to remember, but lost them all. They brushed her, touched her, then melted away, back into the fog, here and gone again so swift that she could not remember quite what they had been. With the words, the music; wistful and melancholy and full of secrets, pulling at her, crying, whispering promises of a thousand tales untold. All around the room the candles flamed up brighter, and globes of light grew and danced and flowed together until the air was full of color.

Words, music, light; Laren Dorr put them all together and wove for her a vision.

She saw him then as he saw himself in his dreams; a king, strong and tall and still proud, with hair as black as hers and eyes that snapped. He was dressed all in shimmering white, pants that clung tight and a shirt that ballooned at the sleeves, and a great cloak that moved and curled in the wind like a sheet of solid snow. Around his brow he wore a crown of flashing silver, and a slim, straight sword flashed just as bright at his side. This Laren, this younger Laren, this dream vision, moved without melancholy, moved in a world of sweet ivory minarets and languid blue canals. And the world moved around him, friends and lovers and one special woman whom Laren drew with words and lights of fire, and there was an infinity of easy days and laughter.

Then, sudden, abrupt darkness. He was here.

The music moaned; the lights dimmed; the words grew sad and lost. Sharra saw Laren wake in a familiar castle, now deserted. She saw him search from room to room and walk outside to face a world he'd never seen. She watched him leave the castle, walk off towards the mists of a far horizon in the hope that those mists were smoke. And on and on he walked, and new horizons fell beneath his feet each day, and the great fat sun waxed red and orange and yellow, but still his world was empty. All the places he had shown her he walked to; all those and more; and finally, lost as ever, wanting home, the castle came to him.

By then his white had faded to dim gray. But still the song went on. Days went, and years, and centuries, and Laren grew tired and mad but never old. The sun shone green and violet and a savage hard blue-white, but with each cycle there was less color in his world. So Laren sang, of endless empty days and nights when music and memory were his only sanity, and his songs made Sharra feel it.

And when the vision faded and the music died and his soft voice melted away for the last time and Laren paused and smiled and looked at her, Sharra found herself trembling.

"Thank you," he said softly, with a shrug. And he took his instrument and left her for the night.

THE NEXT DAY DAWNED cold and overcast, but Laren took her out into the forests, hunting. Their quarry was a lean white thing, half cat, half gazelle, with too much speed for them to chase easily and too many teeth for them to kill. Sharra did not mind. The hunt was better than the kill. There was a singular, striking joy in that run through the darkling forest, holding a bow she never used and wearing a quiver of black wood arrows cut from the same dour trees that surrounded them. Both of them were bundled up tightly in gray fur, and Laren smiled out at her from under a wolf's-head hood. And the leaves beneath their boots, as clear and fragile as glass, cracked and splintered as they ran.

Afterwards, unblooded but exhausted, they returned to the castle, and Laren set out a great feast in the main dining room. They smiled at each other from opposite ends of a table fifty feet long, and Sharra watched the clouds roll by the window behind Laren's head, and later watched the window turn to stone.

"Why does it do that?" she asked. "And why don't you ever go outside at night?"

He shrugged. "Ah. I have reasons. The nights are, well, not good here." He sipped hot spice wine from a great jeweled cup. "The world you came from, where you started—tell me, Sharra, did you have stars?"

She nodded. "Yes. It's been so long, though. But I still remember. The nights were very dark and black, and the stars were little pinpoints of light, hard and cold and far away. You could see patterns sometimes. The men of my world, when they were young, gave names to each of those patterns, and told grand tales about them."

Laren nodded. "I would like your world, I think," he said. "Mine was like that, a little. But our stars were a thousand colors, and they moved, like ghostly lanterns in the night. Sometimes they drew veils around them to hide their light. And then our nights would be all shimmer and gossamer. Often I would go sailing at startime, myself and she whom I loved. Just so we could see the stars together. It was a good time to sing." His voice was growing sad again.

Darkness had crept into the room, darkness and silence, and the food was cold and Sharra could scarce see his face fifty long feet away. So she rose and went to him, and sat lightly on the great table near to his chair. And Laren nodded and smiled, and at once there was a *whooosh*, and all along the walls torches flared to sudden life in the long dining hall. He offered her more wine, and her fingers lingered on his as she took the glass.

"It was like that for us, too," Sharra said. "If the wind was warm enough, and other men were far away, then we liked to lie together in the open. Kaydar and I." She hesitated, looked at him.

His eyes were searching. "Kaydar?"

"You would have liked him, Laren. And he would have liked you, I think.

He was tall and he had red hair and there was a fire in his eyes. Kaydar had powers, as did I, but his were greater. And he had such a will. They took him one night, did not kill him, only took him from me and from our world. I have been hunting for him ever since. I know the gates, I wear the dark crown, and they will not stop me easily."

Laren drank his wine and watched the torchlight on the metal of his goblet. "There are an infinity of worlds, Sharra."

"I have as much time as I require. I do not age, Laren, no more than you do. I will find him."

"Did you love him so much?"

Sharra fought a fond, flickering smile, and lost. "Yes," she said, and now it was her voice that seemed a little lost. "Yes, so much. He made me happy, Laren. We were only together for a short time, but he *did* make me happy. The Seven cannot touch that. It was a joy just to watch him, to feel his arms around me and see the way he smiled."

"Ah," he said, and he did smile, but there was something very beaten in the way he did it. The silence grew very thick.

Finally Sharra turned to him. "But we have wandered a long way from where we started. You still have not told me why your windows seal themselves at night."

"You have come a long way, Sharra. You move between the worlds. Have you seen worlds without stars?"

"Yes. Many, Laren. I have seen a universe where the sun is a glowing ember with but a single world, and the skies are vast and vacant by night. I have seen the land of frowning jesters, where there is no sky and the hissing suns burn below the ocean. I have walked the moors of Carradyne, and watched dark sorcerers set fire to a rainbow to light that sunless land."

"This world has no stars," Laren said.

"Does that frighten you so much that you stay inside?"

"No. But it has something else instead." He looked at her. "Would you see?" She nodded.

As abruptly as they had lit, the torches all snuffed out. The room swam with blackness. And Sharra shifted on the table to look over Laren's shoulder. Laren did not move. But behind him, the stones of the window fell away like dust and light poured in from outside.

The sky was very dark, but she could see clearly, for against the darkness a shape was moving. Light poured from it, and the dirt in the courtyard and the stones of the battlements and the gray pennants were all bright beneath its glow. Puzzling, Sharra looked up.

Something looked back. It was taller than the mountains and it filled up half the sky, and though it gave off light enough to see the castle by, Sharra knew that it was dark beyond darkness. It had a man-shape, roughly, and it wore a long cape and a cowl, and below that was blackness even fouler than the rest. The only sounds were Laren's soft breathing and the beating of her heart and the distant weeping of a mourning-bird, but in her head Sharra could hear demonic laughter.

The shape in the sky looked down at her, in her, and she felt the cold dark in her soul. Frozen, she could not move her eyes. But the shape did move. It turned and raised a hand, and then there was something else up there with it, a tiny man-shape with eyes of fire that writhed and screamed and called to her.

Sharra shrieked and turned away. When she glanced back, there was no window. Only a wall of safe, sure stone, and a row of torches burning, and Laren holding her within strong arms. "It was only a vision," he told her. He pressed her tight against him, and stroked her hair. "I used to test myself at night," he said, more to himself than to her. "But there was no need. They take turns up there, watching me, each of the Seven. I have seen them too often, burning with black light against the clean dark of the sky, and holding those I loved. Now I don't look. I stay inside and sing, and my windows are made of night-stone."

"I feel . . . fouled," she said, still trembling a little.

"Come," he said. "There is water upstairs, you can clean away the cold. And then I'll sing for you." He took her hand and led her up into the tower.

Sharra took a hot bath while Laren set up his instrument and tuned it in the bedroom. He was ready when she returned, wrapped head to foot in a huge fluffy brown towel. She sat on the bed, drying her hair and waiting.

And Laren gave her visions.

He sang his other dream this time, the one where he was a god and the enemy of the Seven. The music was a savage pounding thing, shot through with lightning and tremors of fear, and the lights melted together to form a scarlet battlefield where a blinding-white Laren fought shadows and the shapes of nightmare. There were seven of them, and they formed a ring around him and darted in and out, stabbing him with lances of absolute black, and Laren answered them with fire and storm. But in the end they overwhelmed him, the light faded, and then the song grew soft and sad again, and the vision blurred as lonely dreaming centuries flashed by.

Hardly had the last notes fallen from the air and the final shimmers died than Laren started once again. A new song this time, and one he did not know so well. His fingers, slim and graceful, hesitated and retraced themselves more than once, and his voice was shaky, too, for he was making up some of the words as he went along. Sharra knew why. For this time he sang of her, a ballad of her quest. Of burning love and endless searching, of worlds beyond worlds, of dark crowns and waiting guardians that fought with claws and tricks and lies. He took every word that she had spoken, and used each, and transformed each. In the bedroom, glittering panoramas formed where hot white suns burned beneath eternal oceans and hissed in clouds of steam, and men ancient beyond time lit rainbows to keep away the dark. And he sang Kaydar, and he sang him true somehow, he caught and drew the fire that had been Sharra's love and made her believe anew.

But the song ended with a question, the halting finale lingering in the air, echoing, echoing. Both of them waited for the rest, and both knew there was no more. Not yet.

Sharra was crying. "My turn, Laren," she said. Then: "Thank you. For giving Kaydar back to me."

"It was only a song," he said, shrugging. "It's been a long time since I had a new song to sing."

Once again he left her, touching her cheek lightly at the door as she stood there with the blanket wrapped around her. Then Sharra locked the door behind him and went from candle to candle, turning light to darkness with a breath. And she threw the towel over a chair and crawled under the blankets and lay a long, long time before drifting off to sleep.

It was still dark when she woke, not knowing why. She opened her eyes and lay quietly and looked around the room, and nothing was there, nothing was changed. Or was there?

And then she saw him, sitting in the chair across the room with his hands locked under his chin, just as he had sat that first time. His eyes steady and unmoving, very wide and dark in a room full of night. He sat very still. "Laren?" she called, softly, still not quite sure the dark form was him.

"Yes," he said. He did not move. "I watched you last night, too, while you slept. I have been alone here for longer than you can ever imagine, and very soon now I will be alone again. Even in sleep, your presence is a wonder."

"Oh, Laren," she said. There was a silence, a pause, a weighing and an unspoken conversation. Then she threw back the blanket, and Laren came to her.

BOTH OF THEM had seen centuries come and go. A month, a moment; much the same.

They slept together every night, and every night Laren sang his songs while Sharra listened. They talked throughout dark hours, and during the day they swam nude in crystalline waters that caught the purple glory of the sky. They made love on beaches of fine white sand, and they spoke a lot of love.

But nothing changed. And finally the time drew near. On the eve of the night before the day that was end, at twilight, they walked together through the shadowed forest where he'd found her.

Laren had learned to laugh during his month with Sharra, but now he was silent again. He walked slowly, clutched her hand hard in his, and his mood was more gray than the soft silk shirt he wore. Finally, by the side of the valley stream, he sat and pulled her down by his side. They took off their boots and let the water cool their feet. It was a warm evening, with a lonely, restless wind, and already you could hear the first of the mourning-birds.

"You must go," he said, still holding her hand but never looking at her. It was a statement, not a question.

"Yes," she said, and the melancholy had touched her, too, and there were leaden echoes in her voice.

"My words have all left me, Sharra," Laren said. "If I could sing for you a vision now, I would. A vision of a world once empty, made full by us and our children. I could offer that. My world has beauty and wonder and mystery enough, if only there were eyes to see it. And if the nights are evil, well, men have faced dark nights before, on other worlds in other times. I would love you, Sharra, as much as I am able. I would try to make you happy."

"Laren . . . " she started. But he quieted her with a glance.

"No, I could say that, but I will not. I have no right. Kaydar makes you happy. Only a selfish fool would ask you to give up that happiness to share my misery. Kaydar is all fire and laughter, while I am smoke and song and sadness. I have been alone too long, Sharra. The gray is part of my soul now, and I would not have you darkened. But still . . . "

She took his hand in both of hers, lifted it, and kissed it quickly. Then, releasing him, she lay her head on his unmoving shoulder. "Try to come with me, Laren," she said. "Hold my hand when we pass through the gate, and perhaps the dark crown will protect you."

"I will try anything you ask. But don't ask me to believe that it will work." He sighed. "You have countless worlds ahead of you, Sharra, and I cannot see your ending. But it is not here. That I know. And maybe that is best. I don't know anymore, if I ever did. I remember love vaguely, I think I can recall what it was like, and I remember that it never lasts. Here, with both of us unchanging and immortal, how could we help but to grow bored? Would we hate each other then? I'd not want that." He looked at her then, and smiled an aching, melancholy smile. "I think that you had known Kaydar for only a short time, to be so in love with him. Perhaps I'm being devious after all. For in finding Kaydar, you may lose him. The fire will go out someday, my love, and the magic will die. And then you may remember Laren Dorr."

Sharra began to weep, softly. Laren gathered her to him, and kissed her, and whispered a gentle "No." She kissed back, and they held each other, wordless.

When at last the purple gloom had darkened to near-black, they put back on their boots and stood. Laren hugged her and smiled.

"I *must* go," Sharra said. "I *must*. But leaving is hard, Laren, you must believe that."

"I do," he said. "I love you *because* you will go, I think. Because you cannot forget Kaydar, and you will not forget the promises you made. You are Sharra, who goes between the worlds, and I think the Seven must fear you far more than any god I might have been. If you were not you, I would not think as much of you."

"Once you said you would love any voice that was not any echo of your own."

Laren shrugged. "As I have often said, love, *that* was a very long time ago."

They were back inside the castle before darkness, for a final meal, a final night, a final song. They got no sleep that night, and Laren sang to her again just before dawn. It was not a very good song, though; it was an aimless, rambling thing about a wandering minstrel on some nondescript world. Very little of interest ever happened to the minstrel; Sharra couldn't quite get the point of the song, and Laren sang it listlessly. It seemed an odd farewell, but both of them were troubled.

He left her with the sunrise, promising to change clothes and meet her in the courtyard. And sure enough, he was waiting when she got there, smiling at her, calm and confident. He wore a suit of pure white; pants that clung, a shirt that puffed up at the sleeves, and a great heavy cape that snapped and billowed in the rising wind. But the purple sun stained him with its shadow rays.

Sharra walked out to him and took his hand. She wore tough leather, and there was a knife in her belt, for dealing with the guardian. Her hair, jet-black with light-born glints of red and purple, blew as freely as his cape, but the dark crown was in place. "Good-bye, Laren," she said. "I wish I had given you more."

"You have given me enough. In all the centuries that come, in all the sun-cycles that lie ahead, I will remember. I shall measure time by you, Sharra. When the sun rises one day and its color is blue fire, I will look at it and say, 'Yes, this is the first blue sun after Sharra came to me.'"

She nodded. "And I have a new promise. I will find Kaydar, someday. And if I free him, we will come back to you, both of us together, and we will pit my crown and Kaydar's fires against all the darkness of the Seven."

Laren shrugged. "Good. If I'm not here, be sure to leave a message," he said. And then he grinned.

"Now, the gate. You said you would show me the gate."

Laren turned and gestured at the shortest tower, a sooty stone structure Sharra had never been inside. There was a wide wooden door in its base. Laren produced a key.

"Here?" she said, looking puzzled. "In the castle?"

"Here," Laren said. They walked across the courtyard, to the door. Laren inserted the heavy metal key and began to fumble with the lock. While he worked, Sharra took one last look around, and felt the sadness heavy on her soul. The other towers looked bleak and dead, the courtyard was forlorn, and beyond the high icy mountains was only an empty horizon. There was no sound but Laren working at the lock, and no motion but the steady wind that kicked up the courtyard dust and flapped the seven gray pennants that hung along each wall. Sharra shivered with sudden loneliness.

Laren opened the door. No room inside; only a wall of moving fog, a fog without color or sound or light. "Your gate, my lady," the singer said.

Sharra watched it, as she had watched it so many times before. What world was next? she wondered. She never knew. But maybe in the next one, she would find Kaydar.

She felt Laren's hand on her shoulder. "You hesitate," he said, his voice soft.

Sharra's hand went to her knife. "The guardian," she said suddenly. "There is always a guardian." Her eyes darted quickly round the courtyard.

Laren sighed. "Yes. Always. There are some who try to claw you to pieces, and some who try to get you lost, and some who try to trick you into taking the wrong gate. There are some who hold you with weapons, some with chains, some with lies. And there is one, at least, who tried to stop you with love. Yet he was true for all that, and he never sang you false."

And with a hopeless, loving shrug, Laren shoved her through the gate.

DID SHE FIND HIM, in the end, her lover with the eyes of fire? Or is she searching still? What guardian did she face next?

When she walks at night, a stranger in a lonely land, does the sky have stars?

I don't know. He doesn't. Maybe even the Seven do not know. They are powerful, yes, but all power is not theirs, and the number of worlds is greater than even they can count.

There is a girl who goes between the worlds, but her path is lost in legend by now. Maybe she is dead, and maybe not. Knowledge moves slowly from world to world, and not all of it is true.

But this we know: In an empty castle below a purple sun, a lonely minstrel waits, and sings of her.

≫•≪

In Yoon Ha Lee's story, the High Fleet of the Knifebird is still fighting the war that strategist Niristez promised to win. She has lost a match, but there is still a game—perhaps more than one—to play.

THE KNIGHT OF CHAINS, THE DEUCE OF STARS

Yoon Ha Lee

THE TOWER IS A BLACK SPIRE upon a world whose only sun is a million starships wrecked into a mass grave. Light the color of fossils burns from the ships, and at certain hours, the sun casts shadows that mutter the names of vanquished cities and vanished civilizations. It is said that when the tower's sun finally darkens, the universe's clocks will stop.

But the sun, however strange, is not why people make the labyrinthine journey to the tower. The tower guards the world's hollow depths, in which may be found the universe's games. Every game played among the universe's peoples was once trapped in the world's terrible underground passages, and every one was mined and bargained for by some traveler. It is for such a game that the exile Niristez comes here now, in a ship of ice and iron and armageddon engines.

This is the hand Niristez played long ago: The Ten of Theorems; the Knight of Hounds; the Nine of Chains, the bad-luck symbol she uses as a calling card; and she kept two cards hidden, but lost the round anyway.

Niristez carries the last two cards with her. They come from a deck made of coalescent paper, which will reveal the cards drawn when she chooses and not before. Today, the backs show the tower in abbreviated brushstrokes, like a needle of dark iron plunging into an eye. Coalescent cards are not known for their subtlety.

She may have lost that match, but it's not the only game she's playing, and this time she means to win.

THE TOWER HAS A WARDEN, or perhaps the warden has a tower. The warden's name is Daechong. He is usually polite. It was one of the first lessons he learned. Most people don't first notice the warden when they meet him, or the rooms crowded with agate-eyed figurines, flowers of glass, cryptochips sliced into mosaics. They first notice the warden's gun. It is made of living bone and barbed wire and smoke-silver axioms. It would have a stock of mother-of-pearl, if pearls were born from gangrenous stars. It has a long, lustrous barrel forged in a bomb's hellheart. And along the barrel is an inscription in whatever language your heart answers to: *I never miss.*

When he is human-shaped, Daechong is modestly tall, with a narrow face and dark hair cut short. His hands move too quickly to be reassuring, even if he always keeps them in sight. He wears gray, although sometimes his definition of "gray" has more in common with the black static that you find on the other side of your eyelids.

Daechong has been chained to the tower since the tower came into existence. He remembers his first visitors. It took him very little time to understand that he couldn't leave, and so he murdered them. After that, for a long time, he was alone. When more visitors started to arrive, he was very careful with them, having learned that silence is wearisome company.

Anyone who desires to descend into the world with its unmined games must persuade him to let them pass. Daechong is not recalcitrant, precisely, but he likes to challenge his visitors to games himself. It is possible, although not easy, to defeat him. Sometimes defeat carries a small penalty, sometimes a great one, according to his mood.

It is inadvisable to threaten him, and especially inadvisable to attempt to separate him from his gun. The gun admits no bullets and speaks no words of fire or fission. It gives forth no smoke, no sparks, no suppurating oil.

Yet the gun always hits what Daechong intends to shoot. Killing is one of the few pleasures available to him, and he indulges either as part of a wager or in self-defense. It doesn't matter whether the target is in front of him, or behind him, or in another galaxy, behind the ash-shroud of stars that failed to be born. Sometimes, when he fires, a quantum sentience shudders apart into spin-states pinned to forever zeros. Sometimes a city inverts itself, plunging its arches and cobweb skyroads into the earth, leaving its citizens to suffocate. The story goes that the sun-of-starships was Daechong's response to some reckless admiral bent on conquering the tower, although Daechong refuses to say anything definite on the matter.

It has been a long time since Daechong feared anyone. When he learns that Niristez of the Nine of Chains has asked for an audience, fear is not what he feels. But after all this time, he is still capable of curiosity; he will not turn her away.

THERE IS AN OLD STORY you already know, and a variant on it that you have already guessed.

Take a chessboard, eight squares by eight squares, sixty-four in total. Play begins with the first square being paid for with a single death. On the second day, fill in the next square with two deaths. On the third day, four; on the fourth day, eight. The sequence continues in this manner. The question is when both parties will find the toll of deaths such that they can no longer stomach the price of play.

We use chess—with its pieces intimating knights and kings and castles, sword-crash wars of old—for convenience, although it could be anything else. And we restrict ourselves to powers of two for convenience as well, although the mathematics of escalation knows no such boundary.

DAECHONG WAITS for Niristez in one of the highest rooms of the tower. He doesn't know what she looks like, and he declines to watch her enter by the door that will admit her but which will not allow him to leave. Besides, he can hear her footsteps wherever she is in the tower, or on the world. She has a militant reputation: he can tell that by the percussion of her boots.

This room contains musical instruments. He doesn't know how to play any of them, but he can tune and maintain them. His current favorite is a flute made of pipe scavenged from some extinguished city's scrap heap. There's a great curving harp, a lithophone, two bells. On occasion, one of his visitors breaks an instrument, and then he burns up the fragments; that's all.

The footsteps slow. She's reached the room. The lights in the tower will have told her where to go. On occasion, some visitor strays, and then he has to fetch them out of the confusion of hallways and shadows. It is sometimes tempting to let them wander, but by now the habits of courtesy are strong.

Niristez knocks once, twice. Waits.

"The door is unlocked," Daechong says.

He regards her thoughtfully as she enters the room. She is taller than he is, and her hair is like a banner. In the intolerable aeons of her exile, she has gone by many names, but Niristez is the one she prefers. It means *I promise.* The name is a lie, although most people know better than to mention it to her face. Once she had a reputation for always keeping her promises. Once she swore to win an unwinnable war. Then she fled her people, and the war has not, to this day, been won.

Her most notable feature, aside from her reputation, is not her height, or the gloves made from skinned fractals, or even the sword-of-treatises knotted at her side. It is her eyes, whose color cannot be discerned in any light but corpselight. In her eyes you can see a map forever drawing and redrawing itself, a map that knows where your flaws may be found, a map that knows how your desires may be drowned. Long ago, she was a strategist for the High Fleet of the Knifebird, and while no one now refers to her by her old rank, people remember what her eyes mean. Daechong isn't concerned by them, terrible though they are. She will already have charted his greatest weakness, and she doesn't need her unique form of vision to do so.

Niristez isn't looking at his gun, which is easily within his reach. That isn't saying much. No matter where it lies, the gun is always within his reach. But its presence is like a splinter of black dreaming, inescapable.

Niristez is, however, bearing a bottle of amber-green glass, with a cork whose eye stares unblinking at Daechong. "I thought," she says dryly, "it would be ungracious if I didn't bring a gift, considering that I am here to bargain for a favor."

"It's very considerate of you," Daechong says. "Shall I open it here?"

Niristez shrugs. "It's yours now, so you may as well suit yourself."

He keeps glasses in a red-stained cabinet. She's not the first person to bring him liquor. He picks out two spiraling flutes, with gold wire patterns reminiscent of inside-out automata and melting gears. It's tempting to shoot the bottle open, but that would be showing off, so he picks the cork out with his fingers. He's killed people by digging out their eyes; this isn't so different.

The liquor effervesces and leaves querulous sparks in the air, spelling out hectic inequalities and the occasional exclamatory couplet. Daechong looks at it longingly. "Would you be offended if I burn it up?" he says. Anything for a taste of the world outside. "I can't actually drink."

"I can't claim to be difficult to offend," Niristez says, "but as I said, it's yours now." She takes a sip herself. The inequalities flare up and die down into first-order contradictions as they pass her lips.

Daechong taps the rim of the glass. For a moment, nothing happens. Then the entire glassful goes up in smoke the color of lamentations, sweet and thick, and he inhales deeply. "You must find my tastes predictable," he says.

Niristez smiles, and shadows deepen in her eyes. "Let's say it's something we have in common."

"You mentioned that you wished to bargain," he says. "Might I ask what you're looking for?" Ordinarily he would not be so direct, but Niristez has a reputation for impatience.

"I want what everyone wants who comes here," Niristez says. "I want a game. But it's not just a game." It never is. "You know my reputation, I trust."

"It would be hard to escape it, even living where I do," Daechong says.

"On this world is the stratagem that will enable me to keep my promise." Niristez's eyes are very dark now, and her smile darker still. "I wish to buy the game that contains it from you. I've spent a great deal of time determining that this game must exist. It will win me the war of wars; it will let me redeem my name."

Daechong taps the glass again. This time it chimes softly, like a bell of bullets. Some of the musical instruments reverberate in response. "I'm afraid that you are already losing my interest," he says. "Games that admit an obvious dominant strategy tend not to be very interesting from the players' point of view." It's difficult to be a warden of games and not feel responsible for the quality of the ones that he permits to escape into the outside world. "I could let you root around for it, but I assume you're after a certain amount of guidance."

Although he is not infallible, Daechong has an instinct for the passages. He knows where the richest strata are, where the games sought are likeliest to be found. When people bargain with him, it's not simply access that they seek. Anyone can wander through the twisty passages, growing intoxicated by the combinatoric vapors. It's another matter to have a decent chance of finding what they want.

"That's correct," Niristez says. "I have spent long enough gnawing at the universe's laws and spitting out dead ends. I don't intend to waste any more time now that I know what I'm after." She leans forward. "I am sure that you will hear me out. Because what I offer you is your freedom."

Daechong tilts his head. "It's not the first time someone has made that claim, so forgive me for being skeptical."

He cannot remember ever setting foot outside the tower; it has a number of windows almost beyond reckoning, which open and close at his desire, and which reveal visions terrible and troubling. Poetry-of-malice written into the accretion disks of black holes. Moons covered with sculptures of violet-green fungus grown in the hollowed-out bodies of prisoners of war. Planets with their seas boiled dry and the fossils bleached upon alkaline shores. These and other things he can see just by turning his head and wishing it so.

Yet he thinks, sometimes, of what it would be like to walk up stairs that lead to a plaza ringed by pillars of rough-hewn stone, or perhaps gnarled trees, and not the tower's highest floor with its indiscriminate collection of paintings, tapestries, and curious statuettes that croak untrue prophecies. (More gifts. He wouldn't dream of getting rid of them.) What it would be like to travel to a gas giant with its dustweave rings, or to a fortress of neutronium whispers, or to a spot far between stars that is empty except for the froth of quantum bubbling and the microwave hiss. What it would be like to walk outside and look up at the sky, any sky. There isn't a sky in the universe whose winds would scour him, whose rains would poison him, whose stars would pierce his eyes. But his immunity does him no good here.

"Call my bluff, then," she says, her smile growing knife-sweet. "You like a challenge, don't you? You won't see me here again if you turn me down. If nothing else, it's a moment's diversion. Let's play a game, you and I. If I win, you will tell me where to find my stratagem. If I lose, I will tell you how you can unshackle yourself from this tower—and you can set me whatever penalty you see fit."

"I don't remember the very beginning of my existence," Daechong says softly. "But I was made of pittances of mercy and atrocities sweeter than honey. I was made of carrion calculations and unpolished negations. They say your shadow is shaped like massacres, Niristez. You haven't killed a fraction of the people that I have. Are you sure you want to offer this? I am not accustomed to losing, especially when the stakes matter to me."

He doesn't speak of the penalties he extracts when people lie to him. For all the dreadful things he's done, he has always respected honesty.

"I am sure," she says.

"The High Fleet of the Knifebird is still fighting the war you promised to win. It would not be difficult for me to shoot the key players into cinders."

The lines of her face become sharper, keener. "I know," she says. "But I made my promise. This is the only way to keep it. I will attempt the gamble. I always keep my promises."

Niristez has been saying this for a long time, and people have been tactful when she does so for a long time. Daechong, too, is tactful. It does him no harm. "If you are certain," he says, "then let us play."

AT THIS POINT, it is worth describing the war that the High Fleet of the Knifebird has been fighting for so long, against an opponent that is everywhere distributed and which has no name but the name that particles mutter as they decay. The High Fleet has not yet raised the redshift banner that indicates defeat, but the fact that they have been fighting all this time without much in the way of lasting gains is hardly a point of pride.

High Fleet doctrine says that they are finite warriors fighting an infinite war, and the stakes are nothing less than control of the universe's laws. Each small war in the continuum is itself a gamepiece in the war of wars, placed or extinguished according to local conditions. The value of each piece is contextual both in time and in space. A duel between two spindleships at the edge of an obscure asteroid belt may, at times, weigh more heavily than a genocidal war between a dozen star empires.

In the game of Go, it is possible for players to play such that alternating captures of single stones would cause repeating positions. In principle, these moves could be played forever, and the game would never end. However, the rule called ko prevents such repetition from happening immediately.

There exists a type of ko situation, the ten thousand year ko, which is often left unresolved—sometimes until the game's conclusion—because the player who enters the battle first does so at a disadvantage. The war of wars is widely held to have run afoul of something similar.

You may speculate as to the application to the ex-strategist Niristez's situation, although most people believe that she is not capable of such subtlety. Indeed, it's not clear why she would be interested in prolonging the war of wars, unless she intended it as revenge for her loss of status. Even if she meant only to force the universe into an asymptotic cooldown rather than a condensed annihilation, this would hardly be an unambiguous victory for her or her former allies. But then, if she were skilled enough to carry out this gambit anyway, surely she wouldn't have fallen in the first place.

DAECHONG ALLOWS NIRISTEZ the choice of game, since she is the petitioner. The choice itself might tell him something about her, although he doubts it will be anything he couldn't already have figured out. He is surprised, then thoughtful, when she requests a linguistic game played upon competing lattices. Its name means something like "the calculus of verses." He would not have suspected her of a fondness for poetry, even the poetry of eradication. It is likely that the game has real-world manifestations, not that he has any way of checking.

The game has a deployment phase, in which they breed pensive sememes and seed rival phonologies, braid the syntactical structures that they will be pitting against each other. "Do you have the opportunity to read much?" Niristez asks him, no doubt thinking of varieties of literature to wield against him.

"On occasion people bring me books," he says. Sometimes they are tattooed on wafers of silicon. Sometimes they come bound in metal beaten thin from the corpses of deprecated clocks. Occasionally they have pages of irradiated paper. He is especially fond of the neutron variety. "I don't often read them, however." He reads fastest by—surprise—burning up the books, and while he did that a few times by accident in the early days, he saves that now for special occasions.

"Well," Niristez says, "the universe is infested with words of all kinds. I can't blame you for being choosy." She does something exceedingly clever with the placement of a cultural singularity to urge her budding language to better readiness for the engagement.

Daechong's deployments are conservative. In his experience, people who focus too much on the setup phase of the game tangle themselves up during the match proper. "I am fluent in very many languages," he says, which is an understatement. He has always assumed that the knack is a requirement, or perhaps a gift, of his position. "But I enjoy talking to people more."

"Yes," she says, "I imagine you would."

They are quiet through the rest of the deployment phase, although Daechong pours Niristez another glass of the wine she brought him, since she appears to be thirsty. She sips at it little by little, without any sign of enjoyment. He considers having another glass himself, but the smoke is still pleasantly strong in the air; no need yet.

When the game begins in earnest, the lattices light up in the colors of drifting constellations and burning sodium and firefly sonatas. Niristez's first move gives her entire language an imperialistic focus. His response is to nurture a slang of resistance.

"I am not familiar with the High Fleet's customs," Daechong says while she considers a typological imperative. "Will it be difficult to secure your reinstatement?"

This is not, strictly speaking, a courteous thing to bring up; but they are playing now. She will expect him to try to unsettle her.

Her laugh is so brief he wonders if he imagined it. "That's an open question. Tell me, Warden, if you get free of this place, where will you go?"

A predictable riposte. "I don't know," he says, although people have asked him before. His answer always changes. "The universe is a very large place. I expect that wherever I start, I can find something new to see. At the moment, I wouldn't mind visiting a binary star system. Something simple and ordinary."

That's not it at all. He likes the thought of stars that have companions, even though he knows better than to think that such things matter to stars.

Niristez seeds the plebeian chants with prestige terms from her own language, denaturing his slang. "What if you find that you were happier here?"

"There's always that risk, yes."

"The possibility doesn't bother you?"

She's asking questions she knows the answers to, which is also part of the game. "Of course it bothers me," Daechong says, "but if I never leave, I will never find out." He initiates a memetic protest. Unstable, although it has the advantage of propagating swiftly.

"I have seen a great deal of the world outside," Niristez remarks. For a moment, he can almost see what color her eyes are. "There are people who wall themselves away deliberately, you know. Ascetics and philosophers and solitude artists. Some of them would give a great deal to take your place."

"As far as anyone knows," Daechong says, "I have been here since the first stars winked open. My time here has hardly been infinite, but it's still a long time, as finite numbers go. I have no reason to believe any successor of mine would spend less time here."

She studies his move's ramifications with a slight frown, then glances around as though seeing the instruments for the first time. Nevertheless, it doesn't escape his attention that she singles out the flute for scrutiny. "Your imprisonment has given you unprecedented access to the games of the universe," she says. "Or do you take no pleasure in the things you guard?"

He considers his answer while she puts together a propaganda campaign. Blunt, but perhaps that's to be expected of someone with a military background. Still, he can't let down his guard. She may be covering for a more devious ploy. "I can't claim that the position hasn't been without its privileges," he says mildly.

Daechong has played games on involute boards, games of sacrifice and skullduggery and smiling assurances, games where you keep score with burning worlds. He has played games with rules that mutate turn by turn, and games where you bet with the currency of senescent ambition, and games that handicap the stronger player with cognitive manacles. Most of the time, he wins, and he never throws a match, even when he's tempted to just to see what would happen.

After a few moments, he counters the propaganda campaign with a furtive renaissance of the musical forms that he put in place during deployment. It's early to do this, but he'd rather respond now than give Niristez's tactic a chance to play out fully. People are sometimes startled by his comfort with music, for all that he plays no instrument. Music has its own associations with games and sports: battle hymns, marches, aggressive rhythms beaten upon the space-time membrane.

They test each other with more such exchanges. Niristez's fingers tap the side of the table before she manages to still them. Daechong doesn't take that lapse at face value, either. "In the old days, it was held that my vision meant I could not be defeated," she says abruptly, "although that has never been the case. Seeing a no-win situation opening its jaws in your direction isn't necessarily helpful."

"Have there been many of those in your career?"

"You only need one," she says, not without humor. "And even then, I've orchestrated my share of dreadful battles. Gravitational tides and neutron cannons and the slaughters you get when you use a thermodynamic vise on someone's sputtering sun. Doomships that intone stagnancy-curses into the ecosystems of entire planets. Civilizations' worth of skeletons knit together with ligatures-of-damnation and made to fight unsheathed in the crackling cold void. Dead people everywhere, no matter how you count the cost."

She's either trying to warn him or distract him. They might be the same thing. "You wouldn't have been at personal risk?" he asks. Although he's spoken with soldiers of all sorts, the staggering variety of military conventions means that he is cautious about making assumptions. In any case, he's met very few Knifebird officers.

"Not as such," she says, "although there's always the risk of an assassination attempt. A few have tried." She doesn't bother telling him what happened to them. In this matter, anyway, they are similar.

Niristez's attacks are starting to give way before Daechong's tradition of stories handed down mouth to mouth, myths to succor insurrection. A myth doesn't have to roar like dragons or fight like tigers. A myth can murmur possibilities with fox words. A myth can be subtle.

He doesn't point this out, but he doesn't have to. The rueful cast of her mouth tells him she is thinking it.

Niristez redoubles her efforts, but her early-game deployment has locked her into rigid, not to say tyrannical, stratagems. Unless she comes up with something extraordinary, they are nearing the point where the game is effectively over, even if a few of the lattices' regions can still be contested.

At last Niristez picks up a hollowed-out demagogue node and tips it over: surrender. "There's no sense in dragging this out any further," she says.

Daechong is starting to become alarmed: Niristez should be afraid, or resigned, or angry; anything but this calculating alertness. It does occur to him that, by choosing her strategy so early, she dictated his. But that was only part of the game, and in the meantime, they have their agreement.

He doesn't reach for the gun—not yet.

"It doesn't matter anyway," Niristez says. The side of her mouth tips up, and there are fissures like needles in her irises. "We both win."

He doesn't understand.

"I never needed to go into the passages," she says, and her voice is very steady. "I'm looking at what I seek already. Because the game the tower plays is you, Warden."

A myth can be subtle, and some regard Daechong as one himself; but he isn't the only myth in the room.

"Explain yourself," Daechong says, quiet and cutting.

"Everyone has been mining the planet for its games," Niristez says, "but no one has been looking at what's been right in front of them all this time. In a way, you are a game, are you not? You are a challenge to be met. You have rules, give rewards, incur penalties.

"I don't know who mined you out of the dark depths. It was probably long ago. You must have been one of the first games after the universe's very machinery of equations. And when they realized just what they had let loose into the world, when they realized your name, they locked you up in the tower. Of course, it was too late."

Niristez doesn't tell him what his name has to be. He is figuring that out for himself. The gun's presence presses against his awareness like an attar of carnage.

"You promised me my freedom," Daechong says after a long, brittle silence. "Or is that a trick, too?"

"Only if you think of it as one," she says. "You could have left at any time if you'd only known, Warden. You're only trapped here so long as you are a prisoner of your own nature. As the warden, you alone can determine this. If you choose to be a game no longer, you can walk out at any time."

Now she looks at the gun. At the dull bone, at the spiky wires, at the inscription: *I never miss.* "Destroy the gun," she says, "and walk free. It's up to you."

"If you had won," Daechong says, "you would have demanded that I come with you."

He rises. She tilts her head back to meet his gaze, unflinching. Of all things, her eyes are—not kind, precisely, but sympathetic. "Yes," she said. "But this way you have a choice."

"You're implying that, when I leave, all the wars end. That the game of war ceases to exist."

"Yes," she says.

All wars over. Everywhere. All at once.

"I can only assume that at this point in time, such a suspension of hostilities would leave the High Fleet of the Knifebird in a winning position," Daechong says.

Her eyes darken in color. "Warden," she says, "if I have learned one thing in my years of exile, it is that there are victors in war, but no one *wins.*"

"I could wait for a position unfavorable to your cause," he says. "Thwart you." They're playing for higher stakes now.

"You could try," she says, "but I know what passes outside this tower, and you don't." The map in her eyes is fractal-deep, and encompasses the universe's many conflagrations.

"You played well," Daechong says. He isn't merely being polite, and he doesn't say this to many people. "I should have been better prepared."

"The difference between us is this," she says. "You are a tactician, and you fought the battle; but I am a strategist, and I fought the war. *I keep my promises.*"

"I don't concern myself with ethics," Daechong says, "but I am surprised that you would think of something as far-reaching and devastating as war to be nothing more than a game."

"It's all in how you define the set," she murmurs.

The gun is in his hand. He points it at the wall, not at Niristez, and not at himself. (This is habit. In reality, this doesn't make Niristez any safer.) It is beautiful in the way of annihilated stars, beautiful in the way of violated postulates. And she is telling him that he would have to extinguish it forever.

"It comes down to this," Niristez says. The smile is gone from her mouth, but it kindles in her eyes. "Is thwarting my promise in the war of wars more important to you than the freedom you have desired for so long?"

IN THE GAME OF GO, groups of stones are said to be alive or dead depending on whether or not the opponent can kill them. But sometimes the opponents have two groups that live together: Neither can attack the other without killing itself. This situation is called *seki*, or mutual life.

THE TOWER IS A BLACK SPIRE upon a world whose only sun is a million starships wrecked into a mass grave. There is no light in the starships, and as time goes by, fewer and fewer people remember when the sun-of-starships gave forth any radiance at all. The shadows still mutter the names of vanquished cities and vanished civilizations, but of course the world is nothing but shadow now, and the few inhabitants remaining find it impossible to hear anything else.

Now and again people make the labyrinthine journey to the tower, which plunges into the world's hollow depths. But the tower no longer has any doors or any windows, or a warden to greet visitors, and the games that might have been dug out of the dark passages are trapped there.

Two cards of coalescent paper can, however, be found before the tower. Even the wind dares not move them from where they rest. One of them displays the Knight of Chains reversed: shattered fetters, unsmiling eyes, an ornate border that speaks to a preference for courtesy. The other card is the Deuce of Stars. It is the only source of light on the planet.

Even with the two cards revealed, Niristez would have lost the round; but that wasn't the game she was playing anyway. In the meantime, she likes to think of the former warden looking up at a chilly sky filled with enough stars to sate the longest nights alone, his hands forever empty.

≫•≪

Virtue Kana is a warrior to the extent that she defends those for whom she feels responsible—her partner, Dayva, and her former partner, General— and what is hers: Artace, *her hover boat. But Jessica Reisman reveals Virtue has a secret: someone intended her to be something other than a salvager, and that something would have led to frequent combat.*

BOY TWELVE

Jessica Reisman

THE TWELFTH CLONE of Virtue Kana's dead lover came to call one day while Virtue and her partner prepped for a salvage run. The light-drenched tranquility of Jumka Docks, on the Coreyal Sea of Samjadsit Space Station, had, until that moment, seemed as remote from Virtue's home world of Piranesi as the Coreyal from the fabled seas of Earth.

Spreading dark and sinuous to the white-sugar crust of glow along the upcurve of station horizon, the Coreyal's waters were luminous. The glow came through station wellcore from Samjadsit system's young sun, to which the vast space station was oriented, axis-wise, like a gaudy bead on a festival stick.

On the deck of the *Artace*, Virtue readied equipment for a run to the Fortunate Isles for dust while her partner Dayva fed numbers into the nav comp.

"Seems to me I recall hearing someone say that the day she agreed to salvage dust would be the day they could pack her in—let me see," Dayva held up one hand, "what was it?—'pack her in the *Artace*'s carapactic hull and spit her off station into the solar winds.'"

"What?" Virtue looked around at her partner. "Why are you ragging on me?"

"Because you're grinding your teeth and it's getting on my nerves."

Dayva had come up out of the gravity well of a little planet named Asp. She had a straight back, a penchant for darkside philosophy, the face of a dark angel, and a fine-boned frame that seemed better suited to dance, or something equally courtly, than the rough work on a hover boat.

A wind frisked along the beach. The whisper of bronze silicate-sand sliding over itself hissed into the air as the *Artace* rocked at her mooring. Virtue finished a check of the utility skiff and moved to the salvage equipment. Filtered illumination came up through the Coreyal's waters and reflected warmth along the hulls of other rigs, up into her face as she worked, the scent of heated metal and deep water making her mildly euphoric.

Dayva stretched from her hunched position at nav, dark fingers spread to the station sky. "Be a shame to grind those fine teeth down to nubs, girl."

"Nothing better to do than kive my offhand comments in your head, D?"

Dayva snorted, delicately—something Virtue had only seen Dayva manage. "You're the most stimulating company I've been able to scare up since coming to this misbegotten slag heap of a space station."

"Take it up with the tourist board, D."

"Come clean, Virtue, you took this job just because General threatened to give it to Turner, didn't you?" She glanced down at the comp as it spit out the numbers kive, then sat in one of the seating hollows and leaned elbows on knees, peering up at Virtue. "You're a competitive headcase, you know that, right?"

Virtue opened her mouth to answer, but out past Dayva, a spot of motion turned into someone heading down the docks toward them.

Someone wearing dark clothes, looking over his shoulder every few steps, like some other someone might be following him.

Which predisposed Virtue not to like him.

Dayva came up behind her. "Friend of yours?"

Virtue shrugged. "Yeah, you may have noticed, I've got so many." Then she muttered, "What's it want with us, that's the issue."

Their visitor reached the *Artace* and stepped down on the dock, looking up. He trailed off, uncertain, took a step back at what must be showing in her face.

The grip of her knuckles was white.

Their visitor looked up past her, at Dayva, back to Virtue. He tilted his head, as if to say, well, you're rude, but I'm a forgiving sort. Then he quirked his mouth like he might say something funny. "Should I go away and come back later? You're obviously . . . busy."

The red tide crested and washed through her, leaving a puddle of toxins to shiver her muscles and trace an ache behind her eyes. Virtue swallowed, feeling the shakiness in her limbs. She was still hanging on to the *Artace* as if they'd just come through a stormwall of heavy weather.

The Rage was hard—supposedly impossible—to subdue.

She pulled her hand, trembling, off the hull, and folded her arms. "Why would Horatio send someone? He has a perfectly good uplink."

The clone shrugged one shoulder. "He had something he wanted to send personally—not on a delivery transport, I guess. I wanted to get off Piranesi, see some of the universe." A slightly embarrassed, crooked smile.

Wind riffled across the deck.

It was so familiar, that smile, it slipped behind all of Virtue's defenses.

She imagined she could hear the infinitesimal whirr and click of biochemical mechanisms. There was that chance, of course, that his puzzlement was genuine, his candor real—so far as he knew. That he didn't know he was a clone, whose clone, or why he'd been sent to Virtue.

"What's your name, brother's messenger?"

"Tao-Jin James."

Virtue pictured the registry data, in some code-locked, vaulted compfile. James Xu, what—five, ten, thirteen? How many clones had her brother decanted by now?

She leaned forward on the rail. She'd play, until she knew what was behind this latest sally of her brother's.

"So, what's he sent?"

The kid slid a sphere the size of an apricot out of his hip pocket. The sphere glinted opalescent cloudy gray, like a brakfish's eye. A Shiralsky-Deek Modular Coded Comp Messaging Holo. *Shiral*, for short. A baroque technology, rarely used and fabulously expensive. Horatio used them as an idiosyncratic tic that he wanted to be seen as an eccentricity.

"Virtue—" The tone in Dayva's voice brought her attention off the problem standing on the dock below her. She followed the slant of Dayva's gaze and saw Lobren, the Jumka bursar, coming along the dock toward them. Wanting their one-day-past-due dock fee—which they didn't have, currently. "Void." Virtue looked down at Tao-Jin James, chewed her lip. Then, what Dayva called her toffish perversity kinked into play. Damn all if she'd let Horatio Kana get any satisfaction out of this. Send her a copy of James, would he? And think to pull her strings thereby?

"Power up, Dayva," she said. "We're moving. So, Tao-Jin—you want to go salvage dust in the Fortunate Isles?" She sensed, rather than saw, Dayva's brows come frowning down as she keyed code into the *Artace* and the hover boat came to life. Tao-Jin James blinked, trying to read her.

"Either climb on or toss me Horatio's toy. We're on a schedule."

He gave her a hard look, suspicious even. But he slid the shiral back into his pocket, wrapped one hand around the lowest rung and pulled himself aboard in an easy, agile motion.

How well Virtue remembered that agility.

The *Artace* almost threw him the next moment, though, as the hover turbs kicked in, so she gave him a hand the last rung up.

Shiver of visceral memory as their hands connected. He got a startled look. Virtue's expression was grim.

IN THE FOURTEEN GENS it had taken for the slowly built sections of Samjadsit Station to accrete into a unity the size of a small moon, some unintended materials had slipped into the mix. Legend had it that in the tenth gen of construction, the sixth region of what would become the Coreyal basin had been caught in the protomatter—whatever that was when it was at home—of a passing galactic phenomenon. The stuff had crusted into the unfinished matrix and never been removed.

Over the course of time and through the working of various chemistries, something came to exist in the isles. Dust. Its properties were variously believed to be restorative, mutative, miraculous.

La Cabeza Azul was offering more than respectable pay for a cache of the stuff—something Virtue definitely needed. Both the *Artace* and Virtue's former partner, General, needed new parts—not to mention the dock fees. General, an old station relic before he'd ever become Virtue's partner, needed them most. It was General who'd asked her to take the run; General who'd offered her his most precious possession—the route to an untapped cache of dust; General who'd cajoled, challenged, and, finally, threatened to give the route to another hover boat operator, Jake Turner. Dayva was right—Virtue was competitive and she didn't like Turner.

The *Artace* sailed the air just above the water. Occasional displacements sent a spume of drops over the boat's pale leading curve.

The vast network of the Fortunate Isles grew slowly closer, a vivid fringe of green under the distant station sky. The numbers General had given them were for a spot deep in the isle network.

"Tell me again," Dayva said, removing the ear and eye pieces of her kive link to the ship and frowning into the slowly glooming distance, "why it's a good idea to go so deep in? No one else does, not in a hover the *Artace*'s size."

"That's the spot General gave us," Virtue shrugged. "The dust caches in the outer isles are all tapped, anyway." She kept a hand to the *Artace*'s rudderpad, linked to comp, surveyed her partner's face. "Scared?"

Dayva nodded. "You should be, too, crazy bitch."

Tao-Jin James sat leaning over the *Artace*'s hull, face into the wind. Virtue was used to Dayva muttering unflattering things about her, but he looked around, from one to the other of them.

"What's wrong?"

Dayva cast Virtue a glance that said, clearly, that's your piece of ass, you want me to talk to it? Then she did anyway. "The deep parts of the isles are spawning ground for brakfish. It's near spawning time."

Tao-Jin tilted his head.

"What Dayva means," Virtue said, "is that salvage isn't usually a fish-fighting danger sport and she's no harpoonist."

He leaned forward, frowning, moved one hand in a gesture that echoed into her memory.

"So the fish are dangerous?"

Dayva laughed.

"The brakfish," Virtue said, "is a monster of ichthyofauna, a speciation unique to Samjadsit Station, one which no one knows or claims the breeding and introduction of. The Fortunate Isles are brakfish spawning grounds."

Dayva rolled her eyes at Virtue's imitation of a tourist kive and Tao-Jin James smiled.

"Brakfish grow three times bigger than the *Artace*, and wily with it." Virtue found she had to look away from James' smile. She gestured. "Teeth long as my forearm. There are hunting regattas every year, people coming from all over to kill the unexpected miracle of accidental evolution."

"Usually," Dayva added, "some one or two hapless humans die in the course of the hunting, too."

"So that's a yes," Tao-Jin concluded. "And they're from the same place as this dust." He glanced out toward the isles.

"Maybe that's why *Azul* wants some." Dayva rose to lean near Tao-Jin and peer into the wind. She looked like an icon, with her short white hair and long dark self.

"Why?" Tao-Jin asked.

"To grow something prodigiously large." She raised one elegant hand, graceful bones turning, and put inflection on her words, drawling a bit. Tao-Jin's gaze followed her hand, then he laughed. They all laughed.

For all the universe like friends on a joy spin, Virtue thought and then her thoughts snagged on the shiral in Tao-Jin James' pocket. She wondered if she ought to listen to it. Later, she decided, because the air felt good and Horatio's voice would take all the joy out of it.

They hit the outer isles shortly after the core went to ninety-five percent polar for station night. The intense radiance melted from the upcurve, fading to a soft, mellow limning; illumination left the water, the solar relays giving only a faint veining of wispy fire to the dark.

Tao-Jin James had been studying Virtue, surreptitiously. He met her gaze, though, when she turned her most impassive stare on him. Eventually he lowered his eyes.

Dayva slowed the *Artace* as the isles rose around them. The hover boat's nightlight picked out the bristling shapes of ranga trees and formstone monoliths in the dark, one after another, an endless-seeming depth of them hinted at beyond its scope. The waterways narrowed. Insects spoke from within dense copses. A night bird swept from one isle to another, long silvery feathers briefly etched from the darkness.

Samjadsit Station was large enough, and one of the system's planets near enough, that the Coreyal possessed tides. The station's tide and spin motion stabilization systems—what Virtue thought of as the slosh compensators—were in a permanent state of repair and adjustment. There was a betting pool, on the docks, long standing, on whether and when it would be the erosion or the slosh that sent the station critical.

The scents on the Coreyal's back were never those of a planetary sea. For one thing, the Coreyal was fresh water, not salt; but there was a dense, overcharged feeling to the air Virtue had never known on another station, nor on Piranesi, the planet she left when she was fifteen. Where Tao-Jin James had lately come from, emissary of her brother, who held the strings to a fortune she hadn't touched since leaving, and—he thought—to things by which he could call her back.

The *Artace* tracked the specs Dayva had fed to comp until the numbers ran out. Full nav shifted to Virtue's rudderpad.

"Watch for a jut of formstone that looks like a fat woman," General had said, lying in his bed, shaping the air with one hand. His other hand, and the rest of him, was looped, plugged, or cybered into various bio support. His voice wheezed out, soft and fragile as ancient cloth. "Just after the breakaway—that comes up sudden-like. Narrow waters there. Skinnier than the Drift Witch's gullet. Then comes the inlet, all covered over with ranga branches. Skinny, skinny—hard to get through. She'll groan at you, but the *Artace* can do, if any can."

They were in narrow channels now, ranga and other flora, colorless pale in the *Artace*'s light, rising to either side, closing above in places.

"Dayva, slow her to point five and disengage the hovers."

Dayva didn't move for a moment, than said quietly, stating the obvious, "That means setting down in the water."

"Yes."

"That'll—"

"Yes."

She muttered, but turned back to comp and did it. The hover turbs slowed, disengaged, and the *Artace* set down gently in a puff of air and a slap of water. Then it was the low hum of the engines, and the slip of water across the hull.

Tao-Jin James looked out into the isles, intent. Virtue could see his nostrils flare as he took in the unfamiliar scents. The posture was echo, mirage. Hair shorter than James ever kept his. He was younger than her memory of James.

None of that mattered.

General's breakaway loomed, and just beyond it, hidden by a curve of ranga branches and a swarming of vines, his formstone fat woman loomed, a giant figure of rock, seeming to leer at them as they passed. The *Artace*'s light passed right over the inlet beyond it. Invisible, if you weren't looking.

Maneuvering the *Artace* into a passage she could only take on faith to actually be there, Virtue grimaced as ranga roots groaned against the hull, leaf and branch scratching and whining over the upper carapace. It went on for long moments, her hand tense on the rudder, sweat dripping down her sides. The *Artace* could lead with any end of her curve-framed self, nimble as hover ships came, but a root or vine in the engines would be bad, especially in brakfish waters. Dayva bent over comp; the ship bucked and creaked until, with a final groan, they were through. Both Virtue and Dayva breathed out, relieved.

Skinny passage for a bit, then the channel opened out, widened, deepened, and they were slipping down a tunnel made incandescent by the hover boat's beam.

"Kill the light, Dayva."

She did and it was suddenly very dark, the five percent of relayed sun's light that filtered through the night polar blocked here by the thickness of roots below, branches above. The *Artace*'s running lights, motes of yellow reflection on the water, didn't touch the darkness of the isles.

They drifted in the dark, silent. Slowly, here and there on either side, something began to singe at the edges of their sight: a burning of blue threads and embers in the depths of the isles. More and more, until there was enough of the blue glow to see the suggestion of ranga trunks and formstone shapes. Virtue locked the rudder.

Awareness of his presence was like heat on her skin—she couldn't help herself. She looked over at Tao-Jin. His eyes were wide, lips parted. See the universe's many wonders, adventure and excitement, you bet. Then he shook his head, at some thought, turned to look at her.

"Dust?"

"Dust."

"It looks like something out of an Irdish fable."

She found she had nothing to say to that and turned away to prep the equipment. Dayva set the anchor and started lowering the skiff to the water, the crank whining softly.

Virtue pulled a duck suit over her jump, belted it, hung a palm flash and a catchnet containing three preserving boxes and a scraping tool to the belt; last, she tucked the suit's long gloves into the belt, leaving the filter hood down around her shoulders. Dust was toxic in its unprocessed state.

"Thirty minutes," Dayva said. "Then you're back here."

"Forty-five." She slid over the side and climbed down, jumping the last step off the ladder to land in the skiff. Now she could feel the water under her, close and alive in a way it never was on a hover. Over the *Artace*'s hull edge, two faces peered down at her, Dayva mostly just white hair and brows.

"Don't forget the hood, Virtue," she gestured.

Virtue grunted, but her attention drifted to the figure beside Dayva. "My brother send you to talk me into going back to Piranesi?"

"He sent me to bring you the shiral. But—yes, he asked me to try." He hesitated for a second, like he was going to say more, then didn't.

"And you don't know why he might have chosen you—someone I don't know?"

Tao-Jin shook his head. "Horatio just said—I might do." His voice carried softly: so, so familiar Virtue forgot to breath until her chest hurt. "It was free passage off Piranesi," he said. "I'd never have afforded it on my own."

She wished he was telling the truth, but knew he wasn't. "When I get back," she said, "I want a better reason than that. You think about it."

Dayva shifted beside him, looking nervously up and down the channel. "Virtue—over the side of the hull isn't the place for this conversation." She

waved her hands in a shooing motion, looking like a witch doing incantation
in the blue light. "Get moving."

Tapping a code into the skiff's rudderpad to unlock it, Virtue set one palm to
its surface. The skiff parted water. A short, silent, gliding while later it bumped
up against the jagged formstone that passed for a shore. She knotted a line to
a low hanging branch. One glance back to the *Artace*, the two faces, distant in
the dim, still watching her.

She wondered what they'd talk about, and what Dayva made of the whole
thing. The things she'd never told Dayva—anyone. General knew, some of it,
but the old man had figured it out for himself, knowing a thing or two about
the trade on Piranesi. With these thoughts for company, she headed into the
ranga copse, ducking branches as she went. It was hard to gauge where the dust
was, its burning blueness seeming to float in the darkness, fooling about with
the distances. Shining a light on it made dust disappear—poof, nothing there.
Dust salvage was strictly a night cycle activity.

Climbing over roots and formstone she could barely see, the roots smoothly
gnarled, the stone cool and rough beneath her hands, the mineral scent of stone
and soil was in her nose, and the blue burnings swam at the edges of her sight,
beginning to seem more and more like ghost fire in her head.

Then she put her duck suited foot down in the ghost fire, slipped and caught
herself. A little cloud of blue sizzled up into the air.

A cache of dust spread around her, in the ranga roots, over the soil, in
the crevices of the formstone. Belatedly, she remembered to draw the filter
hood over her head, pull on the gloves. The sound of her own breath filled
Virtue's ears; the hood's disinfectant smell, that made her want to sneeze or
retch, burned in her throat.

General had explained the collection of dust in detail—along with gifting
her this location, held secret to himself for half his lifetime. Dust was found
mostly in tiny caches, little bits of the stuff that amounted to no more than a
palmful. Most of the known salvage spots were scraped clean.

Virtue was standing in an unbelievable cache.

Preserving boxes set out and scraping tool in hand, she dug the thin layer of
blue fire off a root, scooping it into the first of the boxes. Fibrous when the tool
first went in, on contact with it the stuff mutated into a clinging, viscous dust.

By the time the third box was filled with oily, burning blue dust, her skin
was sticky with sweat, jump clinging beneath the duck suit. She shook out a
cramp in her hand and a twinge in her shoulder. Three boxes full and there was
plenty of dust left among the roots, over the soil and formstone.

The lid on the last box sealed with a hermetic hiss and Virtue loaded up to go, the catchnet swinging heavy. Midway back, sudden light leaned through the ranga trees and disappeared the dust—Dayva's way of calling time.

At isle's edge, the skiff waited, bumping roots on a gulp of disturbed water. Virtue's skin prickled and she surveyed the area, but the channel was flat again, netted by the white and gold blaze of the *Artace*'s main and running lights.

Dayva, with Tao-Jin James lending a hand, hauled the skiff up, rivulets streaming off it in luminous beaded strings. Setting the catchnet on the deck, Virtue stripped off the duck suit and gloves and dropped them in the detam unit. A bitter oily smell clung to the suit and lingered in the air.

"This it?" Dayva looked down at the three preserving boxes in the catchnet.

"That's it." They exchanged a silent look. Sitting on the deck was a fortune. More scrip than they might have expected to earn off a job in twenty years.

And there was Tao-Jin James, unknown quantity, in and of whom Virtue suspected any number of things. He stood by the dripping skiff, watching them. Virtue couldn't tell what she was thinking—wasn't, maybe. Not, Athra knew, with any portion of her anatomy that thought clearly.

COMING BACK THROUGH the narrow inlet, roots scraping, leaves scratching, hull groaning, tension rode Virtue with steel talons in her shoulders. Tao-Jin leaned over the edge, observing the backwash.

Then they were through, back into the narrow channel they'd come down earlier.

"Hover turbs?" Dayva wanted to know.

Virtue shook her head. "Wait till we get to wider passage. I don't want to risk her now."

The channel widened slightly. Then Virtue heard a sound, the ghost of a *thump*.

"What was that?" Tao-Jin asked. He peered off what was currently the stern.

It came again, under the engine's low hum, a ghost of a sound, like something big moving water.

"Dayva—"

"Yeah," she said, fingers moving quickly over comp. They gained speed in suddenly rolling water.

A distinct *thump*, then, to that portion of the ship under water, like distant, wrong direction thunder. The *Artace* rocked.

The brakfish rose, off to port, a great shifting just under the water's surface as it turned back toward them, scales sheened and reflective, an impressive roll of water cascading from a flip of tailfin big as the *Artace*.

"Engaging hover turbs." Dayva didn't ask if it was okay now.

Just as they gained hover, the brakfish bumped the *Artace* again. The hover turbs went offline and the ship tilted crazily, sending Virtue, Tao-Jin James, and the heavy boxes of dust tumbling across the deck. Dayva hung on to comp with both hands as the *Artace* hit the water hard, half on her side, then bobbed back.

Flashes of pain as Virtue took the hull hard in one shoulder, then one of Tao-Jin's elbows in her side. She got a grip on the hull's edge and pulled herself up in time to see a great shimmer-scaled monstrosity rising out of the Coreyal, water streaming back from a mouth full of teeth.

Teeth definitely longer than her forearms.

The fish dove into them again, screech of those teeth across the hull and again they rocked hard.

"Virtue!" Dayva yelled and flung the harpoon bow at her. The alloy frame hit one palm; she let go of the hull to scramble for it, then wedged herself into one of the seating hollows. Dayva was trying to get some maneuvering room as Virtue pried off the safety, loaded a dart from the chamber and sighted toward the water as the brakfish came round for another pass.

She squeezed the trigger; the shock of recoil punched through her. The dart sailed through the air to wreak no more damage than a rip in the flirting tailfin. Then she had to hang on through another charge. Her hip took the brunt of the hull this time and she almost went over, drowning in a wave of water and losing track of up from down. A hand got hold of her jump and hauled her back.

James.

He ripped the harpoon out of her hands, turned, sighted, and shot as the brakfish leapt, streaming water. The harpoon stood out of the center of one wide, glassy dark eye as the fish floated on the air a moment before them.

Then another screech of teeth, the ship rocked, and they were thrown back under another drenching. Virtue came up onto her knees, coughing, and found the harpoon under her hands. James' clone was climbing to his feet over across the deck. She was about to give him the 'poon back, considering his skill with it, when Dayva said, in a tense voice, "Virtue."

She pointed: another fish was coming down the narrow channel. Another fish.

"Bloody void," Virtue breathed.

James tugged the harpoon from her grip and fell to his knees, sighting over the hull. Rather than watch to see what damage the clone might do with the 'poon, Virtue flung around to scrabble at one of the seat hollow storage areas. Her fingers found what she wanted quickly, two small chem charges she used for blasting in salvage work.

She turned with one in her hand to see the first brakfish falling back to the water with two more 'poon shafts bristling from the same eye as the first. The first fish hit the water heavily, suddenly graceless, just as the second came for its go at them, mouth open, long teeth bristling.

Her focus narrowed down as her fingers primed the charge. The fish rose and she flung the charge in a sure arc, straight for the dark behind long ivory teeth.

A low-pitched, eeling whine filled the air, and before the *Artace* had stopped rocking from the last attack, the second brakfish was blown out of the water. A breathless moment later, large pieces of fish rained down. Backsplash washed across the deck, chunky with dead fish and blood; the deck streamed water back into the Coreyal. The smell was atrocious.

Dayva still clung to comp, wet and coughing. James was just gaining hands and knees, having been washed clear across the deck. Virtue, thrown to her back, rolled, found the harpoon bow under one hand, gripped it as she rose, barely conscious of doing so.

She eyed the channel, dripping, her thoughts running ahead and behind, circling.

"Dayva?"

"Working on it."

"What's happening?" James coughed the words up with water, climbing to his feet.

"Mother—" Dayva pounded on the comp console.

Virtue's jump clung uncomfortably, her hair plastered to her cheeks, down her neck.

"Someone put a lure signal on us," she said softly.

Dayva looked up. "What? How do you figure that?"

"Brakfish don't hunt in pairs. And they don't usually hunt ships unless the ships have a lure signal on them—like they use in the regattas. So, someone planted a lure on us. It's the only explanation that makes sense."

She saw the clone's hand go to the hip pocket of his drenched jump, where the shiral was, a look of horror crossing his face.

As they left the dead brakfish, one floating, a huge raft of scale, the other so much flesh and gore in the water, further and further behind, Virtue regarded Tao-Jin James, standing on her deck, watching her.

"Are you going to shoot me?" he asked.

She cast a blank look down at the harpoon bow still in her grip. Ignore him, she decided, with a desperate, half-rational thought.

"How's it coming, Dayva?" She went past James to the skiff, unlocked the crank with a savage, left-handed yank, started to lower it. She could smell her own sweat, in the wet jump, and the lubricant in the crank mechanism. Red, red, red, the edges of things, and the center was going dark.

"About ready to go online."

Virtue heard Dayva, distantly, through deep static.

The skiff hit water with a splash and she waved the harpoon at James' clone, gesturing down to the skiff she could barely see through red darkness. "Get in."

Dayva looked over.

He lifted a hand, lowered it, shook his head once. "I didn't know about the tracer."

The harpoon was slick with sweat in her grip. "Get. In."

"Virtue—"

"Dayva, shut up."

The clone shook his head again. "Captain—"

It's for your own damn good, she thought, but couldn't verbalize it. There was too much red; she was going to break apart around it. Holding herself in place was like holding—she didn't know, but it was hard and it hurt and she didn't know if she could do it if he didn't—

"Virtue, what the void are you—" Dayva began, but she put her hand on Virtue's arm and for a breath, just the thought of a breath, Virtue stopped holding it in and there was a loud crack of sound, a surprised sound—

—then a feel of wind across her wet skin—

—and Dayva was sitting on the deck a few feet away, looking surprised, one long-fingered hand spread over her cheek.

And oh drift, oh void, no—

—and she clamped it back down and forced one sentence out of her mouth. "Get him off my ship."

Something passed between the clone and Dayva; he set the shiral on the deck and scrambled over the side into the skiff.

He was a dot behind them on the Coreyal, left behind in the dark, when Virtue thought to unprime the harpoon and set it back in the rack. Her hand ached, but it was distant.

There was quiet over in the direction of Dayva, the noisy kind of quiet. After awhile, though, she said, "He doesn't know the code for the rudder."

"He should have thought of that before," Virtue answered.

She picked up the shiral in a hand that only shook slightly. First she found the tiny transceiver that was emitting the infrasonic brakfish lure, pulled it off and ground it into the deck under one foot.

Then she pressed her thumb into the center of the shiral's cloudy opal eye. It identified her chemical signature and a line of light chorused through the sphere as it cleared to a brilliant, hard-edged depth in which her brother Horatio appeared, perfect tiny miniature in her palm.

"Virtue." Just that, for a moment, his tiny, perfect image regarding her. "I'd like to you to come home now. I have some reorganizing to do among the associations." It was his voice out of the shiral, as if he were there: clipped, creamy tones. It made the skin on her back twitch.

"Your unique gifts can't be comfortable off Piranesi. Surely you see that you're better off here. Eventually someone is going to put you down like a rabid dog. Oh, and if you haven't figured it out already, James Twelve brought a nice little fish lure with him. I hope you don't kill him too messily—or, I'm sorry, have you already?"

"Hold." She set the sphere down, carefully, though there was red rage in her eyes and arms, tidal as the Coreyal's engineered sea. Red as Horatio's reorganizing of Piranesi's associations.

Several breaths strung like water on air, in the dark, bloody, shoreless place. After a minute she could see again. Her hands shook as if with palsy, and familiar pain twisted, bitter with the unreleased Rage that had been building for the last half hour. That she hadn't unleashed on Tao-Jin James. Horatio would be amazed and chagrined. Now, though, her hands were shaking, hard. The red washed slowly from the air. She was crying, it hurt so much.

He'd wanted her to unleash it on James. Again.

That became clear in the lucid moments that usually followed a Rage. If she'd torn James' clone apart, come out of the fit to see what she had done—Horatio would have had her. Murder. Off Piranesi such things didn't go unremarked.

At the very least she would have been sent to an Aggregate stew; more likely there'd have been regen for the emotional wreckage killing James again would have left of her.

Or shipped back to Piranesi, where she'd be safe from the retributions of relatively sane society. Horatio would have been sure to have that option covered.

It would have been the second time she killed James.

It gave Virtue a moment of cold joy to know how it must vex Horatio that she'd taken her genetic file when she'd skipped out.

"That was your brother?" Dayva had set comp on auto and come to lean against the slope of the *Artace*'s upper carapace. A puffy swelling marred the dark skin of her angled cheek where Virtue had hit her. Her voice was stiff, eyes slanted away.

Virtue considered her, let her own gaze slide away. "Rearranging the world from his little gravity sink, yes."

Dayva was thinking, one silvery brow lifted high, still not looking at Virtue, anger and hurt shading her eyes. "You're engineered?"

"Yes."

"To what?"

"Kill."

Dayva barked a laugh, then gave a sharp shake of her head. "Waste of genetic tinkering. Plenty of ways to kill without making a specialty human to do it. Why?"

"Have you ever been to Piranesi, Dayva?"

"Is that the answer?"

Virtue nodded.

"I see." Maybe she did. "You really going to leave that kid out there in the skiff?"

Virtue shifted away, shook her head.

"What about the brakfish?"

Stretching her arms, shoulders cracking, Virtue shook her hands out. "If he's quiet, they won't notice him." She turned to Dayva and said, softly, "I'm sorry."

Dayva looked at her finally. "Explain it to me." She didn't need to add: or forget this partnership. The words were clear as day without the speaking.

"The Rage is triggered by certain sets of circumstances, particular goads or spurs. Evidence of betrayal will do it. It's . . . very hard . . . to contain it once it's triggered. It's supposed to be impossible. You interrupted me at the wrong moment." She shrugged one shoulder. "I'm sorry, Dayva. I . . . " Falling silent, she looked away. "I'd never . . . not for the world."

Dayva shifted. Then she said, "Don't do it again. Ever."

"Never." Virtue considered whether she could actually promise that, then said, "Dayva, maybe . . . maybe it would be better if you found another gig."

Dayva folded her arms, stared out into the dark over the water. "I'll keep that in mind. Stay for now. My choice." The staccato statements drifted through soft air. Then she said, "Virtue, not my business, maybe—but I talked to that kid some while you were down in the ranga digging dust. I don't think he knew about the tracer. Or what it is that's got you so kinked about him."

"He knows—that, at least. He must. He was raised in my brother's household and he was being paid, by my brother. About the tracer, you're right, he probably didn't know."

Dayva snorted. "So he's not a saint. What is it about him, anyway? Still not my business, but you did nearly get me killed—and you hit me. You owe me."

"Slim payment."

"I'm a philosophical girl. That's what you like about me."

Virtue stared down at her hands, still trembling. "I loved someone named James Xu. My brother didn't like the influence James had with me. So he triggered the Rage with the original James in the kill path. Tao-Jin is one of James' clones."

Silence, the slur of water under hovers, race of wind. Her hair was almost dry, whipping into her face.

"Hido has said that the more primitive human chemical responses are at war with our most advanced bio-technologies," Dayva said, apropos of what, Virtue wasn't entirely sure.

"The esteemed Hido has his philosophical head up his ass." She wiped her hair back and twisted it into a knot. "Anyway, Horatio secured the rights to James' gene set when he saw what a good control for yours truly the model was. James died . . . I killed him. But Horatio keeps bringing him back."

She glanced at Dayva as she fisted and stretched her hands, shook them out once more. "He uses them like one-shot kive chips, disposable, trying to get me to come back to be his personal berserker."

"Mother void," Dayva said, and that was all for a good minute or two. Then, "But the Megrath Reversal overturned ownership rights on adult-formed clones."

"Except on Piranesi."

"Oh." That probably told her more about Piranesi than she wanted to know. "So what happened to the other eleven?"

Virtue closed her eyes, opened them, said evenly, "He tortured one and sent me kives of it. Others might not have been a close enough match, psychologically, or they failed before full realization." She rubbed at the back of her neck, the corded muscles tense. "There's a sixty to seventy percent failure rate."

The Coreyal sped beneath them, silver from their light, away into lucid dark and the upcurve of distance. The ache in her hip and shoulder, and one on her hand from hitting Dayva, all throbbed dully. She needed food and was starting to shudder with that need; the Rage used carbs like air.

"You a clone, Virtue?"

She blinked at Dayva. "No."

"You sure?"

"Yes." She frowned, her voice going stiff. "I'm quite sure."

Dayva chewed her lip. "Maybe that kid knows he's a clone, Virtue, maybe not. And even if he does—"

"Right, he didn't know about the tracer," she said, finally thinking it through. "If Horatio meant me to kill him, he wouldn't have told him much. James is a smart set. He'd have tracked this whole encounter differently if he'd known. He'd have run the second he was off Piranesi."

She picked up the shiral, turned it once in her fingers; it had gone cloudy opal again. She heaved it overhand with a grunt, didn't listen for the splash. Maybe a brakfish would eat it.

THEY WENT BACK for him the next day.

It was full day. The light and heat bouncing back and forth between the water and station sky made it brutal hot at mid-cycle. You couldn't drink Coreyal water: the first and most frequent warning a tourist got.

His skin was burned, lips swollen slightly; he sat in the bottom of the skiff, knees up, arms loosely clasping them, head down, shirt off, wet and draped over him. He looked up only slowly when Virtue caught the skiff with a hook. She tossed him a water flask and leaned above him on the *Artace*'s deck. Dayva was over by comp, listening.

"You think of a better answer yet?" She watched him remember what she meant, and the words echoed in her own head.

"And you don't know why he might have chosen you—someone I don't know?"

"Horatio just said—I might do . . . It was free passage off Piranesi," he said. *"I'd never have afforded it on my own."*

"When I get back," she said, "I want a better reason than that . . . "

Now he drank some of the water, squinting up at her through swollen lids. He said slowly, "I knew. About you and my . . . predecessor. Not that Horatio ever told me. Remember Famke?"

Virtue nodded.

"Well," he coughed, drank another sip of water, wiped his face with trembling fingers. "She told me, some of it. So, I knew. And I knew your brother wasn't sending me for any reason that would make you happy. But . . . I never let on . . . how much I just wanted to escape. I was a very obedient clone." The bitterness sounded almost mild.

"You could have just run, not brought me his message at all."

He cast another look up at her. "I was curious. About you. The story Famke told me . . . "

"You didn't know about the tracer?"

He shook his head, swallowed. "No. Void—I'd never have . . . No."

Virtue flicked her fingers against the hull. "How long have you been, Tao-Jin James?"

"Ten years."

"What's your cell age?"

He touched a blister on his lower lip, gave her an opaque look. "Twenty-five."

"Does my brother have a hold on you?"

"Besides money, power, and registry title?"

"Title's not good off Piranesi."

"Then, no." He blinked, then grinned with cracked lips. "Not that I know of, anyway."

Virtue nodded and reached a hand down to him. "Come aboard, then. And welcome."

≫•≪

Kristine Kathryn Rusch's story is set in her Diving Universe. Tory Sabin, captain of the Geneva, *is a professional warrior who serves the Fleet. The Fleet has been around for thousands of years—always moving forward, never looking (or going) back.*

THE APPLICATION OF HOPE

Kristine Kathryn Rusch

1.

"REQUESTING SUPPORT. The *Ivoire*, just outside of Ukhanda's orbit. Need warships."

The calmness in the request caught Captain Tory Sabin's ear before the name of the ship registered. She had stopped on the bridge just briefly, on her way to a dinner she had sponsored for her support staff. She wasn't dressed like a captain. She had decided to stay out of her uniform and wear an actual dress for a change.

At least she had on practical shoes.

But she felt odd as she hurried across the nearly-empty bridge, covered in perfume, her black hair curled on the top of her head, her grandmother's antique rivets-and-washers bracelet jingling on her left wrist. She grabbed the arm of the captain's chair, but didn't sit down.

Only three people stood on the bridge—the skeleton crew, all good folks, all gazing upwards as if the voice of Jonathon "Coop" Cooper, captain of the *Ivoire*, were speaking from the ceiling.

Then Lieutenant Perry Graham, a man whose reddish-blond hair and complexion made him look continually embarrassed, leaned forward. He tapped the console in front of him, so that he could bring up the *Ivoire's* location.

It came up in a two-D image, partly because of the distance, and partly because Graham—the consummate professional—knew that Sabin preferred her long-distance views flat rather than in three dimensions. The best members of any bridge crew learned how to accommodate their captain's quirks as well as her strengths.

She moved closer to the wall screen displaying the image. The ship, marked in shining gold (the default setting for the entire Fleet), showed up in small relief, traveling quickly. Like Coop had said, the *Ivoire* wasn't too far from the planet Ukhanda. Whatever was causing the crisis wasn't readily apparent from this distant view, but Sabin could tell just from Coop's voice that he had been under attack.

Coop was one of those men, one of those *captains*, who didn't ask for help if he could avoid it. Much as she teased him about this, she knew she fell in that category as well.

Sabin didn't have to tell Graham to zoom in. He did, more than once, until the *Ivoire* looked huge. Around it were at least a dozen other ships, so small and feathery that they almost seemed like errors in the image.

"What the hell?" said Second Lieutenant Megan Phan. She was tiny and thin, her angular face creased with a frown. She probably hadn't even realized that she had spoken out loud.

Sabin doubted the other two had realized it either. Phan's words probably echoed their thoughts. In all her years in the Fleet, Sabin had never seen ships like that.

On screen, they looked too small to do any damage. If they were firing on the *Ivoire*, it wasn't obvious. But their position suggested an attack, and a rather vicious one.

"Let Captain Cooper know we're on the way," Sabin said to Graham.

"Yes, sir," Graham said, and sent the word.

The *Geneva*'s current rotation put it in the front line of defense for the Fleet, but the Fleet was in a respite period, which was why Sabin only had a skeleton crew on board. The Fleet had rendezvoused near an unoccupied moon. Six hundred of the Fleet's ships were engaged in maintenance, meetings, and vacations, all on a rotating schedule.

She'd been in dozens of respite periods like this one, and she'd never needed more than a few officers on the bridge.

Until now.

"Captain Cooper sends his thanks," Graham said, even though everyone on the bridge knew that Coop had done no such thing. Someone on his staff had. If Coop had done so, he would have spoken on all channels, just like he had a moment ago.

"We need other front line check-in," Sabin said. Technically, she wasn't the senior captain for all the front line ships on this shift, but no one took front line seriously during a respite period. Everyone had dinners and relaxation scheduled. Most bridges, even in the front line ships, were minimally staffed.

The only difference between a minimal staff in a front line ship and the other ships during a respite period was that the front line ships had top-notch crews manning the bridge, in case something did go wrong.

"Already done, sir," Graham said. "The captains are reporting to their bridges."

"What about our crew?" she asked. She felt almost embarrassed to ask. Graham was one of her most efficient crew members and she knew he had most likely pinged the bridge crew.

But she had to make sure—even in this respite period—that the crew was following protocol.

"Notified, and on the way," Graham said.

"Good, thank you." She sat in the captain's chair, and winced as the bow on the dress' back dug into her spine. A bow. What had she been thinking?

She knew what. The dress' tasteful blue fabric and demur front had caught her eye. But she had loved that bow for its suggestion of girlishness, something she wasn't now and would never be.

"Let's hear the check-in," she said.

Graham put the captains' responses overhead. In addition to the arrivals—all twenty of them—the captains seemed to believe it important to engage in a discussion of Coop's motives. A request for support was the lowest level request a captain could issue. Normally, a captain in distress asked for a battalion of a particular type, not a general support request of warships.

So it was curious, but it spoke more to Coop's conservatism than to the situation at hand. Besides, no one seemed to acknowledge that the *Ivoire* had gone to Ukhanda at the request of one of its nineteen cultures. The Fleet had agreed to broker a peace deal between the Xenth and the Quurzod, but didn't know enough about either to do a creditable job.

The *Ivoire,* which had the best linguists in the Fleet, had gone into Quurzod territory to learn more about that culture in advance of the actual peace conference three months away. The *Alta*, the Fleet's flagship, apparently believed that the Fleet knew enough about the Xenth to do more limited preparation.

It had only been a month since the *Ivoire* had sent a team to the Quurzod. Apparently things had not gone well.

She shifted, the dress' shiny fabric squeaking against the chair's seat. She wasn't sure she had ever sat in her chair without wearing regulation clothing—at least, since she had become captain. As a little girl, she used to sit in her father's captain's chair on the *Sikkerhet.* This dress made her feel that young and that out of place.

Stupid chatter from the other captains surrounded her. They were still speculating on what Coop wanted and whether or not this was a legitimate request. They hadn't made the transition from respite to action. And there was another issue. Coop's message was low-key.

Only people who knew him well understood that he was worried.

"Open a channel," she said, unable to take the chatter any longer.

Graham nodded. Then he signaled her.

"Coop's asked for support," Sabin said in her most commanding voice. "Stop arguing about why, and haul your asses out there."

The chatter stopped immediately. She had a hunch she knew how the other captains had reacted: a straightening of the shoulders, a nod, a deep breath as they all gathered themselves, a momentary flush of embarrassment as they realized they had conducted themselves like people on vacation instead of captains on a mission.

She didn't like respite periods, so she didn't understand the vacation mindset. But a lot of these captains believed in relaxation, and believed the crap that the civilians on the various ships peddled, that a rested crew was a healthy crew.

She believed a practiced crew was an efficient crew.

She followed regulations, gave her staff the proper amount of time off, and no more.

Because this respite period was so long—months, really, as the Fleet prepared for the work around Ukhanda—she had her first officer, Charlie Wilmot, continually run drills. Each department had to run drills as well.

Her crew was going to remain the most disciplined crew in the Fleet. If a member of the crew complained, that crew member got transferred. Often, she'd trade that crew member for someone else on a different ship. She'd stolen more good officers from other ships than any other captain. The good officers, she believed, were the ones who wanted to work, not party at every opportunity.

Wilmot had just arrived on the bridge. His uniform looked crisp and sharp. He glanced at her dress and his lips turned upward just enough to register as a smile to anyone who knew him. Fortunately, no one else on the bridge watched him.

"The *Ivoire*'s in trouble," she said to him. "Graham will catch you up."

Wilmot nodded, then walked to his station not too far from hers. As he did, he looked up at the screen, frowned, and glanced at her again. But he didn't ask anything, because she had already told him to figure out what was happening from Graham.

As if Graham knew. No one on the bridge did, and it was clear that no one on the other front line ships did either.

She tapped the right arm of her chair, bringing up the captain's holographic console. She'd designed this so she didn't have to move to another part of the bridge to get information.

Before she'd followed the captain's training route, she'd started in engineering. While she loved design, she hated the lack of control the engineering department had. Plus, she was a captain's daughter, and she had Ideas from the start on the way a well-run ship worked.

Most of the ships she had served on were not well run. So she had gone back to school, and had risen through the ranks until she got the *Geneva*. That was fifteen years ago. Even though she occasionally designed upgrades for her baby—upgrades that other engineers eventually brought to their ships—she hadn't really looked back.

She preferred being in charge.

Which was why, as the five other members of her team took their places on the bridge, she looked up those small, feather-shaped ships herself.

The ships weren't in the database, no matter how she searched for them. She searched by the ships' image, the design, and the area's history. She also searched through the images of Ukhandan ships, not that there were uniform ships on a planet that housed so many different cultures. Not all nineteen cultures were space-faring, but five of them were, according to the database, and those five had no ships like this.

Small, efficient, and capable of swarming.

She wanted to contact Coop, but she would wait. He would let her—and the other front line ships—know if something had changed.

She almost closed the console, when something caught her eye. She had images of the ships for five cultures, but the information before her contradicted itself. Five cultures had ships, but six cultures had been gone into the space around Ukhanda.

The sixth culture, the Quurzod, were the ones that the *Ivoire* had gone to Ukhanda to study before the peace talks.

Her stomach clenched.

Clearly, something had gone very, very wrong.

"How far out are we?" Sabin asked Lieutenant Ernestine Alvarez, who was running navigation.

"Even at top speed, we're half a day away," Alvarez said.

Too close to use the *anacapa* drive with any accuracy. The *anacapa* was the thing that enabled the Fleet to negotiate long distances. It put a ship in foldspace, and then the ship would reappear at set coordinates. The problem was that the ship would reappear blind, and in a battle situation, that wasn't optimum.

Plus, time worked differently in foldspace, and while the best crews could predict the time differences down to the second, sometimes even the work of the best crews went haywire. Engineers claimed the problem was with sections of foldspace itself; scientists believed the problem was with certain *anacapa* drives.

Even with centuries of study and upgrades, neither group could come to a complete agreement. In Sabin's opinion, the Fleet had forever messed with something it did not understand when it started using the *anacapa* drive.

She wasn't going to use it on something like this. Nor was she going to order the rest of the front line to do so—not unless Coop sent out a major distress signal, which he had not yet done.

She wasn't going to explain herself to her crew, but if she had to, she would tell them what she always told them—that portion of the truth that they needed to know. It was the same truth every time they considered using the *anacapa* drive. The *anacapa* put a strain on the ship and on the crew that Sabin couldn't quite quantify. She hated using it for that very reason, just like most of the captains did.

Which was probably why Coop hadn't used his drive yet. The *anacapa* also worked as a shield. The ship would jump to foldspace for a moment, and then return to its original coordinates. Depending on how the *anacapa* was programmed, the return could happen seconds later or days later, without much time passing on the ship at all.

"Another twenty-five ships have just left Ukhanda's orbit," Alvarez said.

"That settles where the ships are from, at least," Graham said.

"It was pretty obvious that the ships were from Ukhanda," Phan said. "The question is which culture controls them."

That *was* the question. It would have an impact on everything: how the front line ships would proceed, how they would fight back, *if* they would do more than simply rescue the *Ivoire*. If they needed to rescue the *Ivoire*. Coop might get away on his own.

Sabin hoped Coop would get away on his own.

She asked Graham, "Have you sent a message to the *Alta*, asking if they know which culture owns these ships? Because we need to get some diplomats on the mission here, to ensure we don't make things worse."

The *Alta* was twice as large as all of the other ships in the Fleet, including the warships, and it housed the Fleet's government when that government was in session.

"I notified them as soon as we got Captain Cooper's message," Graham said. "I trust that they're monitoring the *Ivoire* as well."

Sabin was about to remind Graham that one should never "trust" someone else to do anything important, when Wilmot snapped, "Don't make assumptions, Lieutenant."

He sounded a bit harsh, even for him. Sabin glanced at him. That small smile had disappeared, and she saw, for the first time, how tired he looked. She wondered what he'd been doing during respite, besides running drills.

His uniform was so crisp she knew he had put it on right after the call to the bridge. So he'd been either asleep or doing something else when the call came in.

"Sorry, sir," Graham said, sounding just a bit contrite.

"I want identification on those ships," Sabin said. "We have time—half a day, you said. So let's see if we can cut that time short, and see if we can figure out who or what we're dealing with. The other cultures on Ukhanda are a mystery to me. Maybe they developed some technology of their own that we're not familiar with."

"Do you want me to send for Sector Research?" Meri Ebedat spoke up for the first time. She usually handled navigation, but she'd been doing some maintenance on the secure areas of the bridge during the respite period. She had a streak of something dark running along her left cheek, and her eyes were red-rimmed. Her brown hair had fallen from its usually neat bun.

She had to be near the end of her shift, although now, she wouldn't be leaving. She was a good all-around bridge crew member, and Sabin would need her as the mission continued.

"Yeah, do it," Sabin said, "although I doubt Sector Research knows much more than we do. We haven't had enough time to study Ukhanda. That was one reason the *Ivoire* was there."

"You think they did something wrong?" Wilmot asked her softly, but the entire bridge crew heard.

She knew what he meant: he meant had the *Ivoire* offended one of the cultures in a severe way.

But she gave the standard answer. "By our laws, probably not," she said.

He gave her a sideways look. He wanted a real answer, even though he knew the real answer. They all did knew the real answer.

Had the *Ivoire*—or, rather, its on-planet team—offended one of the cultures? Clearly. And if Coop didn't act quickly, the entire ship might pay the price.

2.

"Do you ever question it?" Coop asked Sabin months before, his hands behind his head, pillows pushed to the side, strands of his black hair stuck to his sweat-covered forehead.

They were in a suite on Starbase Kappa. They had pooled their vacation funds for the nicest room on the base—or at least, the nicest room available to someone of a captain's rank. Sabin hadn't stayed anywhere this luxurious in her entire life—soft sheets, a perfect bed, a fully stocked kitchen with a direct link to the base's best restaurant, and all the entertainment the Fleet owned plus some from the nearby sector, not that she had needed entertainment. She had Coop.

The two of them weren't a couple, not really. They were a convenience.

It was almost impossible for captains to have an intimate relationship with anyone once they were given a ship. Coop's marriage to his chief linguist—a marriage that began when they were still in school—hadn't made it through his first year as captain.

Sabin had never been married, and she hadn't been in love in decades. At least that was what she told herself. Because the people she interacted with on a daily basis were all under her command. She didn't dare fall in love with them or favor them in any way.

It wasn't against Fleet policy to marry or even sleep with a crew member (provided both had enough years and seniority to understand the relationship, and provided both had signed off with all the various legal and ethical departments), but it didn't feel right to her to sleep with and then command another person.

It didn't feel right to Coop either. They'd discussed it one night, decided they were attracted enough to occasionally scratch an itch, and somehow the entire convenience had improved their friendship rather than harmed it (as they had both feared it might).

Ever since, they would communicate on a private link between their ships, and when their ships had a mutual respite period, they got a room and scratched that itch, sometimes repeatedly.

She had been about to get out of bed and order some food when Coop spoke. She had the covers pulled back, but his tone caught her, and she lay back down.

"Do I question what?" she asked, grabbing one of his pillows and propping it under her back.

"Our mission," he said. "Or at least part of our mission."

She felt cold despite the blankets and the perfect environmental setting. She hadn't heard anyone question the Fleet's mission since boarding school. At that point, everyone questioned, just a little. They were encouraged to.

"You don't believe in the mission any more?" she asked, turning on her side to face him. If Jonathon "Coop" Cooper no longer believed in the Fleet, well, then the Fleet might as well disband. Because the universe had shifted somehow and the rules no longer applied.

"Part of it," he said. "Although to say that I don't believe might be too strong. Let's just say I'm worrying about things."

He didn't look at her. He was staring at the ceiling, which was covered with a star field she didn't recognize. Starbase Kappa was old, built by her grandfather's generation and much of the base paid homage to places the Fleet had been almost a century ago. The Fleet usually liked to leave its past behind. Even the feats of bravery and the victories (large and small) became the stuff of legend, not something that the old-timers discussed as if they were meaningful events.

"What are you worrying about?" She propped herself up on her elbow so that she was in his field of vision.

He glanced at her, then smiled almost dismissively, and looked back up at the ceiling.

"What makes us so smart?" he asked.

She blinked, not expecting that.

"You and me?" she asked, thinking about their captains' duties.

He sat up, shaking his head as he did so. The blanket slid down his torso, revealing the dusting of black hair that covered his chest and narrowed on its way down his stomach.

Normally that would have distracted her, but his mood changed everything. She wasn't sure she had ever seen Coop this focused, even though she knew he was capable of it.

"Not you and me," he said. "The Fleet. We've been traveling for thousands of years. We go into a sector and if someone asks for help—or hell, if we figure they *need* help even if they don't ask—we give them assistance. We advise them, we make them see our point of view. We give them whatever they need from diplomatic support to military back up, and we stay as long as they need us, or at least until we believe they'll be just fine."

She'd been in hundreds of these kinds of conversations throughout her life, but never with another full adult vested with the powers of the Fleet. Always with children or teenagers or discontented civilians who traveled on the various ships.

Never with another captain.

"We never go back and check, we have no idea if we've done harm or good." Coop ran a hand through his hair, making it stand on end. "We continually move forward, believing in our own power, and we never test it."

"We test it," she said. "The fact that we've existed this long is a test in and of itself. We've been the Fleet for thousands of years. We've lived this way forever. We know the history of various regions. That's just not normal, at least for human beings."

"Because we never stick long enough to be challenged," he said. "And we 'weed' out the bad elements, giving them crappy—and sometimes deadly— assignments or we leave them planetside someplace where we convince ourselves they'll be happy."

Her breath caught. Finally, a glimmer of what might have caused this mood.

"Did you have to leave someone behind, Coop?" she asked softly.

"*No*," he said emphatically, then gave her a look that, for a moment, seemed filled with betrayal. "Haven't you wondered these things?"

She hadn't. She wasn't that political. She stayed away from the diplomats and the linguists and the sector researchers. She didn't like intership politics or the mechanics of leadership.

She knew what she needed to know to run her ship better than anyone else in the Fleet—better than Coop, although she would never tell him that—and she left the rest to the intellectuals and the restless minds.

She had never expected such questioning from Coop. If anything, she found it a bit disappointing. She didn't want him to doubt the mission.

She had thought better of him than that.

She wasn't sure how to respond, because anything she said would probably shut him down. It might even interfere with the comfortable convenience of their relationship.

But he expected an answer. More than that, he seemed to need one.

"In my captaincy," she said after a moment, after giving her self some time to think, "the *Geneva* has never had an on-planet assignment. We've been front line or support crew or the occasional battleship. We don't get the diplomatic missions."

"You haven't thought about what we do, then," he said flatly.

"Not since school, Coop," she said, finally deciding on honesty.

"Not once? This mission from God or whatever is causing us to move ever forward, spreading the gospel of—what? A culture that we've never lived in and we no longer know existed?"

He sounded wounded, as if all of this were personal. She had to think just to remember what he was talking about. The Fleet left Earth thousands of years ago, and supposedly did have a mission, to find new cultures and to help them or something like that.

She had never paid attention to mythology and history in school. She didn't think it pertained to anything she was doing.

She still didn't.

"I think," she said gently, "we have our own culture now. The Fleet doesn't live on planets or moons. Its world is the ships. That's what we are. The ships. And everything else is what we do to maintain our ships. We do explore, we do encounter other peoples, but that's not the Fleet's main job. The Fleet's main job is to maintain the Fleet."

He slouched in the bed. "Oh, hell, that's even more depressing."

"Why do you question?" she asked.

He gave her that betrayed look again, then threw the covers back.

"Why do you breathe?" he asked, and left the room.

3.

"Captain," Graham said, "I managed to modify our visuals just a bit. Those little ships *are* firing."

Sabin stood so that she could see the screen better. She had assumed that the little ships were doing something to the *Ivoire*, but, she realized as she watched, she hadn't thought of it as *firing* on the larger ship for two reasons.

The first reason was that something that small couldn't have weapons that would damage the *Ivoire*—not individually, anyway, and to her, somehow, that meant that any shots those little ships did take would be harmless. The second reason she hadn't thought the little ships were firing was that the *Ivoire* didn't seem to be reacting as if it were being shot at.

Why wasn't Coop shooting back? He could blow those things apart.

But the modified view showed little rays of light, coming from the small ships and hitting the *Ivoire* with a flare. The light and the flare were clearly constructs that Graham had designed to make the shots visible.

Still, they seemed creepy and a little overwhelming, rather like being stung continually by tiny insects. Pinpricks in isolation were annoying. Continual pinpricks weren't just annoying, they became painful.

"Have those ships been targeting more than one area on the *Ivoire*?" she asked. The answer wasn't readily apparent from the images that Graham had designed.

"I don't know," he said, "but if they are, the *Ivoire's* in real trouble. From what I can tell, those ships have a lot of firepower."

The weapons she understood, the ones that worked against great ships like these, required a lot of space and often their own power system away from the ship's engines. She had never seen ships so tiny with repeated firepower, the kind that could do damage on something like the *Ivoire*.

That wasn't entirely true. It was possible, if the ships gave up something, like speed. But these little ships kept up with the *Ivoire* and had powerful weapons.

"How is that possible?" she asked.

"I don't know," Graham said. "They're not like anything we've ever encountered before."

"And," Phan said, "they don't seem to be anything our various allies have encountered either."

"What about the Xenth?" Sabin asked. The Xenth weren't really allies, but they were the ones who suggested the brokered peace conference.

"I'm not getting anything from Sector Research," Phan said. "They're scrambling for information from the *Alta*. But they're not finding anything."

"Which might mean that there's nothing to find," Wilmot said.

He seemed unusually pessimistic. Sabin frowned at him. He didn't look at her. He was bent over his console, working furiously on improving their speed so that they could get to Coop faster.

"Captain." The single word cut through all the discussion. It was Alvarez. "Look at the *Ivoire*."

Sabin looked. It seemed to glow.

"Is that your effect, Perry?" she asked Graham.

"No, sir," he said. "That's the *Ivoire*."

Sabin had never seen anything like that before. "What the hell is that?"

The *Ivoire's* glow increased and then the ship vanished.

"Tell me they activated their *anacapa*," she said, hoping she didn't sound as worried as she felt.

"They did," Graham said, "but I only know that because I just got a transmission from them a few minutes ago, announcing their intention to do so."

"That transmission should be simultaneous with the *anacapa's* activation," Sabin said. "We should have gotten it as the *Ivoire* vanished."

"Yes, sir," Graham said, his tone speaking to the problem more than his words did.

"Keep this screen open, but show me what happened when that transmission was sent," she said.

Another screen appeared next to the main screen. On it, the ships—all of them, including the *Ivoire*—were in slightly different positions.

The little rays of light kept hitting the *Ivoire* in various places all over its hull.

"Dammit," Ebedat said.

"What?" Sabin said. She hadn't seen anything. But her eye kept getting drawn to the scrum of little ships left in the *Ivoire's* wake. The *Ivoire's* disappearance seemed to have confused them. Or maybe they were automatic, and unable to cope with a target that suddenly vanished.

"I think," Ebedat said, "and let's put an emphasis on 'think,' okay? I *think* that six shots hit the *Ivoire* as it activated the *anacapa*."

"That shouldn't cause a problem," Wilmot said.

"Not with weapons we understand," Ebedat said, "but these didn't show up on our system without some tweaking from Lieutenant Graham."

"Good point," Sabin said, wanting to shut down dissent while Ebedat had the floor.

"And look." Ebedat froze the frame, then went over to it and pointed. "Three of those shots hit the general vicinity of the *anacapa* drive."

"The most protected drive on all the ships," Wilmot said. "You can't hit the *anacapa* without penetrating the hull."

"Do we have proof that the hull was penetrated?" Alvarez asked.

"There's no obvious damage," Graham said.

Sabin frowned at it all. "We don't know what kind of weapons they're using. They might have penetrated the hull without damaging it."

"That's not possible," Wilmot said.

"Most cultures would say the *anacapa* isn't possible either," Sabin said, "and almost everyone we've encountered hasn't figured out that foldspace exists."

The bridge was silent for a moment. The second screen's image remained frozen. On the first screen, the little ships swarmed the spot where the *Ivoire* had been, almost as if they were trying to prove to themselves that it hadn't become invisible.

"The *anacapa* couldn't have malfunctioned and created that light," Wilmot said, but he didn't sound convinced.

"We don't know if that light came from the weapons," Sabin said. "The *Ivoire* is probably in foldspace right now. Did Captain Cooper send us a window? How long does he plan to be in foldspace?"

"That part of the message was garbled," Graham said. "Give me a moment to clean it up."

"How long would you remain in foldspace, Captain, if this were happening to the *Geneva*?" Phan asked.

"The *Ivoire* knew support was half a day out," Sabin said. "That would seem like a blip in foldspace. They could return without worrying about the little ships."

She hoped that was what Coop had done. Just because one captain would do it didn't mean another would. It was logical, though. And then they could all take on the problems caused by those little ships.

"They'll also get a chance to assess damage," Wilmot said, "and maybe recalibrate their own weapons to take out those little ships."

Sabin frowned. Coop hadn't fired on those ships, that she had seen anyway.

Maybe he had other reasons that he couldn't do so. Maybe his weapons systems weren't working. Maybe he already knew that the weapons had no effect on those little vessels.

"He planned a twenty-hour window, sir," Graham said. "At least I think that's what the *Ivoire's* message said. I'm coordinating with several others in the front line. We'll let you know if that estimate is wrong."

"It sounds right to me," Sabin said. "It gives the *Ivoire* enough time to do some work on its own and it gives those small ships enough time to give up on the *Ivoire* and think it gone."

"And it also gives enough time for us to arrive," Wilmot said.

"Is he leaving this mess for us to clean up?" Phan asked, a bit too bluntly.

But Sabin knew what she meant. "The Fleet is operating diplomatically on Ukhanda. Once fire is exchanged, diplomacy ends."

"Yeah, so why wouldn't we fire?" Phan asked.

"I mean, once *we* fire, diplomacy ends," Sabin said.

"So we're supposed to take it when someone shoots at us?" Phan asked.

Had Phan never been in a battle? Sabin couldn't remember. It had been a long time since the *Geneva* had been under fire.

"Sometimes," Sabin said. "But we're generally not a diplomatic ship. Captain Cooper's weapon components would be different for this mission, and his orders would be constrained."

"Twenty hours," Wilmot said, clearly wanting to change the conversation. Protecting Phan? Sabin couldn't tell. "Does he want us there early to take the action he couldn't take?"

"He probably wants the show of force," Graham said. "It's one thing for a bunch of tiny ships to go after a large ship. It's another to face twenty ships from our front line."

Graham had a point. And Sabin had a job to do. She had to get her ship to that location, but she also needed clear instructions from the *Alta*. The diplomatic mission might be important or it might be something that the front line could scrub.

"I'm going to change," Sabin said, "and while I'm in my cabin, I'm going to see if I can get clear orders from the *Alta* on what we need to do when we get to Ukhanda. The last thing we need to do is blunder our way into a crisis."

Phan looked at her, expression serious. This time, however, Phan didn't say anything.

Wilmot was still staring at the screen as if he were trying to understand it.

"For the moment, Charlie," Sabin said to him, "you have the comm. Notify me if anything changes. And do your best to get us to that spot as fast as we can go, would you?"

"Yes, sir," Wilmot said.

She tugged on her bracelet as she left the bridge. To tell the truth, she was relieved that the dinner wouldn't happen. She liked action. She liked doing her job, not talking about trivial things.

She was worried about Coop, but he could take care of himself.

Her most important job now was to make sure the *Geneva* didn't screw up the Fleet's plans for the region.

She needed guidance, and she needed it now.

4.

It only took Sabin a few minutes to remove the dress and put on her uniform. Her uniform felt like a second skin to her. She glanced at the bed, her dress with its bow and fancy fabric splayed on top of the coverlet and wondered what she had been thinking. She expected her crew to be prepared on front line.

She should have been too.

Her quarters were the largest on the *Geneva*, not because she reserved the best for herself, but because regulations insisted. She had to put up with a certain amount of ceremony as captain, and she didn't like it any more than she liked the dress.

But she appreciated her quarters this evening. Because, unbeknown to most of the crew, the captain's quarters had a back-up control area, along with its own private communication network. And to get into that area took several layers of identification and approval. Once she was inside—alone—no one else could get in without even more identification and approval from her.

The area was just off her bedroom. A panel in the wall hid the entrance to the back-up control area.

She finger-combed her hair, then went through the various protocols that opened the panel. It slid back, revealing a small space that looked more elaborate than the back-up controls in engineering. In addition to the back-up navigation, piloting, and weaponry, there was an entire console for communications.

She closed the panel, then settled in, facing the communications console. This was where she had usually contacted Coop. In fact, he was the person she spoke to the most from this room.

It felt odd not to contact him at all.

The thought made her just a little shaky. She wasn't sure why she was so on edge about his message, even though her counselor at the academy would tell her why she was. He would have said that it had to do with her father.

Sabin set that aside.

She took a deep breath, feeling the calm she was known for descending on her.

She put a message through to Command Operations on board the *Alta*. Command Operations guided the Fleet. It was an organization of top-ranked officials, most of whom had served with distinction as captains of their ships once upon a time. They were the ones who essentially ran the Fleet.

There was a civilian government, but because the Fleet's origins were military, the power structure remained so. The civilian government took care of general management and often took care of diplomatic relations, but in situations like this one, Command Operations took charge.

Sabin identified herself, and then she said, "I realize I'm not senior captain for the front line, but so far, the senior captain hasn't checked in."

And she hoped that message got through: the front line's senior captain was so far away from his duties that he could come to a support request in a timely fashion.

"We're heading toward the *Ivoire's* position as per Captain Cooper's request. We'll be there in less than twelve hours. But we all have some questions about the mission."

Finally the screen across from her winked on, revealing the faces of several members of Command Operations. She had met two of them, including General Zeller who had been the first to question her abilities to captain, more than twenty years ago. The other three faces looked familiar, of course, and even if she hadn't known them by reputation, the listing of names and credentials below their images would have helped her understand who she was talking to.

The faces seemed to float against a black background. Long ago, Command Operations had established its communications imagery to show only the pertinent information and nothing more. In conversation with a captain, only the faces had been deemed pertinent.

"Your mission or Captain Cooper's?" asked General Nawoki, the other person that Sabin had met personally. She barely knew General Nawoki, although she admired Nawoki's military record. Nawoki was one of the few officers who had defended her ship—with no loss of life—in a four-day prolonged battle after her *anacapa* had broken down. At one point, overrun by the enemy, she managed to stave off boarding and ship capture by reengineering half of the lifepods into weapons.

"I'm interested in both missions," Sabin said. "According to what little we saw of the attack, Captain Cooper did not fire on the ships. Speculation from our Sector Research team is that these ships are Quurzod, and we know that the *Ivoire* was on a pre-diplomatic mission to the Quurzod. I need to know—the entire front line needs to know—if we're not to fire on those ships, or if the diplomatic mission is off."

The members of Command Operations did not look at each other—that she could tell, anyway. She had no idea how the cameras were set up in Command Operations. She didn't even have a high enough rank to enter the level on the *Alta* that housed Command Operations, let alone ever go into the room.

"Anything else?" Nawoki asked.

"When we arrive," Sabin said, "who runs the mission? The front line commander or Captain Cooper?"

"Why do you care now?" Zeller asked.

Sabin glanced at him. His face had more lines than it had when she was in school, but his eyes remained the same. Steel gray, flat, and cold. She had tried not to hate him back then. Given the resentment she felt now as she looked at him, she wondered if she had been successful.

"It will make a difference as to how we plan our response. A cursory study of the ships on front line tells me that none of us have the kind of diplomatic experience that the crew of the *Ivoire* have, and if this is still a diplomatic mission, then—"

"We will get back to you," Nawoki said, and the images vanished from the screen. The contact had been severed.

Sabin stood and let herself out of the room, leaving the panel open in case Command Operations responded immediately. She didn't want anything to record the expression that she had barely been able to keep off her face inside that room.

She knew why Zeller had asked her why she cared now. The bastard thought she was panicking. Even after fifteen years of exemplary command, he thought some ship slipping into foldspace made her panic.

Then she let out a long breath. Maybe she was misjudging him. Maybe the problem was something else entirely, a diplomatic problem that no one in Command Operations could discuss in front of her.

She stretched, trying to relax her muscles, and willed herself to focus on the moment.

The past did not matter, whether it was her past relationship with General Zeller or the disappearance of her father.

What mattered was this mission, and how she would handle it. How her crew would handle it. How the front line would handle it.

And whether or not they would imperil a diplomatic mission.

And if anyone in Command Operations asked her about her reasons for asking questions, she would not be defensive. She would answer honestly. She would tell them she wanted to do what was best for the Fleet.

Because she did.

5.

HER FIRST ENCOUNTER with George Zeller had come more than two decades before, when he was still a major. He reluctantly ran the counselors in the evaluation section of the academy's officer training program and, she later learned, he had taken no interest in the psychological evaluations or their necessity until she enrolled.

Correction: until she enrolled and did well.

Then, apparently, Major George Zeller made it his business to prove that she wasn't fit to command anything larger than an engineering staff on a third-class Fleet vessel.

He had been younger then, not just in age or experience, but in manner. He had red hair and green eyes that flashed when he was angry, which to her, seemed like all of the time.

He was the one who mentioned her father's disappearance to the academy staff, he was the one who believed that disappearance would cause problems, and he was the one who insisted on psychological training so rigorous that Sabin had to go without sleep for days to complete the testing and her schoolwork. When she complained to the head of her department, he moved the testing to dates between the school terms, enabling her to at least get some rest.

She always tested well, but Zeller kept accusing her of gaming the system. She finally reported him to his superior, one Colonel Gaines who would eventually disappear himself in an *anacapa* accident two years later. She never quite got over the irony of that; Zeller never got over the fact that she went over his head.

He might have overcome it, had she failed in Officer Training, but she had graduated first in her class, with high honors, the only person in twenty years to get a perfect score on all of the final term tests—including the physical ones.

She never quite figured out what Zeller had against her; other students had lost parents to accidents, disappearances, and explosions, and Zeller had never taken an interest in them.

Just her.

It wasn't until years later, after she had become a captain, that she found a reference to Zeller in her father's file. The record itself was mostly redacted. What did exist was deliberately vague.

After that discovery, she told herself that Zeller's reactions to her came from survivor's guilt, but she never really wanted to test that theory. So she avoided him whenever possible.

In fact, she had avoided him for more than a decade.

Until now.

6.

A SOFT, ALMOST INAUDIBLE *CHEEP* let Sabin know that the screen had activated. She slipped back into her chair, letting the panel close behind her.

Only one face floated in the blackness—that of General Nawoki. She looked tired, but Sabin didn't know if that was her natural state.

"We are getting conflicting reports from Ukhanda," Nawoki said. "The Xenth claim that the Quurzod killed all but three of the team members the Ivoire sent to the Quurzod. The Quurzod claim that the *Ivoire's* team violated Quurzod law and declared war. Word from some of the other cultures on Ukhanda is that the Quurzod are quick to offend and even quicker to use violence to punish the offenders. Unfortunately, the *Ivoire* herself has not sent us their report on the incident, so we have no way to assess the truth of the interaction. In other words, hold back until the *Ivoire* returns from foldspace, and let Captain Cooper lead the response."

It sounded like a mess and reinforced to Sabin, yet again, that she wanted nothing to do with actual diplomatic missions.

"Captain Cooper said he would keep the *Ivoire* in foldspace for twenty hours. We'll arrive eight hours before he returns. Should we stay out of the area until we have word of the *Ivoire*?"

Nawoki's lips thinned. She glanced over her shoulder at someone or something that Sabin could not see. Either Nawoki disagreed with the command she was about to give, or she was giving that command over the disagreements of others.

Sabin had no way to know which was true, only that Nawoki seemed as uncomfortable about the situation as Sabin felt.

"If those small ships remain, then stay out of the area," Nawoki said.

"And if they show up after we enter the same area?"

"Try to ascertain whose ships they are. See if they will negotiate or explain their position."

Sabin's breath caught, and she had to struggle to hold back her initial reaction. She had hoped that Command Operations had known to whom those ships belonged.

"Do we have any theories about who the ships belong to?" she asked.

"The Xenth say they are Quurzod ships, but our other sources on Ukhanda cannot confirm," Nawoki said.

"And forgive me, sir, but why aren't we trusting the Xenth?"

"Because we are getting conflicting signals from them. They claim they want peace with the Quurzod, but they are building their own military. Our Sector Research Team is also locating some evidence that the breaches of previous agreements might have come at the instigation of the Xenth rather than through the general warlike nature of the Quurzod."

Coop's voice echoed in Sabin's mind: *Do you ever question it? Our mission. Or at least part of our mission. What makes us so smart?*

"Were we planning to broker on the side of the Xenth?" Sabin asked, feeling like Phan—naïve and a bit out of her depth, and hoping the General wouldn't notice or would take pity and answer her.

"We believed we could bring peace to Ukhanda," Nawoki said primly.

What makes us so smart? The memory of Coop's voice floated through Sabin's mind. She had to concentrate to keep his doubts from infecting her.

"We believed, sir?" she asked.

"Something went wrong, Captain," Nawoki said. "And after we recover the *Ivoire*, we will figure out what that something was."

7.

THE REST OF THE TRIP to the Ukhandan part of the sector was uneventful. Captain Seamus Cho of the *Bellator* finally took over his role as commander of the front line. He had, apparently, been holding a bachelor party for a crew member and hadn't heard the summons in all of the ruckus.

In Sabin's opinion, Cho did not seem concerned enough about the *Ivoire* or the situation near Ukhanda. But he was operating under the same orders that Sabin was, and so she knew he would at least wait, the way she would have, for the *Ivoire* to reappear.

Coop would be sensible, and he would know what to do.

As the front line approached an hour sooner than planned, the small ships remained, patrolling the area as if they expected the *Ivoire* to return.

Most ships with strong sensors left a fighting region shortly after a Fleet ship disappeared. The sensors would show that the Fleet ship had left somehow and was not cloaked. Even ships that had poor sensors would get the message after eleven hours.

Either these small ships knew how the Fleet used their *anacapa* drives or the commanders of those ships were extremely stubborn, holding that small region of space as proof that they had conquered it.

Cho ordered the entire front line to remain just outside of standard sensor range—close enough to join any fight should the *Ivoire* return suddenly, but far enough away for a battle to be a struggle for any ships with planetside bases.

Finally, after eighteen hours, the small ships gathered into a V-shaped pattern and headed back toward Ukhanda. The entire front line tracked them, but did not see the ships go back to a base on the planet. Instead, they went past Ukhanda toward a small satellite that looked like it was part of an uninhabited sister planet.

Cho should have sent a ship to investigate, but he didn't. He believed their mission was to rescue the *Ivoire*, not to pursue the *Ivoire's* attackers.

Sabin couldn't argue with him. She might have made the same call herself, had she had command of the front line. It seemed as if Cho was as leery of getting involved in any diplomatic incident as she had been.

Finally, thirty minutes from the twenty-hour mark, he ordered the front line to prepare to defend the *Ivoire*. The front line would move slowly forward, not enough to attract attention from Ukhanda, but enough to get them in better range of the *Ivoire*.

They had covered half the distance to the *Ivoire's* last location when twenty hours came.

And went.

No one panicked. The *anacapa* drive could be finicky, and all of the captains had miscommunicated or misestimated their time in foldspace at one point or another.

Twenty-one hours passed.

Then twenty-two.

And finally, the front line got nervous.

Cho gave the standard search orders. A standard three-dimensional search pattern should have used twenty-four ships, but the front line didn't have that many. Besides, a few had to remain in position, in case the *Ivoire* returned later.

Cho assigned sixteen ships to the grid search, and left three ships in a waiting position. The fourth ship would go to an area not to far from the *Ivoire's* return site—close enough to be a bit dangerous, but far enough to prevent most collisions from happening.

That ship would be the most vulnerable: if the *Ivoire* returned to slightly different coordinates and the other ship's failsafes did not work, the ships might collide. But it was a standard risk at this point in delayed *anacapa* response.

Cho contacted Sabin before making the assignment. He used a private channel so that the other ships couldn't hear their conversation, even though the bridge crew could.

He turned up on her screen, tall and stately in his uniform. He had zoomed out the image so that she could see his entire bridge crew, who looked as busy and focused as hers.

"I want to assign you to the on-site investigation spot," he said. "You have the most experience. However, General Zeller told me that you might not want the task. I don't believe in taking one person's word for another's possible reaction, especially when the other person is available. You're the best person for the job, Tory. Do you want it?"

"Of course I do," she said, keeping her voice calm. The momentary flash of annoyance at Zeller's name and remark had already faded. Zeller was a problem for another day. "Do you want me to do a grid search or an area search?"

"See if you can find traces of the *Ivoire*," Cho said. "Barring that, see if you can figure out exactly what they did."

Something in his phrasing seemed strange to her.

"Don't you think they used their *anacapa* drive?" she asked.

"I do, but I've never seen one take so long to engage, and I've never seen a ship light up like that," he said. "I'm worried that they disappeared, not because of the *anacapa* but because those little ships used a weapon we don't understand."

Sabin felt chilled. She hadn't even thought of that possibility. In that case, Coop—and his entire crew—were already dead.

But she shouldn't guess. Guessing was the enemy in any search for information.

"If those ships used such a powerful weapon," she said, "why would they have remained in the area?"

"I don't know," Cho said. "I don't think they would have. But I can't rule out anything at the moment. We need to search."

She agreed. "I'll do my best to figure out what happened here," she said. "I'll let you know when we have news."

She had almost said *if we have news*, and had caught herself just in time. Normally, she wasn't a pessimist, but something was odd here, something she could feel but couldn't see.

She wasn't usually a gut commander. She liked facts and hard information. But she also knew that sometimes hard information took too much time to acquire and gut became important.

She hoped this wasn't one of those times.

8.

ON THE DAY HER FATHER DISAPPEARED, they pulled Tory Sabin out of class on the *Brazza* and took her to the observation deck. She always remembered it as "they" because try as she might, she couldn't remember who took her from class, how she got to the observation deck, how many people spoke to her along the way, or what anyone expected of her.

She was all of thirteen, precocious and opinionated, one month into her new school—a boarding school, which was unusual at her age. Boarding school for most students started when they qualified for the final four years of mandatory education. She tested way ahead of her peers, and so got assigned to a special school for children her age who were on a fast-track.

Her father was proud of her. No one had bothered to tell her mother.

But someone had told her mother that Sabin (whom everyone called Tory back then) was alone on the *Brazza*, waiting for news of her father, because her mother swooped in as if she would rescue everyone.

Her mother always wore impractical flowing garments, the kind of thing that confirmed she wasn't, nor would she ever be, part of the Fleet's military structure. She was an artist who worked in fabric. Her art changed each time she visited a new culture or planet, so her work became quite collectible among a certain group in the Fleet. She couldn't replicate patterns or materials once she ran out of whatever she had purchased in her (actually, the Fleet's) travels, so her pieces became—of necessity—limited editions.

Tory hadn't seen her mother in more than six months, even though the ship her mother lived on, the *Krásný*, never left the Fleet on any kind of mission. Most of the Fleet's civilians ended up on the *Krásný*, partly because the military presence was smaller on that ship. The ship specialized in environments and environmental systems, and that included the interior design that kept the people on board all of the ships entertained, stimulated, and sane.

Her mother sat beside Tory on a bench in the center of the room, enveloping her in lavender perfume. The bench was built so that the occupant had a 360-degree view of the space outside. Plus the domed ceiling was clear so that she could see everything above her.

Tory wanted to slide away. Her mother's perfume was overwhelming, but more than that, her mother's golden gown was made of some kind of shiny but rough fabric, and just being near it made Tory itch.

"They don't understand the *anacapa*, you know," her mother said conversationally, as if they'd been talking all along. No hello, no hug, no how-have-you-been, or even a comforting he'll-be-all-right. Nothing. Straight into the old arguments, with Tory standing in for her father. "It's dangerous to use them, and your father promised, back when we married, that he never would—"

"Fortunately, you're divorced," Tory said and stood up, arms crossed. "He's overdue by five hours. That's all, Mom. You can go back to whatever thing you're designing. I won't be mad at you. *I'm* not worried. Daddy's good at his job."

Her mother stood, and this time, wrapped her arms around Tory. Tory thought of elbowing her mother hard and viciously so that her mother would never hug her again, then suppressed the response and squirmed out of her mother's embrace.

"They don't remove a child from school or contact her remaining parent because they think this is routine," her mother said—so not comfortingly.

"I'm smart enough to know that, Mother," Tory said.

"They think you need me."

"They're wrong." Tory stepped closer to the observation window. "Daddy will be just fine. The *Sikkerhet* will return, and he and I will get on with our lives. *Without you.*"

Her mother tilted her head just a little, a dismissive *you can't mean that* look she had used as long as Tory could remember.

"I divorced him, not you," her mother said.

"Funny," Tory said, "I couldn't tell."

"I contacted your father about a visitation schedule. He never responded," her mother said.

On purpose, Tory almost said but didn't. He wanted to see if Tory's mother would push the visitation, wanted to see if she would make contact, if she would hire a lawyer to enforce the terms of the shared custody.

Her mother had done none of those things. In fact, she hadn't even done what was on her schedule—a series of internship calls that were supposed to happen every Friday night. Instead, she'd send apologies, usually about work-related distractions, and finally, she stopped apologizing altogether.

Tory's father had been surprised; he had thought Tory's mother was a different person, maybe from the beginning. Tory attributed his blindness to both love and to the fact that he hadn't spent much time with his wife once he got on a career track. It was only after he kept finding Tory on her own, in the engineering and maintenance areas of the ship, at an age when the crew would report Tory's appearance (because it was dangerous) that he finally realized his family couldn't stay on the ship when he had an actual mission.

When he broke that news to Tory and her mother, her mother had shrugged and said they would move to the *Krásný*. Tory had burst into tears, begging to stay, and her father, for once, had listened. Not that he could have missed the campaign. Because others on the ship said that Tory shouldn't—couldn't—stay with her mother. Not and have actual parental care.

"What happened between you and Daddy isn't my business," Tory said. "I—"

"It is your business, darling," her mother said. "If your father had—"

"I don't want to discuss it. In fact, I don't want you here. Daddy will return, and I'll be fine, and even if I'm not fine, you're not the kind of person who can take care of anyone. If you don't leave right now, I will."

Her mother stared at her as if Tory had betrayed her.

"You need me right now," her mother said. "I thought you were smart. No one misses an *anacapa* window without a reason, a serious reason. In the history of the Fleet, those who miss the window by an hour or more usually do not return. You have a scientific brain. You should understand—"

"Shut up," Tory said, her hands balled into fists. "Shutupshutupshutup."

"Tory—"

Tory waved her hand at her mother, effectively silencing her. Then Tory shook her head, and ran for the door. Tory had no idea where she was going to go—if she went back to her room, her mother would find her—but she had to get away.

Just like she had to get away when she was a child.

And like she had when she was a child, she found herself heading toward engineering, the only place on any ship with concrete answers.

The only place she had ever felt safe.

9.

SABIN'S SEARCH FOUND EVIDENCE that Coop had used the *anacapa* drive. Sabin was relieved and not relieved at the same time. In fact, she couldn't remember a moment when her emotions over one event had been so mixed.

The fact that he had used the *anacapa* proved that those small ships didn't have some kind of miracle weapon that destroyed the *Ivoire*. But the fact that he used the *anacapa* and wasn't back in the same spot at the time he had mentioned meant he was in trouble.

Sabin's mother had been right all those years ago: those who miss the window by an hour or more usually did not return.

Sabin sent the information to Cho and asked if he wanted her to contact all the sector bases still in operation. Sometimes a ship having trouble with its *anacapa* wouldn't show up in the spot it was supposed to; it would instead go immediately to the nearest sector base for repair.

The failsafe also took ships to sector bases, usually the most active one. If the crisis had been really bad, no one at the base would have thought of contacting the front line—if, indeed, the base even knew that the front line had moved.

Cho promised to check, and after he did, he requested a private audience with her. He wanted to talk to her nowhere near her crew or his.

She didn't think that unusual. She thought it sad. Because she knew part of what he was going to say.

Her ship had a small communications area just off the bridge. She had built that as well, for moments just like this one. When she thought about it, she realized she had made major modifications to every single ship she had served on, and on none more than the *Geneva*.

She slipped inside the communications area. It was larger than the one in her cabin. Ten people could fit in here comfortably, even though, if she needed that many people to hear something, then they would usually go to the conference area or listen on the bridge.

The communications into this section of the ship were scrambled and encoded, more private than anything else on the *Geneva*.

Screens covered all the walls. Everything could become holographic if needed, but she never used that feature. The table in the middle of the room felt out of place. She didn't sit at it.

Instead, she leaned on it, and contacted Cho.

He showed up on the screen in front of her, in a room similar to her own. His ship had been redesigned after she made modifications to hers.

Cho looked tired. Some of that might have been because of the bachelor party and the change of focus, but some of it was a man trying to cope with hard news, news that upset him, news he wanted to treat dispassionately, even though it was impossible.

"You think they're dead," she said without introduction. She had almost said, *you think* he's *dead*, which was an insight into her own mind that she didn't want and she certainly didn't want Cho to hear.

Either she thought Coop was dead, or she feared it, or she cared about it too much. After all, there were more than five hundred souls on that ship. She should care about all of them equally.

"What I think doesn't matter," Cho said, which was clearly his version of yes. "They haven't shown up at any of the active sector bases or starbases. The *Alta* tells me that experts have pinged the older sector bases, and there's been no activity, at least activity that has shown up in the logs. Experts tell me that they shouldn't have gone back to sector bases that the *Ivoire* hasn't used in the past twenty years, so that double-check was a long shot."

She knew that. No ship had shown up on old decommissioned sector bases unless that ship had used or visited the sector base some time in its recent history.

"The *Alta* wants us to do a few things," he said. "They want us to wait until the *Taidhleoir* arrives. That ship will handle the situation on Ukhanda."

The *Taidhleoir* was another ship that specialized in diplomatic missions. It wasn't as top of the line as the *Ivoire*, but it would do.

"They figured out, then, who the ships belonged to?" Sabin asked.

"The Xenth say that the ships are Quurzod, but the Quurzod aren't acknowledging anything, and apparently the *Alta* can't confirm. It's a mess, and they don't want us in the middle of the diplomatic part of the mess. The front line has to remain, though. The show of force is going to show everyone on Ukhanda that the Fleet isn't to be messed with."

"Even though someone probably think they successfully harmed one of our ships," she said, more to herself than to Cho.

"Even though," Cho said, in the tone that captains used when they didn't approve of the path their higher ups were taking. "They also want us to do some investigating along the trails left by the small ships and near that spot where the *Ivoire* lit up so oddly."

"I have been," Sabin said.

"Not for an indication of *anacapa* use, but to see if there are other energy signatures that we're unfamiliar with, or maybe even ones we are familiar with. In other words, they want our investigators to figure out what those ships were attacking the *Ivoire* with."

"Reverse engineer it?" she asked. She'd been part of teams that had done such things in the past. They were usually used in war situations, when one of the participants had developed a new weapon. "We can't just ask someone on Ukhanda or capture one of the ships?"

Cho visibly shrugged, and he looked away for a moment. When he glanced back at her, his dark eyes held sadness and something else. Frustration? She didn't know him well enough to be able to tell.

"They think something really bad happened on that planet," he said, "and they believe it's going to take some work to deal with it. Work we can't do in a time frame that will enable us to rescue the *Ivoire*."

If they could rescue the *Ivoire*. He didn't even have to add that part for her to hear it.

"You didn't have to tell me all of this in private," she said. "You know our bridge crews could have kept this quiet. What else is there?"

"I wanted you to make a choice. Not your crew, not the *Alta*. You." Now his gaze met hers, and she almost felt him in the room. He was scared. She rarely had that thought about other captains, and she had never seen such emotion from Cho. Not that he was showing much now. His mouth had thinned a bit. Anyone who didn't know him would have thought he was just a little more concerned than normal, a little preoccupied.

But she could feel it: He was scared.

Was he scared of her response? Or something else entirely?

"Here's the thing, Tory," he said, his tone confidential. "I talked to some of the generals directly. We all know that time is of the essence in tracking a lost ship in foldspace. But General Zeller wants us to wait until some of the foldspace investigative and rescue ships arrive. He doesn't trust you."

Of course he didn't. He hadn't from the moment he met her.

"Trust me to what?" she asked, although she had a hunch she knew.

"Search foldspace." Cho spoke tersely as if he wanted to get this part of the conversation over with. And as she was about to respond, he added, "I don't understand it, Tory. You're the one who developed the search method that we've used for the past thirty-five years. You're the one who understands it the best. I know you and Zeller have issues, and I assume it's none of my business—"

"He thinks I'm too emotional about this," she said. "And you know, on this one thing, he might be right."

10.

OLDER THAN HER YEARS, brilliant, and obsessed. That was what Sabin's evaluations all said. She had hacked into them on the night before the very first test mission began.

Her years were all of twenty, too young to do much in the Fleet, but old enough to be considered an adult. She had already gone to two boarding schools. She had worked her way through some of the most difficult engineering degree programs in the Fleet, plus she had done some work with the Dhom, one of the more advanced cultures they were lucky enough to find two years ago.

The scientists there taught her things about dimensional theory that no one in the Fleet had contemplated before. After they heard the Dhom scientists, some of her professors postulated that the Fleet had lost a lot of its research into dimensional theory. The professors claimed that the *anacapa* drive couldn't have been developed without it.

Some of her professors were a little naïve, in Sabin's opinion anyway. She could have pointed to a dozen points in the history of science and technology, points she knew, where something got developed accidentally and no one quite knew how it worked.

Granted, however, such things rarely inspired confidence, and she didn't need to point out that there were parts of her theories that were just guesses as well. Guesses based on research, but as she could have pointed out to anyone who listened (as she would argue sometimes inside her own mind), theories needed testing before they became quantifiable.

Her test missions were the transition between theory and fact. Or at least, between narrower, more apt theories, and something approaching fact.

What she couldn't admit to anyone—not her mentors, not the professors, not the captains running the ships would take these risks—was that she really didn't care about ancient history, *anacapa* development, or even dimensional theory.

She cared about finding her father and his crew.

And if her theories were right, then even now, she might find them, trapped in foldspace for only a few hours or days. Even if seven years had gone by for them, as those seven years had gone by for the Fleet, she might still discover some remnant of the ship. Maybe the *Sikkerhet* had gone to a nearby planet and settled. Maybe it had simply refueled and waited, trying to figure out how to return to what the Fleet called "real space," which was, the current space and time.

The one thing the Fleet had done was build a long-term future trajectory. The Fleet knew where it was going. It was heading into what, for it, was uncharted space. It had advance ships to either map the area or to double-check the maps provided by the locals of the sector the Fleet was currently in.

The only thing uncertain in the Fleet's map was the timeline. The Fleet had none. It would spend months near some planet, learning the culture. It would spend years helping a new ally fight a war.

If her father knew the trajectory, he might be waiting for the Fleet *ahead* of where the Fleet currently was. She doubted that, though, since the *Alta* had sent large ships as well as exploratory vessels ahead, searching for the *Sikkerhet*.

If her father had gone too far into the trajectory, she might never see him again. The version of the Fleet that greeted him or the descendants on his ship might be populated by her grandchildren's generations—if, indeed, she ever had grandchildren.

The method she had devised, the method that ultimately got tested, was a three-part grid search inside foldspace. The Fleet had never done foldspace grid searches for lost ships before, not in all the millennia of its existence.

Part of that was a simple disagreement as to what foldspace was. Some theorists believed that foldspace was a different point in time—the future, the past—some*when* else. But a lot of the practical military, those who'd actually flown into foldspace through their *anacapa* drives, didn't believe that.

The star maps in foldspace were significantly different than the star maps from the area where the ship had left. It usually took something catastrophic to change star maps in the same area—not even the explosion of a planet would change a star map so drastically as to be completely unrecognizable.

So most theorists believed that foldspace was either an alternate reality that somehow the ships tapped into with the *anacapa* or a fold in space, an actual place that the ships could somehow access.

What Sabin privately believed was that the *anacapa* sent a ship far across the universe, into another galaxy altogether, and then back again. But the scientists told her that the *anacapa* didn't have the energy for that. Nothing did.

Which left her with dimensional theory. One of her professors claimed that foldspace was another dimension, one that hadn't yet been charted and wasn't understood. Some of the work done by the scientists on Dhom pointed to that theory being correct.

She had been contemplating all of that when she realized that none of it mattered. *What* the ships went into wasn't important. What it *seemed like* was.

And what it seemed like was a sector of space like all other sectors of space, except for the different star maps. Except for the fact that none of the equipment that the Fleet had could track the ships down in that sector of space. None of the equipment that any other culture had could track those ships either.

So she decided to do what all the scientists of the *anacapa* had done before her—not question how it did what it did—but accept the reality that it worked.

In that reality, the ships went somewhere that looked like this reality.

And those realities could be searched.

If she could find the right point in foldspace, the same entry point that a missing Fleet ship had taken.

The same entry point that the *Sikkerhet* had taken.

The same entry point that her father had taken—and disappeared.

11.

"Oh, come on," Cho said in a tone she'd never heard him use before. "Zeller's unreasonable. Everyone knows that. They're just waiting for him to retire."

Sabin blinked at him, forcing herself to come back for a moment in her own past. A quick escape in her own mental foldspace.

The small control room was hot. She pushed a strand of hair off her face, and resisted the urge to smile grimly. Cho was staring at her with something like sympathy, which she would not have expected from him.

"I know they're waiting for him to retire," she said. "They think he's old-fashioned. But he's not entirely unreasonable."

Cho frowned. He looked like he was about to disagree, when she said, "He's lived through a lot, Seamus. Sometimes we don't respect that enough."

"I can't believe you're agreeing with him, after the way he treats you."

Her smile was thin. "Yeah, I know," she said. "But I think I don't treat him well either."

12.

WHEN SABIN WAS TWENTY-ONE, she hadn't known who Zeller was. He'd just been a crew member on the *Rannsaka*, one of the ships that had used her grid system to explore foldspace in search of her father's ship.

Zeller had simply been a face in the crowd when she boarded the *Rannsaka*, heading to its largest crew dining room for a briefing.

What she encountered was a celebration.

Over two hundred crew members applauded her as she walked into the room. The captain, a severe woman who until this point rarely seemed to smile, had led the cheers, then surprised Sabin by saying,

"And thanks to Tory Sabin, we now know what happened to five of our vessels. Five, considered lost, and now found."

Sabin's breath caught. She'd been running so-called test missions of the grid search for more than a year. The missions were no longer tests, really. Everyone knew they worked on some level. But so far none of the ships found had been the *Sikkerhet*. All had disappeared at different times, and in different sectors of space. None had had crew members that anyone knew, and indeed, the ships themselves had been empty for a long time. There weren't even bodies on board, although no one knew if the crews had left voluntarily or not. Most of the ships were open to space. Those ships could have been raided, abandoned, or simply suffered through the passage of time.

As of yet, no one had even tried those ships' *anacapa* drives or even tried to boot up the other equipment. The ships had piggybacked on the science vessels and had been taken to Sector Base T so that they could be studied.

Four of those ships anyway.

Sabin hadn't known about a fifth.

She turned to the captain and said softly, "There's a fifth?"

"Yes," the captain said with a smile. "We found it at the very end of our search and it's already at Sector Base T. And this one's mostly intact."

Sabin knew better than to ask the captain why no one had contacted Sabin. Gradually the mission was changing from testing to something run by the military, and the military rarely gave out information.

The entire crowd had grown silent. Maybe they saw Sabin's reaction, a tentative response, not quite the joy everyone had expected.

She had gotten the news on the other four in her command headquarters on the *Pasteur*, and she had been with her team. They knew she had been searching for one ship in particular, so her mixed reactions hadn't bothered them.

She wished she could remain as calm as a scientist should in such circumstances, but her heart rate increased. Her face was slightly flushed and she knew she looked just a bit too eager.

"What ship is it?" she asked, suspecting she knew the answer. After all, why would they throw a celebration if it weren't the *Sikkerhet*?

"The *Moline*," the captain said, "and the good news is that she's mostly intact."

The ship's name rolled around in her head for a long moment. *Moline. Moline.* She hadn't even heard of that ship. She had heard of two of the others before they were found, but the *Moline* wasn't one that had any obvious known history.

She could feel her intellect trying to wrap itself around the news, while her heart sank. She needed to leave the room, she needed to be alone with this, but she also needed to acknowledge everyone's good work.

"That's excellent," she said and hoped she sounded enthusiastic.

"And," the captain said with that unbelievably cheerful sound in her voice, "I wanted to let you know that the *Alta* has decided that your foldspace searches are now going to become part of the Fleet's regular systems. We'll design ships to do the searches, train people, everything. Your program is official now!"

The crew cheered and applauded. Sabin smiled at them—at least, she hoped she smiled. How come no one had told her this personally? Why were they doing this kind of "celebration"? Didn't they know this wasn't about the old ships or even the program? It was about her father.

At the thought of him, the frustration she'd been holding back welled up. She knew better than to react here. Instead she smiled, waved some more, and then nodded once, fleeing the room.

She made it halfway down the corridor before she burst into tears. She had known things would change at some point, but she figured she'd find her father first. The search wasn't refined enough yet. She couldn't pinpoint where a ship disappeared and where it had gone to in foldspace. The grid search had used *anacapa* signatures to track ships, yes, but they weren't ships that anyone had been searching for. They had disappeared long ago; their crews would have been dead now, anyway.

Some of the *Rannsaka*'s crew came through the corridor. She turned away, unable to go farther, and hid her face against the wall, hoping no one would stop for her.

One man did. He touched her back, asked if she was all right.

"Yes," she had lied. "Yes. Just tired."

She had no idea if she knew him or if he knew her. She never ever learned who he was. But later, she'd come to suspect Zeller. Zeller, who realized how broken up she had been over not finding her father's ship, about effectively being removed from running the program she had started.

Or maybe that man had been someone else, and she had given Zeller too much credit. Maybe the man—whoever he had been—had no memory of an incident that loomed so large in her own mind.

The next day, she asked to search for her father's ship. Her request was denied. Apparently Command Operations on the *Alta* wanted to examine the five recovered ships before searching for any more.

They told her to put in a request for a future search, and they would get back to her.

They commended her for her service. They designed an entire group of ships to search foldspace, based on her plans. They offered to promote her.

She let them.

And six months later, she was moved from foldspace search to engineering, where she was supposed to improve the *anacapa* design.

Five years after that, after applying and reapplying to search for her father's ship to no avail, she applied to the academy for officer training.

And, it turned out, only Zeller had figured out why.

13.

"I HAVEN'T RUN A SEARCH since the very first one, decades ago," Sabin said to Cho. "Things have changed, procedures have changed, and honestly, I haven't kept up with most of it."

She shifted in her chair. The room had closed in on her.

Cho nodded. "I glanced at the information, and from what I can tell, the only time we recovered a ship in foldspace right after the ship missed its window, we had gone in within twenty-four hours."

She closed her eyes. She could almost picture Coop, grinning at her over a private dinner in their suite on Starbase Kappa, teasing her about the changes in protocol on something or other. He had once told her that she jumped in too early, in his opinion, that a captain needed caution to protect his crew.

She had told him that a captain also had to know when to take a risk.

Cho said something, but she held up her hand to silence him. She needed a moment to think. He was going to explain risks to her that she understood, risks she invented for god's sake.

Ships had to dive in and out of foldspace just to do the grid search, and each trip into foldspace, each search, put the rescue ships at risk. The best grid search took the coordinated effort of five or more ships, exchanging information, going in, coming out, never staying in foldspace longer than a minute or two to gather information.

Because a minute or two in foldspace could be an hour or more outside of it.

Sixty minutes or sixty-five or sixty-three. The correlation was never entirely precise, which was what made foldspace so very dangerous.

In fact, there were three main things that made foldspace dangerous. The first was that no one entirely understood it, so the sensible captains were leery about using it. The second was that the sensors did not work between foldspace and real space. So returning from or going to foldspace meant that a ship might land on top of something else, like an asteroid or, in the case of real space, another ship.

And of course the final great risk was the one she dealt with right now: the longer a ship stayed in foldspace, the more unreliable the time of return became. No one could predict the exact moment the ship would come back, only that it would come within a time frame. That was why Coop said twenty hours, but he didn't specify down to the minute or second.

The biggest problem Sabin had now was this: the front line didn't have five ships to spare. She knew that, and Cho hadn't mentioned any others. The crew of her ship was going to have to do something it wasn't trained for, and she would be risking her crew to save another.

Jumping in too fast.

She had a hunch Coop would have waited until the investigative team arrived. She wouldn't.

She opened her eyes. Cho was watching her patiently, as if he expected her to say no. He had given her time, and she appreciated that, especially since his time was so valuable.

Just like hers was.

Like Coop's was.

"I think we need at least two ships to do this," she said. "And if there are crew members on any ship in the front line who used to work foldspace investigation and rescue. I'd like them to join my team for this rescue attempt."

Cho's jaw moved just a little, as if he started to say something and then held it back.

"The *Alta* didn't approve two ships for this," he said.

She started to argue, but it was his turn to hold up his hand.

"But," Cho said with great force. "I agree with you. If we're going to mount a rescue, we're going to do the best we can to get it right."

She grinned at him, and felt—astonishingly—a prickle of tears behind her eyes. Dammit, she cared more than she wanted to.

She probably should have admitted that as well, but she didn't. Besides, she suspected Cho understood.

She suspected his willingness to countermand the orders from the *Alta* had more to do with Coop and the *Ivoire* than it did any kind of common sense.

She appreciated it, but she didn't tell Cho that.

She suspected he already knew.

14.

IT TOOK HALF AN HOUR to prepare for the rescue. The *Geneva's* partner ship on this mission was the *Pueblo*, commanded by Captain Jakoba Foucheux. Foucheux had spent two months in foldspace investigation and rescue before asking for a transfer. The reason for the transfer remained classified, a procedure that usually meant some issue with a superior officer, and usually one that never got properly resolved in any kind of arbitration.

Sabin didn't have any time to dig deeper. She was relieved to have Foucheux, whom she liked, as her partner, but disappointed that Cho had only found ten other crew members who'd worked in foldspace investigation and rescue. Of those ten, only five were available to transfer to Sabin's ship. The others were too far away on the search near Ukhanda to get back in time to start this mission.

The mission was deceptively simple. Once Sabin finished the math confirming what she believed Coop had done considering the information he had given, the telemetry that the *Ivoire* had automatically sent to the Fleet, and the time he'd been gone, she could—within a limited range—figure out the coordinates in foldspace.

The foldspace investigation and rescue section had a formula for all of this, and since they were the ones that had actually discovered recently missing ships in the past, she had two of the borrowed crew members use that formula as well.

All three people—the crew members and her, using her old system—had come up with the same location, which cheered her. If they had been searching for a ship disappeared long ago, they would have a lot more trouble coming up with the same location. They'd probably come up with three different locations, and maybe more, depending on how they all tweaked their formulas.

Once they had a location, the ships would work in tandem. First the *Geneva* would head to that part of foldspace and immediately scan the area. The *Geneva* would stay no more than a minute, and reappear, sending all of its scanned information to the *Pueblo*.

The *Pueblo* would do the same thing, scanning a slightly different swath of foldspace, and the two ships would continue to work in tandem until they found something, or until the actual investigation and rescue ships arrived.

The problem was that there were no guidelines on which direction to proceed once the searching ships moved beyond the scans of the original location. That was why five ships was better, and more than five desirable. The ships would partner, and go in *all* directions, doing so quickly, then moving to cover as much of that region of foldspace in the shortest amount of time.

Sabin had to pick a direction after the third set of tandem jumps, and she didn't like that. She hoped the *Ivoire* would be easy to find, that it would show up—even as a speck—on the nearest grid search. But she knew that hope and reality often failed to collide.

15.

THE FIRST JUMP into foldspace felt like any other. First, the thrum of the *anacapa* drive, which she barely heard or felt on a normal day, faded. Then the screens blanked. Sabin knew that if she were watching the navigation controls, they would flicker for just a moment.

The entire ship would bump, only once and very slightly. If she were in a vehicle on the ground, she would think that vehicle had hit a small rock, sending a tiny reverberation through the entire system.

Then the screens reappeared, the navigation controls clicked back full force, and that reverberation disappeared, replaced by the thrum of the *anacapa*.

Sabin had jumped into foldspace so many times, she usually didn't notice the details. In fact, she could only remember noticing a few times in her past: on her first trip doing a grid search, on her first jump as chief engineer, and then the first time she piloted a vessel, as a lieutenant on the path to full command.

So, Sabin watched herself react here as if she were standing outside herself. Paying attention to those tiny details, common details, meant three things. She was worried about this grid search. She was worried about her ship.

And she was worried about Coop.

The images on the screen were a star map she didn't recognize. Even though that happened with every jump into foldspace, it was still something she noticed. She liked knowing exactly where she was, and in foldspace, she never did.

"Rapid grid search," she ordered, even though Wilmot, Phan, and Ebedat were already bent over their consoles. Sabin wanted to be in and out of foldspace as fast as she could.

"We have it, sir," Wilmot said.

"Good," Sabin said. "Let's go back."

Alvarez activated the *anacapa*.

As the screens blanked for the second time in less than a minute, Sabin said, "Graham, the millisecond we return, you need to send that information to the *Pueblo*. Even before we analyze."

"Yes, sir," Graham said.

By the time he finished speaking, the *Geneva* had returned to real space.

"Done, sir," Graham said and as he spoke, the *Pueblo* vanished.

Sabin let out a small breath.

"Any ships?" she asked Wilmot.

"Not obviously in this first grid," he said. "How deep a search do you want?"

"It's all we've got at the moment, so keep some part of the system probing as deep as possible," she said. "The better the search, the better our luck will be."

And as she said that, the *Pueblo* returned in the same place it had been a few minutes before.

"Okay," she said, "let's go again."

And they did.

16.

Twenty-five searches later, Wilmot said, "Sir, the *Pueblo* may have found something."

Sabin's heart rose, but she made herself take a deep breath and tamp down the emotion. "May" was not definitive enough, and Foucheux was the kind of woman who would be accurate in her descriptions.

"Tell the *Pueblo* that we'll delay our search to see what's on the grid. Let's compare notes."

Sabin knew that speed was of the essence. The true investigative team wouldn't be here for a while, so the *Geneva* and the *Pueblo* needed to act. But they had to act together, and as accurately as they could.

Sabin had the five former members of foldspace investigation and rescue evaluate the information. She did the same.

And she discovered that Foucheux was right: there was something at the edge of the *Pueblo*'s last grid search that looked like one of the Fleet's ships. Oddly, it didn't have an active signature, but that could mean many things.

It could mean that the *Ivoire* was dead, with no power at all.

It could also mean that what they were looking at was a ship, but not one of the Fleet's.

"Is the computer finding anything else on its deep searches?" Sabin asked Wilmot. "Are we getting other strange readings?"

"No, sir," he said. "This is the only thing that could be a ship, according to the data we've analyzed so far."

No analysis could be complete in such a short period of time. There could be other things in the grid that they'd missed because of their focus on the *Ivoire*.

But all of that—if there was anything at all—would have to wait for the foldspace investigation and rescue team.

She needed to make a decision now.

"Tell the *Pueblo* we're going to focus our search on that part of the grid, and we're going to take a maximum of three minutes per search inside foldspace instead of one minute."

"Sir?" Wilmot asked. "The time—"

"I am aware of the time," Sabin said. "We don't have enough ships to double up, so we have continue doing this as best we can."

Her heart was pounding. Three minutes in foldspace would seem like forever to the ship outside of foldspace. But it would also give her time—and Foucheux time—to figure out what, if anything, that reading on the sensors was.

"Take us into the last place the *Pueblo* was," Sabin said to Alvarez. "Then prepare to move quickly toward that blip. If we read it as anything but one of our ships, we move back into position, and return to real space. Got that?"

She wanted everyone clear on the mission before they went in.

"Let the *Pueblo* know we're heading in," she said, and gave the order.

17.

WHEN THEY WERE INSIDE FOLDSPACE, the blip on the *Pueblo*'s search grid did not seem like a blip at all. It looked solid.

Sabin's bridge crew worked quietly and quickly, shouting out information only when necessary.

The ship wasn't that far away from their position, and as they approached, it became clear they *were* looking at a ship.

One of the Fleet's ships.

But not the *Ivoire*. The *Ivoire's* design was sleeker, with some of the design tweaks that Sabin herself had helped engineer.

Her heart continued to pound as they approached the ship.

It had no power; that was evident. And its *anacapa* wasn't working at all. No matter what system the *Geneva* used to see if the ship had an energy signature, they could find nothing.

It took less than a minute to get close enough to get a full visual on the ship.

Its center was gone; only the outer edges remained, giving it a ship-like shape, but no real heart.

No wonder she saw no evidence of the *anacapa*. There was no *anacapa* at all. The bridge was gone, engineering was gone, the heart of the ship was gone.

And it looked, from a cursory glance, as if the entire ship had somehow been ripped open. At some point, probably when the ship arrived in foldspace, it had hit something, done the thing everyone feared, and landed on top of, in the middle of, something else—an asteroid, space debris, or another ship.

No one survived.

Even if they had survived in the outer edges of the ship, they would not be alive now. Without that center core of the ship, the crew would have had only a few weeks to live. And judging by the design—what she could see of the design—those few weeks had expired years ago.

"Captain." Wilmot's voice was tight. "Look."

He zoomed on a section of the damaged ship, showing that section only to her. The name of the ship registered on her screen:

The *Sikkerhet*.

Sabin had finally found her father.

18.

SOMEHOW, SABIN REMAINED CALM. That detached feeling she'd had earlier when the *anacapa* first activated had returned. She knew that she had to captain the *Geneva*, and she had to continue on her mission.

Only the mission had changed.

They did have a ship to recover as well as one to find.

But their time had run out. They also had to return to real space.

Sabin got the *Geneva* back. Then she contacted Foucheux. Sabin almost asked for a private conference, but knew that was for her. It wasn't necessary and it would take to much time.

Foucheux appeared on one screen to the left of Sabin. Foucheux was tall and thin, and seemed more so on a two-dimensional screen. Her mocha-colored skin looked a bit gray, but that might be the lighting or the imagery.

Or she might be tired from the interruption of the respite period, just like everyone else had been.

She stood with her hands clasped behind her back. That posture, and the way that she had pulled back her black hair, made her seem more severe than usual.

"It's not the *Ivoire*," Sabin said, even though she suspected Foucheux had already seen the data. "It's the *Sikkerhet,* and it was destroyed long ago. I have no idea how it got to this part of foldspace or what that even means. The *Sikkerhet* has been missing for decades, and it was nowhere near this section of real space when it disappeared."

Her voice remained calm, normal, in control. She felt like three people— the captain of the *Geneva*, a little girl who had just realized her father was really and truly dead, and the woman who watched them both.

"Regulations require us to continue the search for the *Ivoire* and let recovery teams handle the *Sikkerhet*," Sabin said. Wilmot was watching her. She had a feeling that Charlie expected her to countermand regulations. "And in this instance, regulations absolutely apply. The *Sikkerhet* is beyond help, and any crew that survived either took lifepods elsewhere long ago, or expired when the ship got destroyed."

Her voice still remained calm. She felt calm. Or at least the captain part of her did, as did the observer part. The little girl had a metaphorical fist against her mouth to prevent an outburst, and wanted nothing more than to flee to her cabin right now.

There was no right now, not for grieving. Technically, Sabin should have done that a long, long time ago.

"So," Sabin said, "let's maintain our initial plan for the grid search and our initial timeline. I'll send the location of the *Sikkerhet* to the foldspace investigation and rescue team."

Foucheux nodded. Her posture didn't change, but her expression had softened. "I was going to suggest the same thing. But, let me be the first to say to you that I'm sorry."

Sabin had nearly interrupted. She didn't want her crew to know the meaning of the *Sikkerhet*. Nor did she want any more sympathy.

"Thank you," she said, and this time she had just a bit of wobble in her voice. "Now, let's get back to the search."

"We're on it," Foucheux said and signed off.

After a moment, the *Pueblo* disappeared into foldspace.

Sabin took a deep breath and sat down.

"Captain, did I miss something?" Ebedat asked. "Did something—"

"Nothing's amiss," Sabin said, trying to forestall the questions. "We continue the search. Please make sure that both Captain Cho, the *Alta*, and foldspace rescue know about the *Sikkerhet*."

"Yes, sir," Ebedat said. "Already done, sir."

"Good," Sabin said, and forced herself to focus, as she waited for the *Pueblo* to return.

19.

"IF I COULD DISCOURAGE YOU from this path, I would," Major Zeller said, on the day he became her advisor.

They were sitting in his office on the *Brazza*, a blue-and-white planet visible through the gigantic window on the left side of the room. The *Brazza* was in orbit, while the Fleet tried to decide if the planet would become the next sector base location. A series of postdoctoral students were taking part in the studies, so someone in command believed it easier to have the *Brazza* in orbit than in its usual place near the bulk of the Fleet.

"You should go back to engineering, designing, and numbers," Zeller said. "You have a gift for them, and we need someone like you there."

Sabin hadn't expected his negativity, particularly since he was to be her advisor for the next few years.

"I tested well," she said. "In fact, I tested higher than anyone else this year."

"You did," he said. "Tests aren't everything."

"I know that," she said. "But I come from a long line of commanders. My father was a captain. My grandfather made general. My great-grandmother—"

"I'm aware of your family's history," Zeller said. "That's why we're talking. It's your family's history that makes me think you're not captain material."

She felt the shock all the way through her. No one had spoken to her like this before. Until this moment, everyone she had encountered, all of the administrators, instructors, and so many others believed she belonged in command.

"Excuse me?" she said, because she didn't know how else to respond.

"Ever since your father disappeared, you've been on a single-minded mission to find him," Zeller said. "Along the way, you have helped the Fleet. Your design for searches in foldspace is genius. The tweaks you've made to the *anacapa* systems and use are valuable. The designs you've added to the ships are both luxurious and comfortable. But none of that will make you a good leader. In fact, I think you'll be a terrible one."

Her face warmed. If she got angry now, though—or, at least, let him see how angry she already was—she would prove him right.

"My father has been gone a long time," she said.

"Yes, he has," Zeller said. "But I know how this goes. I've lost people too. I was on the first team sent—using your methods—to try to find the *Sikkerhet*. I volunteered because I had family on that ship."

His expression changed just a little, saddened, then hardened again. This was not a man with whom she could speak of shared sympathy.

"The hardest part of being a leader, Victoria," Zeller said, using her real first name, which no one ever did. It made her feel even smaller, "is not decisions, but the attrition. You will lose people. They will fall away like parts off a damaged ship. They will get angry and move planetside, they will transfer, or they will die in battle."

She knew that. She had already lived through it. Even children lost friends when ships went down. The losses had been part of her life, like they were part of everyone's life here in the Fleet.

"But some of them, Victoria, will disappear. Literally disappear. You won't know what happened to them ever. They will be like ghosts who haunt you through your entire career."

"I know that," she said.

He gave her a contemptuous smile. "No, you don't. You think you do because we all lose people, we lose things, we lose ships. But you don't, because you've never been responsible for the loss. You've never ordered a ship to go into a dangerous maneuver or into foldspace or into a battle where no one emerges alive. The responsibility is what's different, Victoria. And the responsibility makes you second-guess everything."

She willed herself not to move. She suspected this conversation was more about him than it was about her. He was probably moved off the career track into academic administration because he couldn't handle the results of his own orders.

"When you start second-guessing," he said, "everything you do, everything you are, is about that ghost. Every captain has one. Generals have dozens. But they acquire them during their commands. They lose people. And not every leader mentally survives those losses."

She was convinced now: this was about him, not her. But she listened.

She had no other choice.

"You already have a ghost," he said. "One that you can't let go of. Your entire life has been about finding your father, and he can't be found. He is *gone*, Victoria, and nothing you do, no search patterns you develop, no tweaks you make to the *anacapa* drive, no command you give when your ship needs to go to foldspace, will ever change that."

She wasn't sure if she should respond. But he had paused for several seconds now, so she said, "I know that, sir."

"Intellectually, yes, you know that. Emotionally, you do not. And someday, you will risk your entire crew because of your father. You will make a decision that has nothing to do with now, and everything to do with that loss. It might not seem obvious. It might seem totally unrelated. But it won't be. And more people will die."

She wanted to say sarcastically, *Thank you for your belief in me, sir*, but she didn't. Instead, she silently vowed she would prove him wrong.

"I'm not leaving the officer training program," she said. "If I wash out, fine. But I want to do this. I think I'll be good at it. I think I'll be better at it than anything else I've ever done."

He shook his head slightly, as if he couldn't believe her arrogance. Well, she couldn't believe his. Who was he to tell her who she was and who she would be?

"I'm going to be watching you," he said. "The moment I see that ghost making decisions for you, I'm pulling you out. Is that clear?"

She wondered how he would know. Would he fudge results? Would he see a "ghost" where there was none?

But she knew better than to ask. She remained as still as she possibly could, so he wouldn't see her steeling herself for battle with him.

"Yes, sir," she said calmly. "That's clear."

Technically, she should have thanked him. Technically, she should have told him that he was doing the entire Fleet a favor by keeping an eye on her.

But that was admitting weakness.

She wasn't going to admit weakness. Especially not now.

She wanted to command—and she would.

And she would be so much better than Zeller ever was, than Zeller ever could be.

But she didn't tell him that either.

Instead, she would show him. Every single day, for the rest of her life.

20.

THE *GENEVA* AND THE *PUEBLO* continued the grid search, but Sabin knew after the fiftieth iteration they would find nothing. No trace of the *Ivoire*.

She tried not to feel dispirited, and when the emotion threatened to overwhelm her, she privately blamed it all on the confirmation of her father's death.

She didn't let any emotion show. She did her job, coldly and efficiently, knowing she could tend to her emotions later.

Even after the foldspace investigation and rescue team arrived, even after they failed to find the *Ivoire* with a thorough by-the-books search, she held her emotions back.

They did her no good. They certainly didn't help her, or anyone, find Coop.

The *Geneva* took part in a lot of the background investigation, providing support, ferrying teams to various parts of the Ukhandan sector.

And all the while, the foldspace investigation and rescue team searched, doing the math over and over again, trying to find a hole in the logic, replaying the telemetry sent by the *Ivoire*, the coordinates, the estimates—and finding nothing.

Just like the ships that searched for the *Sikkerhet* found nothing all those years ago.

When it became clear that the *Geneva's* role would be downsized, Sabin took some time off—actual time off.

She got some sleep. And she spoke to a mandatory grief counselor. She was proud of herself; she didn't lie. She said the discovery of her father's ship brought everything back up, and created as many questions as it answered.

The remaining information systems on the *Sikkerhet* were corrupted, the life pods were in place in the intact portions of the ship, but all of that meant nothing considering how much time had passed.

The foldspace investigation and rescue team brought the *Sikkerhet* back to real space, and would take it to Sector Base V for study. There they would figure out what the information systems said, what happened in the last few hours of the ship, and how it got to that part of foldspace.

For all anyone knew, that part of foldspace was the part ships went to when they activated the *anacapa* decades ago. Or maybe it was easily accessed from the part of real space where the *Sikkerhet* had been when it disappeared.

No one knew, but they did know they had to answer some questions. Sabin knew that she needed the questions answered as well.

Because, she figured, if they found out what happened to the *Sikkerhet*, they might end up with more information in their search for the *Ivoire*.

That search would continue for months, maybe years. Already a mathematics and theoretical physics team had come in to watch the imagery of the *Ivoire* in the moments before it vanished. They were timing the last message, and figuring out why it had reached the ships before the *Ivoire* vanished, since those two things should have happened simultaneously.

The hope was that they would figure out the differential, use it in the equations that sent ships into a particular part of foldspace, and find the *Ivoire*.

The *Alta* had sent another diplomatic ship to work with the Xenth in locating the ships that had attacked the *Ivoire*. If a team from the Fleet got to investigate those ships' weapons systems, they might figure out how the weapons interacted with the *Ivoire's anacapa*, *if* those weapons did indeed interact with the *anacapa*, and maybe come up with some answers that way.

The *Geneva* was to help transport the *Sikkerhet* to Sector Base V. Sabin knew that she had received a charity mission, one that would let her find some answers slowly, and for once in her life, she didn't care.

Because she had finally come to some conclusions.

As the *Geneva* traveled back to Sector Base V, she asked for a private conference with General Zeller.

She spoke to him from her private communications room in her captain's suit, the same room she had spoken to Coop night after night after night.

She didn't miss the sexual side of her relationship with Coop—that had happened only a few times per year—but she missed the friendship, the ability to consult with someone who had a similar job but a different point of view.

She felt alone now, in a way she had never felt alone before.

But she didn't tell Zeller that.

Instead, when his disapproving face appeared on her screen, she actually smiled at him.

"I'm finally going to do what you want, General," she said, after the initial niceties ended.

His gaze kept moving away from her image, as if something else in the room interested him more than any conversation with her could. "And that would be?"

"I'm resigning my commission. I'm stepping down as captain of the *Geneva*."

His entire posture changed. His gaze snapped forward, meeting hers.

"That is not what I want," he said. "You have become one of the best captains in the Fleet. You proved me wrong long ago, Captain Sabin, and even on this most difficult mission, you kept your focus on the task at hand, setting your personal problems aside and rising to a standard that few captains achieved."

She had waited years for praise like that from him. Her cheeks warmed as her face flushed. But the praise was no longer relevant.

"Thank you, General," she said, "but I realized on this last trip that you were right: my father's disappearance has haunted me. It still does. We don't entirely understand what happened—"

"We're pretty sure that the ship collided with something in foldspace as it arrived," Zeller said. "Every captain's nightmare."

"Yes," Sabin said. "It is, and they're probably right. But I want to know."

"You can get reports. Your talents would be wasted working on the remains of the *Sikkerhet*. Let the technicians do it—"

"General," she said gently. "I've acquired a new ghost on this trip."

To his credit, he stopped speaking and frowned. "Someone on the *Ivoire*?" he asked, keeping the question both professional and delicate.

"Captain Cooper and I were good friends," she said, unwilling to explain more. "I believe if I return to foldspace and *anacapa* research, I might be able to find him."

"We've lost one excellent captain on this trip," Zeller said. "We can't lose you as well."

A month ago, these comments would have angered her. She would have wanted to know why he hadn't said such things to her before, why he had kept his evaluations to himself.

Or she would have demanded to know why he believed her good now, instead of earlier. She could almost hear her own voice, strained, angry: *Am I a better captain now that you're short a captain, General? Or are you supposed to say this to keep me in line?*

But she didn't have the energy or the desire for that kind of confrontation.

"General," she said gently, "my full attention will never again be on the *Geneva* and that, by definition, will make me a bad captain. I'm going to resign my commission, and you can't talk me out of it. If you value my work, please help me secure a good spot on the teams investigating the *Sikkerhet* and the disappearance of the *Ivoire*."

His expression was flat. Only his eyes moved, as if he could see through the camera into her soul.

"I have never understood you," he said. "I always thought I did, but I don't."

"I disagree, General. You believed me obsessed with my father's disappearance, and I was. When I realized I could learn no more, I put myself in a position to emulate him. And now that we have information again, I want to return to research."

Zeller shook his head. "Your father wouldn't understand this."

"Probably not," she said. "I think it would make him angry."

She didn't add the rest. She had finally realized that she was her mother's daughter as well as her father's. Unlike her mother, Sabin thrived in a military environment. But unlike her father, she had to choose her own path, and if that path deviated from the norm, she had to follow the new path instead of trudging along the old.

Amazing that a double loss—learning her father was truly dead and suspecting that Coop was as well—would help her discover who she really was.

Perhaps that was what living was all about, using the good and the bad to determine the essence of one's self.

"I'll be more useful in research," she said. "Of course, I will remain on the *Geneva* until the Fleet can provide a suitable replacement."

"I don't think anyone has resigned a captain's commission after such a success, Sabin," Zeller said. "Not in all the years of the Fleet."

She didn't believe that was true. There were centuries of Fleet history, and so much had disappeared into legend.

"I don't consider what happened in foldspace a success, sir," she said. "We lost the *Ivoire.*"

"And found a ship that we had thought gone forever, Captain," Zeller said. "We wouldn't have found it without you. The foldspace rescue team says they might have dismissed that blip on their equipment. They think you and Captain Foucheux saw things they did not, and they must change their algorithms accordingly."

This was one of the reasons that Sabin had to return to research and foldspace investigation. The method of doing things had become more important than the purpose for doing those things.

The teams no longer thought of the lives hanging in the balance. They thought about the probabilities for success.

And with that realization, she finally understood what Zeller was telling her.

There was only one person who could have found the *Sikkerhet* on this mission, one person whose thinking was both rigid enough to conduct a grid search and creative enough to explore all the possibilities.

That was why he considered her mission a success.

"I am going to see if we can invent a new position for you, Captain," Zeller said. "We need something better in investigations, and we need someone of command rank who can run that new system. Tell me you'll keep your captain's commission and accept the reassignment."

"Only if I may focus on research, sir," she said.

"Research, investigation, and the technology itself. I'll see if we can change the *Geneva's* designation so she can be the ship in charge of that part of our team."

"Sir, the *Geneva's* not equipped for the kind of work we would need to do," she said. "We would need a newer ship, one outfitted especially for us."

His eyes narrowed, that disapproving look she knew so well. He had once accused her of taking what little she was offered, and ungratefully asking for ten times as much.

She had just done so now.

But she didn't take back her request.

"My instinct is to say no, Captain," he said. "But I have learned that my instinct always discounts you. So I will see what I can do."

"Thank you, sir," she said as he signed off.

She sat in her small back-up control room for several minutes afterward, staring at the blank screen.

For the first time in their careers, neither Zeller nor Sabin had won the argument with each other. They had compromised in a way neither of them would have thought possible two decades before.

She was starting something new, remaking something old into a brand new part of the Fleet.

And, sadly, the first thing she wanted to do was tell Coop. He might not understand her choice, but he would give her an intelligent and lively discussion. He would let her know what she hadn't thought of, and what she needed to do to make the experiment work.

She closed her eyes for just a moment.

She would remain a captain, and the loneliness would still be a large part of her life.

Maybe even larger now, without Coop.

As a young girl, she had needed her father back. She couldn't imagine life without him.

As an adult woman, she wanted Coop back. But she could easily imagine life without him. It wasn't just something she would have chosen.

None of this was.

And here was the difference between her childhood and now: If her research found Coop alive, she still would retain a job in research and foldspace investigation. If they had found her father before she quit school, she would have become someone else.

Funny how the events of one's life changed that life.

Coop understood that. He seemed to fathom how wisdom was hard-earned, not something someone else could impart and believe that another person would get.

Maybe that was why the Fleet's insistence on stepping into life in other cultures bothered him so much. Because he hadn't even been certain he understood his own life.

She wished she could tell him that she finally realized what he had been telling her all those months ago.

And, in acknowledging the feeling she had, she realized also that she believed, deep down, she would never get the chance to tell him. Even if her research led to his ship's discovery forty years from now, she suspected Coop would not be on it, just like her father hadn't been on his ship.

Hard-won understanding.

It wasn't quite the death of hope—part of her still hoped that Coop was alive somewhere.

It was more like the application of hope.

She wanted to make sure that no one else—child, adult, crew member, captain—would ever lose a loved one to foldspace again.

It was probably a vain hope.

But it would keep her going, for at least another forty years.

≫•≪

The Confederation fights only because the baffling Others continue to battle them. Staff Sergeant Torin Kerr's aim is to keep both her superiors and her motley crew of space marines alive as they deal with lethal missions in defense of the galaxy. Tanya Huff's story is set in her Valor Confederation universe.

NOT THAT KIND OF A WAR

Tanya Huff

"WE STILL HAVE ONE HELL of a lot of colonists to get off this rock before we can leave." Captain Rose frowned at Sho'quo Company's three surviving second lieutenants and the senior NCOs. "And every ship going up is going to need an escort to keep it from being blown to hell by the Others so we're on Captain Allon's timetable. Given the amount of action up there . . . " He paused to allow the distant crack of a vacuum jockey dipping into atmosphere to carry the point. " . . . we may be down here for a while. Bottom line, we have to hold Simunthitir because we have to hold the port."

"The Others have secured the mines," Second Lieutenant di'Pin Arver muttered, her pale orange hair flipping back and forth in agitation, "you'd think they'd be happy to be rid of us."

"*I'd* think so. Unfortunately, they don't seem to." The captain thumbed the display on his slate and a three dimensional map of Simunthitir rose up out of the holo-pad on the table. "Good news is, we're up against a mountain so, as long as our air support keeps kicking the ass of their air support, they can only come at us from one side. Bad news is, we have absolutely no maneuvering room and we're significantly out-numbered even if they only attack with half of what they've got on the ground."

In Staff Sergeant Torin Kerr's not inconsiderable experience, even the best officers liked to state the obvious. For example: *significantly out-numbered.* Sho'quo Company had been sent off to this mining colony theoretically to make a statement of force to the Others' scouts. They'd since participated in a rout and now were about to make one of those heroic last stands that played so well on the evening news. No one had apparently told the enemy that they were merely doing reconnaissance and they had, as a result, sent two full battalions— or the Others' equivalent—to take the mines.

"Lieutenant Arver, make sure your remaining STAs . . ."

And what fun, they'd already lost two of their six surface-to-air missiles.

" . . . are positioned to cover the airspace immediately over the launch platform. See if you can move one of them up here."

A red light flared on the targeting grid overlaying the map.

"Yes, sir." The lieutenant keyed the position into her slate.

"Set your mortars up on level four. I want them high enough to have some range but not so high any return fire they draw may damage the port. You're going to have to take out their artillery or we are, to put it bluntly, well and truly screwed. Staff Sergeant Doctorow . . ."

"Sir."

Doctorow's platoon had lost its second lieutenant in the first exchange.

" . . . I want all accesses to the launch platform in our hands ASAP. We don't need a repeat of Beniger."

With the Others beating down the door, the civilians of Beniger had rushed the ships. The first had taken off so over-loaded it had crashed back, blown the launch pad and half the port. Granted, any enemy in the immediate area had also been fried but Torin figured the dead of Beniger considered that cold comfort.

"Lieutenant Garly, I want one of your squads on stretcher duty. Get our wounded up into port reception and ready to be loaded once all the civilians are clear. Take position on the second level but mark a second squad in case things get bad."

"Sir."

"Lieutenant Franks . . . "

Torin felt the big man beside her practically quiver in anticipation.

" . . . you'll hold the first level."

"Sir!"

Just on the periphery of her vision, Torin saw Staff Sergeant Amanda Aman's mouth twitch and Torin barely resisted the urge to smack her. Franks, Torin's personal responsibility, while no longer a rookie, still had few shiny expectations that flared up at inconvenient moments. He no longer bought into the romance of war—his first time out had taken care of that—but he continued to buy into the romance of the warrior. Every now and then, she could see the desire to do great things rise in his eyes.

"You want to live on after you die, Staff . . . " He danced his fingers over his touchpad, drawing out a martial melody. *" . . . do something that makes it into a song."*

Torin didn't so much want Lieutenant Franks to live on after he died as to live on for a good long time so she smacked that desire down every time she saw it and worried about what would happen should it make an appearance when she wasn't around. The enemy smacked down with considerably more force. And their music sucked.

The captain swept a level stare around the gathered Marines. "Remember that our primary objective is to get the civilians out and then haul ass off this rock. We hold the port long enough to achieve this."

"*Captain.*" First Sergeant Chigma's voice came in on the company channel. "*We've got a reading on the unfriendlies.*"

"On my way." He swept a final gaze over the Marines in the room and nodded. "You've got your orders, people."

Emerging out of the briefing room—previously known as the Simunthitir Council Chamber—the noise of terrified civilians hit Torin like a physical blow. While no one out of diapers was actually screaming, everyone seemed to feel the need to express their fear. Loudly. As if maybe Captain Allon would send down more frequent escorts from the orbiting carrier if he could only hear how desperate things had gotten.

Captain Rose stared around at the milling crowds. "Why are these people not at the port, First?"

"Port Authorities are taking their time processing, sir."

"Processing?"

"Rakva."

Although many of the Confederation's Elder Races took bureaucracy to a fine art, the Rakva reveled in it. Torin, who after twelve years in the Corps wasn't surprised by much, had once watched a line of the avians patiently filling out forms in triplicate in order to use a species-specific sanitary facility. Apparently the feathers and rudimentary beaks weren't sufficient proof of species identification.

"They're insisting that everyone fill out emergency evacuation forms."

"Oh for the love of God . . . Deal with it."

Chigma showed teeth—a distinctly threatening gesture from a species that would eat pretty much anything it could fit down its throat and was remarkably adaptable about the later. "Yes, sir."

"Captain . . . " Lieutenant Franks' golden brows drew in and he frowned after the First Sergeant. "Begging your pardon, sir, but a Krai may not be the most diplomatic . . . "

"Diplomatic?" the captain interrupted. "We've got a few thousand civilians to get off this rock before a whole craploud of Others climb right up their butts. If they wanted it done diplomatically, they shouldn't have called in the Corps." He paused and shot the lieutenant a frown of his own. "Shouldn't you be at the first level by now?"

"Sir!"

Torin fell into step at his right shoulder as Franks hurried off the concourse and out onto the road that joined the seven levels of Simunthitir into one continuous spiral. Designed for the easy transportation of ore carriers up to the port, it was also a strong defensive position with heavy gates to close each level off from those below and the layout ensured that Sho'quo Company would maintain the high ground as they withdrew to the port. If not for the certain fact that the Others were traveling with heavy artillery—significantly heavier than their own EM223s—and sufficient numbers to climb to the high ground over the piled bodies of their dead, she'd be thinking this was a highly survivable engagement. Ignoring the possibility that the Others' air support would get off a lucky drop.

"Well, Staff, it looks like we've got the keys to the city. It's up to us to hold the gates at all costs."

And provided she could keep Lieutenant Franks from getting them all killed—but *that* was pretty much business as usual.

"ANYTHING HAPPEN WHILE I WAS GONE?"

Sergeant Anne Chou shook her head without taking her attention from the scanner. "Not a thing. Looks like they waited until you got back."

Torin peered out over the undulating plain but couldn't see that anything had changed. "What are you getting?"

"Just picked up the leading edge of the unfriendlies but they're packed too close together to get a clear reading on numbers."

"Professional opinion?"

The other woman looked over at that and grinned. "One fuck of a lot, Staff."

"Great." Torin switched her com to command channel. "Lieutenant, we've got a reading on the perimeter."

"Is their artillery in range?"

"Not yet, sir." Torin glanced up into a sky empty of all but the distant flashes of the battle going on up above the atmosphere where the vacuum jockeys from both sides kept the other side from controlling the ultimate high ground. "I imagine they'll let us know."

"Keep me informed."

"Yes, sir."

"You think he's up to this?" Anne asked when Torin tongued off her microphone.

"Since the entire plan is that we shoot and back up, shoot and back up, rinse and repeat, I think we'll be fine." The lieutenant had to be watched more closely moving forward.

Anne nodded, well aware of the subtext. "Glad to hear it."

The outer walls of Simunthitir's lowest level of buildings presented a curved stone face to the world about seven meters high, broken by a single gate. Running along the top of those buildings was a continuous line of battlement fronted by a stone balustrade about a meter and a half high.

Battlements and balustrades, Torin thought as she made her way to the gate. *Nothing like getting back to the basics.* "Trey, how's it going?"

The di'Taykan Sergeant glanced up, her hair a brilliant cerulean corona around her head. "She's packed tight, Staff. We're just about to fuse the plug."

They'd stuffed the gate full of the hovercraft used to move people and goods inside the city. Individually, each cart weighed about two hundred kilos, hardly enough to stop even a lackluster assault, but crammed into the gateway—wrestled into position by the heavy gunner's and their exo-skeletons—and then fused into one solid mass by a few well placed demo charges, the gate would disappear and the city present a solid face to the enemy.

As Trey moved the heavies away, Lance Corporal Sluun moved forward keying the final parameters into his slate.

"First in Go and Blow, eh?" Lieutenant Franks said quietly by Torin's left shoulder.

"Yes, sir." Sluun had kicked ass at his TS3 demolition course.

A trio of planes screamed by closely followed by three Marine 774's keeping up a steady stream of fire. Two of the enemy managed to drop their loads—both missed the city—while the third peeled off in an attempt to engage their pursuers. The entire tableau shrieked out of sight in less than minute.

"I only mention it," the lieutenant continued when they could hear themselves think again, "because there's always the chance we could blow not only the gate but a section of the wall as well."

"Trust in the training, sir. Apparently Sluun paid attention in class."

"Firing in five . . . "

"We might want to step back, sir."

" . . . four . . . "

"Trust in the training, Staff?"

"... *three* ..."

"Yes, sir. But there's no harm in hedging our bets."

"... *two* ..."

They stopped four meters back.

"... *one. Fire in the hole.*"

The stones vibrated gently under their feet.

And a moment later ... *"We've got a good solid plug, Lieutenant."* Trey's voice came over the group channel. *"They'll need the really big guns to get through it."*

Right on cue: the distinctive whine of incoming artillery.

This time, the vibrations underfoot where less than gentle.

Four, five, six impacts ... and a pause.

"Damage?"

"Got a hole into one of the warehouses, Staff." Corporal Dave Hayman's voice came over the com. *"Demo team's filling in the hole now."*

"Good." She tongued off the microphone. "Everything else hit higher up, sir. I imagine we've got civilian casualties."

Frank's lips thinned. "Why the hell isn't Arver pulsing their targeting computers?" he demanded grimly.

Shots seven, eight, and nine missed the port entirely.

"I think it took them a moment to get the frequency, sir."

Ten, eleven, and twelve blew in the air.

Confident that the specialists were doing their jobs, the Marines on the wall ignored the barrage. They all knew there'd be plenty to get excited about later. Electronics were easy for both sides to block, which was why the weapon of choice in the Corps was a KC-7, a chemically operated projectile weapon. Nothing disrupted it but hands-on physical force and the weighted stock made a handy club in a pinch. Torin appreciated a philosophy that expected to get pinched.

Eventually, it would come down to flesh versus flesh. It always did.

As another four planes screamed by, Torin took a look over the front parapet and then turned to look back in over the gate. "Trey, you got any more of those carts down there?"

"Plenty of them, Staff."

"All right, lets run as many as will fit up here to the top of the wall and send those that don't fit up a level."

"Planning on dropping them on the enemy?" Lieutenant Franks grinned.

"Yes, sir."

"Oh." Somewhat taken aback, he frowned and one of those remaining shiny patches flared up. "Isn't dropping scrap on the enemy, I don't know ..."

Torin waited patiently as, still frowning, he searched for the right word. "UnMarinelike?"

Or perhaps he'd needed the time to make up a new word.

"Look at it this way, sir, if you were them and you thought there was a chance of having two hundred kilos dropped on your head, wouldn't you be a little hesitant in approaching the wall?"

"I guess I would . . . "

He guessed. Torin, on the other hand, knew full well that were the situations reversed, Lieutenant Franks would be dying to gallantly charge the port screaming *once more into the breach!* And since her place was beside him and dying would be the operative word, she had further reason to be happy they were on this side of the wall. If people were going to sing about her, she'd just as soon they sang about long career and a productive retirement.

THE OTHERS CAME OVER THE RIDGE in a solid line of soldiers and machines, the sound of their approach all but drowning out the scream of the first civilian transport lifting off. Marine flyers escorted it as far as the edge of the atmosphere where the Navy took over and the Marines raced back to face the bomber the Others had sent to the port. One of Lieutenant Arver's sammies took it out before it had a change to drop its load. The pilot arced around the falling plume of wreckage and laid a contrail off toward the mountains, chased away from the massed enemy by two ships from *their* air support.

According to Torin's scanner, these particular soldiers—fighting for a coalition the Confederation referred to as the Others—were mammals; two, maybe three, species of them considering the variant body temperatures. It was entirely possible she had more in common physically with the enemy than she did with at least half of the people she was expected to protect—the Rakva were avian, the Niln reptilian, and both were disproportionately represented among the civilian population of Simunthitir.

The odds were even better that she'd have an easier time making conversation with any one of the approaching enemy than she would with any civilian regardless of species. Find her a senior non-com, and she'd guarantee it. Soldiering was a fairly simple profession after all. Achieve the objective. Get your people out alive.

Granted, the objectives usually differed.

Behind her in the city, in direct counter-point to her thoughts, someone screamed a protest at having to leave behind their various bits of accumulated crap as the remaining civilians on the first level were herded toward the port. It never failed to amaze her how people hung on to the damnedest things when running for their lives. The Others *would* break into the first level. It was only a question of when.

She frowned at an unlikely reading.

"What is it, Staff Sergeant?"

"I'm not sure . . . " There were six, no seven, huge inert pieces of something advancing with the enemy. They weren't living and with no power signature they couldn't be machinery.

The first of Lieutenant Arver's mortars fired, locked on to the enemy's artillery. The others followed in quick succession, hoping to get in a hit before their targeting scanners were scrambled in turn. A few Marines cheered as something in the advancing horde blew. From the size of the explosion, at least one of the big guns had been taken out—along with the surrounding soldiers.

"They're just marching into an entrenched position," Franks muttered. "This won't be battle, this will be slaughter."

"I doubt they'll just keep marching, sir." Almost before she finished speaking, a dozen points flared on her scanner and she switched her com to group . . . "It's about to get noisy, people!" . . . and dropped behind one of the carts. Lieutenant Franks waited until the absolute last moment before joining her. She suspected he was being an inspiration to the platoon. Personally, she always felt it was more inspiring to have your lieutenant in one piece, but hey, that was her.

The artillery barrage before the battle—any battle—had one objective. Do as much damage to the enemy as possible. Their side. The other side. All a soldier could do was wait it out and hope they didn't get buried in debris.

"Keep them from sneaking forward, people!" It wasn't technically necessary to yell, the helmet coms were intelligent enough to pick up her voice and block the sound of the explosions in the air, the upper city, and out on the plains but there was a certain satisfaction in yelling that she had no intention of giving up. She pointed her KC-7 over the edge of the wall. "Don't worry about the artillery—they're aiming at each other not at you!"

"Dubious comfort, Staff!"

Torin grinned at the Marine who'd spoken. "It's the only kind I offer, Haysole!"

Ears and turquoise hair clamped tight against his head, the di'Taykan returned her grin. "You're breaking my heart!"

"I'll break something else if you don't put your damned helmet on!"

The di'Taykans were believed to be the most enthusiastically non-discriminating sexual adventurers in known space and Private Haysole di'Stenjic seemed to want to enthusiastically prove he was more di'Taykan than most.

While allowances were made within both branches of the military for species specific behavior, Haysole delighted in stepping over the line—although in his defense he often didn't seem to know just where the line was. He'd made corporal twice and was likely never going to get there again unless casualties in the Corps got much, much worse. Given that he was the stereotypical good-humored, well-liked, bad boy of the platoon, Torin was always amazed when he came out of an engagement in one piece.

"Staff." Corporal Hollice's voice sounded in her helmet. His fireteam anchored the far end of the wall. *"Picking up unfriendlies approaching our sector."*

Torin glanced over at the lieutenant who was obviously—obvious to her anyway—fighting the urge to charge over to that sector and face the unfriendlies himself, mano a mano. "Mark your targets people, the official number seems to be one fuck of a lot and we're not carrying unlimited ammo."

"Looks like some of them are running four on the floor. Fuck, they can really motor!"

"What?"

"Uh, sorry Staff, old human saying. One group has four legs and they're running really fast."

"Thank you. I'm guessing they're also climbers or they wouldn't be first . . ." And then she was shouting in the sudden silence. " . . . at the wall," she finished a little more quietly. "Stay sharp."

"Artillery seems to have finished smashing things up," Franks murmured as he cautiously stood and took a look around.

The two lower levels were still more or less intact, the upper levels not so much. The question was, had the port survived. And the answer seemed to be yes as a Marine escort screamed in and another civilian carrier lifted off.

The distinct sound of a KC-7 turned Torin's attention back to the plains.

"Our turn," Franks murmured. "Our turn to stand fast and say you shall not pass."

Had that rhymed? "Sir?"

His cheeks darkened slightly. "Nothing."

"Yes, sir."

All Marines qualified on the KC-7. Some of them were better shots than others but every single one of them knew how to make those shots count. The problem was, for every one of the enemy shot, another three raced forward to take their place.

"I hate this kind of thing." Franks aimed and fired. "There's no honor in it. They charge at us, we shoot them. It's . . . "

"Better than the other way around?" Torin suggested.

He shrugged. Aimed. Fired. "I guess so."

Torin knew so.

The enemy wore what looked like a desert camouflage that made them difficult to see against the dead brown grasses on the plains. Sho'quo company was in urban camouflage—black and gray and a dirty white—that hopefully made them difficult to see against the walls of Simunthitir. Most were on foot but there were a scattering of small vehicles in the line. Some the heavy gunners took out—the remains of these were used as cover at varying distances from the wall. Some kept coming.

Torin pulled the tab on a demo charge, counted to four, leaned over the wall and dropped it. The enemy vehicle blew big, the concussion rattling teeth on the wall and windows behind them in the port. "I suspect they were going to set a sapper charge."

"Odds are good, sir."

"Why didn't you drop a cart on them?"

"Thought we'd best leave that to the end, sir. Get a few carts stacked up down there and they'll be able to use them to get up the . . . Damn!"

The quadrupeds were climbers and they were, indeed, fast. One moment there were only Marines on the wall, the next there was a large soldier with four heavily clawed legs and two arms holding a weapon gripping the edge of the parapet. One of the heavies went down but before the quad could fire again, Lieutenant Franks charged forward and swung his weapon so that the stock slammed in hard between the front legs and then shot it twice in the air as it fell backwards off the wall.

He flushed slightly as Marines cheered and almost looked as though he was about to throw himself off the wall after it to finish the job. "I was closest," he explained, returning to Torin's side.

He wasn't. She hid a smile. Aimed. Fired. Hid a second smile as the lieutenant sighed and did the same. He wanted deeds of daring and he got target practice instead. Life was rough. Better than the alternative though, no matter how little the lieutenant might think so. *Do or die* might have more of a ring to it but she much preferred *do and live* and did her damnedest to ensure that was what happened for the Marines under her care.

Another civilian carrier lifted off. So far they were three for three.

"Artillery seems to have neutralized each other," Franks murmured, sweeping his scanner over the plain. "That's some nice shooting by Arver's . . . What the hell?"

With the approaching ground troops dug in or pulling back, Torin slaved her scanner to the lieutenant's. The inert masses she'd spotted earlier were being moved forward—no, *pushed* forward, their bulk shielding the pushers from Marine fire.

"Know what they are, Staff?"

"No idea, sir."

He glanced over at her with exaggerated disbelief, as he activated his com. "Anyone?"

"I think they're catapults, sir."

"*Cat*—apults, Corporal Hollice?"

"Yes, sir, it's a pre-tech weapon."

"And they're going to what? Throw cats at us?"

"No, sir. Probably rocks."

Franks glanced at Torin again. She shrugged. This was new to her.

"They're going to throw rocks at us?"

"Yes, sir."

"I'm not reading a power source, Hollice."

"They use, uh, kind of a, uh, spring thing. Sir."

"You have no idea, do you Corporal?"

"Not really, sir. But I've read about them."

Franks took another look through the scanner. "How do the mortars target something with no energy read?"

"Aim and fire, sir. They're not that far away."

"Not so easy with an emmy, Staff." Franks mimed manually aiming one of the mortars and Torin grinned.

Then she stopped grinning as the first of the catapult things fired and watched in disbelief as a massive hunk of ore laced rock arced overhead and slammed into level five. The wall shattered under the impact flinging debris far and wide.

"Cover!"

Then BAM! BAM! BAM! BAM! Not as deafening as artillery but considerably more primal.

Most of the rock screamed over their heads, aimed at the remaining emmies now beginning to return fire from level four.

Most.

One of the rocks grew larger, and larger, and . . .

The wall bucked under foot, flexed and kicked like a living thing trying to throw them off. A gust of wind blew the rock dust clear and Torin saw that a crescent shaped bite had been taken out of the top of the wall. "Chou?"

"Two dead, three injured, Staff. I'm on it."

What if they gave a war and nobody died . . . Never going to happen. "Listen up, people, next time you see a great hunk of rock sailing toward you, get the fuck out of the way! These things are moving a lot slower than what we're used to!"

Only one emmy spat back an answer blowing one of the incoming rocks out of the sky.

"Oh for . . . COVER!" A piece of debris bounced off Torin's helmet with enough force to rattle her teeth and a second slammed into her upper back, fortunately moving fast enough that her vest absorbed most of the impact.

"Arver!" Spitting out a mouthful of blood from a split lip, Franks screamed the artillery lieutenant's name into his com. "You want to watch where you're dropping that shit!"

"You want to come up here and try and aim this thing manually?"

"I don't think you're going to have time for that, sir." Torin nodded out over the wall. Under cover of the rocks, which were probably intended to be as much of a distraction as a danger, the Others had started a second charge, the faster quadrupeds out front once again and everyone else close behind.

The odds of deliberately hitting a randomly moving object were slim. The Marines switched to full automatic and sprayed rounds into the advancing enemy. Bodies started hitting the dirt. The enemy kept coming.

"As soon as you can take out multiple targets, start dropping the carts!"

Out of the corner of one eye, Torin saw Juan Checya, one of the heavy gunners, sling his weapon, flick on a hovercraft, and, as it lifted on its cushion of air, grab the rear rail with both augmented hands and push it to the back of the wall. As soon as he had the maximum wind-up available, he braced himself and whipped around, releasing the cart at the front of the arc. It traveled an impressive distance before gravity negated the forward momentum.

The quadrupeds closest to the casualties keened at the loss of their companions and seemed to double their speed. Torin found it encouraging, in a slightly soul deadening way, that they grieved so obviously. Grief was distracting. Unfortunately, not only distracting for the enemy. "Sir . . . "

Franks rubbed a grimy hand over his face, rock dust mixing with sweat and drawing vertical gray streaks "I'm okay, Staff."

"Never doubted it, sir."

Above and behind them, a fourth civilian carrier rose toward safety.

"One carrier remaining." Captain Rose's voice on the command channel. Torin almost thought she could hear screaming in the background. She'd rather face a well-armed enemy than civilians any day. *"Lieutenant Franks, move your*

platoon back to level three and take over stretcher duty from Lieutenant Garly who will hold level two!"

"Captain!" Lieutenant Franks slid two steps sideways and blew a biped off the wall. Although it might be a new species, Torin missed any other distinguishing features—after a while, the only thing that registered was the uniform. "Unfriendlies have broken the perimeter!"

"That's why we're moving the perimeter, Franks. Fall back!"

"Yes, sir! Staff . . . "

"Sir! Fall back by numbers, people! You know the drill! Keep low so the second level has as clear a shot as possible! And Amanda, I want that covering fire thick enough to keep out rain!"

"You got it, Torin!"

The word retreat was not in the Corps vocabulary. Marines fell back and regrouped. In this particular instance it wasn't so much back as down. The heavies leapt off the wall into the city and then joined in providing covering fire so that those without exo-skeletons to take up the impact could come off the wall a little more slowly. And then it was a fast run up the lowest level of the spiraling street, squads leapfrogging each other as Lieutenant Garly's platoon swept the first level wall, keeping the enemy too occupied to shoot down into the city.

Given the fire from the second level, a number of the enemy decided that the safest thing to do was to follow the Marines down to the street.

Also, without Marines on the outside wall to keep the sappers away . . .

The explosion smelled like scorched iron and filled the street with smoke and dust. Swearing for the sake of swearing, Torin ducked yet another rain of debris.

"They're in!"

Squad one made it through the second level gate. Torin and the lieutenant crouched behind a rough barricade as squad two followed. As a clump of the enemy rounded the curve of a building, a hovercraft sailed off level two, plummeted downwards, and squashed half of them flat.

"I think that's our cue, Staff."

"Works for me, sir."

They moved back with the squad, Torin keeping herself between the lieutenant and the enemy. The largest part of her job was, after all, keeping him alive.

They were no more than four meters from the gate when a pair of the quadrupeds charged over the wreckage of the hovercraft, keening and firing wildly as they ran. Their weapon was, like the KC, a chemically powered projectile. The rounds whined through the air in such numbers that it almost seemed as though they were being attacked by a swarm of angry wasps. No choice but to dive for dirt and hope the distinctly inadequate cover would be enough.

Shots from the second level took the quads out just before they reached the squad.

Torin scrambled to her feet. "Let's go before more show up."

No one expected the quads to have riders: smaller bipeds who launched themselves from the bodies. One of them died in the air, the other wrapped itself around Haysole and drew its sidearm. Haysole spun sideways, his helmet flying off to bounce down the street, and got enough of an elbow free to deflect the first shot. Between the frenzied movement, and the certainty that taking out the enemy would also take out Haysole, no one dared shoot. Torin felt rather than saw Franks charge forward. He was a big man—because he was a second lieutenant she sometimes forgot that. Large hands wrapped around the enemy's head and twisted. Sentient evolution was somewhat unimaginative. With very few exceptions, a broken neck meant the brain was separated from the body.

Turned out, this was not one of the exceptions.

"You okay?" Franks asked as he let the body drop.

"Yes, sir."

"Then let's go . . . "

They stepped over the body, which was when pretty much everyone left on the street noticed that harness strapped to the outside of the uniform was festooned with multiple small packets and what was obviously a detonation device.

Rough guess, Torin figured there were enough explosives to take out the gate to the second level. The high ground didn't mean much if you couldn't keep the enemy off it.

Franks gave Haysole a push that sent him stumbling into Torin. "Move!" Then he grabbed the body by the feet and stood, heaving him up and into the air. The explosion was messy. Loud and messy.

It wasn't until Franks slumped onto her shoulder as she wrestled him through the gate that she realized not all the blood soaking his uniform had rained down out of the sky.

He'd been hit in the neck with a piece of debris.

As the last squad through got the heavy metal gate closed and locked, he slid down her body, onto his knees, and then toppled slowly to the ground.

Torin grabbed a pressure seal from her vest but it was too late.

The lower side of his neck was missing. Veins and arteries both had been severed. He'd bled out fast and was probably dead before he hit the ground. There were a lot of things the medics up in orbit could repair; this wasn't one of them.

"Damn, the lieutenant really saved our asses." Sergeant Chou turned from the gate, ignoring the multiple impacts against the other side. "If they'd blown this sucker we'd have been in a running fight to the next level. Is he okay."

Torin leaned away from the body.

"Fuck." Haysole. The di'Taykan had a way with words.

Chou touched her shoulder. "Do you . . . ?"

"I've got it."

A carrier roared up from the port, its escort screaming in from both sides.

"That's it, Marines, we're out of here!"

"Staff . . . "

"Go on, I'm right behind you."

They still had to make it up to the port but, holding the high ground as they did, it shouldn't be a problem. She spread the body bag over Second Lieutenant Franks and sealed the edges as Lieutenant Garly's platoon started spending their heavy ordinance. From the smell of things, they'd dropped something big and flammable onto the street behind the gate.

This wasn't the kind of war people made songs about. The Confederation fought only because the Others fought and no one knew why the Others kept coming. Diplomacy resulted in dead diplomats. Backing away only encouraged them.

But perhaps a war without one single defining ideology was exactly the kind of war that needed an infinite number of smaller defining moments.

Torin smoothed out the bag with one bloody hand then sat back and keyed the charge.

Maybe, she thought as she slid the tiny canister that now held Lieutenant Franks into an inner pocket on her combat vest, maybe it was time they had a few songs . . .

>•≪

In Sharon Lee and Steve Miller's Liaden Universe® series, one of the primary missions of the ace-pilot Scouts is to seek out odd, lost, or hidden knowledge and old technology. Scout Montet sig'Norba inadvertently finds herself on a quest to find the one "warrior" who can truly wage cosmic "battle."

NARATHA'S SHADOW

Sharon Lee & Steve Miller

"For every terror, a joy. For every sorrow, a pleasure. For every death, a life. This is Naratha's Law."

—from *Creation Myths and Unmakings, A Study of Beginning and End*

"TAKE IT AWAY!" The Healer's voice was shrill.

The Scout leapt forward, slamming the lid of the stasis box down and triggering the seal in one smooth motion.

"Away it is," she said soothingly, as if she spoke to a child instead of a woman old in her art.

"Away it is not!" Master Healer Inomi snapped. Her face was pale. The Scout could hardly blame her. Even with the lid closed and the seal engaged, she could feel the emanation from her prize puzzle—a grating, sticky malevolence centered over and just above the eyes, like the beginnings of a ferocious headache. If the effect was that strong for her, who tested only moderately empathic as the Scouts rated such things, what must it feel like to the Healer, whose gift allowed her to experience another's emotions as her own? The Scout bowed. "Master Healer, forgive me. Necessity exists. This . . . *object*, whatever it may be, has engaged my closest study for . . . "

"Take. It. Away." The Healer's voice shook, and her hand, when she raised it to point at the door. "Drop it into a black hole. Throw it into a sun. Introduce it into a nova. But, for the gods' sweet love, *take it away!*"

The solution to her puzzle would not be found by driving a Master Healer mad. The Scout bent, grabbed the strap and swung the box onto her back. The grating nastiness over her eyes intensified, and for a moment the room blurred out of focus. She blinked, her sight cleared, and she was moving, quick and silent, back bent under the weight of the thing, across the room and out the door. She passed down a hallway peculiarly empty of Healers, apprentices, and patrons, and stepped out into the mid-day glare of Solcintra.

Even then, she did not moderate her pace, but strode on until she came to the groundcar she had requisitioned from Headquarters. Biting her lip, feeling her own face wet with sweat, she worked the cargo compartment's latch one-handed, dumped her burden unceremoniously inside, and slammed the hatch home.

She walked away some little distance, wobbling, and came to rest on a street-side bench. Even at this distance, she could feel it—the thing in the box, whatever it was—though the headache was bearable now. She'd had the selfsame headache for the six relumma since she'd made her find, and was no closer to solving its riddle.

The Scout leaned back on the bench. "Montet sig'Norba," she told herself loudly, "you're a fool." Well, and who but a fool walked away from the luxury and soft life of Liad to explore the dangerous galaxy as a Scout? Scouts very rarely lived out the full term of nature's allotted span—even those fortunate enough to never encounter a strange, impulse-powered, triple-heavy something in the back end of nowhere and tempt the fates doubly by taking it aboard.

Montet rested her head against the bench's high back. She'd achieved precious little glory as a Scout, glory arising as it did from the discovery of odd or lost or hidden knowledge.

Which surely the *some*thing must carry, whatever its original makers had intended it to incept or avert.

Yet, six relumma after what should have been the greatest find of her career, Montet sig'Norba was still unable to ascertain exactly what the something was.

"It may have been crafted to drive Healers to distraction," she murmured, closing her eyes briefly against the ever-present infelicity in her head.

There was a certain charm to Master Healer Inomi's instruction to drop the box into a black hole and have done, but gods curse it, the thing was an artifact! It had to do something!

Didn't it?

Montet sighed. She had performed the routine tests and then tests not quite so routine, branching out, with the help of an interested if slightly demented lab tech, into the bizarre. The tests stopped short of destruction; the tests, let it be known, had not so much as scratched the smooth black surface of the thing. Neither had they been any use in identifying the substance from which it was constructed. As to what it did or did not do . . .

Montet had combed, scoured, and sieved the Scouts' not-inconsiderable technical archives. She'd plumbed the depths of archeology, scaled the heights of astronomy, and read more history than she would have thought possible, looking for a description, an allusion, a hint. All in vain.

Meanwhile, the thing ate through stasis boxes like a mouse through cheese. The headaches and disorienting effects were noticeably less when the thing was moved to a new box.

Gradually, the effects worsened until even the demented lab tech—no empath, he—complained of his head aching and his sight jittering. At which time it was only prudent to remove the thing to another box and start the cycle again.

It was this observation of the working of the thing's . . . aura that had led her to investigate its possibilities as a carrier of disease. Her studies were, of course, inconclusive. If it carried disease, it was of a kind unknown to the Scouts' medical laboratory and to its library of case histories.

There are, however, other illnesses to which sentient beings may succumb. Which line of reasoning had immediately preceded her trip to Solcintra Healer Hall, stasis box in tow, to request an interview with Master Healer Inomi.

"And much profit you reaped from that adventure," Montet muttered, opening her eyes and straightening on the bench. Throw it into a sun, indeed!

For an instant, the headache flared, fragmenting her vision into a dazzle of too-bright color. Montet gasped, and that quickly the pain subsided, retreating to its familiar, wearisome ache.

She stood, fishing the car key out of her pocket. *Now what?* she asked herself. She'd exhausted all possible lines of research. No, check that. She'd exhausted all orderly and reasonable lines of research. There did remain one more place to look.

THE LIBRARY OF LEGEND was the largest of the several libraries maintained by the Liaden Scouts. The largest and the most ambiguous. Montet had never liked the place, even as a student Scout. Her antipathy had not escaped the notice of her teachers, who had found it wise to assign her long and tedious tracings of kernel-tales and seed-stories, so that she might become adequately acquainted with the Library's content.

Much as she had disliked those assignments, they achieved the desired goal. By the time she was pronounced ready to attempt her Solo, Montet was an agile and discerning researcher of legend, with an uncanny eye for the single true line buried in a page of obfuscation. After she passed her Solo, she opted for field duty, to the clear disappointment of at least one of her instructors, and forgot the Library of Legends in the freedom of the stars.

However, skills once learned are difficult to unlearn, especially for those who have survived Scout training. It took Montet all of three days to find the first hint of what her dubious treasure might be. A twelve-day after, she had the kernel-tale. Then it was cross-checking—triangulating, as it were—trying to match allegory to orbit, myth to historical fact. Detail work of the most demanding kind, requiring every nit of a Scout's attention for long hours at a time. Montet did not stint the task—that had never been her way—and the details absorbed her day after day, early to late.

Which would account for her forgetting to move the thing, whatever it was, from its old stasis-box into a new one.

"THIS IS AN ALERT! Situation Class One. Guards and emergency personnel to the main laboratory, caution extreme. Montet sig'Norba to the main laboratory. Repeat. This is an alert . . . " Montet was already moving down the long aisle of the Legend Library, buckling her utility belt as she ran. The intercom repeated its message and began the third pass.

Montet slapped the override button for the lift and jumped inside before the door was fully open.

Gods, the main lab. She'd left *it*, whatever it was, in the lab lock-box, which had become her custom when she and the tech had been doing their earnest best to crack the thing open and learn its inner workings. It should have been . . . safe . . . in the lab.

The lift doors opened and she was running down a hall full of security and catastrophe uniforms. She wove through the moving bodies of her comrades, not slackening speed, took a sharp right into the lab's hallway, twisted and dodged through an unexpectedly dense knot of people just standing there, got clear and stumbled, hands over her eyes.

"Aiee!"

The headache was a knife buried to the hilt in her forehead. Her knees hit the floor, the jar snapping her teeth shut on her tongue, but that pain was lost inside the greater agony in her head. She sobbed, fumbling for the simple mind-relaxing exercise that was the first thing taught anyone who aspired to be a Scout. She crouched there for a lifetime, finding the pattern and losing it, beginning again with forced, frantic patience. Finally, she found the concentration necessary, ran the sequence from beginning to end, felt the agony recede—sufficiently.

Shaking, she pushed herself to her feet and faced the open door of the lab.

It was then she remembered the stasis box and the madcap young tech's inclination toward explosives. "Gods, gods, gods . . . " She staggered, straightened, and walked—knees rubbery, vision white at the edges—walked down the hall, through the open door.

The main room was trim as always, beakers and culture-plates washed and racked by size; tweezers, blades, droppers and other hand tools of a lab tech's trade hung neatly above each workbench. Montet went down the silent, orderly aisles, past the last workbench, where someone had started a flame on the burner and decanted some liquid into a beaker before discovering that everything was not quite as it should be and slipping out to call Security.

Montet paused to turn the flame down. Her head ached horribly, and her stomach was turning queasy. All praise to the gods of study, who had conspired to make her miss the mid-day meal.

The door to the secondary workroom was closed and refused to open to her palmprint. Montet reached into her utility belt, pulled out a flat thin square. The edges were firm enough to grip, the center viscous. Carefully, she pressed the jellified center over the lockplate's sensor and waited.

For a moment—two—nothing happened, then there was a soft *click* and a space showed between the edge of the door and the frame. Montet stepped aside, lay the spent jelly on the workbench behind her, got her fingers in the slender space and pushed. The door eased back, silent on well-maintained tracks. When the gap was wide enough, she slipped inside.

The room was dim, the air cool to the point of discomfort. Montet squinted, fighting her own chancy vision and the murkiness around her.

There: a dark blot, near the center of the room, which could only be a stasis box. Montet moved forward, through air that seemed to thicken with each step. Automatically her hand quested along her utility belt, locating the pinlight by touch. She slipped it out of its loop, touched the trigger—and swore.

The stasis box lay on its side in the beam, lid hanging open. Empty.

Montet swallowed another curse. In the silence, someone moaned.

Beam before her, she went toward the sound and found the charmingly demented lab tech huddled on the floor next to the further wall, his arms folded over his head. She started toward him, checked, and swung the beam wide.

The thing, whatever it was, was barely a dozen steps away, banked by many small boxes of the kind used to contain the explosive trimplix. The detonation of a single container of trimplix could hole a spaceship, and here were twelves of twelves of them stacked every-which-way against the thing.

"Kill it," the tech moaned behind her. "Trigger the trimplix. Make it *stop*."

Carefully, Montet put her light on the floor. Carefully, she went out to the main room, drew a fresh stasis box from stores and carried it back into the dimness. The tech had not moved, except perhaps to draw closer round himself.

It was nerve-wracking work to set the boxes of trimplix gently aside until she could get in close enough to grab the thing and heave it into the box. It hit bottom with a thump, and she slammed the lid down as if it were a live thing and likely to come bounding back out at her.

That done, she leaned over, gagging, then forced herself up and went over to the intercom to sound the all-clear.

PANOPELE SETTLED HER FEET in the cool, dewy grass; filled her lungs with sweet midnight air; felt the power coalesce and burn in her belly, waking the twins, Joy and Terror. Again she drank the sweet, dark air, lungs expanding painfully, then raised her face to the firmament, opened her mouth and sang.

Amplified by Naratha's Will, the song rose to the star-lanes: questing, questioning, challenging. Transported by the song, the essence of Panopele, Voice of Naratha, rose likewise to the star-lanes: broadening, blossoming, listening.

Attended by four of the elder novices, feet comforted by the cool grass, strong toes holding tight to the soil of Aelysia, the body of Panopele sang the Cycle down. Two of the attendant novices wept to hear her; two of the novices danced. The body of Panopele breathed and sang, sang and breathed. And sang.

Out among the star-lanes, enormous and aquiver with every note of the song, Panopele listened and heard no discord. Expanding even further, she opened what might be called her eyes, looked out along the scintillant fields of life and saw—a blot.

Faint it was—vastly distant from the planet where her body stood and sang, toes comfortably gripping the soil—and unmistakable in its menace. Panopele strained to see, to hear more clearly, hearing—or imagining she heard—the faintest note of discord, the barest whisper of malice.

Far below and laboring, her body sang on, voice sweeping out in pure waves of passion. The two novices who danced spun like mad things, sweat soaking their robes. The two who wept fell to their knees and struck their heads against the earth.

Panopele strained, stretching toward the edge of the song, the limit of Naratha's Will. The blot shimmered, growing, the malice of its answering song all at once plain.

Far below, the body of Panopele gasped, interrupting the song. The scintillance of the star-lanes paled into a blur; there was a rush of sound, unsonglike, and Panopele was joltingly aware of cold feet, laboring lungs, the drumbeat of her heart. Her throat hurt and she was thirsty.

A warm cloak was draped across her shoulders, clasped across her throat. Warm hands pressed her down into a chair.

In her left ear the novice Fanor murmured, "I have water, Voice. Will you drink?"

Drink she would, and drink she did, the cool water a joy.

"Blessings on you," she rasped and lay her left hand over his heart in Naratha's full benediction. Fanor was one of the two who wept in the song.

"Voice." He looked away, as he always did, embarrassed by her notice.

"Will you rest here, Voice? Or return to the temple?" That was Lietta, who danced and was doubtless herself in need of rest.

Truth told, rest was what Panopele wanted. She was weary, drained as the song sometimes drained one, and dismayed in her heart. She wanted to sleep, here and now, among the dewy evening. To sleep, and awake believing that the blot she had detected was no more than a woman's fallible imagining.

The Voice of Naratha is not allowed the luxury of self-deceit. And the blot had been growing larger.

Weary, Panopele placed her hands on the carven arms of the chair and pushed herself onto her feet. "Let us return," she said to those who served her.

Lietta bowed and picked up the chair. Fanor bent to gather the remaining water jugs. Panopele stopped him with a gesture.

"One approaches," she told him. "You are swiftest. Run ahead and be ready to offer welcome."

One glance he dared, full into her eyes, then passed the jug he held to Dari and ran away across the starlit grass.

"So." Panopele motioned and Zan stepped forward to offer an arm, her face still wet with tears.

"My willing support, Voice," she said as ritual demanded, though her own voice was soft and troubled.

"Blessings on you," Panopele replied, and proceeded across the grass in Fanor's wake, leaning heavily upon the arm of her escort.

THERE WAS, OF COURSE, nothing resembling a spaceport on-world, and the only reason the place had escaped Interdiction, in Montet's opinion, was that no Scout had yet penetrated this far into the benighted outback of the galaxy. That the gentle agrarian planet below her could not possibly contain the technology necessary to unravel the puzzle of the thing sealed and seething in its stasis box, failed to delight her. Even the knowledge that she had deciphered legend with such skill that she had actually raised a planet at the coordinates she had half-intuited did not warm her.

Frowning, omnipresent ache centered over her eyes, Montet brought the Scout ship down. Her orbital scans had identified two large clusters of life and industry—cities, perhaps—and a third, smaller cluster, which nonetheless put forth more energy than either of its larger cousins.

Likely, it was a manufactory of some kind, Montet thought, and home of such technology as the planet might muster. She made it her first target, by no means inclined to believe it her last. She came to ground in a gold and green field a short distance from her target. She tended her utility belt while the hull cooled, then rolled out into a crisp, clear morning.

The target was just ahead, on the far side of a slight rise. Montet swung into a walk, the grass parting silently before her. She drew a deep lungful of fragrant air, verifying her scan's description of an atmosphere slightly lower in oxygen than Liad's. Checking her stride, she bounced, verifying the scan's assertion of a gravity field somewhat lighter than that generated by the homeworld.

Topping the rise, she looked down at the target, which was not a manufactory at all, but only a large building and various outbuildings clustered companionably together. To her right, fields were laid out. To her left, the grassland continued until it met a line of silvery trees, brilliant in the brilliant day. And of the source of the energy reported by her scans, there was no sign whatsoever.

Montet sighed gustily. *Legend.*

She went down the hill. Eventually, she came upon a path, which she followed until it abandoned her on the threshold of the larger building. Here she hesitated, every Scout nerve a-tingle, for this *should* be a Forbidden World, socially and technologically unprepared for the knowledge-stress that came riding in on the leather-clad shoulders of a Scout. She had no *business* walking up to the front door of the local hospital, library, temple, or who-knew-what, no matter how desperate her difficulty. There was no one here who was the equal—who was the master—of the thing in her ship's hold. How could there be? She hovered on the edge of doing damage past counting. Better to return to her ship quickly, rise to orbit and get about setting the warning beacons.

And yet . . . the legends, she thought, and then all indecision was swept away, for the plain white wall she faced showed a crack, then a doorway, framing a man. His pale robe was rumpled, wet and stained with grass. His hair was dark and braided below his shoulders; the skin of his face and his hands were brown. His feet, beneath the stained, wet hem, were bare.

He was taller than she, and strongly built. She could not guess his age, beyond placing him in that nebulous region called "adult." He spoke; his voice was soft, his tone respectful. The language was tantalizingly close to a tongue she knew.

"God's day to you," she said, speaking slowly and plainly in that language. She showed her empty hands at waist level, palm up. "Has the house any comfort for a stranger?"

Surprise showed at the edges of the man's face. His hands rose, tracing a stylized pattern in the air at the height of his heart. "May Naratha's song fill your heart," he said, spacing his words as she had hers. It was not quite, Montet heard, the tongue she knew, but 'twould suffice.

"Naratha foretold your coming," the man continued. "The Voice will speak with you." He paused, hands moving through another pattern. "Of comfort, I cannot promise, stranger. I hear a dark chanting upon the air." Well he might hear just that, Montet thought grimly, especially if he were a Healer-analog. Carefully, she inclined her head to the doorkeeper. "Gladly will I speak with the Voice of Naratha," she said.

The man turned and perforce she followed him, inside and across a wide, stone-floored hall to another plain white wall. He lay his hand against the wall and once again a door appeared. He stood aside, hands shaping the air. "The Voice awaits you." Montet squared her shoulders and walked forward.

The room, like the hall, was brightly lit, the shine of light along the white walls and floor adding to the misery of her headache. Deliberately, she used the Scout's mental relaxation drill and felt the headache inch, grudgingly, back. Montet sighed and blinked the room into focus.

"Be welcome into the House of Naratha." The voice was deep, resonant, and achingly melodic, the words spaced so that they were instantly intelligible.

Montet turned, finding the speaker standing near a niche in the left-most wall.

The lady was tall and on a scale to dwarf the sturdy doorkeeper. A woman of abundance, shoulders proud and face serene. Her robe was divided vertically in half—one side white, one side black. Her hair was black, showing gray like stars in the vast deepness of space. Her face was like a moon, glowing; her eyes were black and insightful. She raised a hand and sketched a sign before her, the motion given meaning by the weight of her palm against the air.

"I am the Voice of Naratha. Say your name, Seeker."

Instinctively, Montet bowed. One would bow to such a lady as this—and one would not dare lie. "I am Montet sig'Norba," she said, hearing her own voice thin and reedy in comparison with the other's rich tones.

"Come forward, Montet sig'Norba."

Forward she went, until she stood her own short arm's reach from the Voice. She looked up and met the gaze of far-seeing black eyes.

"Yes," the Voice said after a long pause. "You bear the wounds we have been taught to look for."

Montet blinked. "Wounds?"

"Here," said the Voice and lay her massive palm against Montet's forehead, directly on the spot centered just above her eyes, where the pain had lived for six long relumma.

The Voice's palm was warm and soft. Montet closed her eyes as heat spread up and over her scalp, soothing and—she opened her eyes in consternation.

The headache was gone.

The Voice was a Healer, then. Though the Healers on Liad had not been able to ease her pain.

"You have that which belongs to Naratha," the Voice said, removing her hand. "You may take me to it." Montet bowed once more.

"Lady, that which I carry is . . . " she grappled briefly with the idiom of the language she spoke, hoping it approximated the Voice's nearly enough for sense, and not too nearly for insult. "What I carry is . . . accursed of God. It vibrates evil and seeks destruction—even unto its own destruction. It is . . . I brought it before a . . . priestess of my own kind and its vibrations all but overcame her skill."

The Voice snorted. "A minor priestess, I judge. Still, she did well if you come to me at her word."

"Lady, her word was to make all haste to fling the monster into a sun."

"No!" The single syllable resonated deep in Montet's chest, informing, for a moment, the very rhythm of her heartbeat.

"No," repeated the Voice, more quietly. "To follow such a course would be to grant its every desire. To the despair of all things living."

"What *is* it?" Montet heard herself blurt.

The Voice bowed her head. "It is the Shadow of Naratha. For every great good throws a shadow which is, in its nature, great evil."

Raising her head, she took a breath and began, softly, to chant. "Of all who fought, it was Naratha who prevailed against the Enemy. Prevailed and drove the Enemy into the back beyond of space, from whence it has never again ventured. The shadows of Naratha's triumph, as terrible as the Enemy's defeat was glorious, roam the firmament still, destroying, for that is what they do." The Voice paused. The chant vibrated against the pure white walls for a moment, then stopped.

This, Montet thought, was the language of legend—hyperbole. Yet the woman before her did not seem a fanatic living in a smoky dream of reality. This woman was alive, intelligent—and infinitely sorrowful.

"Voices were trained," the Voice was now calmly factual, "to counteract the vibration of evil. We were chosen to sing, to hold against—and equalize—what slighter, less substantial folk cannot encompass. We were many, once. Now I am one. Naratha grant that the equation is exact."

Montet stared. She was a Liaden and accustomed to the demands of Balance. But this—"You will die? But, by your own saying, it wants just that!"

The Voice smiled. "I will not die, nor will it want destruction when the song is through." She tipped her massive head, hair rippling, black-and-gray, across her proud shoulders. "Those who travel between the stars see many wonders. I am the last Voice of Naratha. I exact a price, star-stranger."

Balance, clear enough. Montet bowed her head. "Say on."

"You will stand with me while I sing this monster down. You will watch and you will remember. Perhaps you have devices that record sight and sound. If you do, use them. When it is done, first bring the news to Lietta, First Novice, she who would have been Voice. Say to her that you are under geas to study in our library. When you have studied, I require you to return to the stars to discover what has happened . . . to the rest of us." She paused.

"You will bring what you find to this outpost. You will also initiate your fellow star-travelers into the mysteries of Naratha's Discord." The wonderful voice faltered and Montet bent her head.

"In the event," she said, softly, "that the equation is not entirely precise." She straightened. "I accept your Balance."

"So." said the Voice. "Take me now to that which is mine."

THE VOICE STOOD, humming, while Montet dragged the stasis box out, unsealed it and flipped open the lid. At a sign from the other woman, she tipped the box sideways, and the thing, whatever it was, rolled out onto the grass, buzzing angrily.

"I hear you, Discord," the Voice murmured, and raised her hand to sign.

Montet dropped back, triggering the three recorders with a touch to her utility belt.

The Voice began to sing. A phrase only, though the beauty of it pierced Montet, heart and soul.

The phrase ended and the space where it had hung was filled with the familiar malice of the black thing's song.

Serene, the Voice heard the answer out, then sang again, passion flowing forth like flame.

Again the thing answered, snarling in the space between Montet's ears. She gasped and looked to the Voice, but her face was as smooth and untroubled as glass.

Once more, the woman raised her voice, and it seemed to Montet that the air was richer, the grassland breeze fresher, than it had been a moment before.

This time, the thing did not allow her to finish but vibrated in earnest. Montet shrieked at the agony in her joints and fell to her knees, staring up at the Voice who sang on, weaving around and through the malice: stretching, reshaping, *reprogramming*, Montet thought just before her vision grayed and she could see no longer.

She could hear, though, even after the pain had flattened her face down in the grass. The song went on, never faltering, never heeding the heat that Montet felt rising from the brittling grass. Never straining, despite the taint in the once clean air.

The Voice hit a note—high, true, and sweet. Montet's vision cleared. The Voice stood, legs braced, face turned toward the sky, her mighty throat corded with effort. The note continued, impossibly pure, soaring, passionate, irrefutable. There was only that note, that truth, and nothing more in all the galaxy.

Montet took a breath and discovered that her lungs no longer burned. She moved an arm and discovered that she could rise.

The Voice sang on, and the day was brilliant, perfect, beyond perfect, into godlike, and the Voice herself was beauty incarnate, singing, singing, fading, becoming one with the sunlight, the grassland and the breeze.

Abruptly, there was silence, and Montet stood alone in the grasslands near her ship, hard by an empty stasis box.

Of the Voice of Naratha—of Naratha's Shadow—there was no sign at all.

≫•≪

Corporal Josie Two Ribbons is a soldier in the Space Force, but her mission on Janus 4—a planet being terraformed for human settlement—is a personal one. Nancy Kress shows the personal, however, often reveals more universally applicable truths.

EATERS

Nancy Kress

THE GIRL IS TWO DAYS EARLY.

Ellen first sees Josie Two Ribbons crossing the staff mess trailer, several moments before Josie sees her. Ellen's belly goes cold. This is going to be even worse than she has dreaded. Josie wears military fatigues; she scowls so hard that her eyebrows nearly meet. She looks far too much like her father: short, with wide shoulders, spreading nose, glossy black hair cropped into bristles.

Jim Herndon, seated beside Ellen, touches her arm. "Do you want me to—"

"No. No." Ellen has to do this herself. She rises and holds out her hand as the girl stops beside the table. "Corporal Two Ribbons?"

The girl ignores the outstretched hand. Her eyes, as dark as Tom's, sweep away from Ellen, over the other scientists, back again. Ellen drops her hand.

"You bastards," Josie Two Ribbons says.

"SHE WANTS TO GO OUT ALONE," Carlos Sanchez says, "but of course I can't let her do that. Corporate would have my head if she damaged one of our copters. Or herself."

"I know," Ellen says.

"For her to even get permits to come here—just how *did* she do that?"

"I don't know." Although Ellen has her suspicions.

Carlos has called her into his office, which is just as makeshift as everything else human on the base. The office had, a decade ago, been a fuel tank on the ship that brought the first team from Earth. The fuel tank had been flown downstairs, fitted with electronics and with foamcast furniture newly sprayed into existence, and now serves as command station for the Second Terraforming Team of SettlerHome Corporation on Janus 4. The rest of the base, housed in other bits of the ship or in pre-dropped trailers, consists of twenty-four of Ellen's fellow scientists and a great number of very large, very expensive machines, some stationary and some mobile. Twenty-four people to remake a planet for the hordes of colonists to follow.

Not that Janus 4 needs very much remaking. Unlike some other worlds, the profit margin on this one would be large. The atmosphere is already breathable, there is enough fresh water, the small planetary tilt means a fairly stable climate. The gravity is .93 Terran, just enough difference to put a spring in one's step. Janus 4 could be a very popular settlement world. The team's only real problem has been the soil—at least, until Tom Two Ribbons, the junior xenobiologist, had gone out into the bush. And gone, and gone, and gone.

Carlos runs his hand through his hair, which immediately flops back over his forehead. "Ellen, there's no reason for you to be the one to go with her to look for him. In fact, anybody else would be better."

"No, it has to be me."

"So you said. Why?"

Carlos looks straight at her, his no-nonsense-give-me-a-real-answer look. Ellen has always liked Carlos. Whoever said that a team leader needs either charisma or an iron hand was dead wrong. What a team leader needs is a nose for truth, and Carlos—quiet, skinny, occasionally dithering Carlos—has it.

Ellen says quietly, "Because I didn't love Tom. If I had, I'd have tried harder to find out what was driving him, and I didn't. It was all just good-time light-hearted fucking for me. I treated him with the same carelessness that—"

She breaks off, knowing that Carlos knows the rest of the sentence: *with the same carelessness that we treated the Eaters.*

Carlos says, "I really wish you wouldn't go, Ellen."

"I have to."

"I don't think she's dangerous—no history of that, although Chang will run a psych check—but she's completely unedited. Primal."

"I know."

"Also, she's mad as hell."

"Well," Ellen says, shifting her gaze to the window, where two Eaters have wandered too close to the force fence, "she has reason to be. He's her father, he's out there someplace alone, and he's crazy."

"But *not*," Carlos says, with an emphasis unusual for him, "because of us."

Ellen doesn't answer.

IT TAKES TWO DAYS for Josie to pass Chang's mandatory health exam, psych check, and gene scan. After the two days, Chang tells Ellen that Josie is a remarkable physical specimen, that Josie psych-tests as sane, and that none of the medical team can stand her. "I've never seen an angrier human being," Chang says, "and she absolutely refuses editing. It's a good thing that she only has a ten-day planetary permit. Still, it's going to be unpleasant for you." Ellen agrees, thinking it's also good that Josie was not allowed to bring any weapons to a Corporate planet. A second later she's ashamed of this thought; Josie is not a threat, merely "unpleasant."

They leave at dawn of Josie's third day planetside. As the two-seater copter lifts off from the base with Ellen piloting, a herd of Eaters wanders across the ground below, just outside the fence. The alien creatures are spherical, bulky, slow-moving, covered with masses of coarse orange fur.

From this angle Ellen cannot see their legs, which are thin and scaly as a chicken's although they end in broad, hard hooves. She can barely see the Eaters' arms, thin and short and held close to their silly-looking bodies. Furry beach balls bobbing along. Those beach balls are delaying a multitrillion-credit project by at least a decade.

Ellen knows what will happen next, and it does. The left flank of the herd brushes the force-field fence, and half a dozen Eaters crumple to the ground. The rest move on a little more quickly. The copter makes so little noise and flies so low that Ellen can hear their hoofs on the hard ground. How do creatures that are basically sacks of protoplasm on ungulated sticks manage to make so much noise? She braces herself for Josie's rant about the fence deaths, but instead the girl directs her hostility in another direction.

"You're very pretty."

It sounds like a curse. Ellen, not knowing how to respond, says nothing.

"You're exactly the type my father always favored. Soft, feminine. Weak. In fact, you look like a blond version of my mother."

Ellen says dryly, "One can't be all that weak and still belong to a terraforming team."

"I meant emotionally weak. Yielding."

Ellen puts the copter on autopilot and turns to face Josie. "Look, I know you don't like me, or any of us. You resent that we edited your father's memories of what happened. And you resent that until he told us different, we *did* think the Eaters were non-sentient and we did try to exterminate them so they would stop eating the nitrogen-fixing plants. I realize that with your ethnic heritage—"

"Fuck my ethnic heritage."

Ellen stares at her.

"Do you think I give a shit that two hundred years ago your ancestors tried to exterminate the Sioux? Give me a break. Chances are your particular ancestors hadn't even yet emigrated to North America—right, Ellen *Jenssen*? That whole anguish-of-the-Indians thing was my father's bag, not mine. I got off the res as soon as I could and joined the Space Force. The white man won over the Sioux because he had all that advanced tech and so deserved to win. You think I'm going to cry for the losers, just because I carry around some of their genes? It's nothing to do with me. I'm not my great-great-grandparents, and I'm not that sentimental."

Certainly Josie Two Ribbons doesn't look sentimental. She looks hard as the granite boulders forty feet below. The girl still wears military fatigues, boots, and her habitual scowl. Even her bristly dark hair looks aggressive. Ellen feels confused and—yes, admit it!—a little afraid of this ferocious young woman fifteen years her junior.

She says haltingly, "So . . . why . . . why are you here?"

Josie turns the scowl full force on Ellen. "He's my *father*. In the same circumstances wouldn't you go out after your father?"

No. Ellen would not go across town, let alone half a galaxy away, to search for the man who calls himself her father. But she doesn't say it aloud.

"Christ, you people," Josie says, turns her back, and scans the ground.

The base is now out of sight. The copter flies around it in widening spirals, so Josie can look for—what? Ellen doesn't know. But the terrain below is varied and beautiful. Treeanalogs, never more than twenty feet high but full and bushy, purple with the rhodopsin-like photosynthesizer the plants use instead of chlorophyll. Wide slow rivers, which will grow narrower and swifter when they near the mountains, blue among the purple. Outcroppings of pale rock. The tiny, barely visible blue flowers of the native plants, almost lost among the larger white and pink blooms of the bushes introduced by humans. Flora 1 and Flora 2.

Josie says, "So which ones are hallucinogenic?"

"The white ones."

"Those are the ones you guys put here originally? That the Eaters ate?"

"Yes." The Eaters, and Tom. Ellen doesn't want to talk about this. *We didn't know.* But Josie has the right to information—doesn't she? Or is Ellen just doing what she always does, giving in to the stronger personality? She has always felt more comfortable with genes than with their carriers.

"And you're the geneticist who designed the plants, right?"

"Yes."

"What were the plants supposed to do?"

"They do it. They fix nitrogen from the atmosphere into the soil. Without more fixed nitrogen than is native to Janus 4, agriculture would be impossible here."

"And the Eaters lunched on your precious plants, so you guys decided to wipe out the aliens."

"Before we knew they were sentient, yes." The neural pellets falling from the sky—how many drops had Ellen herself made? Although they possess high-phylum nervous systems, the Eaters have no blood. What they have instead is a kind of lymph fluid that permeates every tissue. It transmits nourishment osmotically throughout those beach-ball bodies, as in Terran low-phylum amoebae or sponges. This evolutionary path had made extermination particularly easy. Within an hour of ingestion, the poison had reached all sections of an Eater's body. Then came a rapid breakdown of cellular matter as the lymph-like fluid became an acid bath. The Eater literally fell apart molecule by molecule. Flesh and cartilaginous bones dissolved. In two hours, there was a puddle on the ground. In four hours, nothing left at all.

We didn't know.

Josie smiles. Her smile is just as angry as her scowl. "I guess my father screwed up your big plan, huh? What did he discover about aliens that convinced you all that they're sentient?"

"They communicate through pheromone analogs. They—maybe—pray to some sort of sun god, or at least have rituals that look like prayer. They dance."

"Bees can dance. And so you stopped exterminating the Eaters and instead changed the plant's genes so that the Eaters don't like the taste?"

"Yes."

"Why didn't you just do that in the first place?"

"It's not as easy as you make it sound." Josie probably knows all these answers already, or she wouldn't know what questions to ask. Ellen jabs at the copter's controls.

"You hate this conversation, don't you, Ellen? Just like you hate me."

"I don't hate you."

Josie snorts. "The hell you don't. You hate me for coming here and stirring up your big mistake all over again, all that white-man guilt. Well, I don't give a fuck for your guilt or your big mistake. You moved into the Eaters' ecological niche, and if you can take it over, more power to you. Law of the jungle."

"That's a pretty simplistic view. The moral—"

"Yeah, right. Your guilt is dumb but your hypocrisy is criminal. The weaker culture always goes under, that's just evolution in action. If you're going to participate in evolution, you don't get to also cry about it. Didn't expect philosophy from a dumb Indian soldier, did you? You think—"

"Don't tell me what I think. And don't tell me that your heritage doesn't matter to you."

"It doesn't. I'm an individual, not a defunct tribe."

"Really? How did you get permission to visit a planet in Stage II terraforming? You went to the authorities and played the race card, didn't you?"

Josie doesn't reply, and all at once Ellen is afraid she's gone too far. What does she know about the ethnic feelings of a Native American? Even if Josie is caught in some sort of Stockholm Syndrome, identifying with the victors who destroyed the Sioux, she's still a daughter searching for her lost father. Ellen is contemplating an apology when Josie points to the ground below. "Land there."

It's an oxbow in a river, a U-shaped bend so sharp that only a narrow neck of land protrudes into the river. Eventually the neck will become an island, when the river cuts it off entirely. Dense purple tree-analogs cover the future island. Ellen lands the copter in the closest clearing, and Josie jumps lightly out and disappears into the trees.

An hour later she is back. "Nope. Fly."

Seething, Ellen lifts the copter. She can't think what to say to Josie Two Ribbons: not about her peremptory tone, her rudeness, her astonishingly cold view of what humans on Janus 4 had almost done to the Eaters. Stockholm Syndrome or not, is that callous indifference normal . . . especially coming from a Native American? Or is the girl only pretending indifference, putting on a protective see-if-I-care shell to hide what must be complicated identification with the Eaters' near fate?

Ellen has never been comfortable with tense silence. Despite herself, she tries again. "Growing up on the reservation must have been tough, especially after your parents divorced and—"

"You don't know anything about the res," Josie says, scanning the ground, "or about me. So don't pretend you do. Land there."

"Look, Josie, while we're on this expedition together I insist that at least you treat me with minimal courtesy. Or else don't say anything at all."

Josie says nothing at all.

Ellen lands *there*.

They investigate four more oxbows before nightfall. When Josie wants to land, she flips her wrist in a gesture both indicative and insulting. Ellen swallows her anger and concentrates on the terrain below. The base uses satellite mapping, of course, but as they leave Sector A she is surprised to see how widely both Flora 1 and Flora 2 have spread. The white flowers and the pink both flourish beneath treeanalog canopies and in the shade of boulders. They must have adapted, even mutated, more quickly than she'd counted on. The Eaters are still devouring Flora 1—Ellen sees them doing it—but the hardy plant is flourishing anyway, seeding itself faster than its predator can consume it.

Just before the abrupt sunset of a planet with negligible axial tilt, they make camp. The copter, whose design demands lightness, can sleep two uncomfortably, but the back seats have been removed in order to store equipment and supplies. Ellen sleeps in the copter, curled across two front seats joined by a piece of removable foam. She can't stretch out, but she feels calmer here. Josie pitches a tent beside the copter.

Josie has still not said a single word to her.

SHE IS DANCING, *surrounded by vague shapes under a hot sun. Her bare feet move joyously, her arms wave. The vague shapes are also dancing, pressing close to her . . . closer . . . then away. She laughs. Her feet pound out complex rhythms that she never knew, on a grassy purplish ground that her toes never touched before. She dances faster, they all dance faster, whirling and jumping and shouting in frenzied joy, and still she doesn't tire, she dances and dances and—*

A shot, followed by a high inhuman scream.

Ellen jerks awake and fumbles for the copter's floodlights. In their harsh glare she sees Josie, legs apart and braced, lowering the barrel of a gun. How could Josie have a gun? It takes a moment for Ellen to recognize the weapon. She throws open the copter door.

"You stole that! From the base!"

"Of course I did."

"What in hell did you fire at?"

"An Eater." Josie points at her tent. Something has gashed one side of the tough plasticanvas. Ellen drops to her knees to examine the rip. Impossible that it could come from an Eater, they are herbivorous and at the top of the simple Janus 4 food chain, with no predators. However, Dave Schwartz, the team zoologist, has described Eater mating rituals. Two males kick each other viciously, sometime inflicting considerable damage, until one or the other gives up. This gash could have been made by an Eater hoof, doing . . . what?

Ellen feels dizzy. No Eater has ever attacked a human. If Tom was to be believed, the Eaters didn't even mind when he joined their herd, running with them, dancing with them, feeding with them on Flora 1, the unintended hallucinogenic that destroyed his mind. Ellen herself has seen Eaters ignore the deaths of their fellows who brush against the force-field fence that is the Corporation's grudging, expensive alternative to exterminating the creatures blocking agribusiness on Janus 4. The Eaters may be sentient, but it is a very primitive sentience, and it is not aggressive.

Josie is watching her closely. Ellen raises her head to stare back, but cannot keep it up. Not against that cool, amused disdain. Josie says, "Surprised you, did they?"

"Yes. No Eater has . . . has acted like that before."

"Well, they do now."

Ellen stands. "Give me the gun."

"Do you know how to use it?"

Ellen doesn't, or at least not very well. She says, hating the slight tremor in her voice, "It's Corporate property."

Josie laughs. "It's my property now. We're out here in the bush, Ellen. You can't control me, and you can't edit me to remove any behavior you happen to not like."

Editing removes memories, not behavior, but Ellen doesn't argue the point. "Give me the gun or I'll fly the copter back to base."

"No, you won't." Almost casually, Josie points the gun at her, smiles, lowers the barrel. Oddly, Ellen isn't afraid; she intuits that Josie is only playing with her. Nasty play, but not serious threat. Josie adds, "You can report this, get the second copter after me, file charges with the Space Force, whatever. But I'm not going back until I find my father, and I'm keeping the gun because I'm the one who knows how to use it. Understand?"

Ellen understands. She understands that Josie knows that Ellen will not report the incident, will not destroy Josie's life. Because Ellen has already destroyed Tom's. Guilt is driving her now, the guilt that Josie Two Ribbons so completely disavows. That she leaves to the white man, so ready to accept it, bear it, eat it.

The sky is lightening. Josie packs up her tent and climbs into the copter.

THEY SPEND THE DAY investigating oxbows, and Josie actually offers an explanation: "My father used to take me camping, always on oxbows or oxbow islands. He liked them because they're easier to defend against attack."

Ellen tries to imagine this unknown Tom who was conscious of attack and defense. When she knew him, he seemed a quiet, pacific sort of man, absorbed in xenobiology. But how well had she actually tried to know him? Not very. It was Stan Michaelson whom she was in love with, and Ellen used Tom as both a convenient distraction and a (futile) ploy to incite jealousy in Stan. And when Tom presented his evidence of sentience in the Eaters and the terraforming team had to change strategy, Ellen was just as upset as anyone else. Upset and— yes!—irritated. The entire project was set back years. And then Stan took up with Julia. Ellen hated that, and she stopped sleeping with Tom, and then he went bonkers, running off to live with Eaters—three times!—and each time coming back more delusional, in need of more editing from Chang, gone just completely off the reservation—

Off the reservation. She never thinks in those demeaning clichés—what is wrong with her?

What has always been wrong with her? *Something—*

Josie says, "What the hell is wrong with you? You're red as a boiled lobster."

"Nothing," Ellen says. "I'm going to gather samples."

The have just landed the copter beside yet another oxbow, the sixth one today. They are farther from base than Ellen has ever gone, nearly into Sector D, and yet she can see both Flora 1 and Flora 2 flourishing here. The seeds, designed for wind-scatter, have adapted incredibly well to Janus 4. She climbs out after Josie.

"Stay near the copter," Josie says. "I'm taking the gun."

"Okay."

Ellen gathers samples of both Flora 1 and Flora 2 and brings them back to the copter. She has brought a handheld gene scanner with her. The space in the front seat is cramped, but she prepares samples and runs them through the scanner. When the results are finally ready and she scrolls through the display on the small screen, her heart nearly stops.

There has been massive genetic drift.

Flora 1—white flowers and greenish-purple photosynthesizer, one of Ellen's best recombinant jobs—shows the most genetic mutations. Not surprising— it has been here the longest. But even Flora 2's genes have changed at an astonishing rate. Mutating, jumping, recombining to create new proteins that do . . . what? No way to tell, not in this copter. The scanner can record the simple facts of a shifting genome, the long strings of ATGCs, but the behavior caused by any genome is never simple.

One of her samples of Flora 1 has passed the flowering stage. Ellen touches the little lemon-colored globe of fruit, not yet fully ripe. At her touch, it releases a whiff of sweet perfume. Ingested, it is a powerful hallucinogenic. This is what destroyed Tom's mind, making him think that the terraforming team was still exterminating Eaters after the drops of neural pellets had been discontinued. Making him imagine that psychiatrists back on Earth had arranged the entire tragic extermination merely to help Tom Two Ribbons cope with anger about Indian wars two hundred years ago. Making him believe, finally, that his friends were evil enemies out to destroy him. Chang had edited and edited, trying to cut the poison out of Tom's mind, but drug-induced schizophrenic paranoia is so stubborn . . .

Liquid spurts onto Ellen's hand. She has clutched the lemon-colored globe so hard that it ruptured. "Damn!" She reaches for a wipe, and her gaze focuses through the copter window. A circle of Eaters surrounds her craft.

Human and aliens stare at each other. The aliens' protruding, perfectly round eyes, set above narrow rubbery lips, have no expression, or at least not that Ellen can read. But their orange fur stands straight up, in what Dave has told her is male mating aggression. A long moment passes. Then all together, as if choreographed, the Eaters rush the copter and begin kicking it furiously. Their hooves ring on the light metal. The passenger door, thin since the copter is made of light metal both to save fuel and because there was never a reason for reinforcement, caves inward. Ellen screams.

Gunfire erupts from the woods and two Eaters fall to the ground. The rest run off in a flurry of orange fur. Josie emerges from the trees. The whole episode has taken less than a minute.

This is different from Eaters ingesting neural pellets and quietly dissolving. Josie, apparently an expert shot (Ellen never doubted it), has hit both Eaters in the head. The corpses lay inert, solid, their eyes still open. They will be there until they rot.

Josie yanks open the damaged door of the copter. "What did you do?"

"Nothing!" *And I'm not hurt, thanks for asking.*

"They just attacked without provocation?"

"Yes!" Ellen remembers the juice on her hands and fumbles again for the wipe. Her fingers shake. "Eaters never acted like that before!"

"Well, they do now." Josie climbs into the copter. "Lift off."

"Just . . . just give me a minute!"

Josie does. Ellen cleans off the juice and tosses the wipe into the recycler. She reaches for the flight controls, but instead her hand goes to the cockpit storage compartment and pulls out a flask of whiskey. She doesn't do this very often—

and she never did it before Tom's last disappearance—but there are some nights that it's the only way through. The combination of mellow and burn, as always, steadies her, and she lifts the copter. "We're returning to the base, I presume."

Josie doesn't answer. Ellen glances over at her and finds Josie's eyes locked onto the flask. Josie has not even heard her. Ellen could not have imagined that expression on Josie Two Ribbons' face: could not have imagined that much hunger, that much despair.

Oh, Ellen thinks. *Oh.*

Eventually—and it is a long eventually—Josie again becomes aware of Ellen. The scowl returns. But Josie doesn't try to lie; lying is not her style. Attack is.

"So I'm not the only one bringing along contraband, huh? What is that supposed to be, the back-up plan, the ultimate way to control me? I'll bet Tom told you that my great-great-grandfather died of alcoholism, my great-grandfather was addicted to hallucinogens, and so on. Whiskey for the Indian, huh? What else have you got stowed away here—blankets seeded with smallpox? I thought you were more original than that."

"Fuck you," Ellen says, and immediately realizes she has never said that to anyone in her life. Never. Ashamed, she shoves the flask back into storage and slams the door close. The door bounces open. Josie reaches out and shuts it, but there is something wrong with the gesture: It is too slow and a little clumsy, as if the girl's neural timing is off. Closing that door is costing Josie every gram of will that she possesses.

Her voice comes out harsh. "Where the fuck do you think you're flying?"

"I told you. Back to the base."

"No." She faces Ellen, wrenching her gaze from the storage compartment. "We're going to find my father."

Is such determination a species of courage, or a species of delusion? Ellen can no longer tell.

CARLOS, WITH HIS USUAL democratic leadership, leaves the decision up to Ellen. She suspects he is far more interested in her reports of genetic drift and Eater aggression than in Josie Two Ribbons. Ellen sends him all the data from her handheld and describes the Eater attack to the entire base, gathered in front of the linkscreen to watch and listen.

"Where are you now?" Hélène asks.

"On an open plain. I have the camera and motion detectors turned on so we won't be surprised again. Both Flora 1 and Flora 2 are everyplace, and in the morning I'll gather more samples." She is not going out onto the plain in the dark, motion detectors or no motion detectors. She spends another ten minutes being asked questions, most of which she cannot answer, by scientists concerned with their various fields. Xenobiology, zoology, geology, soil engineering. Ellen discovers that, for the moment, she doesn't care about the answers she doesn't have. She is so tired.

Josie is not present for this conference. She has set up the tent and the instabake outside and heated their meals. In the harsh glare of the copter floodlights, Ellen climbs down and sits on the ground to eat. Every little noise makes her jump. Are they out there? Of course they are. It seems to her that she can smell their hatred, feel it on her skin.

"Sleep in the copter," she says to Josie. "We'll unload enough equipment for me to squeeze back there, and you can have the front."

"Not a chance." The scowl deepens. Ellen sees that this is somehow a matter of stupid pride. Or maybe Josie is just one of those people who cannot stand being cooped up for very long. Somewhere to the east, about a mile away, is a river with a wooded oxbow. Josie will search it in the morning, possibly before Ellen even wakes.

Josie sits in the shadow cast by the copter on the floodlit ground. In that half-gloom, her heritage is somehow sharpened. Despite the military fatigues and bristly hair, she looks Sioux. It's in the cheekbones and nose, the shape of her face, the dark eyes, the still posture. Not for the first time, Ellen wonders about Josie's mother, who had refused to follow Tom to a better life. Who had instead raised her daughter on a reservation, probably in poverty and stagnation. Ellen has read about life on what remains of Indian reservations. When the United States went into steep economic decline, Native Americans were hit even harder than most others. As usual.

Ellen picks up the plates, her excuse to go back into the copter; she puts them in the recycler. Josie stows the instabake and then disappears into her tent. When the flap has closed, Ellen quietly opens the copter door facing away from the tent. She empties the whiskey flask onto the ground, watching the amber liquid disappear into the thick purplish grass.

It reminds her of Eaters' bodies dissolving from neural pellets.

We didn't know. And as soon as we did know, we stopped. As soon as Tom convinced us the Eaters were sentient. That very second, we stopped.

It is the same mantra she repeated to herself in the months that followed Tom's revelation, through all his disappearances, recaptures, therapeutic edits. We didn't know. It was the truth.

Too bad truth could be so inadequate.

When Ellen finally sleeps, she dreams. *She is dancing, surrounded by vague shapes under a hot sun. Her bare feet move joyously, her arms wave. The vague shapes are also dancing, pressing close to her . . . closer . . . then away. She laughs. Her feet pound out complex rhythms that she never knew, on a grassy purplish ground that her toes never touched before. She dances faster, they all dance faster, whirling and jumping and shouting in frenzied joy, and still she doesn't tire, she dances and dances and—*

Alarms shriek. Ellen cries out as she wakes. The motion detector has picked up something. Josie bolts from her tent, gun in hand. But it is not Eaters.

Walking toward the copter from the direction of the oxbow, all alone, is Tom Two Ribbons.

Almost Ellen doesn't recognize him. Although Tom's only been gone for six months, his beard and hair have grown several inches and he is much thinner. But it's not that. Tom had a certain way of walking, a tentative and careful gait that could unexpectedly break into a brief swagger. Both tentativeness and swagger are gone. This man walks across the open plain as if across a well-known room, beyond which there might or might not be something interesting. When he is close enough, Ellen can see the lines of puzzlement cross his sunburned forehead. Something turns over in her chest. She turns off the screaming alarm, opens the copter door, and eases herself to the ground, standing behind and to the left of Josie.

Now Tom stands a few yards from his daughter. He looks from Josie to Ellen; the puzzled lines deepen. Beyond the circle of floodlight, Janus 4 is shadowy and indistinct, but in the east the sky is already paling.

Tom says, "Do I know you?"

Ellen's breath catches. He means both of them. He doesn't recognize Ellen. How much memory had Chang edited out? *"I'll need to take a lot more to cure him of his delusions,"* a somber Chang had told Ellen. She hadn't realized that "a lot more" would include her. And how much else?

Josie says, "You don't know me, no. Not since you just up and left Dakota." The girl's voice is so full of anger and hurt that Ellen winces. The very air around her seems charged. But Ellen doesn't know what to do, and so she does nothing.

"I'm Josie. Remember me, *'Dad'*?" You left when I was seven. You went on to the Space Force and a real life while my mother and me rotted away in that hellhole. And you never even contacted me again to see if I survived it."

The forehead lines deepen. Ellen sees the moment that Josie realizes that her father has no idea what she's talking about. The girl's back goes rigid. Ellen thinks wildly of an ancient Terran myth: people turned to stone by staring straight at Medusa. But that drama of deception and betrayal was Greek. What she is witnessing is an American betrayal, transplanted to the stars.

"I'm Josie," the girl says, and her voice cracks. *"Josie."*

"Josie? I can't . . . I don't think I know anyone named Josie."

"Y-You edited me out, didn't you? Trashed me from . . . from your memory . . ."

Ellen can't stand it. She steps out of the shadow of the copter. Maybe if Josie sees the extent of Tom's editing, she will not take it so personally. "Hello, Tom. Do you remember me? Ellen?"

He studies her—giving it a genuine effort—then shakes his head. "No, I don't think so. Have we met?"

She can't go on. Tom, who always feared editing, has been edited down to nearly nothing. Or maybe it isn't the editing; maybe it is his own fragile mind, forgetting what is too painful to remember. Behind her, in the copter, the linkscreen suddenly leaps to life. She can't see it, but she can hear Carlos' voice, both excited and weary. "Ellen? Ellen? Are you there?"

She says to Tom, "I'm Ellen Jenssen. From the base. Do you remember the base, Tom?"

"The base . . . no, I don't think so."

Josie says, so quietly that it's almost a prayer, "Fuck fuck fuck." Her shoulders tremble.

Carlos' voice says, "We've been up all night with your data, Ellen, along with a lot of other—the results are just—call me right away!"

Tom says politely, "Are you here to study the Eaters?"

Josie chokes out, "You really don't remember, do you? You're not . . . you're not you anymore. They got you."

Carlos' voice says, "Meanwhile, I'm sending you the analysis. Call!"

Josie says, somewhere between anguish and rage, "Damn you! Damn you, Daddy!" She raises the gun and fires.

"No!" Ellen screams. But by the time she reaches Tom, he is already dead. Josie lowers the gun and stares bleakly at Ellen and Tom—one alive and one dead.

"Why?" Ellen screams. "Why?"

Josie says nothing. She starts toward Ellen.

Fear squeezes Ellen's chest. But Josie merely hands over the gun, butt first. She holds out her two hands in a mocking mimicry of being handcuffed, then returns to the copter and climbs into the passenger seat.

The situation has been given to Ellen. She tries to think what to do, can't come up with anything, tries again. Nothing makes sense. Finally Ellen drags

Josie's tent, poles and all, over to Tom's body and covers it. She weights the tent down with boxes of equipment from the copter. Carlos will have to send the other copter to retrieve it all. The sun rises.

A circle of Eaters advances toward her.

Ellen climbs in and lifts the copter. She doesn't think the Eaters will disturb the body, even if they can move the boxes and unwrap the tent. After all, Tom has lived among them for six months, unmolested. Has lived and prayed and danced with Eaters. It's Tom's dreams she has been having, not because there is any sort of psychic connection between them, but because Tom haunts Ellen's mind. And, she realizes, always will.

Josie has calmed down. As the copter skims over the ground, an Eater below munches on a bush of Flora 2. Pink flowers disappear between its rubbery lips. Josie opens the cockpit storage and takes out the whiskey flask. She says, "You thought I'd be into this by now, didn't you?"

Ellen hasn't thought about it at all. Josie is still focused on herself. But her action also reveals that she doesn't realize that Ellen emptied the flask. Ellen risks a glance at the girl. Josie is staring at the opaque flask with the same hunger that Ellen witnessed before, but also with a kind of triumph. Congratulating herself on not giving in.

Neither of them speaks the rest of the way back to the base, where Josie surrenders herself to Carlos Sanchez.

ELLEN REFUSES FOOD, a shower, comfort, discussion beyond what is necessary to tell her story. As soon as possible, she locks herself in her quarters, a Spartan room in the back corner of Trailer A, and accesses the base library. She spends the next hour studying genetic data.

In one long night of feverish work, the team has cross-indexed botanical and zoological data. Flora 1 has diverged enormously from the base genome. Ellen built plasticity into the plant's genes so that it could adapt to many soil conditions on Janus 4, fixing nitrogen over several ecological niches. But plasticity is plasticity, and there was no telling where future mutations might occur. Nor their effects.

The Eaters also possess a highly flexible genome, undoubtedly evolved so that they could digest a wide variety of plants. The lemon-colored globes of the original Flora 1 proved hallucinogenic to them, as to Tom. The mutations in Flora 1 apparently affected Eater nervous systems. It made large changes in what senior xenobiologist Stan Michaelson's previous experiments had determined were Eater processing centers for perception, memory, and communication.

Dave Schwartz has an outstanding record in zoology. He's very good, and his initial determinations ruled out sentience in the Eaters. They showed absolutely no signs of it. But aliens are alien. Eight years and four generations later, Tom observed ritual behavior, worshiping behavior, communicative behavior. Eight years and four generations of eating Flora 1.

Did humans cause that? The beginnings of sentience? *We didn't know*, we told each other, and stopped the genocide. But did we not know because, up to that point, there'd been nothing to know?

"Ellen?" A soft tap at the door, Julia's voice.

"Leave me alone," Ellen says.

"Please, honey, come on out. Don't isolate yourself."

"Go away."

She can hear Julia leave. Ellen turns back to the data. Later Eater specimens have all come from creatures killed by brushing against the force-field fence. Ellen studies the dates carefully. There are progressive changes to the Eater brains, in the areas connected to mating hormones. These are the hormones that produce aggression in Eater males. The changes correlate with the introduction of Flora 2. Flora 2 was designed to taste bad to Eaters, but only a few hours ago, Ellen herself saw Eaters munching pink flowers.

First we trigger their evolution into sentience, Ellen thinks, *and now into retaliation.*

Her eyes burn from reading, and she closes them. If the Eaters become more organized, the result will be the resumption of extermination. Only now it will be justified. The colonists who will be coming to Janus 4 must be protected. SettlerHome Corporation has a right to do that. In fact, it has an obligation to do so. Self-defense is always justifiable. Then, and now, and in times to come, amen.

People are back outside her door, she can hear them: Carlos and Julia and Chang and Stan and David and Hélène. Whispering, arguing, working out their concern for her. Because they care. Her family.

"Damn you, Daddy!" Josie cried just before she shot her father. But Ellen doesn't know what to call Josie's act. Not "murder." Not "mercy killing," either, because the girl had been too angry to be merciful. And Josie, no less than Tom, suffered from delusion: in her case, the belief that you could reject the past. However, to reject one's past, you first had to be able to remember it. Tom was beyond that. Josie could do nothing with the blank space that Tom had become: not confront it, not rescue it, not stand looking at it. And Josie held the gun.

"The weaker culture always goes under."

"Ellen," Carlos says, with what passes here for stern leadership, "open the door. Please."

Ellen rises from her chair. If she doesn't open the door, she knows, they will break it down. Carlos is not about to lose another member of his team, thus compounding his error with Tom. Everyone feeds on something: Carlos on his own competence, the scientists on their guilt, the Corporation on profits. The Eaters on Flora 1 and Flora 2. Josie Two Ribbons on her enormous anger, now about to receive a massive infusion of nutrients from a court martial and imprisonment.

"Ellen!"

"I'm coming."

No, you could not stop the clash of cultures, nor the weaker one going under. All you could do was resist. As Josie had resisted both the whiskey and thinking of herself as an ethnic victim, as Tom had resisted the base's convenient genocide of a sentient species. Ellen deplores Josie's anger, Tom's mental fragility. But they had resisted, and so were . . . what? Admirable, in some twisted way?

She doesn't know. This is unfamiliar territory for Ellen, and she hates having to inhabit it. But she is absolutely clear on one thing, at least.

Ellen opens the door. They are all there, huddled together, her friends and colleagues. The sharers of her guilt. They will, of course, suggest editing. She will not accept it.

Gently, but firmly enough so that there is no possibility of being misunderstood, she says to Carlos, "You need to find another botanical geneticist. I'm leaving Janus 4 tomorrow. I resign."

≫•≪

When warriors return home from war, they are not the same as they were before; those they left behind have changed as well. An Owomoyela's tale is about a mother who became a war machine, and her resentful daughter who possesses the only thing that can restore her humanity.

AND WASH OUT BY TIDES OF WAR

An Owomoyela

I AM SITTING at the top of the spire of the Observance of the War, one of three memorials equidistant from the Colony Center. The soles of my runners' grips are pressed against the spire's composite, they're traction engineered at a microscopic level. But I'm not going to push off. I'm 180 meters up, and while I could drop and catch the festoons—my gloves get as much traction as my grips—that's not what I want. I want to freefall all 180 meters, and catch myself, and launch into a run.

That's crazy thinking. I'm good, but no human's *that* good; I'm a freerunner, not a hhaellesh.

I shift my center of gravity. The wind is still temperate up here, fluttering cool under my collar. It outlines the spot of heat where my pendant rests against my skin.

The pendant is the size of my thumbnail, and always warmer than it should be. This has something to do with it reflecting the heat of my body back to me, so the pendant itself never heats up. It was built to do this because it's no gem; its brilliant red comes from my mother's cryopreserved blood.

It was, until the Feast of the Return that morning, the only thing I'd known of her.

THE COLONY'S DESIGNED FOR FREERUNNING. The cops all take classes in it. That's what comes of a government that worships the hhaellesh, who can carve their own path through the three dimensions.

I'm not a cop, either.

I end up dropping, twisting so my fingers and toes find the carved laurels, and from there I make a second drop to the Observance's dome. At my hip, my phone starts thumping like an artificial heartbeat. I pause with my fingertips on the gilt, and finally turn to brace my heels against the shingles and lean back into the curve. I clip the hands-free to my ear, and thumb the respond button. Then I just listen.

After a moment of silence, a human voice says, *"Aditi?"*

I let out a breath. "Michel," I answer. He's a friend.

"Are you okay—?"

"I don't want to talk about it." Obviously a hhaellesh could get up to my perch here, and so could Michel—he's from a family of cops, so he's been playing games with gravity for longer than I have. But effective or not, there's a reason I'm nearly two hundred meters up, and that reason has a lot to do with not wanting to talk about how okay I am.

Michel digests that, then says, *"Okay. Did you hear the new Elías Perez episode?"*

My chest fills with a relief indistinguishable from love. I love Michel so much that it's painful, sometimes, to know he's not my brother. I wish the same blood flowed through both our bodies, and without thinking past that, my fingers go to the pendant at my throat. There, my voice catches.

There are moments when I feel so ashamed.

"I haven't," I say. "Put it on."

THE HHAELLESH STAND at least six feet tall, and usually closer to seven or eight. Their skin is glossy black. Their digitigrade feet end in small, grasping pads; their hands end in two fingers and two opposing thumbs which are thin enough to fit into cracks and gaps and strong enough to pierce titanium composite and tear apart the alloys of landships. They are streamlined and swift, with aquiline profiles and a leaping, running gait like a cat or an impala. They can fall from high atmosphere and suffer no injury. They can jump sixteen meters in a bound. They are war machines and killing machines.

They are also human sacrifices.

I envy them.

GODS, IF THERE WAS ANYTHING in the universe Elías couldn't handle, his writers haven't thrown it at him yet. He would know how to tell his best friend about an enlistment option. He could figure out how to deal with a hhaellesh showing up at his door.

Michel starts the playback, and I tweak the audio balance so I can hear Michel breathing while we both listen. The serials are propaganda and we know it, but they're enjoyable propaganda, so that's fine.

[The esshesh gave us the hhaellesh and the hhaellesh handed us the war—but if

we didn't have the hhaellesh, we'd still have Elías Perez,] the canned narrator says, and I lean into the backbeat behind his words. *[Welcome to the adventure.]*

Around me, the colony spreads out in its careful geometry. There's nothing left to chance or whimsy, here, or adapted from the streets and carriageways built by another, more ancient, society. There's no downtown you can look at and say, *this predated cars and light rail.* No sprawling tourist docks with names that hold onto history. This place is older than I am, but not by much; it's only about the age of my mother.

That's why we cling so much to ceremony, I think: it's what we have in place of tradition. We make monuments to an ongoing war, and when the soldiers return home we have feasts, and we plan holidays to rename the Observances to the Remembrances. The war's only just ended and in a month we'll have three Remembrances of the War, in shiny white limestone and black edging in places of honor.

I get it.

Seriously, I do. When you don't have history in the place you live, you have to make it up or go insane.

EARLIER IN THE DAY, my mother'd shown up to the crappy little allotment I cook and sleep in but don't spend much time in. My allotment's on the seventeenth floor of a housing unit, which makes for a perfect launch point, and doesn't usually get me visitors on the balcony. I was on the mat in my room, with my mattress folded up into the wall, doing pushup jump squats. They weren't helping. I'd split my lip just a bit earlier, and since I bite when I get restless, I had the taste of blood in my mouth.

Then there she was, knocking at the lintel, and I split my lip open again.

I did a thirty-second cooldown and made myself walk to the window. If it had been dark, if the light hadn't been scattering off the white buildings and back down from the cyan sky, it might not have glinted on her skin. She might have just been a black, alien shape like a hole in the world.

"I expected to see you at the Feast of the Return," she said. "I registered my arrival."

"I was busy," I lied.

She regarded me, quietly. And although I didn't want to, I invited her in.

WHEN I FIRST MET MICHEL, he was walking along the rails of the pedestrian bridge by the Second General Form School. I was in Second General Form mostly because my father had hired a tutor before we came to the colony; my education in Shivaji

Administrative District hadn't exactly been compatible with the colony's educational tracks. I was new, and didn't know any of my classmates. We knew each other's names from the class introductions, so Michel didn't bother to introduce himself.

"Settle an argument," he said. "I think Elías is in love with Seve, and Seve just thinks he's ridiculous. My cousin thinks Seve loves Elías but doesn't want to show it, and Elías is just friendly and chirpy to everyone, so he doesn't even see anything weird about acting like that at Seve. You should tell her I'm right."

I shook my head. "Elías? Is that the government stuff? I don't listen to that."

"Wha-a-at?" Michel asked, bobbing the *a*. "Come on, *everyone* listens to Elías!"

"My dad says it's just propaganda," I said, and I remember that little preadolescent me felt damn proud of herself and all smart and grown-up to be slinging around words like *propaganda*. "They just make it so people will want to join the war."

"Well, duh," Michel said. "Everybody *knows* that. But it's cool! Come on, lemme tell you about this time that Elías got stuck on this planet; they were trying to make it into a colony, but there was a whole swarm of the enemy and his ship was broken and he couldn't take off . . . "

Elías always found a way through, and by the end of the day, I was listening to the show. I never helped Michel settle his argument, but I came to my own conclusions.

Today's episode opens with the soundscape that means Elías is on the bridge of the Command and Control station in the sector designated as the Front. Meaning he's on the front lines. Last time that happened, he was in a story arc that had him working with the Coalition forces, which he hates to do; Elías isn't really an official sort of guy.

["If our intelligence reports are correct,"] says the voice of Commodore Shah, ["we're about to lose the war."]

The art of the gentle lead-in is verboten in Elías Perez.

["A larger enemy presence than any we've ever seen is massing at Huracán II. We believe they'll use this staging ground to launch a major, unified offensive on the colonies."]

["You want us to what?"] That's Seve, the captain of Elias' ship. She snickers. ["Take out a whole fleet of the bastids? Hah. No bones in that dog."]

"Oh, Seve," Michel says. Seve's got a stack of sayings that only make sense to her—and to Elías, nowadays, though they didn't always. Elías and Seve have been partners since Episode 3, where Elías stowed aboard Seve's pirate ship and ended up saving it when it was infested by the enemy. Seve turned around and said, there, that paid Elías' boarding fee; what was he going to pay for passage?

I'm a fan of Elías and Seve. Love at first uncompromising deal. And she isn't the kind to think the end of the war obligates her into anything.

["If their war force goes unopposed, the enemy will be able to sweep through our territories unopposed. The Coalition doesn't have the fleet strength to stop them."]

There's a subtle swell in the background music, a rumble of drums and solar radio output, and a thrill goes through me. The writers can play drama with our fear of the war: for most of us, it's the fun kind of fear where something is technically possible but pretty damn unlikely, like an asteroid crashing into the colony. After we lost the Painter settlement, the war was always off somewhere *out there*; we sent out troops, we made our hhaellesh, but it's not like we were really under threat of invasion. I don't think our colony even had an invasion plan in place, beyond the esshesh defense emplacements. We all got a little afraid, but the fear was a *what if, on an off-chance, someday . . .* and not a *when, as it will, this happens to us.*

["Okay,"] Elías says, always the good guy, always the hero. *["What's our job? We can barely take one enemy ship in a firefight; a force that size is beyond us."]*

Commodore Shah says nothing, and the delay is striking. The audio play doesn't go for delays. There's another rumble, and another sensation thrills up my spine, but it's not the fun kind of thrill this time.

"Oh, you're not," I whisper.

["As you know,"] Shah says, her voice clipped so regret doesn't make it through. *["Huracán II suffers from a violent geology. Your ship is one of the few with both the range to reach the Huracán system and the maneuverability to penetrate the enemy's lines and engage your jump engines within the planet's red jump threshold."]*

I hear Michel's sucked-in breath, and I'm sitting dumb, myself.

["Blow out the planet and us with it,"] Seve says. *["Jump'll turn the rock into a frag grenade, and the gravity turns my girl's engines into a nova. That what you want from us, Shah?"]*

Shah's always looked after her people. Elías and Seve—they're not official, military types, but Shah looks after them as her own. Problem is, even Shah's people come in second to the war.

["It's not what I want,"] Shah says, and I want to slam my headset down. *["But I don't see another option."]*

"They're doing a finale," I say, my calves and fingers burning again to run. "The war is over, so they're just going to finish Elías Perez."

←----→

"You left when I was three years old," I'd told my mother as she crouched at the edge of the table, as I shuffled through my shelves for a decent tea. I had a couple spoonfuls left of loose-leaf colony Faisal, which I hear is a good substitute for an Earth Assam, which I will never in my life be able to afford unless it goes big and all the importers start shipping it in in bulk. But the urge to make a good impression got in a fistfight with the urge to be petty and spiteful, and I pulled out two bags of a generic colony black and plunked them into mugs.

"I remember," she said. "I braided your hair and you wore your favorite dress. It was the blue of cobalt glass."

Her voice was deep and flanged, and totally factual. All hhaellesh sound alike. At least, the ones on the war reports sounded the same as my mother.

I have an allotment and not a flat because I have a work placement and not a career. I don't care for any of the careers on offer. But the colony's not so much of a fool to let work potential go unexploited, unlike the governments of Earth, which I'm just old enough to remember. I still have images of walking to the subway past the grimy homeless, with my father's hand on the small of my back to rush me along.

That's what I remember of my childhood. My father's protective hand, my father's tutoring after school, my father's anchor mustache with a bit more salt in its pepper every year, my father's voice carefully explaining the war.

"I don't like dresses," I told my mother, and set down the two mugs of tea. Her fingers clicked around the ceramic.

The hhaellesh can eat and drink, but human scientists still don't know how food passes through the suits. We do know that the suits filter and metabolize any toxins—people have tried to poison them before, with everything from arsenic and cyanide to things like strong sulphuric acid, and the hhaellesh just eat and drink it up and are polite enough not to mention it.

I did not try to poison my mother.

"You've grown," she said. "Of course, I expected that."

"Yeah, kids grow up when you disappear on them."

She was quiet for a few seconds. "I did not expect your father to die."

I stared down into my slowly darkening tea.

"I received notice," she said. "I had to make the decision whether or not to come home. The tide of the war hadn't turned yet. I knew the colony would look after you."

I swirled the tea in my mug. Tendrils of relative darkness wavered out from the bag.

"I was one of only eight hundred hhaellesh volunteers at that point," she said.

"Yeah, I know," I finally interrupted. "Without the hhaellesh, we wouldn't've won the war."

THIS IS HOW the hhaellesh happened:

We had a handful of colonies in the Solar system and three outside of it: Gliese, Korolev, and Painter. Then, abruptly, we had a handful of colonies in the Solar system and two colonies in Gliese and Korolev.

We still thought interstellar colonization was a pretty neat thing, and despite centuries of space war fiction, we didn't have the infrastructure or the technology to mount a space war. We were thoroughly thumped.

Then the esshesh showed up and told us that, while war was (untranslatable, but we think against their religion), they had no problems with arming races to defend themselves.

So they gave us the hhaellesh.

THIS IS HOW the hhaellesh work:

There's a black suit that scatters light like obsidian and feels like a flexible atmosphere-dome composite to the touch. A soldier gets inside, bare as the day she was born. The suit closes around her.

In a few minutes, it's taking her breath and synthesizing the carbon dioxide back to oxygen. In a few hours it's taking her waste and digesting the organic components. In a few days it's replaced the top layers of her skin. In a few months it's integrated itself into her muscles. In a few years there's nothing human left in there, just the patterns of her neural activity playing across an alien substrate that we haven't managed to understand yet.

THIS IS HOW a hhaellesh retires:

The suit has a reverse mode. It can start rebuilding the human core, re-growing the body, replacing the armor's substrate material with blood and muscle and bone and brain matter until the armor opens up again, and the human steps out, bare as the day they were born. A body like Theseus' ship.

But to do that, it needs the original human DNA.

Or some human DNA, in any case; hell, I don't know that anyone's tried it, but you could probably feed in the DNA of your favorite celebrity and the hhaellesh suit would grow it for you, slipping your brain pattern in like that was nothing strange. I suppose that should freak me out—y'know, existentially—more than just growing a new copy of a body long ago digested by an alien non-meatsuit.

It probably should, but it doesn't.

THIS IS HOW a hhaellesh tries to *get* the DNA that'll let it retire:

My mother crouched at the side of my table. With the inhuman height and the swept-back digitigrade legs, the chairs weren't designed to accommodate her.

"When I left, I entrusted you with a sample of my DNA," she said, and my hand went to the pendant. "With love, my daughter, I ask for it back."

At that point, I dove out the window.

"THEY *CAN'T* CANCEL ELÍAS," I say. The top-of-spire restlessness is back, and I want to drop, freefall, roll, clamber, climb. My shoulders and thighs are shaking. "The fuck. He's a goddamn cultural phenomenon, by now."

Michel's voice is unsteady as well, but not as much as mine. He doesn't get it. *"To be fair, I feel like after you've won the war you don't need to push people to sign up for the Forces any more."*

"Fuck the war," I say, and there's anger at the pit of my throat. Like: how dare they take this away from us. Like: Elías and his adventures belong to us. Since the beginning of the war they've been how we're meant to see ourselves—clever and active and *go team human.* You can't take away our stories just because we won.

THE FIRST TIME I met my mother—

Except I can't put it like that, can I? You don't really meet your mother. Or I guess maybe you do at the moment of conception, if you think your zygote is you, or maybe it's when the first glimmers of thought show up in your still-developing brain. But I think maybe it doesn't count if there's no chance that little undeveloped you won't retain the memory.

So. The first time I met my mother, I was in a utility transitway. You know, what we have for back alleys.

I've always been the kid with a chip on her shoulder and a grudge against the world and her nose high in the air. The grudge and the pride come from the same thing. Neither made me many friends.

I ran into a bunch of the voluntary-career types in the transitway on the morning of the Feast, just after the big public ceremony. My blood was up and they were them, and, well, the specifics of the argument don't really matter. I started it. And then I was in the comforting beat of a street fight, and with a split lip and three split knuckles, and while one of them was hollering about how he was going to file a complaint for misdemeanor assault, who should show up?

And my heart leapt up and got a grip in my throat, and I thought, *Oh gods, a hhaellesh*, and standing right there, alien and beautiful. Staring at us with a blank, featureless swept-forward face that we all unambiguously read as disapproval.

The fight stopped. The boys stood there, twitching and uneasy, until they worked out that the hhaellesh was only staring at me. Then they slipped away.

And I stood there, frozen in the moment, until *I* worked out why a hhaellesh would single me out and come find me in a utility transitway. The wonder was slapped right out of me. It meant nothing: it wasn't the free choice of an alien intelligence but the obligate bonds of unreliable blood.

I turned my back and sprinted away.

. . . HOLD IT THERE FOR A MOMENT. I realize this makes it sound like I just run from all my problems, and I want to make it clear that that's not true. The truth is that I run from this *one* problem, and looking back at it, I guess I always have.

I was talking about my pride and my grudge, and how they both come down to this pendant at the base of my throat. My mother's blood. My mother the hhaellesh, the guardian of the colonies, the war hero.

All the hhaellesh are war heroes.

What the hell am I?

[*"MY GOTDAMN SHIP,"*] Seve says. They're in the corridors of *her gotdamn ship* now, the soundscape full of mechanical noises and ambiance. There was a behind-the-scenes episode a few months ago back where they talked about those soundscapes, and how they chose the sounds for Seve's ship to be reminiscent of a heartbeat, rushing blood, ventilation like breath, so it'd seem alive. [*"My gotdamn job. Better pilot than you, anyway; I can see this idiot plan through."*] She's pissed-off. I would be. Hell, I am.

[*"I'm a good enough pilot to dodge through a crowd,"*] Elías says. [*"Come on, Seve. The captain doesn't have to go down with her ship."*]

Michel complains a lot that Seve is a boy's name, and I tell him that so were Sasha and Madison and Wyatt, back in the pre-space days known as the depths of history. And then Michel says that of course I would pay attention to the pre-space days, and I say that of course he thinks history started with the erection of the initial colony dome.

Michel is first-generation colony native. He was born here. His parents were in the third or fourth batch of colonists to set down here. We're never quite sure who's supposed to be jealous of whom in this relationship, so mostly we just rib each other a lot.

In my position, it's easy to feel like you don't have a history. Yeah, I'm from Earth, but I don't remember much. My dad knew more, but he naturalized us; the most culture I think he held over was the way he made tea in a pot with colony spices, and his habit of saying *gods* instead of *god*.

I'm the girl with the hhaellesh mother and the blood at her throat. That's who I am. And I was pretty sure no one could take that away.

["Seve, I can't let you die in my place,"] Elías says.

Seven snorts. *["Well, one of us got to."]*

"I enlisted," I blurt out. I swing the words like a fist. And I can hear the change in Michel's breathing on the other end; I can hear how Elías and the finale and how the writers are screwing us over has ceased to matter.

"Say what?"

"I enlisted," I say again. "I got the assessment. They were going to let me into a Basic Training Group and then the war ended."

Michel doesn't know what to say. I can tell because he says *"You—"*, and then *"Oh"* and then *"So . . . what? What now? Are you—"* and then he trails off into silence. I'm pretty sure I've hurt him.

It's a thing, in my family.

"I don't know," I say. All my plans have been derailed. "I can join the colony's military track. Would that be totally pointless? Think I should go? I could just get out of here."

". . . should I know the answer to this?" He gives a nervous laugh—and the laugh is probably fake, now that I think about it. It's not right, anyway. Michel's real laugh is this deep, throaty thing that doesn't sound right when you know that his voice is higher than average and naturally polite.

If Michel was blood family there'd be a reason I could point to as why I felt so close to him, without wanting to screw him. I could have family that meant what family's supposed to mean.

After a moment, he says *"Aditi, if this is about your mother, can we just, maybe, talk about your mother?"*

Michel, Michel, my not-family family. Talking about my mother, my family not-family. I got this far by not looking too close at the contradiction. It's a lot harder to do when it breaks up your fights and shows up to tea.

It's a lot harder to do when it wins *its* fucking war.

←----→

WHEN WE CAME to the Colony, my father and I, we stepped off the transport in a queue of seven hundred other colonists. We waited nearly an hour before it was our turn to go into a white room whose windows let in the blue of the sky and the white of the skyline, and a pleasant-enough woman took our biometric data and verified all my father's professional assessments. She gave him his schedules—for Colony orientation, the walking tour, the commerce and services lecture, the first day at his assigned career—and set up an educational track for me. Through all of it, I was bored but fascinated by the blue-white-green of the outside world, and my father bounced me on his knee.

At the end, the woman bent down and put her face in front of mine. "That's a beautiful piece of jewelry," she said. "What is it?"

I looked her straight in the eye, and said—you know, in the way that some kids don't quite get metaphor, even when they're using it—"It's my mother."

ON MY PHONE, there's a message from the Coalition Armed Forces Enlistment Office. It reads:

> To Aditi Elizabeth Chattopadhyay,
>
> This confirms that your assessment scores were sufficient to place you in a Basic Training Group for Immediate Interstellar and Exo-Atmospheric Combat. However, due to the recent decision of the Colony Coalition Oversight Office and the cessation of hostilities, the Coalition Armed Forces as an oversight unit is being disbanded and the colonies' individual standing military forces are being scaled back.
>
> At your request, your application can be transferred to the Gliese Armed Forces Enlistment Office, where you can enter into their Standing Military career track. If no such request is made, we will consider your enlistment withdrawn.
>
> Thank you for your willingness to serve the safety and security of the Colonies.

The Standing Military career track trains you in an off-surface location with strict access restrictions. I could still get out of here. I have the option. She can't take everything away.

I DIAL BACK the Elías audio to a quiet background murmur. I can't concentrate on it, anyway, and I don't want to. I don't want to hear Elías and Seve argue about who'll sacrifice for the other.

"Aditi," Michel says.

"Why the *hell*," I ask him, "wouldn't you just put your blood in a bank safe if it meant that godsdamn much to you?"

There's a moment when I think that could have used a little more context than I gave it, but Michel finds the meaning fast. *"If I had a kid, I'd want to leave something they could know me by."*

I kinda think there's not a maternal bone in my body, because that just sounds stupid to me. "Yeah, well, I didn't end up knowing her, did I?"

"You can, though. Now. Can't you?"

"She came back for her *blood*," I say. "She never said she came back to get to know me."

Like a slap in the face, Michel laughs.

"What the fuck," I tell him. "Not funny."

"It is, though," Michel says. *"Adi, I swear you just described exactly what you would do. You would go off to war and kick ass and come back home when there was no more ass to kick, and be all 'hi, I'm back, gimme.' Tell me you wouldn't."*

I spluttered.

["Some things are more important than my life, Seve!"] Elías is shouting, though the low volume just makes him sound faraway and muffled like he's already lost.

From the beginning, Seve has said that if she can't save herself, she's not worth saving. And this is propaganda, so the story never goes out of its way to correct her. I like that. I like that she's never needed saving when she couldn't save herself.

I don't like change.

I want to mute the audio.

"I'm not that self-centered," I tell Michel, but my hand is on my pendant and I've convinced myself the blood inside is mine. It's demonstrably *not* mine, and the DNA will prove it. But still. Still.

"Adi, can I tell you something, and not get in a fistfight with you in a utility transitway?"

I've never been in a fight with Michel. "What?"

He takes a moment to put the words together. *"The necklace is just a thing, Adi. Get your mom back. Once you have her, you can replace the blood. Anyway, one necklace for one mom is a pretty good trade."*

Theseus' pendant. I feel a rush of disagreement. I guess that solves that philosophical riddle for me: I really believe that if you replace all the boards, it's not the same ship.

Which means I also believe there's no way to keep the ship from eventually rotting away.

←----→

I NEVER HELPED Michel settle his argument, but that doesn't mean I didn't come to my own conclusions.

I think Elías and Seve love each other, but love doesn't tell you what to do with it. It just shows up like a guest you have to make a bed for, and it puts everything out of order, and it makes demands.

I DON'T HEAR the rest of the episode.

I take my time. I breathe through the anger in my gut and the sense, not exhilarating now, of falling. Then, in the evening, I sync up with the colony directions database and do a search for hhaellesh in public areas.

Five hhaellesh arrived during the Feast of the Return, and two of them aren't hanging out anywhere that the public cams can see them. One of the ones who is is surrounded by children and a lady who looks like their mother, beaming the whole group of them. Of the other two, one is walking the gardens in the Colony Center Plaza, and the other is . . . familiar.

I take the monkey's route, as my father called it. Roof to roof and wall by wall, the colony's engineered and modified design giving me wings. From the feeds I read, the freerunning spirit everywhere means working with your environment, not against it; you have to take your obstacles as opportunities or you'll never get anywhere. Literally, at that.

If there's a lesson to be learned there and applied to the rest of my life, I've yet to learn it.

I pass over alleys and shopways and along the taut wires that traverse the wide boulevards, the places where parades had been held. People see me, but to them, I'm just motion; just another citizen who takes a hobbyist's interest in how to get around. Anonymous. Not Aditi, the girl with the hhaellesh mother, the girl with her mother's blood. They see me as I'm starting to see myself.

I run harder.

AFTER MY FATHER'S FIRST DAY of work, he took me to the breadfruit shop. It's not real breadfruit—it's some native plant the first colony engineers analyzed and deemed edible; something that looked like a breadfruit to whichever one of them named it—but when it's processed and mashed it has a texture like firm ice cream and a taste that takes flavorings well. My father and I got bowls full of big, colorful scoops, and asked one of the other patrons to take a picture of us. They did, and said "Welcome to the colony!" We were that obvious.

We sent the picture to my mother, and that's where I find her today. Sitting at the table we always tried to get, without any of the breadfruit in front of her.

Hhaellesh can eat, but I'm not sure they need to, and I have no idea if they have a sense of taste. You only hear about them eating to accept hospitality.

There's a halo of awed silence around her, and I slink through it and take another one of the chairs.

"I'm sorry," she says, and I let out a breath. Truth was, until she'd said that, I'd had some doubt that it was her. The hhaellesh all look alike.

I grumble something. I don't know how to accept her apology.

"I haven't been a good mother," my war hero says. "I don't know if you want me to start trying now. You've done well without me."

Yeah, if you want to call it that. I serve the minimum work requirements and spend the rest of my time running across the roofs and up the walls. I haven't gone out and won any wars in my free time.

What I've done, what they'll know me for if I touch the history books at all, is that I've carried *her*.

My fingers itch at the tips. I want to touch the pendant, but I don't. "Hhaellesh don't have blood, do they?"

"The armor substrate carries energy and nutrients," my mother says. "We don't need blood, unless . . . "

"Why do you want to be human?" I ask. *I* don't want to be human. I want to be more than what I am.

My mother doesn't answer that, and the stillness of the armor is the stillness of an alien thing: how am I to read it? Then she seems to answer two questions, my own and one she hasn't articulated.

Why don't you?

"I think," she says, and her words are careful, perhaps uncertain, "If you are something, you don't want it. Does that make sense? Because you *are* it, you forget ever wanting it. Or, I suppose, it never comes up."

I shake my head.

"I miss being human," she says. "I miss feeling warm and sleeping in and stretching out sore muscles. I miss holding you. You were so small, when I left." I think she watches me. "You regret not being old enough."

"*Old* enough?" I snap. For what? To remember her leaving?

My mother holds up her hand. "This lit me up like a candle," she said, turning those long, precise fingers. "I was a goddess. A fury, a valkyrie. I wanted this. Now I miss being human."

I grind my fingertips out against the table. "What's going to happen to the suit, if you're not using it?"

My mother lays her hand near mine, which is a disturbingly human gesture coming from something whose hand is a mechanical claw. "It'll go into a museum," she says. "Or on display in one of the Remembrances. I would give it to you if I could."

I rear back, at that.

"Ah," she says, and she can't smile. There's nothing on her face to smile. But I get the impression she's smiling. "You think I'd say, no, it wasn't worth it, in the end. I've learned my lesson and a human life is the most important thing of all. No." Her head bends toward the table. "This is a part of my life; this is me. I will not disavow it. I would give it to you if I could."

THE COLONY is white buildings and boulevards, green growing plants, and the searing blue sky. And then there's the black of the esshesh artillery emplacements, the black edging on the Observances. Red's not a colony color. Red is primal and messy, like blood.

When I went to enlist, they took a hard-copy signature in black ink and a handprint biometric signature as well. I wonder what else the biometrics recorded: my anxiety? My anger? The thrumming of my heart in my veins?

My mother's hands are cool and pulse-less on the table. Black as the artillery. Black as the ink. Black as the space between what stars we see, where the primal brightness of the cosmos has been stretched into infrared by the passage of time.

I REACH BEHIND MY NECK and fumble with the clasp of my pendant. It takes me a bit to work it out; it's stayed against my throat through showers and formal occasions and a hospital stay or two, busted ribs and broken legs. Pulling it off makes me feel more naked than taking my clothes off does. But here I am, baring myself in front of this alien who wants more intimacy than I think she deserves.

"Two conditions," I say. And it's difficult to tell, under the smooth black mask, but I think she's still watching *me* and not the blood. I push on ahead. "One: I want a piece of that armor. Or, I guess, the substrate. Make a pendant out of it."

It's not a replacement for the blood. But it's not something I'll be holding in trust: it's part of my history, now, too, and it's something that'll be *mine*.

My mother nods.

I exhale. Red's no good for the colony anyway. Black's a bit better, if only because black is the color of the hhaellesh, and the security emplacements which grow fractally more close-packed toward the colony's borders: the lines we draw around ourselves to protect us from the enemy.

After Painter, the enemy never set foot on colony land. They're not the thing that scares me. I'm still figuring out what my enemy is.

"Two," I say. And I'm not sure how to say this next part.

But those were her words. *I'd give it to you if I could.*

"I want your stories," I tell her.

>•<

Elizabeth Moon has said that her story "looks at one of the traditional assumptions of military power: the people a soldier protects (at the cost of blood) should be grateful for such protection, that the culture that is saved should serve its saviors. It is not a pacifist or a militarist story; it is a tale of the tangles humans get into when they don't examine their assumptions, emotional as well as political."

HAND TO HAND

Elizabeth Moon

EREZA STOOD IN THE SHADOWS at the back of the concert hall. She had promised to be silent, to be motionless; interrupting the final rehearsal would, she had been told, cause untold damage. Damage. She had survived the bombing of her barracks; she had survived being buried in the rubble for two days, the amputation of an arm, the loss of friends and all her gear, and they thought interrupting a rehearsal caused *damage*? Had it not been her twin onstage, she might have said something. But for Arlashi's sake she would ignore such narrow-minded silliness and do as she was told.

She had seen concerts, of course; she had even attended the first one in which Arlashi soloed. This was somewhat different. From the clear central dome the muted light of a rainy day lay over the rows of seats, dulling the rich colors of the upholstery. The stage, by contrast, looked almost garish under its warm-toned lights. Musicians out of uniform wore all sorts of odd clothes; it looked as if someone had collected rabble from a street fair and handed them instruments. Ereza had expected them to wear the kinds of things Arlashi wore, casual but elegant; here, Arlashi looked almost too formal in purple jersey and gray slacks. Instead of attentive silence before the music, she could hear scuffing feet, coughs and cleared throats, vague mutters. The conductor leaned down, pointing out something to Arlashi in the score; she pointed back; their heads finally moved in unison.

The conductor moved back to his podium and tapped it with his baton. "From measure sixty," he said. Pages rustled, though most of the musicians seemed to be on the right one. Silence, then a last throat clearing, then silence again. Ereza shifted her weight to the other leg. Her stump ached savagely for a moment, then eased. Arla, she could see, was poised, her eyes on the conductor.

His hand moved; music began. Ereza listened for the bits she knew, from having heard Arla practice them at home. Arla had tried to explain, but it made no sense, not like real things. Music was either pretty or not; it either made her feel like laughing, or crying, or jumping around. You couldn't say, as with artillery, what would work and what wouldn't. This wasn't one she knew without a program. It sounded pretty enough, serene as a spring evening in the garden. Arla's right arm moved back and forth, the fingers of her left hand shifting up and down. Ereza watched her, relaxing into the sweetness of the music. This was the new cello, one of only four wooden cellos on the planet, made of wood from Scavel, part of the reparations payment imposed after the Third Insurrection. Cravor's World, rich in military capacity, had far too few trees to waste one on a musical instrument. Ereza couldn't hear the difference between it and the others Arla had played, but she knew Arla thought it important.

Her reverie shattered as something went drastically wrong with the music. She couldn't tell what, but Arla's red face and the conductor's posture suggested who had caused the problem. Other instruments had straggled to a halt gracelessly, leaving silence for the conductor's comment.

"Miss Fennaris!" Ereza was glad he wasn't her commanding officer; she'd heard that tone, and felt a pang of sympathy for Arla. Somehow she'd thought musicians were more lenient than soldiers.

"So sorry," Arla said. Her voice wavered; Ereza could tell she was fighting back tears. Poor dear; she hadn't ever learned toughness. Behind her twin, two other musicians leaned together, murmuring. Across the stage, someone standing behind a group of drums leaned forward and fiddled with something on the side of one of them.

"From measure eighty-two," said the conductor, this time not looking at Arla. Arla had the stubborn, withdrawn expression that Ereza knew well; she wasn't going to admit anything was wrong, or share what was bothering her. Well, musicians were different, like all artists. It would go into her art, that's what everyone said.

Ereza had no idea what measure eighty-two was, but she did recognize the honeyed sweetness of the opening phrase. Quickly, it became less sweet, brooding, as summer afternoons could thicken into menacing storms. She felt breathless, and did not know why. Arla's face gave no clue, her expression almost sullen. Her fingers flickered up and down the neck of the cello and reminded Ereza of the last time she'd played the game *Flight-test* with her twin, last leave. Before the reopening of hostilities, before some long-buried agent put a bomb in the barracks and cost her her arm. Arla had won, she remembered, those quick fingers as nimble on the controls as on her instrument.

Suddenly the impending storm broke; the orchestra was off at full speed
and volume, Arla's cello nearly drowned in a tumult of sound. Ereza watched,
wondering why it didn't sound pretty anymore. Surely you could make something
stormy that was also good to listen to. Besides, she wanted to hear Arla, not
all these other people. Arla was leaning into her bowing; Ereza knew what that
would mean at home. But the cello couldn't dominate this group, not by sheer
volume. The chaos grew and grew, very much like a summer storm, and exploded
in a series of crashes; the man with the drums was banging away on them.

The music changed again, leaving chaos behind. Arla, she noted, had a
moment to rest, and wiped her sweaty face. She had a softer expression now
and gazed at the other string players, across from her. Ereza wondered what
she thought at times like this. Was she thinking ahead to her own next move?
Listening to the music itself? What?

Brasses blared, a wall of sound that seemed to sweep the lighter strings off
the stage. Ereza liked horns as a rule, but these seemed pushy and arrogant,
not merely jubilant. She saw Arla's arm move, and the cello answered the horns
like a reproving voice. The brasses stuttered and fell silent while the cello sang
on. Now Arla's face matched the music, serenity and grace. Other sections
returned, but the cello this time rose over them, collecting them into a seamless
web of harmony.

When the conductor cut off the final chord, Ereza realized she'd been holding
her breath and let it out with a *whoof.* She would be able to tell Arla how much it
meant to listen to her and mean it. She was no musical expert, and knew it, but
she could see why her sister was considered an important cultural resource. Not
for the first time, she breathed a silent prayer of thanks that it had been her own
less-talented right arm she'd lost to trauma. When her new prosthesis came in,
she'd be able to retrain for combat; even without it, there were many things she
could do in the military. But the thought of Arla without an arm was obscene.

The rehearsal continued to a length that bored Ereza and numbed her ears.
She could hear no difference between the first and fifth repetition of something,
even though the conductor, furious with first the woodwinds and then the
violas, threw a tantrum about it and explained in detail what he wanted. Arla
caused no more trouble—in fact, the conductor threw her a joke once, at which
half the cello section burst out laughing. Ereza didn't catch it. At the end, he
dismissed the orchestra and told Arla to stay. She nodded, and carried her cello
over to its case; the conductor made notes on his papers and shuffled through
them. While the others straggled offstage, she wiped the cello with a cloth and
put the bow neatly into its slot, then closed the case and latched it.

Ereza wondered if she should leave now, but she had no idea where Arla would go next, and she wanted to talk to her. She waited, watching the conductor's back, the other musicians, Arla's care with her instrument. Finally all the others had gone, and the conductor turned to Arla.

"Miss Fennaris, I know this is a difficult time for you—" In just such a tone had Ereza's first flight officer reamed her out for failing to check one of the electronic subsystems in her ship. Her own difficult time had been a messy love affair; she wondered why Arla wasn't past that. Arla wisely said nothing. "You are the soloist, and that's quite a responsibility under the circumstances—" Arla nodded while Ereza wondered again *what* circumstances. "We have to know you will be able to perform; this is not a trivial performance."

"I will," Arla said. She had been looking at the floor, but now she raised her eyes to the conductor's face—and past them, to Ereza, standing in the shadows. She turned white, as if she'd lost all her blood, and staggered.

"What—?" The conductor swung around then and saw that single figure in the gloom at the back of the hall. "Who's there? Come down here, damn you!"

Ereza shrugged to herself as she came toward the lighted stage. She did not quite limp, though the knee still argued about downward slopes. She watched her footing, with glances to Arla who now stood panting like someone who had run a race. What ailed the child—did she think her sister was a ghost? Surely they'd told her things were coming along. The conductor, glaring and huffing, she ignored. She'd had permission, from the mousy little person at the front door, and she had not made one sound during rehearsal.

"*Who* told you you could barge in here—!" the conductor began. Ereza gave him her best smile, as she saw recognition hit.

She and Arla weren't identical, but the family resemblance was strong enough.

"I'm Ereza Fennaris, Arla's sister. I asked out front, and they said she was in rehearsal, but if I didn't interrupt—"

"You just did." He was still angry but adjusting to what he already knew. Wounded veteran, another daughter of a powerful family, his soloist's twin sister . . . there were limits to what he could do. To her, at least; she hoped he wouldn't use this as an excuse to bully Arla.

She smiled up at her sister. "Hello again, Arlashi! You didn't come to see me, so I came to see you."

"Is *she* why—did you see her back there when you—?" The conductor had turned away from Ereza to her sister.

"No." Arla drew a long breath. "I did not see her until she came nearer. I haven't seen her since—"

"Sacred Name of God! Artists!" The conductor threw his baton to the floor and glared from one to the other. "A concert tomorrow night, and you had to come now!" That for Ereza.

"Your own sister wounded, and you haven't seen her?" That for Arla. He picked up his baton and pointed it at her. "You thought it would go away, maybe? You thought you could put it directly into the music, *poof*, without seeing her?"

"I thought—if I could get through the concert—"

"Well, you can't. You showed us that, by God." He whirled and pointed his finger at Ereza. "You—get up here! I can't be talking in two directions."

Ereza stifled an impulse to giggle. He acted as if he had real authority; she could just see him trying that tone on a platoon commander and finding out that he didn't. She picked her way to a set of small steps up from the floor of the hall and made her way across the stage, past the empty chairs. Arla stared at her, still breathing too fast. She would faint if she kept that up, silly twit.

"*What* a mess!" the conductor was saying. "And what an ugly thing *that* is—is that the best our technology can do for you?" He was staring at her temporary prosthesis, with its metal rods and clips.

"Tactful, aren't you?" She wasn't exactly angry, not yet, but she was moving into a mood where anger would be easy. He would have to realize that while he could bully Arlashi, he couldn't bully her. If being blown apart, buried for days, and reassembled with bits missing hadn't crushed her, no mere musician could.

"This is not about tact," the conductor said. "Not that I'd expect you to be aware of that . . . Arriving on the eve of this concert to upset my soloist, for instance, is hardly an expression of great tact."

Ereza resisted an urge to argue. "This is a temporary prosthesis," she said, holding it up. "Right now, as you can imagine, they're short-staffed; it's going to take longer than it would have once to get the permanent one. However, it gives me some practice in using one."

"I should imagine." He glared at her. "Now sit down and be quiet. I have something to say to your sister."

"If you're planning to scold her, don't bother. She's about to faint—"

"I am *not*," Arla said. She had gone from pale to a dull red that clashed with her purple tunic.

"You have no rights here," said the conductor to Ereza. "You're just upsetting her—and I'll have to see her later. But for now—" He made a movement with his hands, tossing her the problem, and walked offstage. From that distance, he got the last word in. "Miss Fennaris—the *cellist* Miss Fennaris—see me in my office this afternoon at fourteen-twenty."

"You want lights?" asked a distant voice from somewhere overhead.

"No," said Arla, still not looking at Ereza. "Cut 'em." The brilliant stage lighting disappeared; Arla's dark clothes melted into the gloom onstage, leaving her face—older, sadder—to float above it. "Damn you, Ereza—why did you have to come now?"

Ereza couldn't think of anything to say. That was not what she'd imagined Arla saying. Anger and disappointment struggled; what finally came out was, "Why didn't you come to see me? I kept expecting you . . . Was it just this concert?" She could—almost—understand that preparing for a major appearance might keep her too busy to visit the hospital.

"No. Not . . . exactly." Arla looked past her. "It was—I couldn't practice without thinking about it. Your hand. My hand. If I'd seen you, I couldn't have gone on making music. I should have—after I beat you at *Flight-test* I should have enlisted. If I'd been there—"

"You'd have been asleep, like the rest of us. It wasn't slow reflexes that did it, Arlashi, it was a bomb. While we slept. Surely they told you that." But Arla's face had that stubborn expression again. Ereza tried again. "Look—what you're feeling—I do understand that. When I woke up and found Reia'd been killed, and Aristide, I hated myself for living. You wish I hadn't been hurt, and because you're not a soldier—"

"Don't start that!" Arla shifted, and a music stand went over with a clatter. "Dammit!" She crouched and gathered the music in shaking hands, then stabbed the stand upright. "If I get this out of order, Kiel will—"

Ereza felt a trickle of anger. "It's only sheets of paper—surely this Kiel can put it back in order. It's not like . . . what do you mean 'Don't start that'?"

"That *you're not a soldier* rigmarole. I know perfectly well I'm not, and you are. Everyone in the family is, except me, and I know how you all feel about it."

"Nonsense." They had had this out before; Ereza thought she'd finally got through, but apparently Arla still worried. Typical of the civilian mind, she thought, to fret about what couldn't be helped. "No one blames you; we're *proud* of you. Do you think we need another soldier? We've told you—"

"Yes. You've told me." Ereza waited, but Arla said nothing more, just stood there, staring at the lighter gloom over the midhall, where the skylight was.

"Well, then. You don't want to be a soldier; you never did. And no need, with a talent like yours. It's what we fight for, anyway—"

"Don't say that!"

"Why not? It's true. Gods be praised, Arlashi, we're not like the Metiz, quarreling for the pure fun of it, happy to dwell in a wasteland if only it's a battlefield. Or the Gennar Republic, which cares only for profit. Our people have always valued culture: music, art, literature. It's to make a society in which culture can flourish—where people like you can flourish—that we go to war at all."

"So it's my fault." That in a quiet voice. "You would lay the blame for this war—for that bomb—on me?"

"Of course not, ninny! How could it be your fault, when a Gavalan terrorist planted that bomb?" Musicians, Ereza thought, were incapable of understanding issues. If poor Arla had thought the bombing was her fault, no wonder she came apart—and how useless someone so fragile would be in combat, for all her hand-eye coordination and dexterity. "You aren't to blame for the misbegotten fool who did it, or the pigheaded political leadership that sent him."

"But you said—"

"Arlashi, listen. Your new cello—you know where the wood came from?"

"Yes." That sounded sullen, even angry. "Reparations from Scavel; the Military Court granted the Music Council first choice for instruments."

"That's what I mean. We go to war to protect our people—physical and economic protection. Do you think a poor, helpless society could afford wood for instruments? A concert hall to play in? The stability in which the arts flourish?" Arla stirred, but Ereza went on quickly before she could interrupt. "I didn't intend to lose a hand—no one does—but I would have done it gladly to give you your music—"

"I didn't ask you for that! You didn't have to lose anything to give me music. I could give *myself* music!"

"Not that cello," Ereza said, fighting to keep a reasonable tone. She could just imagine Arla out in the stony waste, trying to string dry grass across twigs and make music. Surely even musicians realized how much they needed the whole social structure, which depended on the military's capacity to protect both the physical planet and its trade networks. "Besides—war has to be something more than killing, more than death against death. We aren't barbarians. It has to be *for* something."

"It doesn't have to be for me."

"Yes, you. I can't do it. You could fight—" She didn't believe that, but saying it might get Arla's full attention. "Anyone can fight, who has courage, and you have that. But I can't make music. If I had spent the hours at practice you have, I still couldn't make your music. If I die, there are others as skilled as I am who could fight our wars. But if you die, there will be no music. In all the generations since Landing, our family has given one soldier after another. You—you're something different—"

"But I didn't ask for it."

Ereza shrugged, annoyed. "No one asks for their talent, or lack of it."

"That's not what I mean." Arla struggled visibly, then shrugged. "Look—we can't talk here; it's like acting, being on this stage. Come to my rehearsal room."

"Now? But I thought we'd go somewhere for lunch. I have to leave soon."

"Now. I have to put my precious war-won wood cello away." Arla led the way to her instrument, then offstage and down a white-painted corridor. Ereza ignored the sarcastic tone of that remark and followed her. Doors opened on either side; from behind some of them music leaked out, frail ghosts of melody.

Arla's room had two chairs, a desk-mounted computer, and a digital music stand. Arla waved her to one of the chairs; Ereza sat down and looked over at the music stand's display.

"Why don't you have this kind onstage? Why that paper you spilled?"

Her attempt to divert Arla's attention won a wry grin. "Maestro Bogdan won't allow it. Because the tempo control's usually operated by foot, he's convinced the whole orchestra would be tapping its toes. Even if we were, it'd be less intrusive than reaching out and turning pages, but he doesn't see it that way. Traditionally, even good musicians turn pages, but only bad musicians tap their feet. And we live for tradition—like my cello." Arla had opened the case again, and then she tapped her cello with one finger. It made a soft *tock* that sounded almost alive. With a faint sigh she turned away and touched her computer. The music stand display came up, with a line of music and the measure numbers above it.

She turned it to give Ereza a better view.

"Do you know what that is?"

Ereza squinted and read aloud. "Artruud's Opus 27, measure seventy-nine?"

"Do you know what *that* is?"

Ereza shook her head. "No—should I? I might if you hummed it."

Arla gave a short, ugly laugh. "I doubt that. We just played it, the whole thing. This—" She pointed at the display, which showed ten measures at a time. "This is where I blew up. Eighty-two to eighty-six."

"Yes, but I don't read music."

"I know." Arla turned and looked directly at her. "Did you ever think about that? The fact that I can play *Flight-test* as well as you, that my scores in TacSim—the tests you had me take as a joke—were enough to qualify me for officers' training if I'd wanted it . . . but not one of you in the family can read music well enough to pick out a tune on the piano?"

"It's not our talent. And you, surrounded by a military family—of course you'd pick up something—"

"Is war so easy?" That in a quiet voice, washed clean of emotion. Ereza stared at her, shocked.

"Easy! Of course it's not easy." She still did not want to think about her first tour, the near disaster of that patrol on Sardon, when a training mission had gone sour. It was nothing she could discuss with Arla. Her stump throbbed, reminding her of more recent pain. How could Arla ask that question? She started to ask that, but Arla had already spoken.

"But you think I picked it up, casually, with no training?"

"Well . . . our family . . . and besides, what you did was only tests, not real combat."

"Yes. And do you think that if you'd been born into a musical family, you'd have picked up music so casually? Would you be able to play the musical equivalent of *Flight-test*?"

"I'd have to know more, wouldn't I?" Ereza wondered where this conversation was going. Clearly Arla was upset about something, something to do with her own wound. *It's my arm that's missing, she thought. I'm the one who has a right to be upset or not upset.* "I'd still have no talent for it, but I would probably know more music when I heard it."

"Yet I played music in the same house, Eri, four to six hours a day when we were children. You had ears; you could have heard. We slept in the same room; you could have asked questions. You told me if you liked something, or if you were tired of hearing it; you never once asked me a *musical* question. You heard as much music as many musicians' children. The truth is that you didn't care. None of our family cared."

Ereza knew the shock she felt showed on her face; Arla nodded at her and went on talking. "Dari can tell you how his preschool training team pretended to assault the block fortress, and you listen to him. You listen carefully, you admire his cleverness or point out where he's left himself open for a counterattack. But me—I could play Hohlander's first cello concerto backward, and you'd never notice. It's not important to you—it's beneath your notice."

"That's not true." Ereza clenched the fingers of her left hand on the arm of the chair. "Of course we care; of course we notice. We know you're good; that's why you had the best teachers. It's just that it's not our field—we're not *supposed* to be experts."

"But you are about everything else." Arla, bracing herself on the desk, looked almost exultant. Ereza could hardly believe what she was hearing. The girl must have had this festering inside for years, to bring it out now, to someone wounded in her defense. "You talk politics as if it were your field—why this war is necessary, why that legislation is stupid. You talk about manufacturing, weapons design, the civilian economy—all that seems to be your area of expertise. If music and art and poetry are so important—if they're the reason you fight—then why don't you know anything about them? Why don't you bother to learn even the basics, the sort of stuff you expect Dari to pick up by the time he's five or six?"

"But—we can't do it all," Ereza said, appalled at the thought of all the children, talented or untalented, forced to sit through lessons in music. Every child had to know something about drill and survival techniques; Cravor's World, even in peacetime, could be dangerous. But music? You couldn't save yourself in a sandstorm or grass fire by knowing who wrote which pretty tune, or how to read musical notation. "We found you teachers who did—"

"Whom you treated like idiots," Arla said. "Remember the time Professor Rizvi came over, and talked to Grandmother after my lesson? No—of course you wouldn't; you were in survival training right then, climbing up cliffs or something like that. But it was just about the time the second Gavalan rebellion was heating up, and he told Grandmother the sanctions against the colonists just made things worse. She got that tone in her voice—you know what I mean—and silenced him. After that he wouldn't come to the house. I went into the city for my lessons. She told the story to Father, and they laughed together about the silly, ineffectual musician who wouldn't stand a chance against real power—with me standing there—and then they said, 'But you're a gifted child, Arlashi, and we love it.'"

"They're right." Ereza leaned forward. "What would a composer and musician know about war? And it doesn't take much of a weapon to smash that cello you're so fond of." She knew that much, whatever she didn't know about music. To her surprise, Arla gave a harsh laugh.

"Of *course* it doesn't take much weaponry to smash a cello. It doesn't take a weapon at all. I could trip going down the stairs and fall on it; I could leave it flat on the floor and step on it. You don't need to be a skilled soldier to destroy beauty: any clumsy fool can manage that."

"But—"

Arla interrupted her. "That's my point. You take pride in your skill, in your special, wonderful knowledge. And all you can accomplish with it is what carelessness or stupidity or even the normal path of entropy will do by itself. If you want a cello smashed, you don't need an army: just turn it over to a preschool class without a teacher present. If you want to ruin a fine garden, you don't have to march an expensive army through it—just let it alone. If you want someone to die, you don't have to kill them: just *wait*! We'll all die, Ereza. We don't need your help."

"It's not about that!" But Ereza felt a cold chill. If Arla could think that . . . "It's not about killing. It's protecting—"

"You keep saying that, but—did you ever consider asking me ? Asking any artist, any writer, any musician? Did you ever consider learning enough of our arts to guess how we might feel?"

Ereza stared at her, puzzled. "But we did protect you. We let you study music from the beginning; we've never pushed you into the military. What more do you want, Arlashi?"

"To be myself, to be a musician just because I *am*, not because you needed someone to prove that you weren't all killers."

That was ridiculous. Ereza stared at her twin, wondering if someone had mindwiped her. Would one of the political fringe groups have thought to embarrass the Fennaris family, with its rich military history, by recruiting its one musician? "I don't understand," she said, aware of the stiffness in her voice. She would have to tell Grandmother as soon as she got out of here, and find out if anyone else had noticed how strange Arla had become.

Arla leaned forward. "Ereza, you cannot have me as a tame conscience . . . someone to feel noble about. I am not a simple musician, all full of sweet melody, to soothe your melancholy hours after battle." She plucked a sequence of notes, pleasant to the ear.

"Not that I mind your being soldiers," Arla went on, now looking past Ereza's head into some distance that didn't belong in that small room. Ereza had seen that look on soldiers; it shocked her on Arla's face. "It's not that I'm a pacifist, you see. It's more complicated than that. I want you to be honest soldiers. If you like war, admit it. If you like killing, admit that. Don't make me the bearer of your nobility, and steal my own dark initiative. I am a person—a whole person—with my own kind of violence."

"Of course you're a whole person—everyone is—"

"No. You aren't. You aren't because you know nothing about something you claim is important to you."

"What do you want me to do?" Ereza asked. She felt grumpy. Her stump hurt now, and she wanted to be back with people who didn't make ridiculous emotional arguments or confuse her.

"Quit thinking of me as sweet little Arlashi, your pet twin, harmless and fragile and impractical. Learn a little music, so you'll know what discipline really is. Or admit you don't really care, and quit condescending to me."

"Of course I care." She cared that her sister had gone crazy, at least. Then a thought occurred to her. "Tell me—do the other musicians feel as you do?"

Arla cocked her head and gave her an unreadable look. "Come to the concert tomorrow, Eri."

"I don't know if I can—" She didn't know if she wanted to. A long journey into the city, hours crammed into a seat with others, listening to music that didn't (if she was honest) interest her that much. She'd already heard it, parts of it over and over. "How about tomorrow's rehearsal?"

"No. The concert. I can get you in. If you want to know how musicians think, and why . . . then come."

"Are the others—?"

"I don't know. Grandmother usually comes to my performances, but the others less often. I wish you would, Eri."

Ereza sat in the back row of the concert hall, surrounded by people in formal clothes and dress uniforms. Onstage the orchestra waited, in formal black and white, for the soloist and conductor.

She saw a stir at the edge of the stage. Arla, in her long swirling dress, with the cello. The conductor—she looked quickly at her program for his name. Mikailos Bogdan.

Applause, which settled quickly as the house lights went down. Now the clear dome showed a dark night sky with a thick wedge of stars, the edge of the Cursai Cluster. The conductor lifted his arms. Ereza watched; the musicians did not stir. His arms came down.

Noise burst from speakers around the hall. As if conducting music, Bogdan's arms moved, but the noise had nothing to do with his direction. Grinding, squealing, exploding—all the noises that Ereza finally recognized as belonging to an armored ground unit in battle. Rattle and clank of treads, grinding roar of engines, tiny voices yelling, screaming, the heavy thump of artillery and lighter crackling of small arms. Around her the others stirred, looked at one another in amazement, then horror.

Onstage, no one moved. The musicians stared ahead, oblivious to the noise; Ereza, having heard the rehearsal, wondered how they could stand it. And *why?* Why work so for perfection in rehearsal if they never meant to play? Toward the front, someone stood—someone in uniform—and yelled. Ereza could not hear it over the shattering roar that came from the speakers, then—low-level aircraft strafing, she thought. She remembered that sound. Another two or three people stood up; the first to stand began to push his way out of his row. One of the others was hauled back down by those sitting near him.

The sound changed, this time to the repetitive *crump-crump-crump-crump* of bombardment. Vague, near-human sounds, too . . . Ereza shivered, knowing before it came clear what that would be. Screams, moans, sobs . . . it went on far too long. She wanted to get up and leave, but she had no strength.

Silence, when it finally came, was welcome. Ereza could hear, as her ears regained their balance, the ragged breathing of the audience. Silence continued, the conductor still moving his arms as if the orchestra were responding. Finally, he brought the unnerving performance to a close, turned and bowed to them. A few people clapped, uncertainly; no one else joined them and the sound died away.

"Disgracefully bad taste," said someone to Ereza's right. "I don't know what they think they're doing."

"Getting us ready to be ravished by Fennaris, no doubt. Have you heard her before?"

"Only on recordings. I've been looking forward to this for decades."

"She's worth it. I heard her first in a chamber group two years ago, and—" The conductor beckoned, and Arla stood; the gossipers quieted. Intent curiosity crackled around the hall, silent but alive.

"Ladies and gentlemen," Arla said. She had an untrained voice, but even so it carried to the back of the hall. "You may be wondering what happened to the Goldieri Concerto. We chose to make another statement about music."

The conductor bowed to her, and signaled the orchestra. Each musician held an instrument at arm's length; at the flick of his baton they all dropped to the floor, the light rattling cases of violins, the softer boom of violas, the clatter and thud and tinkle of woodwinds, brasses, percussion. A tiny round drum rolled along the floor until it ran into someone's leg and fell over with a final loud tap. Louder than that was the indrawn breath of the audience.

"I'm Arla," she said, standing alone, facing a crowd whose confusion was slowly turning to hostility. Ereza felt her skin tingling.

"Most of you know me as Arla Fennaris, but tonight I'm changing my name. I want you to know why."

She turned and picked up her cello, which she had left leaning against her chair. *No,* Ereza thought, *don't do it. Not that one. Please.*

"You think of me as a cellist," Arla said, and plucked three notes with one hand. "A cellist is a musician, and a musician—I have this from my own sister, a wounded veteran, as many of you know—a musician is to most of you an impractical child. A fool." She ran her hand down the strings, and the sound echoed in Ereza's bones. She shivered, and so did the people sitting next to her. "She tells me, my sister, that the reason we're at war right now—the reason she lost her arm—is that I am a mere musician, and need protection. I can't protect myself; I send others out to die, to keep me and my music alive." Another sweeping move across the strings, and a sound that went through Ereza like a jagged blade. All she could think was *No, no, don't . . . no . . .* but she recognized the look on Arla's face, the tone of her voice. Here was someone committed beyond reason to whatever she was doing.

But Arla had turned, and found her chair again. She was sitting as she would for any performance, the cello nestled in the hollow of her skirt, the bow in her right hand. "It is easy to make noise," Arla said. With a move Ereza did not understand, she made an ugly noise explode from the cello. "It takes skill to make music." She played a short phrase as sweet as spring sunshine. "It is easy to destroy—" She held the cello up, as if to throw it, and again Ereza head the indrawn breath as the audience waited. Then she put it down. "It takes skill to make—in this case, millennia of instrument designers, and Barrahesh, here on Cravor's World, with a passion for the re-creation of classic instruments. I have no right to destroy his work—but it would be easy." She tapped the cello's side, and the resonant sound expressed fragility. "As with my cello, with everything. It is easy to kill; it takes skill to nurture life." Again she played a short phrase, this one a familiar child's song about planting flower seeds in the desert.

"My sister," Arla said, and her eyes found Ereza's, and locked onto them. "My sister is a soldier, a brave soldier, who was wounded . . . she would say protecting me. Protection I never asked for, and did not need. Her arm the price of this one—" She held up her right arm. "It is difficult to make music when you are using your sister's arm. An arm taught to make war, not music. An arm that does not respect music."

She lowered her arm. "I can make music only with my own arm, because it's my arm that learned it. And to play with my arm means throwing away my sister's sacrifice. Denying it. Repudiating it." *No,* Ereza thought at her again. *Don't do this. I will understand; I will change. Please.* But she knew it was too late, as it had been too late to change things when she woke after surgery and found her own arm gone. "If my sister wants music, she must learn to make it. If you want music, you must learn to make it. We will teach you; we will play with you—but we will not play *for* you. Good evening."

Again the conductor signaled; the musicians picked up their instruments from the floor, stood, and walked out. For a moment, the shuffling of their feet onstage was the only sound as shock held the audience motionless. Ereza felt the same confusion, the same hurt, the same realization that they would get no music. Then the catcalls began, the hissing, the programs balled up angrily and thrown; some hit the stage and a few hit the musicians. But none of them hurried, none of them looked back. Arla and the conductor waited, side by side, as the orchestra cleared the stage. Ereza sat frozen, unable to move even as people pushed past her, clambered over her legs. She wanted to go and talk to Arla; she knew it would do no good. She did not speak Arla's language. She never had. Now she knew what Arla meant: she had never respected her sister before. Now she did. *Too late, too late* cried her mind, struggling to remember something, anything, of the music.

>•<

Rachael Acks' Charlie enlists in the Allied Earth Special Forces and becomes a weapon as well as a warrior. But like many other veterans of any war, when she leaves military service and returns home, civilian life is not what she expected.

THEY TELL ME
THERE WILL BE NO PAIN

Rachael Acks

"O, me alone! Make you a sword of me?"
—*The Tragedy of Coriolanus*, William Shakespeare, Act 1, Scene 7

COLONEL RATHBONE ATTENDS my final debriefing. I'm wearing a paper hospital gown that doesn't cover my ass; I've got a breeze where no breeze has any right to be, from the back of my neck right down where the good Lord split me. But despite that I'm sweating, the backs of my thighs sticking to the paper covering the hospital table. The metal contacts set all around my head feel cold, sending little shocks that make my teeth itch.

"Sure you don't want to re-up?" the Colonel asks. He's got a deep voice. Jolly. Like a murderous Santa Claus, shaved into military trim. "You've got a solid record, all kills, no collateral, no fails. We sure could use you."

One of those things is a lie and we both know it. I smile at him with my rattling teeth. "Got to go home and take care of things, sir." Got to get out of here, sir.

"Hate to lose you, son." Rathbone calls everyone *son*, whether you got a cock or tits. He digs his datapad out of his pocket, calls up the SMOP and starts to read like a robot. No, worse than a robot, robots sound almost human these days.

Don't you, Phoebe?

" . . . as agreed upon in your contract as signed, upon termination of your service you will return all government property issued to you upon entry, including all surgical and neural enhancements. Do you understand and still agree to these terms?"

I find I've pressed one finger against the visual link terminal on my right temple, like it's the starter on a car. The scent of lemons floods over my tongue. "I understand and agree, sir."

He shuts off the datapad and tucks it back away, claps me on the shoulder. "Then that's that. Good luck on the outside, son." Then he turns to go, broad back in olive drab, his crew cut salt and pepper above the stiff collar.

"Sir?"

"What?" His eyebrows ask me if I'm changing my mind.

"They said it won't hurt."

He gives me a kind, lying goddamn smile. "You did three tours, son. You're tough."

The door shuts behind him and I fiddle, peeling slowly at my hangnails. I used to do manicures with my big sister. Nail polish isn't regulation, not that I could keep from picking it off like I peel away my own skin.

There will be no pain, Phoebe whispers past my ear and into my spine.

"Shut the fuck up."

So this is how it goes, son.

Ten years ago, you're a snot-nosed chicken-shit fast-food drone in the making. Bronze medal in high school track and field, chorus line parts only in high school drama, grades that aren't quite bad enough to justify the way Mommy and Daddy keep cutting back your allowance. Your older sister is the star quarterback of the family team. Full ride to Titan Tech, ships out on the first terraforming mission to Juno, calls home twice a week like a dutiful daughter and runs the hydroponics lab while she watches her kid sister paint her fingernails on the video feed. You still use her soap on days when you miss her; it smells like flowers and baby powder.

You're special, she tells you. Don't listen to anyone else. Join up in the corps, come out to Juno, we'll be partners.

You know what happens next. As far as Earth's concerned, there's only one thing that happened ten years ago. Only one thing that's happened in the last ten years, because every goddamn one of us ripped our shirts off and wrote it across our hearts in blood.

The Drop. July nine. Starfall. Lots of names, one result. A shattered habitat, a woman with wild eyes and a gold cross tattooed on her forehead screaming that her army, they got their authority straight from Jesus Christ Hisself for our racial impurity and hubris, and your big sister, blown out into space, just one of ten thousand meat snowflakes floating in the black. Only you imagine her lying like a broken doll on the floor of the hydroponics lab, tight black curls sprinkled with dust and ice crystals and her fingernails Bahama Coral Pink, tapping faintly in a pool of blood. The same shade she wore the day she took out a pair of tweezers and came at your eyebrows, saying, "Don't be a wuss, this doesn't *hurt*."

And just like everyone else on the goddamn planet, you cheer until your head just *thumps* with it when we make our war of vengeance.

Contract signing, swearing in, intake, ceremonies, first uniform, boot camp, none of that shit matters. It's all standard. The point is to make you into a unit, one little cog in the big machine of the Allied (ha!) Earth Special Forces.

This is the point where it matters. Where it starts to matter. Where it stops mattering.

Head wrapped in bandages, skull aching from newly drilled holes, random flavors running across your tongue (cantaloupe, cayenne, crawdad bake, we're in the Cs now) as the nanowires finish bonding to your neurons, you've got to focus, soldier, *focus*, this is important.

You look at the blank standard-issue datapad screen, shoulders twitching every time a new ghost runs across your vision. A line of green text scrolls up, like you've jumped back to the goddamn twentieth century, but instead of *Want to play a game* or some shit like that, it reads:

Hello, I am your Tactical Analysis and Oversight Guidance (TAOG) system. My name is _____

Fill in the blank. Your right shoulder twists as a metallic screech runs up the scale in your ear.

Well, what other name could you pick? You can only think of one right now, with the wires in your head all scrambled and crossed and reminding you about that one time you called the teacher "Mom" in third grade.

P-h-o-e-b-e.

Hello Charlie, I am your Tactical Analysis and Oversight Guidance (TAOG) system. My name is Phoebe. She whispers that as a formless voice now given form by your choice, past your ear, deep into your meat. *I'm looking forward to working with you.*

That's how it goes, only you're not you, you're me.

And you had a big sister named Phoebe.

Life outside AESF is one big vacation, only the vacation doesn't end and I don't get to go home, because technically, I am home, permanently downside. But I'm enjoying it. Really, I am. I take the train down to the beach every day, because that's what you do on vacation. Brightly colored plastic umbrellas, all shapes and colors and patterns, bob outside, shielding the civilians from the unending assault of the sun.

Take one of those umbrellas, line it with foil, it can be used to hide an explosive or a person from casual drone scans, only it makes a neat circle cut-out in transmissions that screams for attention after you've run your electronic eyes over it a good hundred times.

It's the middle of the day. Seven people on the train as it hums along over its superconductors: three teenaged boys (could be a threat, one of them's got a backpack, who knows what's in that), one young mother with two sub-five-year-olds (probably okay), one old lady with a parasol (sunlight glancing off the gold cross she wears on her neck, is she one of them, one of the sectarians ohshitohshitohshit call it in—)

No response, Phoebe says. They told me my TAOG would go silent after surgery. They also told me removing the neural links wouldn't hurt. *Disconnected, Charlie. Recalibration necessary.*

Breathe. Breathe. That's right. My hands haven't fallen off. I just don't have drones any more. I'm just me. The old lady is just an old lady. She's out for the sunlight on her old bones. But I let her get off the train first, and keep my ass in the seat until I'm two stops down.

Then I go out onto the beach. The sand feels so strange under my shoes, squashing and shushing and kicking up in little clouds. I don't think I've run on anything but concrete or tarmac or metal decking for almost a decade. It feels different, so I smile about that, and my teeth itch in the cool breeze.

THIS IS WHAT IT'S LIKE, the first time you hook into your cloud. Your consciousness shatters into a hundred pieces, one for each module.

There's the eyes and ears (SASbots), jammers (ESIMbots), guns and missiles (TWINs) and you're all of them at once, trying to hold them in formation and run them through patterns. You scream. It's cool. Everyone screams the first time, not because it hurts, but because it's so overwhelming your body pulls a random choice out of: (a) scream, (b) cry, or (c) laugh hysterically. Crying and screaming is better, it doesn't freak your observers out nearly as much.

But then, goddamn, it's the biggest rush in the world. You are a god with a thousand fingers that you can spike down into the ground like lightning. You fly, atmosphere or space, it doesn't matter. Because when you're hooked into your cloud, you're out there with the drones, and your meat is left behind in the closet.

Calibration complete. Phoebe whispers these magical words to rhyme with "I love you."

A taste like blood floods your mouth. It's nauseating. Don't worry. You get used to it.

LIFE OUTSIDE THE DRONE CLOUD is blindness. I can't *see* anything. What kind of bullshit is the visual spectrum after you've gotten used to having infrared, ultraviolet, radio, all piped into your head from over a hundred different eyes? I used to be a fucking titan, heavy armor Mach six in a thousand different directions, and now I'm small, naked. Just meat.

No jobs yet, but I don't need the money. My severance hasn't run out, I just need something to do. Being a drone pilot isn't much of a marketable skill in the real world. Doesn't help you smile at assholes and sell them cars, or new computers, or vacation packages to resorts where the only people who look like you scrub the toilets. Doesn't help with flipping burgers, either. I've developed this really worrying twitch in my left hand, I think it's from one of the nanowires fizzing in my brain. Makes it hard for me to sleep, I'll be drifting off and then suddenly my hand jerks under the covers and I'm wide awake.

It's bad enough I go to the nearest VA hospital, which takes a thirty-minute train ride—

(two workmen, one of them has a hammer and veins bulging out from his bare forearms; typical nuclear family with a kid in a stroller, who knows what's hidden in there; students, more students, more students in navy blue uniform jackets and at least someone's laughing around here but, fuck, why won't they hold still for five minutes; *No threat, no threat, no threat*, Phoebe assures me in a murmur that runs along my jawbone and makes me yawn)

—and then a two-hour wait in a room that smells faintly of sweat and metal. The data signal there is jacked and all the paper magazines are at least three years old, so I just listen to two other vets make stilted conversation about their dogs.

"That's impossible," the doc at the VA tells me once it's my turn in the carefully refrigerated exam room. "They removed all your links before discharge. I've got the signed order from Colonel Rathbone."

"But what if the nanowires are still there?" I can fucking *feel* them, burrowing into my neurons.

The look he gives me is a lot like the manager of the last place I applied at, some joint that makes pizza. *You've got to be kidding, right?*

But they told me a lot of things, in the service. This will be a cakewalk. You'll go home a hero. We'll pull all the wires out of your brain and it won't hurt one bit, you're tough. "What about the TAOG, did they remove that, too?"

His eyes widen slightly. "Are you hearing voices?"

I hold up my hands. The left twitches—See, I'm not just making this up. "No. Shit no. I'm not crazy." I know what happens to people who say shit like that. They go away and never come back. "Look, I just want to know my brain isn't turning into black pudding behind my eyes, okay? I busted my ass for you guys downside for nine years. Cut me a break."

The doctor sighs. "I'll put you in the queue for some testing. It'll take a few weeks, we're pretty overloaded. Though if you can travel—"

Being on the train for hours and hours, people constantly walking in and out and back and forth behind me and beside me and no thanks, man, sounds like hell, I can't keep track of them all, too many threats. *Acquiring targets*—I shake my head. "Got no scratch. Got a form I can fill out for that?"

"Afraid not. All right. I'll send the appointment confirmation to your calendar."

As I slouch on out of the hospital, they run a guy past on a pallet. He's got a cardio pack on his chest, a vent over the lower half of his face, red-soaked bandages at his wrists. His face is the color of unbaked clay. He's also got a circle of white dimples around his head like a crown.

Corporal Dan Weston, Second Battalion, Third Squadron, retired, Phoebe murmurs up through my meat and into my left ear. *No threat, target deceased, permission not needed.*

I press my finger where the visual link used to be on my temple, and find nothing but a smooth, slick dimple of scar tissue.

My teeth itch.

So then you score a berth on a Predator-Class carrier, space-based command and dispatch center. Calories carefully counted, AG coming off perfectly calibrated spin so you can still do full PT every morning. Your body's all tight with wiry muscle for when you put it on the shelf and abandon it ten hours a day.

They assign you the easy missions first, out into the moons. Ones where you just drop dome busters, and the closest you get is doing an infrared check to make sure all the bodies are cooling off in their individual puddles of effluvia. Or you do spy runs, where you run the SASbots around and it's like a video game, and you'll get the high score and the achievement at the end if you find the princess. And by princess I mean the scumbag you paint down with a targeting laser so one of your big brothers can sweep in like justice in an atomized cloud and light that shit up better than Christmas.

But then you get your first real mission. No fanfare, no warning, you just walk in one day, hook into the cloud and launch off. Then Phoebe says, *Target acquired, authorization go.*

And that's it. You take the TWINs out to play, and the bad guys die. *Clean kill, stand down*, Phoebe tells you.

Years. You do it for *years*. Then:

Target acquired, authorization go.

"Getting a lot of noise. Confirm." The SASbots show a place crawling with heat signatures, like they're having a convention in that dumpy little building. Stats and dimensions scroll through your brain.

A green flash shivers over the view. Targeting laser, some new pilot double-checking your shit.

Authorization go, Phoebe repeats. *Insurgents confirmed. Action is justified.*

You are so fucking justified. You send in the TWINs, and you flatten that little hovel. You turn it into a smear of gravel and ash. Then there's a spike of automatic weapons fire a click and a half west. Two SASbots go dead, a little blind spot in your brain.

Secondary threat, authorization go, Phoebe says. *Assistance incoming.*

A second wave of TWINs joins in the bombardment. You make the night go *white*. In the dim recesses of the drone bay, you hear one of the other jocks whoop. Well, look at those accuracy numbers. You sure can't blame him. You feel pretty fucking badass yourself.

You sweep in with SASbots again, check and confirm the kills, catalog what you just took out. You'd rather just send in recordings than fill out the paperwork. Secondary site is closer, so that gets done first. Shredded remains of fifteen adults, explosive residue that doesn't belong to us. First site—

—she's lying in a puddle of blood, eyes wide and white all around, curly black hair stuck to the floor, legs a mist of bone and flesh

—there's kids, there's a goddamn kid, another one with his head half gone, and another, and a woman in an apron like you blew up a fucking daycare, and, and—

Charlie, your heart rate is spiking, Phoebe says. *What's wrong?*

"Kids," you say. "You said this was an authorized target." She told you to do it, told you, said it was okay. But terrorists don't play with plastic horses, don't have pigtails and purple barrettes. "Look at her! She's trying to scream!"

Death is instant, Phoebe calmly whispers into the skin of your neck. *Residual electrical spikes. There is no pain.*

But the girl looks at your hovering thimble-sized SASbot with eyes to drown in and tremblestremblestrembles her fingernails (glittering with nail polish is that Bahama Coral Pink oh fuck me fuck me fuck me) tapping the ground as she gurgles out breath after breath into the poisonous atmosphere.

←----→

THIS IS HOW IT GOES, only you're not you, you're me.

And you (I mean me) realize this terrible truth: Phoebe's just there to tell you it's okay to pull the trigger. She's a wad of ones and zeroes that stands in for your conscience so you don't hesitate.

Phoebe isn't real.

Phoebe is a liar.

Phoebe is a sin eater.

I CAN'T SLEEP ANY MORE. My hand won't stop jumping. Everything I eat tastes like electricity and motor oil. The VA test results say the nanowires in my head don't exist, but I can feel them rotting out and turning my brain into something black and gooey, blood on tarmac while Phoebe whispers battle plans onto the backs of my knees. All I have is vids, I can't focus enough to read any more, not that I was into books before.

And the vids? It's just bullshit bullshit bullshit, plastic people with perfect teeth in clothes worth more than my entire severance having cat fights about their boyfriends, cooking shows, action movies where a single guy with a gun fires more bullets than a clip can hold, softcore porn. It's like there's not even a fucking war on, and I just have to *move* before the tar in my head overflows.

I take the train down to the beach, late at night. The car is full of drunks, big guys, little guys, and they stand too goddamn close and breathe like furnaces. I finger my pocket, the stunted shape of a ceramic pistol. I don't have a drone cloud to protect me anymore. It's just me, just my pathetic meat and Phoebe, and we're never safe.

"Hey there," one of the guys says. "Where you going?" He smells like money and beer.

"Not anywhere you are." I stare straight ahead. My hand twitches at my side. I could snap his neck. He's crowding me.

"Don't be nasty." Leans even closer. "What are those marks on your head? You some kind of holy roller?"

I get asked that all the time. Like no one knows what soldiers look like if we're not dressed up like a GI Joe. Maybe no one bothers watching the news. Maybe they think the clouds of heavily armed robots just fly themselves now, but shouldn't that scare everyone shitless?

He breathes on the side of my head, too close, too close. My teeth itch.

Threat detected. Phoebe breathes on the other side of my head.

I pull the pistol from my pocket, smooth like butter, slam my other fist into the guy's sternum to get him to back off and give me room. My pistol is the only steady thing in the world as I focus down the barrel at his head framed by gum advertisements and the blank windows looking out into black night. "Back off! Back the fuck off!"

"Whoa! Whoa, lady! Chill! Chill!" Suddenly all the drunk guys are shouting.

"All of you! Shut the fuck up! Back off!"

Hands rise around the train car. A dark stain spreads over the front of my target's pants. "Don't do it. I didn't mean nothin'. I didn't mean nothin'!" The train halts, a cool rush of night air as the doors behind me open, I know exactly where they are, always know where your exits are.

Threat detected. Authorization go.

My trigger finger squeezes even as my hand jerks to the side. The bullet only makes a soft pop—I don't like loud noises, I wouldn't buy a loud gun, are you kidding me—and the window behind the man shatters.

Everyone starts yelling all at once. Hands grab at my arm. I scream and break one of my knuckles on someone's nose. Then I run.

It's cold. There are clouds over the moon, so it's just a glowing, indistinct circle, like a puckered scar in the sky. I only notice when I get to the beach because the ground beneath my sneakers starts shushing me. I keep running until I'm not afraid any more.

Who the fuck am I kidding? I'm always afraid.

I walk out by the waves, where I can watch them crest into white foam, and sit on the damp sand. I take my datapad out of my other pocket, and the screen comes back on to the news vid I saw when I decided I had to get the fuck out of my house: *At Last, War Without Death*. I watch the bland-faced narrator silently mouth the words, "AESF reports zero casualties in the last two years of the conflict." Well, no shit. We're all just clouds of robots now.

Targets don't count. That's authorized.

Retired don't count either.

My hand twitches. My teeth itch.

Disconnected, Charlie. Reactualizing neural connections, Phoebe says calmly, laying the words up my spine.

I pull the pistol from my pocket. My head throbs, hot and sharp under the scars. The barrel feels so cool and soothing, pressed against what used to be the visual link terminal on my right temple. The taste of blood floods my mouth.

There will be no pain, Phoebe whispers into my ear.

I close my eyes. "Liar."

I smell flowers and baby powder. *Authorization go.*

>•≪

A graphic violence warning was attached to Kameron Hurley's "Wonder Maul Doll" when it appeared online in podcast form. War is violent. The one Hurley portrays is relentlessly brutal for the soldiers who fight it and the civilians who suffer from it. And, like too many wars, it is tragically senseless.

WONDER MAUL DOLL

Kameron Hurley

WE'D SET DOWN IN PEKOI as part of the organics inquisition team, still stinking of the last city. We're all muscle. Not brains. The brains are out eating at the foreigners' push downtown, and they don't care if we whore around the tourist dregs half the night so long as somebody's sober enough to haul them out come morning. When the brains aren't eating, they're pretending to give us directions in the field, telling us where to sniff out organics. They're writing reports about how dangerous Pekoi is to the civilized world.

We're swapping off some boy in a backwater push the locals cleared out for us. We're sitting around a low table. I pass off another card to Kep. Luce swaps out a suit. She has to sit on one leg to lean over the table. It's hot in the low room, so humid that moths clutter around our feet, too heavy to fly.

The boy's making little mewling sounds again. Somebody should shut him up, but not me. This is my hand. I'm ahead.

Ro's got her feet up on the chair next to me, head lolled back, eyes closed. She's sweating like a cold glass.

Telle finishes up behind the curtain. She took her time with the boy, the kid. Not a kid, I guess. Looks young, too skinny. They're all pale as maggots, here, built like stick figures. She pushes into a seat next to Kep, flicks on the radio tube. It flickers blue-green, vomits up a misty shot of President Nabirye talking trash.

"Turn that up," Ro says. She passes me some sen. Her teeth are stained red.

The boy stumbles past the curtain. He's a little roughed up. Ro throws some money at him.

Kep crowns my king. I steal an ace.

The boy clutches at the money in the mud; moths' wings come away on his hands. There must be something Ro doesn't like, cause she stands and roughs him up some. He starts squealing.

Elections back home are in a month. President Nabirye's nattering about foreign policy in Pekoi. President says we'll be home in six weeks. Three of our squads just got hashed by a handful of local boys and teenage girls.

"They don't pull us out soon, and they'll be shipping us home in bags," Telle says. "Nabirye won't be in that seat in six weeks."

"Nabirye can eat shit," Kep says.

Ro cuffs her. "Watch the yapping." She sits down and starts polishing her boots.

The boy on the floor isn't moving.

We've been here nine months looking for treaty violations, organic dumps. Bags of human sludge.

We haven't found a fucking thing.

There's nothing dangerous in Pekoi.

RO HAS ME and Kep on point. Kep's all right, a talker, doesn't keep the tube on all the damn time like Telle. We're checking out another field the brains sent us out to sniff. Running fire drills, Ro calls it. We're mucking through half-filled ditches, cutting open suspect corpses, raiding contagion shelters.

"So," Kep says, "sister says, I want to marry her like in the books. Like, for love. A pauper. Mother Mai says—"

"Fuck you?" I suggest.

"Yeah, yeah. Mother Mai says, 'You marry for business. It's in the Bible.'"

"Is that truth?"

"Yea. Book of Theclai. Page eighteen. Line ninety-five."

"Thou shalt eat fish?" I say, wondering if we're talking about the same book.

"Hold!" Ro yells from behind us.

Kep and I drop to our bellies in the high grass. We're slathered in bug secretions, but it doesn't keep them away. I can feel bugs boring up under my slick. Yellow and black ticks, hoar ticks, pill ticks. I'll spend all night burning them out.

"Did you see anything?" Kep says.

"Nah," I say. I crunch a bug in my teeth.

Somebody pokes at Kep. Kep nearly sets off a spray. I pivot onto my back, raise my gun. It's just Ro. I flop back over onto my belly. Ro stays crouched.

"We're twenty paces," Ro says.

"I don't see nothing," Kep says.

"Telle and Luce are running scout," Ro says. "Hold."

We wait. The bugs really start to swarm.

"Clear!" Telle's voice, loud.

"Up," Ro says.

Kep and I pace at a half-crouch, our eyes just above the line of the grass. I can see Luce and Telle at the base of a rocky rise overhung in widow's drape and black morvern. They've uncovered a gaping black mouth.

I come up along Telle. Kep flanks Luce.

"Light," Ro says.

Telle snaps a globe off her vest and flicks the release, tosses the globe into the darkness. The globe throws off white light.

Ro points us in. "Kep, Jian," she says.

Kep and I slip into the tunnel. We have to crouch. The floor's smooth. The globe stops rolling at a bend in the corridor. I hear a scuttling sound, like cockroaches.

Kep raises a fist. We stop. Kep kicks the globe around the turn. The globe cracks against the far wall. Something moves.

Kep goes down on one knee. I aim over her head, into the bowl of the stone room. The globe leaves no shadows, so I see them. Hunkered against the stone, clinging to each other, quaking like boats at tide: Pekoi's stashed organics. Their treaty violation. Nabirye might get her seat yet.

"Live!" Kep yells. "Telle!"

The three girls on the floor start crying. They try to bury their heads in their skinny arms. There's no fat on them. I could break all their bones in my bare hands.

Telle thumps in, does a count. "Haul them out!" she says. "I called it in. They want them live."

"The fuck?" Kep says.

So we haul them out, live.

They come kicking and biting, but they're spent by the time they hit air. The littlest one is the fiercest, all teeth and eyes.

Ro looks them over. She's holding Telle's tube. I hear the tinny voice buzzing from Central. Ro clicks the tube off, tosses it to Telle.

The girls start babbling. They're naked, and their accents are bad, but they know what we're saying. They're feeding us some story about hiding from bursts. Dead families, bloated bodies. They say they're not tailored, not dangerous. They don't know anything about organic sludge. I've heard it from every bag. And every bag opens up the same.

"Shut up," Telle says. She steps in, butts the biggest one in the face with her gun.

The little one leaps on Telle and starts tearing at her slick.

Kep and Luce and I drag the girl off. Telle binds the girl's hands, trusses up the other two with plastic wire.

We string them together and make for Central. We're a long way from Central.

We don't talk about that.

"So Mother Mai says—"

"Fuck Mother Mai," I say.

Telle's got watch over the girls. They're huddled around a big cicada tree. Ro's poking at the fire beetles in the stove. Dusk is heavy. The lavender sky goes deep purple, then black. It's like being smothered.

"Mother Mai says, what you gonna do with a womb anyway? It gonna chew your meat for you?" Kep's sitting up on the fallen tree behind me, wiping down her gun. She's got a globe up there, set low. The light's orange, like bad urine.

One of the girls is bleeding, the little one. It's been three cities since I seen a woman bleed. I forgot that some still do it. Telle's still got a grudge against that girl. She's started calling her *Maul*.

"So my sister has it put back in. Nip and tuck," Kep says. "You know what happens?"

Luce is pulling off the heads of powder bugs. She keeps dropping them on me. I pound at her ankles. She kicks away.

"Nothing happens!" Kep says. "She doesn't even bleed, 'cause she's got implants, of course. I thought she'd be crying all the time. Like a boy. No. It's social, my sister says, makes boys so screwed up."

"Your sister should run for a seat," I say. "She sounds like a bleeding heart. Her and all the bleeding hearts can run the whole damn world from the seat. Start wearing their wombs like trophies."

"Yeah," Kep says. She spits sen on her cleaning rag. "Yeah."

Ro yells at Luce and tells her to run a perimeter sweep. Ro kicks me and makes me heat up the pot. I take some over to Telle and the girls. The little one, Maul, bares her teeth at me, but she takes the food in, takes it so fast she vomits it up. One of the others, this big, broad-shouldered mutt, just looks at the pot like she's never seen food before. She goggles at me like a kid. When she looks at me, I hear that boy. The mewling one.

We move at light, after delousing. The girls are sweating too much. Losing too much water. All that uncovered skin. No slicks. They drink too much.

Luce is running scout. She circles at midday, when we're sitting out the worst of the heat.

"Off track," Luce says. "They put up a ward over the road."

Ro spits sen. "Our road?"

"Yeah."

"Pekoi doesn't want us coming back in," I say.

"Or they're just doing road work," Ro says. "Don't think they're savvy. We reroute. Telle?"

Telle flips on the tube and reroutes us. We have six more days in the field, but the reroute gets us two more. Ro puts us on cut rations.

The girls whine about water all night. All but the broad-shouldered one. She has a tangle of curly hair, always hangs her head over. Kep starts calling her *Doll*.

"What we calling the other one?" Telle says.

The third one, the skinniest girl, with a face smeared purple with bruises, holds her arms over herself, bobs her head. I have a boy back home, he bobs his head like that when things get tense. Says he's thinking too much.

"Call her *Wonder*," I say.

The girls slow us down. There are bugs to eat, but the girls keep retching them up.

Kep's on scout next day, comes in, says there's a village a click south. "Maybe two or three dozen bags," she says. "Mostly boys."

Ro gives the nod. "Stock up on water. Be good."

We push. Luce switches out scout with Kep. Kep paces me. Telle's still on girl detail. Ro's taking up the rear.

Kep and I hit dirt first. We scare a group of scraggly girls and kids in one of the bug farms on the edge of the village. The girls slosh up onto the banks of the ponds. I see the roiling forms of giant madillo bugs churning through the muddy water. Some of the girls grab stones as they disappear into the bush, but nobody throws any. They'll hide and wait. Ro tells us to be careful now, look for trips. Don't go in the water.

When we get into the spread of the village, a bunch of girls are there. They're darting back and forth. Carrying stones. A couple have razor bugs mounted on long poles.

Telle's got the language down, tries some bargaining, but they won't have it. Some stones fly. Kep sprays a couple of the closest throwers. They screech. Their skin starts melting off. Telle shouts out again that we want water, a roof.

They send somebody out, some old woman. She brings two boys with her, skinny, sticky things no better than the ones in Pekoi proper. She kneels down, and the boys kneel down next to her. She holds out their hands to us.

Telle says we have to take them. It's a ceasefire offering. I tell her water's better.

Ro grunts, grabs the boys' hands. "A roof," she says, "water."

They put us up in the old woman's hut, a circular mud pit layered over in thatch. Telle turns on the tube. Ro takes up the food they bring in. We stash the boys in a corner and tell them to shut up. The hut's pretty small, and there's a lot of us. It's too crowded. Ro puts Kep and Luce and me outside, tells us to watch point.

Kep squats down against the house, pulls out her cards. I don't like the air we're getting off the locals. They're too used to muscle.

There's a boy watching from the doorway of one of the far huts. He's seven or eight, old enough to be trouble, young enough not to be much trouble. He comes out of the doorway, takes a couple steps forward. I'm keeping an eye as we lop cards. Luce stares the kid straight in the face. He waves at her. Kep adjusts her gun on her shoulder.

Luce yells out at him in the local. Her accent is bad. "You stay there! Stay or we shoot. Understand?"

The boy goes still. His eyes are wide. He's looking past us.

I look at Kep. She's at the corner of the hut. I can't see around it.

I yell, "Kep!"

Kep unshoulders her gun, flops on the ground. She fires around the corner without looking.

Luce is up. I dart around the other side of the hut. I hear the girls inside, screeching. I pace all the way around, duck out and see what Kep hit. There's a couple of screamers. A boy and a woman, maybe his older sister. Their faces are pretty smeared. Black holes for mouths and eyes, flesh running off bone, no noses. They're wiping off their own faces with their hands.

I do a quick sweep. There are half a dozen people out. More coming up from the other end of the village. They've got stones. Somebody's got a writhing basket. Flesh beetles.

"Hold!" I yell. I only know a couple words in local. I got that one down.

But they don't hold. They start screaming. Somebody throws a stone.

Luce sprays the nearest two. They go down.

There's a girl up on a roof. I see her throw, but she's so far off, I don't think she can hit anything.

But her aim is good. Kep goes down, struck right between the eyes. I run toward her. The crowd screeches.

I can hear Ro's voice somewhere behind me.

"Move back!" Luce says, and yanks me away from Kep. I can't shoulder my gun and grab Kep. I'll lose point on the hostiles.

"Cover me," I say.

The girl with the basket dumps her beetles.

Luce sprays her. But the beetles are out. They swarm. Hunched, dark figures, big as my palms. I fall back from Kep, and the bugs overtake her. Kep jerks.

I duck to reach for her flailing arm. One of the bugs jumps on my hand. I try and smash it, but the pincers get me between thumb and forefinger, right through my slick. The bug starts pumping yellowish fluid.

Luce keeps dragging me back.

Ro's up behind me now. She rips off the bug, takes a hunk of my flesh with it. Pain jolts up my arm.

Ro's got her gun out. "Jian, take girl watch. Telle, get out here! I need a translator!"

I hump back around to the front. Telle's already heading my way. I take watch on the girls. They're huddled in the entryway, clinging to each other. Doll is starting to cry.

We're boxed in. We've got hostiles all around. I can see a half dozen more coming up from the ponds. They're running. There's more screaming around the other side. Ro's shouting—

"Spray! Take them out!"

And when the ones from the pond get close enough, I take them out. Their hands are empty, but Kep's dead, and Ro's giving the watch. We're the muscle. Not the brains.

I can't hear the girls anymore, because everyone else is screaming. I slip a knife out of my boot and go and cut the ones I sprayed. Shut them up. I've got my slick on, so the spray stays off me. Their heads are just big globs of goo now.

Luce is running toward me. I'm standing over a half dozen bodies. I wonder how many more hostiles we've got left.

"Orders?" I say.

"Telle's hit!" she yells. "Ro's down."

"Down?"

"Down!"

I stare past Luce. Telle's humping back. There's a heap of oozing bodies behind her. She's got Ro's gun.

"The fuck?" I say.

"She's down," Telle says.

"The fuck you mean she's down?" I say.

"Let's go. Let's get these bags and go," Telle says. She grabs Wonder by the arm, tries to yank her up. The whole lot of them are clinging so tight that when Wonder moves, they move too.

I do a quick count, look for movement. There's the heap Telle and Luce left behind, the heap where Ro and Kep are. I can just see something flickering on a far roof. What have they got left? Kids and kittens?

"I said we're up!" Telle says.

Luce and I share a look. "Luce, run point!" I say, because I can't grab the girls and aim my gun. I'm stronger than Luce, but she's a better shot.

I look back again, at Ro and Kep and the bodies. I can't even tell one from the other.

"Move!" Telle says.

I grab hold of Maul. She bites at my slick, so I throw her over my shoulder. She goes limp, and we move. Luce paces ahead. She sprays anything that moves. Boys, chickens, bugs. She sprays out a path, and there's nothing left living behind us.

We make it to the bug ponds. Maul twists suddenly, so sudden I think she's having a fit. I lose my grip, and she goes over, rolls into the water with a splash.

Luce twists toward the pond, aims her gun at the water.

"Luce, point!" I say, because I've got my own gun out now. She's moved off point.

Wonder and Doll are crying.

I try to switch my gun setting low, but it's been jammed since the last city.

"Go get her!" Telle says. She's got the other two by the hair. Some of it's come out in her hands.

"Fuck you," I say, because she isn't Ro, but Ro's dead. And that leaves her.

The girls' sobs are turning to keening. I can't see a ripple in the dark water.

Luce sets off a spray ahead of us. "I got movement!"

"What are you shooting at, dogs?" I yell.

Telle hits my shoulder with the butt of her gun. I nearly lose my balance, nearly go over.

But Telle had to let go of the girls to do it. Doll's crawling away. Wonder's almost on her feet.

Telle grabs Wonder by the hair. This time, a big hunk of her hair comes away, leaves a bloody scalp. Wonder screeches.

I stumble forward. These bags of sludge are going to come apart. They're going to come apart and vomit on us, hock up a thousand hours of organic tailoring.

I grab Doll by the ankle, pull her toward me. She bites at my slick. Her teeth don't go through. I put my hands around her throat and squeeze. And squeeze. She flails, like Kep flailed, only her face is turning gray.

Telle's with Wonder. Luce is yelling something.

Doll finally goes still. I let her go limp. I stand up. Telle's standing over Wonder. Wonder's curled up into a ball. I take my knife out of my boot.

"Don't cut her!" Telle says.

But I cut her anyway, because Telle can test and bag a corpse better than a live fish, and Ro and Kep are dead.

Wonder bleeds, more than I thought she would. I keep her between my legs, hold her still. She jerks a little. Her eyes go glassy.

I let her go, wipe my knife. "Tag and bag her," I say. "Central gets their proof. They just won't be live."

Telle's staring at me. Luce's still got her gun trained on the trees. I stare out at the water.

Telle rips off her test pack and starts cutting open Wonder's warm body. Wonder jerks some more.

I crouch, point my gun at the pond, and wait. Maul's body finally comes up, floating face down. Telle's hands are elbow-deep in Wonder's corpse.

I chew some sen. "You gonna fish her out?" I ask Luce, but Luce hasn't seen the body yet. One of the big bugs grabs hold of it again, hauls it back under.

Telle sits back on her heels. She wipes her hands on her slick. She stands up. She looks blank.

"What?" I say.

"Body's clean," she says.

"Clean?" I say.

"There's nothing in there," Telle says. "They weren't organics."

"Check the other one," I say.

"I don't need to—"

I point my gun at her. "Check the other one."

Luce licks her lips.

Telle guts the other one. She cracks open the ribcage. The body shudders. She digs around for a while. Her hands come out bloody. No sludge. Clean. She looks up at me.

"Clean," she says.

"Now what?" Luce says.

"We burn them," I say.

They don't have a better idea. So we burn them. And they burn. Like good little girls, my little WMD. They burn.

I chew some more sen. Telle flicks on the tube.

There's nothing dangerous in Pekoi.

WE SHIP OUT three weeks later. We've got a new first, and a new flank. We're the last squad to take off, so we get to see it. It's Telle who's on the tube, Telle who says, "We're clear."

They drop fire on Pekoi. Pekoi burns. Just like anything else.

The brains say Pekoi is too dangerous to the civilized world. Doesn't matter what the muscle says, what the muscle did. It's all about the brains, in the end. What they thought they saw. What they thought they knew.

Telle's got the tube up by her ear. I'm watching the city burn.

"You hear it?" Telle asks our first.

Our first shakes her head.

"Eighty percent of the districts reporting. Nabirye's leading fifty-six to forty."

Luce is wiping moths' wings off her boots, smearing dusty color on her cheeks. She laughs and laughs.

Nabirye flies us to another city.

≫•≪

Aliette de Bodard's Empire has been ripped asunder. Rebels have taken or destroyed all the other numbered planets of the galaxy and are approaching the First Planet. It is a time of betrayal and treachery; there is no way to tell who the true enemies are. But the last of the mindships still has a mission, one that requires a warrior.

THE DAYS OF THE WAR, AS RED AS BLOOD, AS DARK AS BILE

Aliette de Bodard

IN THE OLD DAYS, *the phoenix, the vermilion bird, was a sign of peace and prosperity to come; a sign of a virtuous ruler under whom the land would thrive.*

But those are the days of the war; of a weak child-Empress, successor to a weak Emperor; the days of burning planets and last-ditch defenses; of moons as red as blood and stars as dark as bile.

WHEN THIEN BAO was twelve years old, Second Aunt came to live with them.

She was a small, spry woman with little tolerance for children; and even less for Thien Bao, whom she grudgingly watched over while Mother worked in the factories, churning out the designs for new kinds of sharp-kites and advance needle ships.

"You are over pampered," she'd say, as she busied herself at the stove preparing the midday meal. "An only child, indeed." She didn't approve of Thien Bao's name, either—it was a boy's name that meant "Treasure from Heaven," and she thought Mother shouldn't have used it for a girl, no matter how much trouble she and Father might have had having children at all.

Thien Bao asked Mother why Second Aunt was so angry; Mother looked away for a while, her eyes focused on something Thien Bao couldn't see. "Your aunt had to leave everything behind when she came here."

"Everything?" Thien Bao asked.

"Her compartment and her things; and her husband." Mother's face twisted, in that familiar way when she was holding back tears. "You remember your Second Uncle, don't you?"

Thien Bao didn't: or perhaps she did—a deep voice, a smile, a smell of machine oil from the ships, which would never quite go away. "He's dead," she said, at last. Like Third Aunt, like Cousin Anh, like Cousin Thu. Like Father; gone to serve at the edge of Empire-controlled space, fallen in the rebel attack that had overwhelmed the moons of the Eighth Planet. "Isn't he?"

Those were the days of the dead; when every other morning seemed to see Grandmother adding new holos to the ancestral altar; every visitor spoke in hushed voices, as if Thien Bao weren't old enough to understand the war, or the devastation it brought.

Mother had the look again, debating whether to tell Thien Bao grown-up things. "He was a very brave man. He could have left, but he waited until everyone had finished evacuating." Mother sighed. "He never left. The rebel ships bombed the city until everything was ashes; your aunt was on the coms with him when—" she swallowed, looked away again. "She saw him die. That's why she's angry."

Thien Bao mulled on this for a while. "They had no children," she said, at last, thinking of Second Aunt sitting before the altar, grumbling that it was wrong to see him there, that he had died childless and had no place among the ancestors. But of course, the rules had changed in the days of the dead.

"No," Mother said.

It was a sad thought, bringing a queer feeling in Thien Bao's belly. "She can remarry, can't she?"

"Perhaps," Mother said, and Thien Bao knew it was a lie. She resolved to be nicer to Second Aunt from now on; and to pray to her ancestors so that Second Aunt would find another husband, and have children to comfort her in her old age.

That night, she dreamt of Second Uncle.

He stood in some shadowy corridor, one hand feverishly sending instructions to the structure's command nodes—speaking fast and in disjointed words, in a tone that he no doubt wanted to be reassuring. Thien Bao couldn't make out his face—it was a dark blur against the shaking of the walls; but she felt the impact that collapsed everything, like a spike-punch through reality, strong enough to shatter her bones—and heard the brief burst of static, the silence falling on the coms, as he died.

The dream changed, after that. She was soaring above a green planet, watching two huge attack ships confronting one another. There was no telling who was the rebels and who was the Empire. With the clarity of dreams she knew that one ship was scanning the other for antimatter weapons; and that the other ship, who had none, was preparing pinhead bombs, in the hopes of breaching the hull at its one weak point. Below, on the planet—again, with that strange clarity— people as tiny as ants were evacuating, struggling to fit onto a few aged shuttles that would carry them no further than the minuscule moon above.

They didn't matter—or, rather, they couldn't be allowed to matter, not if the mission were to be accomplished. Somehow, in the dream, she knew this; that, even if she had been ordered to save them, she wouldn't have been capable of it, wouldn't have made the slightest difference.

She floated closer, unfurling iridescent wings as wide as the trail of a comet; and prepared to unleash her own weapons, to put an end to the fight.

The scene seemed to freeze and blur, disintegrating like a hundred water droplets on a pane of glass—each droplet was a character, one of the old fashioned ones from Old Earth that no one save elite scholars knew how to read—column upon column of incomprehensible words in a red as bright as the vermilion of imperial decrees, scrolling downwards until they filled her entire field of vision—and they, too, faded, until only a few words remained—and though they were still in the old script, she knew in her heart of hearts what they meant, from beginning to end.

Little sister, you are fated to be mine.

Mine.

And then the words were gone, and she woke up, shaking, in the embrace of her own cradle-bed.

THERE WERE FOUR MINDSHIPS, *built in the finest workshops of the Empire, in a time when the numbered planets were scattered across dozens of solar systems—when court memorials reached the outer stations, and magistrates were posted in far-flung arms of the galaxy.*

Four mindships; one for each cardinal direction, raised by the best scholars to be the pride of the Empire; their claimers of tribute from barbaric, inferior dominions; the showcase of their technological apex, beings of grace and beauty, as terrible to behold as any of the Eight Immortals.

AFTER THAT, the dreams never stopped. They came irregularly—once a week, once a month—but they always came. In every one of them she was in a different place—above a planet, orbiting a moon, approaching a space station—and every time the war was in her dreams. In every dream she watched ships attack one another; soldiers fighting hand to hand in a desperate defense of a city's street, their faces featureless, their uniforms in bloody tatters without insignia, impossible to differentiate. She scoured clean the surface of planets, rained war-kites on devastated temple complexes, disabled space domes' weapons—and woke up, shivering, staring at the imprint of words she shouldn't have been able to understand.

Mine.

Come to me, little sister. Come to me and put an end to all of this.

And yet; and yet, the war still went on.

By daylight, Mother and Second Aunt spoke in hushed tones of the fall of planets; of the collapse of orbitals; of the progress of rebel forces across the Empire—ever closer to the First Planet and the Purple Forbidden City.

"The Lily Empress will protect us," Thien Bao said. "Won't she?"

Mother shook her head, and said nothing. But later, when Thien Bao was playing *The Battle for Indigo Mountain*, her implants synched with the house's entertainment center, she heard them—Grandmother, Mother, and Second Aunt, talking quietly among themselves in the kitchen around pork buns and tea. She froze the game into a thin, transparent layer over her field of vision, and crept closer to listen in.

"You should have said something," Grandmother said.

"What do you want me to say?" Mother sounded tired; angry, but the scary kind of anger, the bone-deep one that lasted for days or months. "Everything would be a lie."

"Then learn to lie," Second Aunt said, drily. There was the sound of chewing: betel leaf and areca, the only luxury she'd allow herself. "For her sake."

"You think I haven't tried? She's a bright child. She'll figure it out the moment I open my mouth. Her wealthier schoolmates have all left, and she's got to realize what a desert the city is becoming. Everyone is leaving."

"I know," Second Aunt said. "If we had the money . . . "

Mother sighed, and got up to pour more tea into her fist-sized cup. There was no money, Thien Bao knew; all of Grandmother's savings had gone into paying for the watered down food in the markets; for the rice mixed with blackened grit and ashes; for the fish sauce cut with brown coloring, which never tasted right no matter how much lime or sugar Thien Bao added to it.

Mother said, finally, "Money might not matter anymore soon. There's word at the factories—that Magistrate Viec wants to evacuate."

Silence; and then Grandmother, in a hushed voice, "They can't—the rebel fleet is still not in the solar system, is it?"

"No," Second Aunt said. "But it's getting closer; and they have mindships. If they wanted to hit us, they could send those as advance scouts. Wouldn't be enough to take the planet, but it would cost us much."

"The magistrate said the Lily Empress will send her armies next month, after the end of the rainy season." Mother's voice was still uncertain.

"Ha," Second Aunt said. "Maybe she will, maybe she won't. But even if she did; do you truly believe that will be enough to save us, little sister? The armies are badly run, and overwhelmed as it is."

Mother said, at last, "All we need is one victory. One message to tell the rebels that their advance stops here, at the Sixth Planet; that to go further into the Empire will cost them dearly. They're overstretched, too, it wouldn't take much to make them stop . . . " Her voice was pleading.

"They might be overstretched," Second Aunt said, and there was pity in her voice. "And you're right. Maybe all it would take is a crushing victory; but we don't have that within our grasp, and you know it."

There was silence, then, as heavy as the air before the monsoon. Thien Bao turned back to her game; but it all seemed fake now, the units aligned on the artificial landscape, the battles where no one bled, which you could start, again and again, until you succeeded in the assigned mission—where no one ever felt fear like a fist of ice tightening in their guts; or the emptiness of loss, drawing closer with every passing hour.

IN THE FIRST DAYS OF THE WAR, the mindships were lost; their crews scattered by court decrees, recalled in haste to defend planets that had already fallen; their cradle pods neglected by the alchemists and programmers; their missions assigned irregularly, and then not at all.

One by one, they fell.

Golden Tortoise *trying to evade pursuit by a vast rebel fleet, dove into deep spaces with an aged pilot as his only crew; and never re-emerged.*

Azure Dragon *went silent after the Battle of Huong He, plummeting downwards through the atmosphere in a shower of molten metal, her fragments peppering the burnt earth of the prefecture like so many seeds of grief.*

White Unicorn *completed the emergency evacuation of the Twelfth Planet, sustaining his trembling star-drives well past the point of bursting. He landed, shaking, bleeding his guts in machine-oil and torn rivets; and never flew again.*

And as for Vermillion Phoenix—*the strongest, most capable of all four ships . . . she, too, stopped speaking on the Empire's coms-channels; but her missions had been too well defined. She had been given leave to wage war on the Empire's enemies; and in those days when the Empire tore itself apart and brother denounced brother, father slew son and daughter abandoned mother, who could have told who the enemies of the Empire were, anymore?*

Vermillion Phoenix *went rogue.*

IT TOOK TWO MONTHS, in the end, for Magistrate Viec to give the evacuation order. By then, the rebel fleet had entered the solar system; and the first and second moons of the Sixth Planet had fallen. The army of the Empress retreated, its ships slowly growing larger in the sky, trailing the sickly green light of ruptured drives. The few soldiers the magistrate could spare oversaw the evacuation, their faces bored—most of their comrades were up above, fighting the last-ditch battle in the heavens.

Thien Bao stood in the huddle at the spaceport with her family; holding Grandmother's hand while the old woman engaged in a spirited talk with Second Aunt and Mother, complaining about everything from the wait to the noise of their neighbors.

She watched the army ships through the windows—and the growing shadows of the rebel mindships, creeping closer and closer—and wondered when their own evacuation ships would be ready. Around her, people's faces were tight, and they kept looking at the screens; at the queue that hadn't moved; at the impassive faces of the militia.

Ahead was a floating palanquin: an odd sight, since such a thing could only belong to a high official; but those officials would have been able to jump to the front of the queue. Thien Bao tugged at Grandmother's sleeve. "Grandmother?"

"Yes, child?" Grandmother didn't even turn.

"Who's in the palanquin?"

"Oh." Grandmother's gaze raked the palanquin from base to top, taking in the black lacquered exterior, embossed with golden birds; and the crane with spread wings atop the arched roof. "Probably Lady Oanh—you wouldn't remember her, but she and your mother were members of the same poetry club, in the days before she withdrew from public life. Always an eccentric, that woman." She frowned. "I thought she had a mindship of her own, though—funny seeing her here."

"Lady Oanh?"

But Grandmother had already turned back to her conversation with Mother and Second Aunt.

Above, the army ships hadn't moved; but Thien Bao could see the shapes of the rebel mindships more clearly, emerging from the deep spaces just long enough to power weapons. They were going to . . .

She knew it a fraction of a second before it happened—saw the corona of light filling the sky like an aurora above the poles—saw it spread in deathly silence, engulf the largest of the army ships—saw the ship shudder, and crack like an egg shell—the horrible thing was that it still held together, leaking a cloud of darkened fluids that spread across the surface of the sky—that it shuddered, again and again, but did not fall apart, though surely the life support systems had to be gone, with that kind of impact; though everyone onboard had to be dead, or dying, or worse . . .

In the silence that followed, a man screamed, his voice deep and resonant; and the crowd went mad.

Without warning, people pressed themselves closer to the docks; elbowing each other out of the way, sending others sprawling to the floor. Thien Bao found herself crushed against Grandmother, struggling to remain upright against the press—arms pushed against her, separating her from her family, and she was lost amidst unfamiliar faces, pushed and pulled until it was all she could do to stand upright; until it was all she could do to breathe—

The darkness at the edge of her field of vision descended; and the red characters of her dreams scrolled by, resolving themselves into the same, sharp, lapidary message.

Little sister. Call me. Call me, and put an end to this.

She hung in the darkness of space, the ion exhaust of her drives trailing behind her, opening like a vast fan; every part of her sharp, honed to a killing edge—a living weapon, carrying enough firepower to end it all, to make the rebel fleet cinders, to crack them open as they'd cracked open the army ship. All she had to do was call, reach out to the vast, dark part of herself that moved between the stars . . .

Someone grabbed her. Cold hands tightened on her shoulders, and pulled her upwards before she could stifle a scream; and it all went away, the sense of vastness; the red characters and the presence of something other than her in her own mind.

She sat in the darkness; it took her a moment to realize she was inside the palanquin, and that the slightly clearer form in front of her was an old woman.

Lady Oanh.

"Child," the old woman said. Life-support wires trailed from every end of the palanquin, as though she sat on the center of a spider's web. The skin of her face, in the dim light, had the pallor and thinness of wet rice paper; and her eyes were two pits of deeper darkness. "Anh's and Nhu's daughter, is it not? I was a friend of your mother; in a different lifetime."

Everything was eerily silent: no noise from outside, no hint of the riot that had started on the docks—of course the palanquin would have the best ambiance systems, but the overall effect—that of hanging in the same bubble of artificially stilled time—made Thien Bao's skin crawl. "Lady Oanh. Why—?"

Mother and Second Aunt would be freaking out; they'd always told her not to trust strangers; and here she was in the middle of a riot, stuck with someone who might or might not be a friend—but then why would Lady Oanh bother to kidnap her? She was a scholar, a public figure; or had been, once. Nevertheless . . . Thien Bao reached into her feed, and activated the location loop—she'd sworn to Mother she was a grown up and didn't need it any longer, and now she was glad Mother hadn't listened to her.

The old woman smiled, an expression that did not reach into her eyes. "You would prefer to be outside? Trust me, it is much safer here." A feed blinked in the lower left-hand corner of Thien Bao's vision, asking for her permission to be displayed. She granted it; and saw outside.

The palanquin floated on its repulsive field, cutting a swathe through the press of people. Thien Bao knew she wouldn't have lasted a moment out there, that she'd have been mown down as others sought to reach the shuttles before her. But still . . .

Lady Oanh's voice was quiet, but firm. "You looked set to be trampled by the mob."

"You didn't have to—"

"No," Lady Oanh said. "You're right. I didn't."

How old was she? Thien Bao wondered. How long did it take for skin to become this pale; for eyes to withdraw this deep into the face, as if she stood on the other side of death already? And did all of it, this aging, this putting death at bay, confer any of the wisdom of Thien Bao's ancestors?

"A riot is no place for freezing," Lady Oanh said. "Though in someone your age, it can possibly be excused."

She hadn't noticed the trance then; or that anything was wrong. Then again, why should she? She was certainly wise with her years, but wisdom was not omniscience. "I'm sorry," Thien Bao said. But she remembered the sense of vastness; the coiled power within her. If it was real; if it wasn't dreams; if she could somehow answer . . .

Call me, little sister. Let us put an end to all this.

Thien Bao said, "Grandmother said—you had a mindship—"

Lady Oanh laughed; genuinely amused it seemed. "*The Carp that Leapt Over the Stream*? It seemed senseless to hoard her services. She's part of the fleet that will evacuate her. That's where we're going, in fact."

Lady Oanh's eyes focused on something beyond Thien Bao, and she nodded. "I'll send a message to notify your kin that I'm helping you onboard a ship. That should alleviate their worries."

If they didn't all die first from rebel fire; if the remaining army ship held—if if if . . .

A gentle rocking, indicating the palanquin was moving forward again—to the waiting ships, to safety—except that there was no safety, not anywhere.

Outside, the remaining army ship was trying to contain the rebel mindships; shuddering, its hull pitted and cracked. From time to time, a stray shot would hit the spacesport's shields, and the entire structure around them would shudder, but it held, it still held.

But for how long?

"I hate them," Thien Bao said.

"Who? The rebels?" Lady Oanh's gaze was sharp. "It's as much the fault of the Court as theirs, child. If the Great Virtue Emperor and the Lily Empress hadn't been weak, more concerned with poetry than with their armies; if their officials hadn't encouraged them, repeating that nonsense about adherence to virtue being the only safeguard the Empire needed . . . "

To hear her, so casually criticizing the Empress—but then Second Aunt and Mother had done the same. "I wish . . . " Thien Bao sounded childish, she knew; like a toddler denied a threat. "I wish someone were strong enough to stop the rebel armies. To kill them once and for all."

Lady Oanh's face did not move, but she shook her head. "Be careful, child."

How could wanting peace be a bad thing? She understood nothing, that old, pampered woman who didn't have to fight through the crowd, who didn't live with fear in her belly, with the litany of the family dead in her mind—

"Killing is easy," Lady Oanh said. "But that has never stopped the devastation of war."

"It would be a start," Thien Bao said, defiantly.

"Perhaps," Lady Oanh said. She shook her head. "It would take a great show of strength from the Empire to stop them, and this is something we're incapable of, at the present time. The seeds of our defeat were in place long before the war, I fear; and—"

She never finished her sentence. Thien Bao saw nothing; but *something* struck the shields, wringing them dry like wet laundry; and going past them, a network of cracks and fissures spreading throughout the pillars of the spaceport and the huge glass windows.

Look out, Thien Bao wanted to say; but the wall nearest to them shuddered and fell apart, dragging down chunks of the ceiling in its wake. Something struck her in the back of the head; and everything disappeared in an excruciating, sickening crunch.

WHEN SHE WENT SILENT, Vermillion Phoenix *had had an officer of the Embroidered Guard as her only crew—not a blood relative, but a sworn oath-sister, who had been with the ship for decades and would never hear of abandoning her post.*

There is no record of what happened to the officer. Being human, without any kind of augmentation, she likely died of old age, while the mindship—as ships did—went on, unburdened.

Unburdened does not mean free from grief, or solitude. In the centuries that followed, several people claimed to have had visions of the ship; to have heard her voice calling to them; or dreamt of battles—past and present—to which she put a brutal end. There were no connections between them; no common ancestry or closeness in space or time; but perhaps the mindship recognized something else: a soul, torn from its fragile flesh envelope and reincarnated, time and time again, until everything was made right.

THIEN BAO WOKE UP, and all was dust and grit—choking her, bending her to the ground to convulsively cough until her lungs felt wrung dry. When she rose at last, shaking, she saw the ruins of the palanquin, half-buried under rubble; and a few cut wires, feebly waving in the dim light—and the mob, further into the background, still struggling to reach the ships. She'd thought the wall would collapse, but it stood in spite of the massive fissures crossing it from end to end; and for some incongruous reason it reminded her of the fragile celadon cups Father had so treasured, their green surface shot with such a network of cracks it seemed a wonder they still held together.

Around her, chunks of the ceiling dotted the area—and the other thing, the one she avoided focusing on—people lying still or twitching or moaning, lying half under rubble—with limbs bent at impossible angles, and the stained white of bones laid bare at the heart of bleeding wounds; and spilled guts; and the labored breathing of those in agony . . .

Those were the days of the dead, and she had to be strong.

At the edge of her field of vision—as faint as her paused game of *Battle for Indigo Mountain*, in another lifetime—the red characters of her dream hovered, and a faint sense of a vast presence, watching over her from afar.

"Lady Oanh? Mother? Second Aunt?" Her location loop was still running; but it didn't seem to have picked up anything from them—or perhaps it was the spaceport network that was the problem, flickering in and out of existence like a dying heartbeat. It was nonsense anyway; who expected the network to hold, through that kind of attack.

The sky overhead was dark with the shadow of a ship—not the army ship, it had to be one of the mindships. Its hatches were open, spewing dozens of little shuttles, a ballet slowly descending towards them: rebels, come to finish the work they had started.

She had to move.

When she pulled herself upright, pain shot through her neck and arms like a knife-stab; but she forced herself to move on, half-crawling, half-walking, until she found Lady Oanh.

The old woman lay in the rubble, staring at the torn dome of the spaceport. For a moment, an impossibly long moment, Thien Bao thought she was alive; but no one could be alive with the lower half of their body crushed; and so much fluid and blood leaking from broken tubes. "I'm sorry," she said, but it wasn't her fault; it had never been her fault. Overhead, the shuttles were still descending, as slowly as the executioner's blade. There was no time. There was no safety; not anywhere; there was no justice; no fairness; no end to the war and the fear and the sick feeling in her head and in her belly.

A deafening sound in her ears, loud enough to cover the distant sounds of panic—she realised that it was her location loop, displaying an arrow and an itinerary to join whatever was left of her family; if they, like Lady Oanh, hadn't died, if there was still hope . . .

She managed to pull herself upwards—staggered, following the directions—left right left going around the palanquin around the dead bodies around the wounded who grasped at her with clawed hands—days of the dead, she had to be strong had to be strong . . .

She found Grandmother, Mother, and Second Aunt standing by the barriers that had kept the queue orderly, once—which were now covered in dust, like everything else around them. There was no greeting, or sign of relief. Mother merely nodded as if nothing were wrong, and said, "We need to move."

"It's past time for that," Second Aunt said, her gaze turned towards the sky.

Thien Bao tried to speak; to say something about Lady Oanh, but no words would come out of her mouth.

Mother's eyes rolled upwards for a brief moment as she accessed the network. "*The Carp that Leapt Over the Stream*," she said. "Its shuttles were parked at the other end of the terminal, and there'll be fewer people there. Come on."

Move move move—Thien Bao felt as though everything had turned to tar; she merely followed as Second Aunt and Mother elbowed their way through the crowd; and onto a corridor that was almost deserted compared to the press of people. "This way," Mother said.

Thien Bao turned, briefly, before they limped into the corridor, and saw that the first of the rebel shuttles had landed some way from them, disgorging a flood of yellow-clad troops with featureless helmets.

It was as if she were back in her dreams, save that her dreams had never been this pressing—and that the red words on the edge of her field of vision kept blinking, no matter how she tried to dismiss them.

Mother was right; they needed to keep moving—past the corridor, into another, wider concourse that was mostly scattered ruin, following the thin thread of people and hoping that the shuttles would still be there, that the mindship would answer to them with Lady Oanh dead. By then, they had been joined by other people, among whom a wounded woman carried on the shoulder of a soldier—no introductions, no greetings, but a simple acknowledgement that they were all in this together. It wasn't hope that kept them going; it was sheer stubbornness, one foot in front of the other, one breath and the next and the next; the fear of falling behind the others, of slowing everyone down and ruining everything.

Ahead, the mass of a shuttle, seen behind glass windows; getting agonizingly, tantalizingly closer. "This way," Second Aunt said; and then they saw the yellow-clad troops in front of them, deployed to bar the passage across the concourse—and the other troops, too, blocking the passageways, herding people off the shuttle in the eerie silence.

Mother visibly sagged. "It will be fine," she said, and her voice was a lie. "They'll just want to check our identity and process us—"

But it was the soldier with them who panicked—who turned away, lightning-fast, still carrying his wounded charge—and in the dull silence that followed, Thien Bao heard the click of weapons being armed.

"No!" Mother said, sharply. As if in a dream Thien Bao saw her move in front of the yellow-clad soldiers, with no more apparent thought than if she'd been strolling through the marketplace—and she wanted to scream but couldn't, as the weapons found their mark and Mother crumpled, bloodless and wrung dry, her corpse so small it seemed impossible that she had once been alive.

Second Aunt moved at last, her face creased with anger—not towards Mother or the soldier, but straight at the rebel troops. "How dare you—"

There was the sound again; of weapons being armed.

No.

No. No.

Everything went red: the characters from her dreams, solidifying once more in front of her; the voice speaking into her mind.

Little sister.

And, weeping, Thien Bao reached out, into the void between stars, and called to the ship.

←----→

When the child named Thien Bao was born on the Sixth Planet, there were signs—a room filled with the smell of machine-oil, and iridescent reflections on the walls, tantalizing characters from a long lost language. Had the birth-master not been desperately busy trying to staunch the mother's unexpected bleeding, and calm down the distraught father, she would have noticed them.

Had she looked, too, into the newborn's eyes as she took her first, trembling breath, the birth-master would have seen the other sign: the hint of a deep, metallic light in the huge pupils; a light that spread from end to end of the eye like a wash of molten steel, a presage of things to come.

She was vast, and old, and terrible; her wings stretched around entire planets, as iridescent as pearls fished from the depths; the trail of her engines the color of jade, of delicate celadon—and where she passed, she killed.

She disintegrated the fleet that waited on the edge of the killing field; scoured clean the surface of the small moon, heedless of the screams of those trapped upon it; descended to the upper limit of the planet's atmosphere, and incinerated the two mindships in orbit, and the fragile ship that still struggled to defend against them; and the tribunal where the militia still fought the recently landed invasion force; and the magistrate in his chambers, staring at the tactical map of the planet and wondering how to save what he could from the rebels. In the spaceport, where the largest number of people congregated, she dropped ion bombs until no sign of life remained; until every shuttle had exploded or stopped moving.

Then there was silence, and lack of strife, and then there was peace.

And then she was merely Thien Bao again, standing in the ruins of the spaceport, in the shadow of the great ship she had called on.

There was nothing left. Merely dust, and bodies—so many bodies, a sea of them, yellow-clad, black-clad, civilians and soldiers and rebels all mingled together, their blood pooling on the cracked floor; and a circle around her, where Mother lay dead; and the soldier, and the wounded woman; and the rebels who had shot her—and by her side, Second Aunt and Grandmother, bloodless and pale and unmoving. It was unclear whether it was the mindship's weapons they had died of, or the rebels', or both; but Thien Bao stood in a circle of the dead, the only one alive as far as she could see.

The only one—it couldn't—couldn't—

Little sister. The voice of the mindship was as deep as the sea. *I have come, and ended it, as you requested.*

That wasn't what she'd wanted—that—all of it, any of it—

And then she remembered Lady Oanh's voice, her wry comment. *Be careful, child. Be careful.*

I bring peace, and an end to strife. Is that not what the Empire should desire?

No. No.

Come with me, little sister. Let us put an end to this war.

A great victory, Thien Bao thought, hugging herself; feeling hot and cold at the same time, her bones chilled within their sheaths of flesh, a churning in her gut like the beginning of grief. Everyone had wanted a great victory over the rebels, something that would stop them, once and for all, that would tell them that the Empire still stood, still could make them pay for every planet they took.

And she'd given them that; she and the ship. Exactly that.

Come. We only have each other, the ship said, and it was the bitter truth. There was nothing left on the planet—not a living soul—and of the rebel army that had entered the solar system, nothing and no one left either, just the husks of destroyed ships drifting in the emptiness of space.

Come, little sister.

And she did—for where else could she go; what else could she do, that would have made any sense?

IN THE OLD DAYS, the phoenix, the vermilion bird, was a sign of peace and prosperity to come; a sign of a virtuous ruler under whom the land would thrive.

In the days of the war, it is still the case; if one does not inquire how peace is bought, how prosperity is paid for—how a mindship and a child scour the numbered planets, dealing death to rebels and Empire alike, halting battles by bloody massacres; and making anyone who raises arms pay dearly for the privilege of killing.

Meanwhile, on the inner planets begins the painful work of reconstruction— raising pagodas and tribunals and shops from the ashes of war, and hanging New Year's Eve garlands along avenues that are still dust and ruins, praying to the ancestors for a better future; for a long life; and good fortune; and descendants as numerous as the stars in the sky.

There is no virtuous ruler; but perhaps—perhaps just, there is a manner of peace and prosperity, bought in seas of blood spilled by a child.

And perhaps—perhaps just—it is all worth it. Perhaps it is all one can hope for, in the days of the war.

>−•−≪

ABOUT THE AUTHORS

Rachael Acks is a writer, geologist, and dapper sir. She's written for *Six to Start* and been published in *Strange Horizons, Lightspeed, Daily Science Fiction*, and more. Acks lives in Houston with her two cats, where she twirls her mustache, watches movies, and bikes. Her website is rachaelacks.com.

Elizabeth Bear is the Hugo, Sturgeon, Locus, and Campbell award-winning author of twenty-seven novels (her most recent novels are *Karen Memory* and—co-authored with Sarah Monette—*An Apprentice of Elves*) and over a hundred short stories. She lives in Massachusetts.

Aliette de Bodard lives and works in Paris, where she has a day job as a System Engineer. She is the author of the critically acclaimed Obsidian and Blood trilogy of Aztec noir fantasies, as well as numerous short stories, which garnered her two Nebula Awards, a Locus Award, and a British Science Fiction Association Award. Recent works include *The House of Shattered Wings*, a novel set in a turn-of-the-century Paris devastated by a magical war, and *The Citadel of Weeping Pearls*, a novella set in the same universe as her Vietnamese space opera *On a Red Station, Drifting*.

Theodora Goss' publications include the short story collection *In the Forest of Forgetting; Interfictions*, an anthology coedited with Delia Sherman; *Voices from Fairyland*, a poetry anthology with critical essays and a selection of her own poems; *The Thorn and the Blossom*, a novella in a two-sided accordion format; and the poetry collection *Songs for Ophelia*. Her first novel, *The Strange Case of the Alchemist's Daughter*, is forthcoming from Saga Press in 2017. Her short story "Singing of Mount Abora" won the World Fantasy Award. She teaches literature and writing at Boston University and in the Stonecoast MFA Program.

Nalo Hopkinson was born in Jamaica, but has lived in Canada for the past thirty-five years. She is currently a professor of creative writing at the University of California, Riverside. She is the author of six novels (*Brown Girl in the Ring, Midnight Robber, The Salt Roads, The New Moon's Arms, The Chaos*, and *Sister Mine*), as well as two short story collections: *Skin Folk* and the recently published *Falling in Love with Hominids*. She edited fiction anthologies *Whispers From the Cotton Tree Root: Caribbean Fabulist Fiction*, and *Mojo: Conjure Stories*, and co-edited *So Long Been Dreaming: Postcolonial Science Fiction & Fantasy* (with

Uppinder Mehan) and *Tesseracts Nine* (with Geoff Ryman). Hopkinson is a recipient of the John W. Campbell, Locus, World Fantasy, Norton, Aurora, Gaylactic Spectrum, and Sunburst awards.

On the way to the idyllic rural existence she shares with her wife Fiona Patton, numerous cats, and a chihuahua, **Tanya Huff** served three years in the Canadian Naval Reserve and acquired a degree in Radio and Television Arts from Ryerson Polytechnic. Since the *Blood Ties* television series was based on it, Huff is probably best known for her Blood series—*Blood Price, Blood Trail, Blood Lines, Blood Pact, Blood Debt*—but has authored over fifty fantasy and military SF novels. Her most recent novel is a spin-off her Valor Confederation series of five novels and a few short works: *An Ancient Peace: Peacekeeper #1*.

Kameron Hurley is an award-winning author and advertising copywriter with degrees in historical studies from the University of Alaska and the University of KwaZulu-Natal, specializing in the history of South African resistance. Hurley is the author of *God's War, Infidel,* and *Rapture,* a science-fantasy noir series which earned her the Sydney J. Bounds Award for Best Newcomer and the Kitschy Award for Best Debut Novel. She is the winner of two Hugo Awards, and has been a finalist for the Arthur C. Clarke, Nebula, Locus, and BSFA awards. Her latest subversive epic fantasy novels are *The Mirror Empire* and its sequel *Empire Ascendant.* Her first space opera, *The Stars are Legion,* will be published in 2016.

Elaine Isaak is the author of *The Singer's Crown,* and its sequels, as well as the Tales of Bladesend epic novellas series comprising *Joenna's Axe* in full-length, and *Winning the Gallows Field.* As E. C. Ambrose, she writes The Dark Apostle historical fantasy novels about medieval surgery, which began with *Elisha Barber,* and continue with *Elisha Magus, Elisha Rex,* and two forthcoming volumes. A graduate of the Odyssey Speculative Fiction workshop, she has taught there as well. In addition to writing and teaching, Elaine works part time as an adventure guide and rock climbing instructor. Visit TheDarkApostle.com or ElaineIsaak. com to find out why you do not want to be her hero.

The *New York Times* recently hailed **Caitlín R. Kiernan** as "one of our essential writers of dark fiction." Her novels include *The Red Tree* (nominated for the Shirley Jackson and World Fantasy awards) and *The Drowning Girl: A Memoir* (winner of the James Tiptree, Jr. and the Bram Stoker awards, nominated for the Nebula, Locus, Shirley Jackson, World Fantasy, British Fantasy, and Mythopoeic awards). In 2014 she was honored with the Locus Award for short fiction ("The Road of Needles"), the World Fantasy Award ("The Prayer of Ninety Cats"), and a second World Fantasy Award for Best Collection (*The Ape's Wife and Other Stories*). To date, her short fiction has been collected in fourteen volumes, the most recent of which is *Beneath an Oil-Dark Sea: The Best of Caitlin R. Kiernan (Volume Two)*. Currently, she's working on the screenplay of *The Red Tree*.

Nancy Kress began writing in 1976, but achieved greater notice after the publication of her Hugo- and Nebula-winning 1991 novella "Beggars in Spain," which was later expanded into a novel with the same title. Kress has also written numerous short stories and has won six Nebulas, two Hugos, a Sturgeon, and a John W. Campbell Memorial Award. She teaches regularly at summer conferences such as Clarion West and Taos Toolbox. Her collection, *The Best of Nancy Kress*, was published in September.

Tanith Lee was born in the UK in 1947. After school, she worked at a number of jobs, and at age twenty-five had one year at art college. Then DAW Books published her novel *The Birthgrave*. Thereafter, she was a professional full-time writer. Publications total approximately ninety novels and collections and well over three hundred short stories. She also wrote for television and radio. Lee was honored with several awards: in 2009 she was made a Grand Master of Horror and honored with the World Fantasy Convention Lifetime Achievement Award in 2013. Tanith Lee passed away after a long illness on 24 May 2015.

Sharon Lee's most recent solo novel is *Carousel Seas*, the concluding novel in Archers Beach contemporary fantasy trilogy. Lee and her husband, **Steve Miller**, are creators of the star-spanning Liaden Universe® series. *Dragon in Exile* is the eighteenth novel-length entry in the series; the nineteenth—*Alliance of Equals*—will be published in 2016. Numerous novellas and short stories are also set in the universe. Before becoming fiction writers, both worked in various newspaper jobs, which they credit with teaching them the finer points of collaboration. They live in Maine.

Yoon Ha Lee's debut short fiction collection *Conservation of Shadows* was published in 2013. His first novel, *Ninefox Gambit*—the first of a space opera trilogy—will be published in June 2016. He lives in Louisiana with his family and an extremely lazy cat. Neither the cat nor any family members have yet been eaten by gators.

Ken Liu (kenliu.name) is an author and translator of speculative fiction, as well as a lawyer and programmer. A winner of the Nebula, Hugo, and World Fantasy awards. Liu's debut novel, *The Grace of Kings*, the first in a silkpunk epic fantasy series, was published earlier this year. His first collection of short stories, *The Paper Menagerie and Other Stories,* will be published in 2016. The translator of numerous literary and genre works from Chinese to English, his translation of *The Three-Body Problem*, by Liu Cixin, won the Hugo Award for Best Novel in 2015, the first translated novel to ever receive that honor. Liu lives with his family near Boston, Massachusetts.

Seanan McGuire is the author of the October Daye urban fantasies, the InCryptid urban fantasies, and several other works (both stand-alone and in trilogies or duologies). Under the pseudonym "Mira Grant" she's authored two trilogies. Between the two names, she's published around fifty short stories and novellas in the last six years. McGuire was the winner of the John W. Campbell Award for Best New Writer, and her novel *Feed* (as Mira Grant) was named as one of *Publishers Weekly*'s Best Books of 2010. In 2013 she became the first person ever to appear five times on the same Hugo ballot. McGuire lives in a creaky old farmhouse in Northern California, which she shares with her cats, a vast collection of creepy dolls and horror movies, and sufficient books to qualify her as a fire hazard.

Currently the most famous fantasy author in the world, **George R. R. Martin** sold his first story in 1970 and has been writing professionally ever since. He spent ten years in Hollywood as a writer-producer, working on *The Twilight Zone*, *Beauty and the Beast*, and various feature films and television pilots that were never made. In the mid-1990s he began work on his epic fantasy series, A Song of Ice and Fire. The first novel, *A Game of Thrones*, was published in 1996. The fourth volume, 2005's *A Feast for Crows*, was a New York Times #1 bestseller, as was the fifth, *A Dance with Dragons*, in 2011. In April 2011 HBO premiered its first episode of the adaptation of *A Game of Thrones* series and he was named as one of *Time*'s most influential people of the year. *Game* has gone on to be ratings-breaker and winner of a record number of Emmys—including Outstanding Drama Series—in 2015. He lives in Santa Fe, New Mexico, with his wife Parris.

Elizabeth Moon, a Texas native, is a Marine Corps veteran with degrees in history and biology. She began writing stories in her childhood, but did not make her first fiction sale until age forty. She has published twenty-three novels, including Nebula Award-winner *The Speed of Dark*, three short-fiction collections including *Moon Flights*, and over thirty short-fiction pieces. Her most recent novel is *Crown of Renewal*, the tenth novel to be set in her Paksenarrion Universe.

An (pronounce it "on") **Owomoyela** is a neutrois author with a background in web development, linguistics, and weaving chain maille out of stainless steel fencing wire, whose fiction has appeared in a number of venues including *Clarkesworld*, *Asimov's*, *Lightspeed*, and a handful of "Year's Best" anthologies. Owomoyela's interests range from pulsars and Cepheid variables to gender studies and nonstandard pronouns, with a plethora of stops in-between. Se can be found online at an.owomoyela.net.

Robert Reed is the author of a dozen novels, and over two hundred shorter works. He's had stories appear in at least one of the annual "Year's Best" anthologies every year since 1992 and is a perennial favorite in science fiction readers polls. The winner of the Hugo Award and the Grand Prix de l'Imaginaire, Reed has also received nominations for the Nebula, World Fantasy, Sturgeon, Tiptree, and Campbell Awards among others. His novel *Beyond the Veil of Stars* was a *New York Times* Notable Book of the Year. His most recent novel is *The Memory of Sky*. Reed lives in Lincoln, Nebraska, with his wife, Leslie, and daughter, Jessie. An ardent long-distance runner, he can frequently be seen jogging through the parks and hiking trails of Lincoln.

Jessica Reisman's stories have appeared in numerous magazines and anthologies. Her first novel, *The Z Radiant*, published by Five-Star Speculative Fiction, is "thinking reader's sci-fi." She was a Michener Fellow in Fiction in graduate school. See storyrain.com for more.

International bestseller **Kristine Kathryn Rusch** writes under a variety of pen names, but as Rusch, she's best known for her science fiction. As a writer, Rusch has won Hugo, Endeavour, and two Sidewise awards. She edited *The Magazine of Fantasy & Science Fiction* for six years, winning a Hugo Award as Best Professional Editor. Rusch is married to fellow writer Dean Wesley Smith; they have collaborated on several works and operated Pulphouse Publishing (for which they won a World Fantasy Award). This year, she released the remaining six books in her eight-book Anniversary Day Saga, a mini-series inside the larger Retrieval Artist series. Rusch is series editor for a bimonthly anthology magazine,

Fiction River, and is editing anthology *Women of Futures Past: Classic Stories* for release next year. In addition, she's co-editing a series of reprint anthologies with John Helfers, focused on the history of the science fiction field.

Carrie Vaughn is the author of the *New York Times* bestselling series of novels about a werewolf named Kitty, the fourteenth installment of which is *Kitty Saves the World*. She's written several other contemporary fantasy and young adult novels, as well as upwards of eighty short stories. She's a contributor to the Wild Cards series of shared world superhero books edited by George R. R. Martin and a graduate of the Odyssey Fantasy Writing Workshop. An Air Force brat, she survived her nomadic childhood and managed to put down roots in Boulder, Colorado. Visit her at carrievaughn.com.

Jane Yolen, author of over over 335 books, is often called the Hans Christian Andersen of America—though she wonders (not entirely idly) whether she should really be called the "Hans Jewish Andersen of America." She has been named both Grand Master of the World Fantasy Convention and Grand Master of the Science Fiction Poetry Association. She has won two Nebulas for her short stories, and a bunch of other awards, including six honorary doctorates. One of her awards, the Skylark, given by the New England Science Fiction Association, set her good coat on fire, a warning about faunching after shiny things that she has not forgotten.

≫•≪

ACKNOWLEDGMENTS

"They Tell Me There Will Be No Pain" © 2014 Rachael Acks. First publication: *Lightspeed's Women Destroy Science Fiction!* Special Issue, June 2014 (Limited Edition).

"Love Among the Talus" © 2006 Elizabeth Bear. First publication: *Strange Horizons*, 11 December 2006.

"The Days of the War, as Red as Blood, as Dark as Bile" © 2014 Aliette de Bodard. First publication: *Subterranean*, Spring 2014.

"England Under the White Witch" © 2012 Theodora Goss. First publication: *Clarkesworld*, October 2012.

"Soul Case" © 2007 Nalo Hopkinson. First publication: *Foundation #100*, Summer 2007.

"Not That Kind of War" © 2005 Tanya Huff. First publication: *Women of War*, eds. Tanya Huff & Alexander Potter (DAW Books).

"Wonder Maul Doll" © 2007 Kameron Hurley. First publication: *From the Trenches: An Anthology of Speculative War Stories*, eds. Joseph Paul Haines & Samantha Henderson (Carnifex Press).

"Joenna's Axe" © 2010 Elaine Isaak. First publication: *Demons: A Clash of Steel Anthology*, ed. Jason W. Waltz (Rogue Blades Entertainment).

"The Sea Troll's Daughter" © 2010 Caitlín R. Kiernan. First publication: *Swords & Dark Magic: The New Sword and Sorcery*, eds. Jonathan Strahan & Lou Anders (Eos/Harper Collins).

"Eaters" © 2014 Nancy Kress. First publication: *The Book of Silverberg: Stories in Honor of Robert Silverberg*, eds. Gardner Dozois & William Schafer (Subterranean Press).

"Northern Chess" © 1979 Tanith Lee. First publication: *Amazons!*, ed. Jessica Amanda Salmonson (DAW Books).

"Naratha's Shadow" © 2000 Sharon Lee & Steve Miller. First publication: *Such a Pretty Face*, ed. Lee Martindale (Meisha Merlin).

"The Knight of Chains, The Deuce of Stars" © 2013 Yoon Ha Lee. First publication: *Lightspeed*, August 2013.

"In the Loop" © 2014 Ken Liu. First publication: *War Stories: New Military Science Fiction*, eds. Jaym Gates & Andrew Liptak (Apex Book Company).

"The Lonely Songs of Laren Dorr" © 1976 George R. R. Martin. First publication: *Fantastic Stories*, May 1976.

≫•≪